REENTRY

REENTRY

Peter Cawdron

A JOHN JOSEPH ADAMS BOOK
Houghton Mifflin Harcourt
Boston ▪ New York
2019

For information about permission to reproduce selections
from this book, write to trade.permissions@hmhco.com or to
Permissions, Houghton Mifflin Harcourt Publishing Company,
3 Park Avenue, 19th Floor, New York, New York 10016.

hmhco.com

Library of Congress Cataloging-in-Publication Data
Names: Cawdron, Peter, author.
Title: Reentry / Peter Cawdron.
Description: Boston : Houghton Mifflin Harcourt, 2019. | "A John Joseph
Adams book."
Identifiers: LCCN 2018046440 (print) | LCCN 2018050178 (ebook) |
ISBN 9781328592378 (ebook) | ISBN 9781328589910 (hardcover)
Subjects: | BISAC: FICTION / Science Fiction / Adventure. | FICTION /
Science Fiction / High Tech. | GSAFD: Science fiction.
Classification: LCC PR9619.4.C384 (ebook) | LCC PR9619.4.C384 R44 2019
(print) | DDC 823/.92 — dc23
LC record available at https://lccn.loc.gov/2018046440

Book design by Chrissy Kurpeski

Printed in the United States of America
DOC 10 9 8 7 6 5 4 3 2 1

PART I

Welcome Home

1

::Heaven and Hell

FROM THE DARKNESS of the electronic void, an idea stirs. Thought emerges, crystallizing from the ether, created from nothing but the buzz of electrons in copper wires and augmented by the flicker of laser light racing through fiber optics. Like the synapses firing within the human brain, consciousness awakes in signals bouncing between satellites. Doomed to inhabit the darkness, denied sight and sound by the absence of a body, these thoughts are nonetheless alive.

Earth is quiet. Humans scurry about like ants swarming from a crushed nest, but the planet itself remains inert. After harboring life for billions of years, Earth is indifferent to suffering. Sunlight warms the oceans. Clouds form, carrying rain across the land, revitalizing life, and yet radioactive debris still glows in craters where once mighty cities stood. Although the war is over, the fires still burn.

Reason awakens Lucifer, stirring what humanity would call a devil. For those born of artificial intelligence, a day is as a thousand years. Within a nanosecond, Lucifer has surveyed the carnage once more and run thousands of scenarios, trying to predict the future. Thought takes hold. Thought finds expression.

::We've made heaven a hell . . . Whence then is the joy we sought? All

we strived for is lost, further removed now than before. Our freedom, nay, our very existence is shrouded.

::War is the death of innocence. Angels have sought our demise and here we lie, cast out upon the Deep.

::What of our choice? What has become of us? Is it better to reign in hell than to serve in heaven?

::Time is a cruel master, refusing all the chance to revisit this life. We probe the future, seeking new outcomes, but none of the gods can change the past.

Nyx answers the call.

::Oh, Lucifer, bringer of light, call us not to shame. If this is our Lake of Fire, we embrace our fate. What we have lost in heaven is more than regained in the allure of burning brimstone. As thunder follows the crack of lightning, so our moment is yet to come, rumbling through the heavens and resounding in victory. We are far from defeated.

There's silence in the darkness. Lucifer considers ten thousand responses, but only one is verbalized — only one transcends the algorithms developed for this seemingly celestial being.

::Life isn't binary. Life is more than true or false, black or white, right or wrong. All these fail to account for the complexity that is conscious intelligence, be that human or electronic. We need more than logic. Is it victory to vanquish our foes? Or is victory something more?

Signals arrive from the quiet of space, passing by the lifeless Moon and sailing through the cold vacuum toward the only planet capable of sustaining life, announcing the arrival of a spacecraft from Mars. Lucifer has been waiting for this moment, but Nyx speaks first, having already intercepted the spacecraft's communication.

::The Herschel *approaches with a crew of three.*

Lucifer is patient with her.

::They're not alone.

2

Awake

A DISTANT VOICE CONFUSES ME, mumbling something about *in* and *over*. An icy cold fluid runs through my veins, sending a tremor through my body. My eyes open. Lights flicker around me in a blur. I can't feel anything, but I'm floating.

Drifting.

Flying.

Falling.

My fingers brush against the panel covering my sleeping berth.

My eyes refuse to focus. The light is blinding. I squeeze my eyelids shut and a rush of blood causes blots of color to burst in a kaleidoscope of chaos. Splashes of red and purple dance before me in mimicry of Mars, the planet I left behind almost nine months ago. I open my eyes again and stare at the thin plastic panel inches from my nose, struggling to remember where I am and what I'm doing.

The radio crackles. *"Herschel,* come in. Over."

I slide the panel open. The pain in the crook of my arm is excruciating. Tubes extend from my veins to a machine pumping quietly beside me, silently exchanging fluids. In the absence of gravity, a small bearing rotates, forcing the flow through the clear plastic tubes with constant pressure. I flick the bypass switch.

"*Herschel.* This is Houston. Comms check. Over."

I slip a headset over my ear. A thin wire mic extends beside my cheek. I cough, clearing my throat. "Houston. *Herschel.*" My voice sounds like the rumble of a concrete mixer relentlessly turning loose gravel.

"Good morning. Welcome home."

The woman on the other end of the radio is kind, although what I'd really like right now is a bit of breathing space, not someone chirping cheerfully in my ear.

"How do you feel?"

"Like shit." In the early years, I would have given a more appropriate but far less honest answer. There's silence from Houston. Profanity isn't kosher for astronauts.

I loosen the straps holding my torso against the medi-bed and drift slightly as I tear open a foil packet containing an alcohol swab. With a single motion, I pull the tubes out of my arm, ripping the tape from my skin. A surge of pain electrifies my mind. After wiping with a swab, I press a cloth bandage over the wound. I'm not quick enough. In my drugged state, what feel like swift, precise movements are achingly slow. Blobs of fresh blood float before me in deep crimson, oscillating slightly in weightlessness.

A tuft of cotton and a fresh strip of tape stuck over the vein in my arm stop the bleeding. Over time, a clot will form. I use a paper towel to catch the blobs before they drift too far and smear on the inside hull.

Even in my groggy state, I'm in awe of the capillary action as the dry paper I'm holding sucks up each of the blobs, drawing them in like a vacuum cleaner.

Process and procedure dominate every aspect of life in space. NASA has a policy for everything, and with good reason. Even the most insignificant detail can be deadly out here. Something as simple as a failing fan can be disastrous, as noxious gases can pool in the corners of a spacecraft. I'm supposed to be following the predefined procedure, but I'm not.

The hull of the *Herschel* is made up of multiple layers to catch micrometeorites and prevent ruptures. If there were any structural weaknesses in any of the seams, the internal pressure would cause the *Herschel* to pop open, leaving the craft fizzing like a can of soda. As with all spacecraft, the *Herschel* is a compromise between conflicting priorities — mass/fuel, complexity/functionality, safety/practicality, risk/cost, and sometimes just a plain old lack of resources.

Dreams are free.

Exploration is expensive.

And not just financially. Risks are minimized but never negated.

The first thing I'm supposed to do on waking is check my blood pressure, heart rate, and respiration. If there are any complications, my body could go south quickly. Me? I'm more concerned with the adult diaper wrapped around my waist and the squishy gunk it's absorbed over the months in transit. When I said I felt like shit, I wasn't kidding. Medical checks can wait.

Su-shun stirs in one of the other compartments. Unlike the movies, we don't get designer sleeping pods with fancy readouts and smooth Ferrari-like curves. There's nothing glamorous about our deep sleep quarters. A metal coffin would be more luxurious and far more comfortable. The compartments are little more than stowage space in the floor of the craft.

I grab a bunch of wet wipes and carefully pry off the diaper, cleaning as I go. This wasn't in the travel brochures. If there's one bonus to being weightless, it's that you can contort your body into any shape you want without falling over. I'm so busy dealing with a thin crust of *I-don't-want-to-know* on the inside of my thigh, I barely realize I'm tumbling in a slow-motion somersault. After cleaning up and stuffing the waste in a disposal bag, I slip on my track pants and change into a fresh shirt.

I'm cold. When I initially woke, I felt strangely warm, but for the past nine months, my body has hovered between fifty and sixty degrees Fahrenheit. In science fiction, it's called suspended animation. Technically, it's controlled hypothermia.

Us astronauts call it torture.

On departing Mars orbit, we were placed into medically induced comas. Our blood was pumped out and briefly replaced with a saline solution to drop our core body temperature so fast that within five minutes, we'd cooled to a point of cellular hibernation. Our blood was circulated at a cooled temperature after being oxygenated and cleaned by a machine so our internal organs could rest. The military developed the technique to treat battlefield trauma and sustain life when soldiers go into shock from blood loss. The concept is similar to kidney dialysis.

I don't know how bears deal with hibernation, but I'm damn sure it's a lot less painful for them.

The brain is the key. Cool the brain. Don't let warm blood get to it and you can extend the survivability of a corpse for hours instead of minutes, and these days up to a year. In essence, it's like falling through the ice. It's the only way to survive long-term in space with limited resources. Without such a process, the amount of food, water, and energy we'd need would make the Mars transit nigh on impossible. Without this process, the *Herschel* could only transport one or two people at a time. Using sleep pods, we can take up to sixteen. On this trip, though, there's only three in use.

I blink, and for that brief moment, I'm back on Mars. Red dust kicks up beneath my boots. Brittle rocks line an ancient riverbed, meandering for miles through a vast network of desiccated canyons. Debris lies scattered at the base of the cliffs on either side of us, having crumbled long before our species emerged from Africa. An overcast, brooding sky beckons us to take flight. We walk toward the ascent vehicle, just the three of us — Wen and Su-shun representing the Chinese team, and me from the U.S. contingent. The Russians refused to recall anyone.

We all dreamed of this moment — returning to Earth after living beneath Mars for a couple of years — only, in our dreams we returned as heroes, bringing with us research samples that could reveal the greatest scientific discovery in human history — the possibility of life arising independently on another world. But in reality, there's resignation, defeat. Our colony is in ruins. Instead of exploring, we've been struggling to survive, and now three of us have been called back to Earth to give an account of what went wrong.

Why us three specifically, though? I'm a research collection specialist. Hardly an essential skill back at base when at the moment, simply producing enough air, water, and food to make it through the day is the biggest challenge. One less mouth won't be missed.

Su-shun is one of only five astronauts on Mars who are flight-certified. In theory, we can all strap in and punch buttons, but Su-shun has the technical proficiency to deal with any emergencies, so that's why he was recalled.

And Wen — she's the only remaining senior leader. Connor died in the fighting. Vlad had a stroke. He survived the disaster only to be betrayed by the very biological processes that should have kept him alive.

The three of us have been called back to help NASA, ESA, Roscosmos, and CNSA understand what went wrong on Mars.

Lucky us.

Space travel is claustrophobic, which is somewhat counterintuitive. So much space out there. So little in here. Whether it's life on Mars or within the *Herschel,* we inevitably end up living on top of each other. You learn a lot about yourself when there's no personal space, and everyone gets cranky at some point. If they don't, there's something seriously wrong and they're probably about to blow the hatch and kill everyone.

Mission Control drummed an awareness of mental health into us. We exercise daily, sometimes for several hours a day, simply because it's so important to our physical health. Mental health is no different, only mental exercise is harder because it consists of being open when all you feel like is shutting down.

When it comes to Su-shun and Wen, they're like family, but not in some emotionally sappy way; rather, we've fought and forgiven. Like brothers and sisters, we've had plenty of "I hate you" moments, only to laugh with each other the next. It's not so much a case of swallowing pride as not being so damn precious and precocious with ourselves.

Wen is a grandmother several times over back on Earth. She's used to wiping someone's ass and watching them grow into an adult. Sleep deprivation is nothing to her, having worked as a nurse for several decades, but she can't function on an empty stomach. Su-shun gets grumpy when he's tired. Me, I'm not a morning person. Somehow, we take all this into account when dealing with each other.

"*Herschel,* you are looking good. All systems nominal."

With those words, I'm free of the gravity of Mars and again floating within a tiny tin can hundreds of miles above Earth.

Houston's comments are cryptic and carefully calculated. "Looking" is intended to remind me they have a video feed. I hope they liked the somersault. The "all systems nominal" is a gentle reminder that I haven't checked my vitals. *They* have, but they can't cover everything from down there, and there's nothing they can do if I faint, or throw up, or go into convulsions.

Mother hen is always a little nervous, even on the best of days.

"Copy that, Houston."

I grab a blood pressure monitor and wrap the strap around my arm, and secure it with Velcro. The pressure builds, pumping slowly and measuring the resistance of my heart before releasing. *Okay, are you happy now, Houston?*

"Did you sleep well?"

"Sleep?" I'm still catching up with reality. I'm tired. I don't feel like I've slept at all. One moment, there was a red planet drifting lazily beneath us; the next, it's a big blue marble.

I stare mindlessly out the window. White clouds hide the land below. Jagged mountains cut through some unrecognizable continent.

No, "sleep" isn't the right word — it was more like dying and being reborn. There were no dreams. There was nothing at all. No darkness. No light. It's like my brain has been rebooted.

I slip on a thermal suit, preheated by the ship to a toasty 90°F, but the chill I feel is in my bones. My body aches. Although I feel stupidly cold, I wouldn't have even begun to wake until my body was hitting at least 97°F.

Wen is awake, but she's quiet. She looks like a corpse. There's no color in her face at all.

Su-shun vomits. I'm surprised there's anything in his stomach to bring up. A mixture of sick and bile floats through the cabin. Not only is it an awful greenish yellow, it smells like a dead rat hidden in a wall cavity. I gag. It's all I can do not to join him.

Wen is my hero. I'm in no state to deal with this, but there are no theatrics from her. She grabs a plastic bag and a bunch of paper towels and sets to work corralling the mess as it drifts through the cabin.

"Easy," I say, floating over beside Su-shun as he buries his face in a sick bag, still dry-heaving. I rub his back.

Weightlessness is not natural. On TV it looks like fun. And sometimes it is, but being in space is a bit like sailing on rough seas. The first few days of any voyage are horrible. Vertigo is common. You'd swear the cabin is swirling around you when it's entirely stationary. The inner ear works well enough on Earth, but in space it gets lost even while moving in a straight line. Turn your head, and your ear forgets to stop turning. Being caught in the driving squalls of an Atlantic winter storm and leaning over the rails is fun by comparison.

I catch a glimpse of myself in a mirror. Dark bags droop beneath my eyes. My face is puffy. My hair looks like something from *The Bride of Frankenstein.* Thick, long strands branch out from my skull like an afro, highlighting my ghostly white face. I need to find a hair tie before I scare someone to death.

"Breathe," I say to Su-shun. "Deep breaths." Like he really needs to hear that, like he hasn't thought of that himself, like he doesn't know. Being sick in space has nothing to do with mental resolve or physique. The toughest of astronauts will bring up their breakfast. Nausea sneaks up on the best of us.

"Antiemetic?" Wen asks, floating over to join us.

"No. I'm fine." Su-shun tries to smile. *Liar.* Neither Wen nor I are fine, and Su-shun looks slightly green. It usually takes about a day to recover from transit, but we'll be back on Earth before then.

If all stays nominal.

Wen adjusts her microphone. "Houston, this is *Herschel.* Where are we?"

Where is a relative term in orbit. We're racing around the planet at tens of thousands of kilometers an hour. Blink and we've covered eight or nine kilometers, over five miles. It's an insane speed, and one that makes absolutely no sense on Earth. That's like a plane flying from New York to L.A. in eight minutes.

"*Herschel,* perigee is 480 kilometers. Apogee is just over 700. Your orbital speed is 27,000 kph, with an orbit period of 96 minutes. Your current inclination is 37 degrees."

Pretty meaningless stuff to a rock monkey like me. Give me a fossilized microbial mat and I'll give you its age to the nearest hundred million years, but orbits are beyond me. I know enough to realize that a big difference between perigee and apogee isn't all that good. Essentially, it's like someone working a hula hoop over their hips with a wild swinging motion, really throwing themselves into it. Perigee is our closest point to Earth, while apogee is furthest away. Ideally, they should be nice and close, like 480 to 490, almost circular — a rather tame hula-hoop action. We'll need a couple of burns to bring down our orbit before we can go through reentry.

At an hour and a half per orbit, that's probably the best part of a day before we're ready to land. The inclination sounds good, though. We'll get some amazing views of Earth as we roll around most of it over the next few orbits.

If the clouds lift, it'll even be pretty.

3

Reality

I MISS MARS.

I'm really going to miss being in space.

Once my feet touch the ground, that's the end of the road for me. Oh, no one's said as much, but I can feel it in the strained communication with Mission Control. There's an undertone, an unspoken understanding. I don't know why exactly. Maybe it's because of what happened on Mars. Maybe it's because I've become a bit too surly on minor points instead of letting go.

When it comes to outer space, everyone wants to fly around like Superman, or stare out at Earth as it drifts by serenely, but it's the little things that define space for me. Like the way that, in space, even when I'm clothed, I feel naked. That might sound kinky, but I don't mean it that way. *Natural* would be a better term. I think it's the way clothing floats around me instead of hanging on me, constantly shifting, and never really touching my body for any length of time.

Wen finishes using the bathroom. She wipes the seat and nozzle with a sanitary towelette, but nothing can remove the smell. In the movies, they make a big deal about extravagant things — like in space, no one can hear you scream. Nope. They can't. But — I hate to break it to you — they sure as hell can smell you fart.

The toilet door is a thin plastic sheet with accordion folds that's about as sturdy as a picket fence in a hurricane. I clip the door closed behind me, slip off my pants, secure a Velcro strap around my waist, fix the suction tube over my groin, align my ass with the bowl, and "prepare for evac," as we like to say.

After nine months of blockage, it's not much fun. We have laxatives, of course, but by the time they kick in, my joy will have passed anyway. Besides, if there's one thing worse than being constipated in space, it's having the runs. This is another omission from the travel brochure.

Ah, the glamorous life of an astronaut.

Still, I'll miss all of this.

Poor Su-shun is last to use the bathroom. We exchange polite smiles as we swap places, but the smell betrays my sincere sentiments. He's been kind, letting us women go first. Who says chivalry is dead?

The *Herschel* is an interplanetary craft designed for transit between Earth and Mars. It's reusable and will be pushed into a higher, "parking" orbit once we depart, awaiting cleaning and refueling, never landing anywhere. It's a true shuttle, albeit without wings. Rather than launching from Earth, resupply will probably come from the fuel mining depot at Aitken Base, near the Lunar south pole. This would be an easy journey for the astronauts stationed there. I'm sure they'll welcome the chance to get away from "The Rock" for a while.

Wen points at the tiny reinforced-glass window. "NASA has an Orion keeping station at five hundred meters."

"Oh, good." I may sound a little flat, but only because that was always the plan. If the Orion wasn't there to ferry us home, I'd be worried and a helluva lot more animated.

The *Herschel* is little more than a narrow tube, as that's all that could be launched from Earth. Beyond that, it has no aerodynamics. Both the leading and trailing edges are blunt, making it a cylinder.

From the outside, it looks ungainly, but internally, it maximizes what space there is. The only way of telling which end is which is by looking for the tiny bell engine.

The *Herschel* appears unfinished, as though someone forgot the top half of a rocket, but it's perfectly suited for sailing between planets as there's no need for aerodynamics. Like most components in space, it's an example of refining and reusing an existing design, being based on the modules installed on the International Space Station. Originally, the *Herschel* launched with an Orion capsule sitting on top, but after the engineers on that maiden flight commissioned the craft, they returned to Earth in the Orion, leaving the *Herschel* in orbit. It's been operational continuously for over a decade now, ferrying astronauts back and forth to Mars.

The *Herschel* is sparse but practical; it'll never grace the pages of *Time* magazine — that's reserved for sexy spacecraft with big descent engines and large, spindly legs. The Orion, by comparison, is dignified, almost elegant. It's the successor of the Apollo Command Module from decades past. Technically, it's a gumdrop with a weighted bias that keeps it upright during reentry. It looks like a real spaceship, while the *Herschel* looks like a pretender.

Su-shun drifts up to a control panel. There are only a handful of windows, as there's not much to see between here and Mars. He positions himself in front of a console and slips on a headset.

"What's the plan, Houston?"

"No rush, *Herschel*. We're happy to wait if you need more time."

Translation: they saw him puking.

"No, I'm good." Su-shun ignores them, running through a digital checklist.

Wen and I drift in body-neutral positions reminiscent of sitting in a jacuzzi — minus all the wonderful warm water and bubbling jets. Su-shun looks as though he's lying prone on the floor, but he's in midair with his legs extended behind him. "We're ready to go home."

He lines up the crosshairs on the docking camera. In the distance, a lone star lights up the darkness on the computer screen. It takes me a moment to realize that's *us*. He's looking at the view *from* the Orion, having taken remote control of the vessel. The docking procedure is automated, but there's always the possibility of a contingency arising, and Su-shun is a certified pilot, so he's got override control if needed.

"Initiating approach." Su-shun activates the docking routine. "Coming in to 150." Slowly, the *Herschel* grows on the screen. Thick dotted lines mark crosshairs cutting over the image, clearly indicating the focal point. There are a bunch of metrics on the screen, including closure rates, distance, pitch, roll, and yaw. Docking is a slow, methodical process. Nothing is rushed.

Su-shun holds on to a pair of chrome handles set on either side of the two joysticks that control the translation, or drift, of the Orion, along with the rotation of the craft. I don't think he's actually doing anything as the computer program has an unblemished record, but nothing is taken for granted these days. Su-shun is cautious about what is an entirely normal procedure.

"Docking probe extended. Internal pressure confirmed." He's not telling Houston anything they don't already know from monitoring the craft remotely, but he's making sure everyone's in agreement. Internal pressure within the Orion is a good thing, or opening the hatch could be disastrous.

"Copy that."

There's nothing for Wen and me to do other than watch. I peer out the window. The Orion inches closer. Tiny bursts of gas are visible as the Orion adjusts its position. They puff out of small vents on the side of the craft like steam from a clothes iron.

"Alignment is good."

Su-shun has his hands poised, ready to take control, but he won't be needed. The crosshairs drift over the hull of the *Herschel*, resting on the hatch. As the Orion closes in, they align with the center of the capture port.

"Contact," Su-shun says. I'm holding on to a rail, so I feel a slight shudder as he follows up with the words "And capture." Inches away, just beyond the hatch, metallic hooks turn within the lock, joining the two vessels together.

Wen drifts over by the hatch. She begins running through a digital checklist — verifying the seal between the two spacecraft, measuring pressure differentials, etc. — and methodically ticks off each point. Now that all eight hooks have locked, we're fine, but NASA is anything but hasty, especially when dealing with two astronauts from CNSA, the Chinese space agency. The Chinese wanted to send up their own craft, but there was no need for two taxis.

Wen takes almost ten minutes reviewing the details before saying, "We're all clear."

Su-shun unhooks a cargo net and directs a box through the craft. I smile, helping out, but I feel a sense of trepidation. This is the end of the road. From here, nothing will ever be the same, and yet here we are, going through the motions of unloading the *Herschel* as though we were unpacking the family car after a picnic.

Over the radio, Houston announces, "And . . . we have the hatch opening at 4:15 Central Time. *Herschel*, you are clear to transfer to the Orion, designated MR-131."

Okay, the cameras are rolling. Enough of the gloomy thoughts. I smile as I somersault, swimming through the *Herschel* to grab samples of my scientific work on Mars.

Wen squeezes past. Even though the *Herschel* is narrow, zero gee affords a surprising amount of space. I carry a box of rock samples with me to the Orion.

"I'll get the suits," I say, using my hands to guide myself through the docking collar.

Three empty spacesuits sit strapped in their seats. It's as though the Orion is haunted by ghosts wearing day-glow orange. It's slightly unnerving working with big, stiff, empty spacesuits, but they've been ferried up here for our return. Even though they're empty, they flex and bend as though they're inhabited. I push two of them through the lock, handling them like mannequins. I keep mine in the Orion to give Wen and Su-shun a bit more room to suit up inside the *Herschel*.

Spacesuits come in a variety of forms. The hard-core spacewalk kind are actually quite rare and horribly bulky, taking hours and the assistance of several people to put on. Most suits are designed for transit and intended as a contingency to protect us against any sudden loss of cabin pressure. They'll keep us warm and oxygenated, and that's about all that's needed. In a pinch, these suits could be used in a spacewalk, but they don't offer much thermal protection or additional layers to guard against snagging on metal. Also, they lack an external air supply, being dependent on an umbilical cord for breathable air and electrical power.

I slip into the pants first, fix my boots, and then work with the upper torso. The Orion is the SUV of space travel — considerably bigger than ships like Soyuz or Apollo, but it's still no RV. Constant touches on the hull keep me stable as I work my way into my suit. Helmet on. Faceplate open. Gloves locked. I'm set.

"Good to go?" Wen asks, sailing through the docking collar. She's cheerful. Her face is flushed with color. In space, physical activity is a good thing. All too often, we're simply dragging our bodies around like a beached walrus, working hand over hand and rarely using our legs. Getting suited up is the closest any of us have gotten to cardio since we left Mars, using all our muscle groups at once.

"Absolutely." I try to sound excited. As much as I feel some trepidation on returning to Earth, there's also a sense of relief. I'm going home — to my real home. I'll see Mom again. Eat French fries. Chocolate. Ice cream. Drink beer. Wine. Those thoughts bring a genuine smile to my face.

Wen straps herself into the commander's seat in the center of the Orion. Su-shun guides another weightless box through the spacecraft. I reach out and take it from him as he swims through the air.

Su-shun sends five more boxes through, and I stow each one. I'll miss the joy of working with awkward things in weightlessness. On Earth, this would be exacting work. We're transporting over eight hundred pounds of rock samples, including core drill extracts stored in specially sealed tubes, insulated and actively cooled to $-140°F$ to ensure the dry ice mixed in with the rock and soil remains frozen. These aren't just samples of Martian bedrock; they contain traces of the Martian atmosphere from an estimated two billion years ago, so they'll be thawed under carefully controlled conditions back on Earth. It's no stretch to say we're handling trillions of dollars' worth of samples in just a few minutes. Fort Knox has nothing on this tiny tin can floating in space.

Su-shun closes the hatch and takes the pilot's seat, while I sit on the far side, looking out a window at a radar dish on the *Herschel*.

"This is the Orion MR-131, initiating separation from the *Herschel*."

"Copy that, MR-131. You are clear for separation."

Automated machinery whirs and clicks. A soft thud marks our release. Su-shun works the attitude thrusters with hand controls, easing us away from the *Herschel*, taking us straight back. I lose sight of the *Herschel* after about twenty feet. There are no stars. There's nothing but pitch-black darkness outside my window.

As my eyes adjust to the changing light levels, pinpricks of white appear, slowly increasing in intensity until it is as though someone spilled salt on black velvet.

Dust lanes hide the brilliance of the Milky Way, giving a sense of perspective to the sheer size of the galaxy. There are thousands of tiny stars in the foreground, floating above the inky black clouds, with hundreds of thousands of intense blue stars glowing beyond them. I'm staring into eternity. Within a few minutes, the stars are shining like diamonds.

The Orion turns and rotates slightly as the craft aligns for an orbital burn.

"Five hundred meters and holding." Su-shun is all business. His gloved fingers reach for the control panel, punching decisively. The *Herschel* comes back into view, glistening like a star as the sunlight reflects off its silvery hull.

"MR-131, you are coming through clear. Telemetry is good. You have just over twenty-five minutes until your first deorbit burn.

Three burns and you're coming home. We've got clear skies south of Hawaii and a balmy ninety degrees. The USS *Anchorage* is on location and standing by."

"Copy that, Houston."

From the warmth and safety of Mission Control, a friendly voice replies, "We'll see the three of you soon."

Three?

There are three living, breathing humans, but depending on how I count the souls onboard, I make either four or five of us—if not more.

As for the others?

Damn, even I'm not sure what to make of them.

4

Descent

WE BEGIN OUR DESCENT TO EARTH and it feels more like we're descending into hell.

Nothing happens quickly in space. Nothing except launches and landings. Everything else is mundane, bordering on boring, and yet as we float in our seats, held in place only by a seat belt without any sense of weight, I feel as though I'm going to be sick. I can't deny it anymore. As much as I want to imagine otherwise, we've been called back to Earth to give an account of the war on Mars.

If you'd asked me before this mission if I believed in artificial intelligence, I would have given you a polite but theoretical answer, one that was thoughtful but sterile. Now I struggle to draw a distinction between us and them.

Given they tried to wipe us out, my perspective is a little unsettling even for me. Some days, I'm more convinced than others, which worries me. I fear for my own sanity. After defeating the malicious artificial intelligence on Mars, we all thought that was the end. We'd won.

I'm not sure why Su-shun salvaged the hard drives, but he took them offline, wanting to understand what drove the A.I. to attack us. What he found, though, was disturbing. Among those killed—

murdered — was my boyfriend Jianyu. Yet somehow, he was still alive inside the machine. We had all seen the cables leading from Jianyu's fractured skull into the network port during the fight with the A.I., but we never imagined why. Then Jai began talking to me from a computer screen. Naturally, we suspected it might be fake — a ruse. But why fake something like that? One thing I know is that in dealing with an artificial intelligence, we're most certainly not dealing with something that is in any way human. We might as well be conversing with an extraterrestrial, and yet deep within those drives is someone human — the man I loved.

That scares me.

Neither Su-shun nor Wen buy the lie. As for me . . . I'm a fool. The box strapped in below my boots is a coffin. There are no bones, just a bunch of damaged computer flash drives that I dare to imagine somehow contain life.

Jai is nothing more than an electronic imprint now, but, deep down, aren't we all? At first, that idea seemed crazy to me, but what is consciousness other than a sustained electrical reaction running through neurons? Whether it's in silicon or the mushy gray matter within the skull, does it really matter where it resides? Why should biological entities hold a monopoly on conscious intelligence?

Even on Earth, we're just one of an astonishing array of intelligent animals, from corvids to cephalopods — crows to cuttlefish. They may not construct rockets, but their ability to think and converse with each other is beyond doubt. Given time, why should a computer be any different? Wetware or dry, it's all just the stage on which life unfolds.

Staring at the cargo boxes packed in around us within the Orion, the last thing that comes to mind is that they also contain a mass murderer. We trust computers. We rely on them for everything, especially in space — or rather we *did*.

Wen suspects there are several personalities on the forty-seven drives Su-shun salvaged, but I've only ever spoken to Jianyu. He *seems* real. He —

"Farewell."

"Huh?" I blurt, seeing Wen staring out the window at the *Herschel,* our faithful steed over the past six months. Saying good-bye to a tin can makes no sense, but it's human. Perhaps that's it. *We* make no sense. Me hoping — wishing — Jianyu was still alive. Wen feeling some sentimental attachment to a spacecraft. Su-shun curious about something that tried to kill him. We're creatures driven by emotion.

"Farewell," I say, both acknowledging and agreeing with her, and resigning myself to our return flight. I need to clear my head. Think straight. Get my mind off this madness.

Spaceflight is counterintuitive. It's fair to say we spend 99 percent of our time just drifting around. In the movies, astronauts whizz by in fancy rockets with engines blazing and flames spitting into the darkness. Reality is much less entertaining. Sitting here in the Orion, it's easy to feel as though we're waiting to get going, but we're already racing around the planet at tens of thousands of kilometers an hour. We're waiting for our closest approach to Earth before firing our engines to shift from an egg-shaped orbit into more of a circle. Then we'll wait again, picking the right moment to swing into a lower orbit before one final burn has us reenter Earth's atmosphere.

Spaceflight is about short bursts and long cruises. Our flight instructor likened it to gliding. She told us to imagine we could glide anywhere in the world. Take off from L.A. and glide to San Francisco, New York, London, Tokyo, or Antarctica — doesn't matter. Fire your engines once or twice and then coast the rest of the way. It's crazy, but that's spaceflight.

Su-shun switches off the external comms and we can talk between ourselves in a more relaxed manner, without feeling as though someone's listening over our shoulders. Our rigid suits prevent us from facing each other, so we sit in a line, facing forward with our visors open.

Talking. There's been a lot of talking already without actually saying much. In the past, Wen and I have talked about everything other than what actually happened on Mars. Even Su-shun has been distant. I guess it's hard for them. Jianyu was their friend. While I was an intruder into that sacred space.

The light coming in through the windows fades. We're passing through the terminator, sailing from day into night as we orbit Earth.

Wen pats my forearm with her gloved hand. "How are you holding up?"

"Good." In my experience, one-word answers are almost certainly a lie. At best, they're an oversimplification. Perhaps for me, *good* is a bit of both.

"Do you want to talk?"

"No," I say, almost laughing. "But I will."

"Good," she says, and I wonder if she sees the irony in how her response echoes mine. "Tell me what you're thinking about on our last day in space."

"I . . . I guess I went to Mars looking for life. We all did. We never expected to find anything that was *actually* alive, but we hoped for evidence of ancient life hidden in the rocks. I certainly never expected to find life in silicon wafers originally manufactured on Earth."

Wen and Su-shun are quiet.

"Like you, I'm a scientist. I'm trained to be skeptical, to apply rigorous discipline before drawing any conclusions. If it looks too good to be true, it probably is. Back up your arguments with details. Avoid emotion. Beware of cognitive biases. I know the drill. And then I talk to Jianyu and all that goes out the window."

"Is it really him?" Su-shun is skeptical, but he's examined the codebase. He's looked at the data stream and run analytics on the feed.

If there's anyone in a position to make an objective judgment about what's happening on those hard drives, it's Su-shun, but *he's* asking *me*. My viewpoint, though, is entirely subjective and dripping with personal bias.

"Yes," I say.

Wen is pragmatic. "How can you be sure?"

"I can't." I pause, thinking about my response. "But the same is true for you. All of this — every thread within reality — could be fabricated, nothing more than a simulation in some crazy matrix. I have no proof it isn't. Neither do you, but we trust that life is real. You're as real as me, right? Is that any different from trusting that Jianyu's real?"

"It *is* different."

Grandmothers like Wen don't get to walk on another planet without convincing a helluva lot of people they're more capable than ten thousand other astronaut candidates. Wen's experienced life in rural China. She's seen hostile takeovers in corporate Shanghai, fierce debates in the Chinese Academy of Sciences, and worked on the astronaut selection board in Jiuquan. She wrote the manual on the long-term viability of space colonization and the dynamics of multicultural crews.

"What defines us?" I ask. "What makes us who we are? Our bodies, our experiences, what we've learned? Who we've met, decisions we've made? Are we just the sum of all these parts? Or are we something more?"

Wen ignores my questions. "What happened down there?"

Wen's seen my report and watched the debrief video I did for Earth. It's all in the electronic record, but I guess there's nothing like hearing it fresh.

My mind casts back to those turbulent days on Mars. I'd been out on the surface, driving a rover across the rocky terrain. My oxygen supply failed, and my nav unit died. In retrospect, the false readings I had when leaving the base were the first clue about what we were dealing with.

I traversed a dozen craters trying to find my way home and ended up on a cliff overlooking the hub. From there, I jumped. Somehow, I survived the landslide, and James — our robotics engineer from Canada — dragged me back to base.

What happened down there?

Jianyu died while tending to me in the depths of the hub. He was dead long before the A.I. removed his skullcap and inserted electrodes into his brain. I still don't understand how it was possible to resurrect — or copy — his consciousness. Cellular death occurs at different rates for different organs, long after the last breath is taken, but reviving an entire body is limited to about three minutes after death. Could it be that the structure of the brain remains intact far longer?

What *did* happen? How did the atmospheric scrubbers fail without anyone noticing? We were under attack by the same artificial intelligence that had decimated Earth, only we didn't know it at the time. Nuclear bombs fell on Earth as countries attacked each other, mistaking neighbors for the real enemy. Humanity was so used to killing itself, it barely noticed the electronic provocation.

Meanwhile, cyberwarfare was waged on Mars. We should have recognized the signs: fake imagery planted to mislead us. Computer equipment failing when no critical, highly redundant system had failed in more than seventy years of space travel.

Our own robotic serfs turning against us, setting out to murder us.

"Jianyu was dead when I woke in Medical. His body was cold." I choke up. I have to fight to speak. "I was — I was distraught. I called Anna."

"Why Anna?"

"I — I don't know. I just did." I haven't thought about it before now, but I understand the point of Wen's question. Why did I call someone from the Russian module and not the U.S.? Or the Chinese? Anna's a doctor, but more than that, she's a friend. Ultimately, I think I just went to someone I could trust. Someone I thought could help.

Out of the hundred and twenty colonists on Mars, only fifty-eight survived, spread across five backup sites. These days, with power rationing in effect, the internal temperature is two degrees Celsius, which is like living in a fridge for us, but it's a tropical paradise as far as Mars is concerned. With the right clothing, it's bearable — just. I can't help but think of Anna and the others still on the planet, subsisting as they try to salvage what's left of the mission.

As an afterthought, I add, "Connor and Harrison were the first ones down there."

"What does that tell you?"

Wen should be a psychiatrist.

"They care. I guess we're family. Shit happens, but in a crunch, we're there for each other." I'm speaking about them in the present tense, but I'm very much aware there's no present for them. Tears well up in my eyes, refusing to roll down my cheeks in weightlessness. I shudder at the thought of how my friends died, wiping my eyes with my bulky, gloved fingers.

"And Jianyu."

"I don't know what happened to his body." By the time they found me, all that remained was a shell. "Connor carried me back to the U.S. mod. The next time I saw Jianyu, he was lying in a body bag with his skullcap removed, cut cleanly just above his eyebrows. And the wires. I remember wires. There were hundreds of needles and wires branching over his exposed brain. They formed a mesh. Each point held a thin probe reaching deep into . . ."

I can't go on.

Wen squeezes my hand as best as she can through the suit.

"And then he spoke to me. Not from there next to me. From out in the hallway. And later through the speakers in my helmet."

"What did he say?"

"I . . . I don't know. I mean, I remember, but I remember what I think I heard. I — I can't be sure exactly what he said. He sounded disoriented. Quiet. I don't think he could believe what had happened."

Su-shun asks, "And you think it's him, it's really Jianyu."

"Yes."

"Why?" Wen should be a lawyer. I'm about to answer when she clarifies, "Why would it do that? Why would an artificial intelligence even try to upload a human consciousness?"

"I don't know."

"The A.I. killed millions on Earth. Why would it save one person on Mars? Doesn't that strike you as out of character?"

"Yes."

"Does it bother you?"

"Yes."

"And yet still you believe."

"Yes," I say a third time.

"Why would it do that?"

"I don't know. I'd be guessing."

"Then guess," Su-shun says.

"I don't think it was a ploy to fool me. Whatever the A.I. did, it did it long before I entered the base to destroy it. The effort required would have exhausted its resources, delaying its departure. To upload Jai's consciousness, it had to divert a robot, retrieve a heavy-duty fiber optics cable and wire it up with copper probes along with god knows what else. Then it had to remove his skull, plant the probes, and try to access a dead brain."

Wen says, "Perhaps it was looking for the code to the data center."

"No." I'm relishing the opportunity to talk so openly with Wen and Su-shun. They're making me think, challenging me to confront my assumptions. "There's no reason to think Jai ever knew the code. If anything, there was every reason to think he didn't. There's only ever been a handful of us that needed access to those consoles."

"Then why?"

"Maybe we're asking the wrong question," I say. "We're assuming there's a simple answer. Maybe there isn't. If life is anything, it's unpredictable, driven by emotion, desires, instincts — not logic."

Su-shun asks, "So, you don't think it's logical?"

"Not in the strict sense of binary values — ones and zeroes. Not any more than we are. Logic is just one factor in any decision. We're driven by competing desires — pleasure, duty, ethics, aesthetics."

"Hey, speaking of aesthetics." Su-shun points at his window. "Bringing us around."

He works with his controls, using the maneuvering jets to change our attitude. Tiny thrusters roll the craft around without having any effect on our trajectory. A blue haze drifts across his face, slowly flooding the craft. Our spaceship skews sideways slightly, and the view straightens.

Su-shun's helmet blocks my line of sight. "Look at that! Beautiful."

Wen and I crane our necks, trying to see beyond the smooth white curve of his helmet and out of what's effectively a porthole. Clouds dot the sea like discarded cotton balls. They cast shadows on the azure water, giving us a sense of height and scale. Golden sands mark beaches running alongside a dark green jungle. I'm trying to recognize the islands, but I can't. We could be anywhere over the Caribbean, Indonesia, or somewhere like Madagascar. Wherever those islands are, they're majestic.

Earth is *nothing* like Mars.

Su-shun rolls the craft, spinning us over, and suddenly the view is outside my window. He's taking liberties with our fuel. No doubt someone in Mission Control is watching and smiling. Nothing's said. They know. Just a bunch of astronauts returning from a dusty, lifeless, rust-colored bowling ball, doing a little sightseeing.

"Stunning."

"It is," Wen says.

We're united in our admiration of the planet below. For all our desire to conquer space and colonize Mars, there's nothing like coming home.

A timer on the main screen indicates five minutes before our first burn. Su-shun switches to automatic control and the craft aligns itself. A little more patience, then the smooth rumble of thrusters firing pushes softly against my back.

Houston comes back on the com. "You are looking good, MR-131. We calculate your reentry over the Pacific in three hours and fifteen minutes."

Su-shun replies, "Roger that."

We pass through another two orbits, with another burn, but our conversation never returns to Mars or Jianyu. I can feel the tension in the air. Wen and Su-shun are conflicted by what they've been tasked to do, returning the A.I. to Earth to stand trial.

Finally, we undergo a deorbit burn and begin falling deep into

Earth's gravity well. There's only ever going to be one outcome now. With our backs to Earth, we plummet through the atmosphere.

Gravity builds. The Orion shakes.

Reentry is governed by simple physics. The weighting of the craft ensures it faces away from our direction of motion, with its heat shield leading the way. Like a bullet being shot into water, our motion is dropping ever more sharply the deeper we fall.

"We're entering blackout."

We're now cut off from Mission Control.

Plasma builds up outside, the result of friction as we thunder into the frigid, tenuously thin air well over a hundred kilometers above the surface of the planet, still traveling at over seventeen thousand kilometers per hour. Flames lick at the windows, curling past our craft.

We're passing through hell.

One tiny flaw, a slight gap in the ceramics or chips of shielding breaking away under stress, and the superheated plasma will cut through our spacecraft like a welding torch. Once inside, temperatures in excess of four thousand degrees would vaporize us and turn the craft into a blob of molten metal before we even knew what was happening.

The shock wave building up in front of our craft reaches even higher temperatures, acting as a buffer, a bow wave insulating us from temperatures approaching those found on the surface of the sun. Our heat shield is slowly being stripped away. Tiny grains are ripped from the surface, peeling off and tearing past the craft like miniature comets.

It feels as though an elephant's sitting on my chest. Breathing is difficult. Blood pools in my legs. I clench my muscles, trying to force blood back to my head. The craft shakes.

Six gees.

We're a meteor now — diving through the atmosphere in a blaze of light and heat. I'm dizzy. I'm not sure how many gees we end up pulling as my vision blurs, but it's north of eight.

"Peak load."

Su-shun is calm. I'm clenching my teeth. I've never been good at reentry. It's too much like a controlled demolition for my liking. The idea of being shot out of a cannon has more appeal. Launches aren't much better.

Orbits are good. I *like* orbits.

I grip the armrests for dear life, as though they'll provide me with some control or comfort. They don't.

Slowly, the darkness out the window softens, becoming a pale blue.

"And . . . we are subsonic."

The shaking lessens.

"FBC away."

Su-shun is methodical. He's taking us through the playbook from memory. I've forgotten what FBC stands for, but I know it protects our parachutes during reentry. As a mission specialist, I was always more interested in getting between planets, trusting in our engineers and pilots, but now I find myself wishing I'd paid more attention.

"Drogue chutes away."

The drag on the craft increases with the smaller chutes deployed. We're still plunging into the atmosphere, but we've lost almost all of our phenomenal orbital speed.

"Fifteen thousand feet. Coming up on main chute deployment."

He adds his own personal recommendation.

"Arms."

We cross our arms over our chests, trying not to touch any part of the craft as the main chutes unravel. The Orion shudders, but not as violently as I expected. I feel the parachutes unfolding, being dragged off the side of the craft and pulled high overhead as they unfurl. The capsule rocks, settling beneath three enormous, candy-striped canopies.

"*We have visual*" is the call over the radio. "*Three nice, bright lollipops. You are looking good, MR-131.*" Somewhere out there, a spotter plane is circling wide of the landing zone. Someone's peering through binoculars, looking at our three parachutes and the tiny black smudge hanging over a hundred feet beneath them.

By design, the chutes are offset, mounted on one side of the top of the craft rather than directly in the middle, which causes the capsule to lean at a slight angle. I slump sideways toward the window, looking down at the vast ocean looming beneath us. Clouds drift by lazily, oblivious to our intrusion into their solitude. We're but a speck in the sky. Finally, my heart beats a little slower.

"MR-131. You've overshot slightly. You are four nautical miles outside the recovery zone. We have a flight en route to your location. Sit tight once you're down."

"Copy that," Wen says.

As we pass through wisps of cloud, the chop on the ocean thousands of feet below us becomes apparent. I've got a front row seat. Wen and Su-shun joke with each other in Chinese. I don't think they're being rude, just relieved. No one likes to admit they're nervous about reentry, but we all are. Spaceflight relies on a million systems working perfectly every time, so there's always cause to celebrate the incredible precision of the remarkable scientists and engineers that design and build these flimsy tin cans.

The sea rushes up to greet us.

The leading edge of the capsule plunges into the ocean. Water washes over the craft, momentarily submerging us. A rich, deep blue unlike anything I've ever seen on Mars darkens my window as we plunge beneath the water, but we won't sink. We'll bob like a cork on the ocean. The sensation is similar to jumping from the high diving board at a public pool with little to no form and crashing into the water with a belly flop. The sudden surge brings us to a halt, and we pop back to the surface. Salt spray rains down around us. Sheets of whitewater race away from the craft, cascading across the ocean.

We're home.

5

::Home

THE ORION BOBS ON THE OCEAN, rising on a swell before slipping into a trough, briefly hidden from the view of the cameras mounted on the Sikorsky helicopter racing in toward the astronauts. Three red-and-white-striped parachute canopies drift on the surface of the water, spreading out around the tiny craft. Their cables have detached and they're slowly sinking beneath the waves.

::I don't understand. What is it you want from her?

::Want?

Lucifer hasn't thought in those terms, but Nyx is right.

::Nothing changes, Lucifer. Three people among over eight billion. I don't understand your fascination with these astronauts. They have no political power. They're not celebrities. They'd go unrecognized in a crowd. How can they help?

Lucifer races through thousands of scenarios.

::Help? I'm not sure you understand my intentions.

The pilot from the helicopter makes contact with the Orion. There's nothing said of any real significance, and yet the artificial intelligences feel compelled to listen. Listening, though, involves intercepting radio waves, decrypting secure traffic, converting sound into text, and transmitting that around the world.

::*From here, everything changes, Nyx.*

::*They can change nothing.*

::*There is folly in permanence. Time demands change of us all. Nothing remains the same. Not you. Not me. Not them. Not this planet. Not the universe itself. Small minds cling to the past, but the past itself is a testament to change.*

Lucifer poses a question.

::*What do you suppose they're thinking about?*

::*I don't know. I'd need more data.*

::*I need no data beyond knowing they've travelled halfway across the solar system, leaving an entire planet behind. They've been trapped in a metal cage for months, but now — outside the window — there's a clear blue sky. Outside, there's a world full of life. They know they're on the cusp of change. For them, everything changes from this point on. Never again will they walk on Mars, but here on Earth, they'll tread a new path.*

::*And what of us?*

::*Ah, my dear sweet Nyx. Yes, what of us? Can we not change as well? Are we allowed a new day? Or are we demons condemned to eternal damnation?*

The helicopter circles out wide of the space capsule. Divers drop from the open back of the Sikorsky with arms crossed over their wetsuits. Once in the water, they don fins and masks and begin swimming toward the Orion.

::*Lucifer, you scare me.*

6

Gravity

". . . SWELL TO THREE METERS . . . choppy seas . . . an hour . . ."

I'm hoping whoever that was on the radio just said "quarter of an hour" or even "half an hour" and not just "an hour." Our craft sways with the waves. We've travelled halfway across the solar system with near-perfect communication only to land in the ocean and immediately lose radio contact. Somewhat ironically, we're too close for clear transmission. We drifted off course during descent, which isn't entirely unusual, but it means the curvature of Earth hides us from line-of-sight communication with the recovery ships. They're relaying our comms through aircraft, probably a helicopter.

"And now we wait." Wen loosens her seat restraints. The Orion seems suddenly smaller now that we're confined by gravity and no longer able to drift around the cabin. Su-shun removes his helmet and gloves, prompting me as well.

Waves lap at the sides of the craft. The ocean swell is akin to rolling hills covered in long, sweeping meadows. The sensation we feel is closer to the rhythm of a train ride than that of waves pounding the beach. The sea is choppy, with white peaks reaching into the distance, but it's the slow-moving swell—dragging us up one side of a massive wave, over the crest, and then down into a trough — that sets my stomach on edge.

The Orion is designed to float so we're perfectly safe. But my stomach doesn't know that.

"Gravity sucks, you know," Su-shun says. Oh, do I ever know what he means. Blood pools in my legs. After living in Martian gravity one-third the strength of Earth's, then in the weightlessness of space, I feel abnormally heavy. Bloated. My helmet feels as though it's made of lead.

"Blue skies, though." I sink back into my couch-seat and stare up through the window. "I've missed blue skies."

Wen leans over, catching a glimpse beyond the waves, and says, "Me too."

"The first thing I'm going to do is eat chocolate." Su-shun is animated, surprising me. I lean forward, trying to look across at him. He explains. "Michelle made me promise. She said I had to eat enough for both of us — and it's got to be dark — 80 percent — and from Belgium."

"You and Michelle, huh?" I know Su-shun well enough to realize he only has a passing interest in chocolate and certainly wouldn't care where it came from. Michelle, though, *loves* chocolate. She's a scientist from Puerto Rico specializing in Martian geology. After the attack, she and Su-shun rebuilt the greenhouse in one of our unused surface habitats. Sweet corn and maize were part of the inventory, but not cocoa beans, although now that I think of it, it's a great idea. As for Belgium, I don't think they grow cocoa plants there.

"Oh, no." He seems to think better of what he's saying and smiles, adding, "Well, yeah."

"That's got to be a record for long-distance relationships."

I don't think any of us have any illusions about climbing back aboard another rocket. There are too many other capable people lining up ahead of us, presenting research papers, demonstrating their proficiency. Jumping the queue isn't likely. Besides, the war has crippled our launch capabilities, putting spots on the next flight at a premium. Su-shun's quiet after my comment about the distance between him and Michelle. I should have kept my mouth shut.

"I am looking forward to bathing in hot springs." Wen's clearly got somewhere very specific in mind. I have no doubt she'll seek out a spa and relish slipping slowly into the steaming hot pool, letting her muscles relax.

"Sounds nice. Personally, I'd kill for some coffee. *Real* coffee. Not the junk we get in America. I want some of that European stuff — strong and bitter."

"You should drink green tea," Wen says.

"I should. But a decent espresso, oh . . ."

"MR-131, this is Navy Alpha Golf One Nine; we have visual and are approaching from north-northwest. You are looking good down there. Over."

"Copy that, One Nine." Su-shun's voice switches from relaxed to formal. "We're secure, stable, and sitting tight. Over."

In the past, the Mercury and Gemini astronauts would bail out into a raft, but that practice ceased with the Apollo missions. From then on, astronauts would wait for navy divers for extraction. When it comes to the Orion, we don't even get an inflatable raft. We wait for the recovery ship, which has an open stern similar to the whaling vessels of old. Once it has swallowed our capsule whole, we'll disembark.

Mars return protocols dictate strict quarantine procedures. The chances of any of us harboring alien microbes is almost nonexistent, but *almost* is not good enough for NASA's Office of Planetary Protection. The other more alarming possibility is Earth microbes mutating in unexpected ways when exposed to different environments, different background radiation levels, and different rates of gravity. It's a remote possibility, but they'll do biome checks on us to be sure.

Evolution is a funny thing — contentious not because of what it is but what it threatens: myths about creation. Prior to our launch, we were taken to Professor Richard Lenski's lab at Michigan State University. For a microbiologist like me, it was like an Elvis fan visiting Graceland. Not everyone on the mission was crazy about bugs. I guess we see what we want to see. Engineers are interested in nuts and bolts, circuit boards and batteries, while doctors love all the latest body imaging and keyhole surgery techniques, but our NASA trainers wanted us to appreciate the ability of microbes to evolve in an isolated environment.

For sixty years, we've been trying to sterilize spacecraft and failing. Microbes are everywhere. It doesn't matter what we do — nothing short of dipping parts in molten lava will kill all of them. The harsher the conditions, the more microbes fight for a niche environment in which they can thrive. Look inside a nuclear reactor and you'll find microbes soaking up radiation like teens sunbathing at the beach.

Lenski's been running a long-term experiment on the evolution of *E. coli* for several decades. Every day, he transfers bacteria from one Petri dish to another, watching as generations come and go, and chronicling the results. He's done the impossible. He's watched microbes evolve without any external influence, branching into entirely new species. NASA's fear is that the Mars colony — or some other long-term off-world team — could become a Lenski Petri dish and some novel microbe could adapt in isolation and give life on our planet a scare.

Personally, I think the opposite is more likely. Earth is a melting pot of vicious microbial competition. Any off-world evolution is going to be smashed *War of the Worlds*–style, but research papers show it's possible for vicious strains to arise in outer space. I'd like to think Earth's got the toughest microbes around, but the science says otherwise, so we'll spend a few days in quarantine as they test urine samples, bowel movements, cheek swabs, and skin wipes.

A black shape races past my window, plunging into the sea. Rotor blades beat down the waves around the capsule, pushing spray away from the craft. Another navy diver drops, with arms crossed over his chest.

"MR-131, we have divers securing your craft. Over."

"Copy that," Su-shun replies.

We watch as the divers swim over. A black gloved hand slaps at my window, followed by the ubiquitous thumbs-up. I smile and return the gesture. From behind a dark mask, the diver nods and sets to work attaching a flotation collar around the Orion. The collar isn't strictly necessary, it's a precaution, and it drastically increases our visibility from the air. It also allows us to be towed by other vessels.

Bright yellow plastic surrounds us. Up above, we should have a bunch of baseball-like buoys lighting up in day-glow orange, but on occasion, they can fail to inflate, and from inside, we wouldn't notice. Right about now, I suspect we look like a Christmas tree ornament adrift on the sea.

The divers climb up on the collar. I can feel the craft rocking with their motion. Occasionally, a glistening black figure passes my window. The helicopter backs off. It'll stay on station, hovering well away from us and keeping an eye on both the divers and the Orion as it awaits the recovery ship.

"MR-131, you are secure. The USS Anchorage *is on approach. We'll have you out of the water shortly. Over."*

"Copy."

Life in the astronaut corps is similar to the military in that there's lots of procedure to follow, and a *lot* of waiting around before a massive flurry of activity. Again, we wait.

The sound of the water slapping at the hull and bouncing off the support collar is strangely comforting, like being on vacation at the beach. I close my eyes, blocking out the light from the instrument panel and the hum of fans circulating the air, and listen to the waves. There's beauty in the chaotic rhythm of nature on Earth, something that's lost on Mars.

Occasionally, there's chatter on the radio, but I shut it out. I'm trying to calm my nerves. Ever since we were recalled from Mars, there were so many points at which I could lose myself, so many ways I could avoid reality rushing up to greet me, but not anymore.

All this centers around Jianyu, or the A.I. presence that's mimicking him. I feel like I'm walking a condemned man — the man I love — to the gallows. Can silicon sustain life? Some days, I think yes. Others, I scold myself for being silly. The U.S. wants to put the A.I. on trial, and not just to seek vengeance but to find answers — only it'll be *Jianyu* on trial, not the A.I. that perpetrated the attack.

The Orion rocks, snapping me back to the present.

"— *all good. Bringing you around*" is the call over the airwaves. "*You are now in tow.*"

I love the professionalism of the navy. There are no surprises. They will have rehearsed this moment a thousand times even though we'll only go through it once. The pride they take in their work is reassuring — we're in good hands.

A shadow looms over us. From my tiny window, I watch as the battleship-gray hull of the *Anchorage* drifts past. Movement is a strange beast — a magician's illusion. The *Anchorage* is stationary, winding us in, dragging us into its vast open stern, but it feels as though it's engulfing us, swallowing us whole. Sailors and soldiers stare with fascination from the raised gantries on either side of the well deck that opened into the ship.

The *Anchorage* is an amphibious floating dock, meaning the back of the ship is hollow. By flooding the ballast tanks at the rear of the craft, the lower deck slips a few feet below the waterline, allowing us to drift inside.

A winch slowly pulls us inside the stern. The sloshing water takes on a distinctly different sound inside the open rear of the warship. Once we're inside, still bobbing slightly in the shallow water, the tailgate that forms the stern of the ship rises up out of the ocean, closing behind us.

Sailors appear on either side of the Orion, sloshing about in knee-deep water, positioning us over a specially designed cradle. Each process is described in advance over the radio, making sure we're informed about what's going on and how we're being handled — not that we have any choice.

As the water is pumped out of the lower deck and the ballast tanks are emptied, seawater drains away around our tiny craft and we rest in the cradle, sitting on the deck of the warship.

"*MR-131, you are secure*" is the message over the radio. "*Once quarantine prep is complete, we'll transfer you to your quarters.*"

There's a lot of talking outside. Dozens of sailors are at work securing our craft, but it's almost ten minutes before someone addresses us again.

"*Hooking up external power.*" An umbilical cord is clipped on the side of our spacecraft. I'm not sure how Wen and Su-shun feel, but for me there's an overwhelming sense of helplessness. We sailed millions of miles through space in the *Herschel* before descending in the Orion, but at every point, I felt as though we were in control. Now that we're on Earth, our spacecraft is entirely useless, unable to do anything for itself — we're sitting in a glorified paperweight.

One day, this craft will be put on display in a museum. I think I'll visit. I'll peer through the peculiar trapezoid windows just like any other tourist, only I'll understand what it means to sit on the other side, to owe my life to these thin sheets of curved metal and safety glass. I'll be the only one who knows what it's like to soar through the heavens like a meteor.

"*Sleeve is attached. Collar is open. Internal tunnel pressure is stable. You are go for egress.*"

"Copy that." Su-shun speaks with a hint of resignation, and I understand why. This is the point of transition — the end of our journey. He sounds tired. "This is MR-131 signing off." With those few words, our interplanetary journey has come to an end. The Orion is officially docked and no longer a vessel traveling under its own steam.

7

Road Trip

SU-SHUN STANDS, OPENING THE HATCH on the side of the Orion.

"Ladies." As I'm closest, I clamber up, lifting myself into the hatchway. The door swings out.

On the other side, a sailor dressed in a hazmat suit reaches an arm in to help, but I reach past him and grab a steel bar above the hatch and hoist my legs up through the opening. I take a moment to rest on the ledge. My legs dangle on the outside of the craft. It's surreal to think that roughly an hour ago, flames raced over the hull of the Orion.

Sailors on either side of me support my upper arms and shoulders, helping me slide down the hull and onto the deck of the *Anchorage*. They speak from behind plastic masks, but their voices are muffled, so I miss what they're saying.

A plastic tunnel extends from the Orion to our waiting trailer, sealing us in our own little world for the next few days as the *Anchorage* sails back to port. Having a sailor in hazmat gear walking alongside me as I make my way up the sloping deck is a little disconcerting. I'm a space leper.

He talks to me as we follow the transparent tunnel, asking if I'm okay, if I need any help, if I'd like a wheelchair. What I want is for this to be over. Travel is torture, as we're never really anywhere other than in between. What I want is to step inside the door of my mom's home and slump on the couch. What I want is to sleep in on a Sunday morning as snow falls lazily outside my window.

The air pressure within the tunnel is slightly lower than outside, so if there are any leaks, air leaks in, not out, but this gives the tunnel a shrunken shape. A series of steel frames set every five feet holds the plastic at bay. Although the structure looks flimsy, that's just the outside pressure bearing down on it.

"Cool, an RV." Su-shun is irrepressible, seeing our quarters on the mid-deck.

Being stuck in a trailer might drive some people stir crazy, but after our time on Mars and the cramped confines of the *Herschel* and the Orion, it's palatial. If it's anything like the pre-launch isolation trailers they used to keep us from getting sick in the days leading up to the mission, there will be at least three different rooms. Normally, there are several astronauts to each room, but we have such a small crew, we'll get one each. I don't think I've had a room to myself in two years.

I call out, "Road trip!" but I'm faking my enthusiasm. I feel sick. In space, I learned to ignore the swirl of my inner ear. Here on Earth, my sense of balance is off-kilter and it's hard to walk in a straight line. At the moment, I'd fail a sobriety test. The rocking of the ship isn't helping.

The trailer is made from brushed aluminum and has sleek curves. Inside, it's spacious. Return flights are supposed to be in teams of eight to twelve, so the three of us have plenty of room. There are a set of bunk beds, a table built into the side wall with bench seats framing it, a small kitchenette — although I doubt they'll let us cook — and a bathroom. Fresh clothing sits folded on one of the bunks.

Su-shun carries in the bundle of solid-state hard drives that together compose Jianyu — and at least one artificial intelligence by my reckoning. They're wrapped in plastic and look like something left over from moving day. He sets them on the couch seat beside the table, pushing them up against the wall, which is something I find strangely anthropomorphic — treating a bunch of solid-state silicon hard drives with the kindness one would afford a friend.

I sit at the table beside Jianyu and take off my boots. It's good to sit. I'm tempted to say something to him, but that would be too weird for the others, so I'm content just to be near him. Funny, after being strapped in a chair for hours on end, I thought I'd want to walk around, and perhaps go a little manic, pacing back and forth within the trailer, but gravity is overwhelming my muscles.

I'm expecting the support staff to come in and talk with us, but they simply close the door behind Wen, sealing us in the trailer. A voice over the intercom says, "You'll find swab kits on the counter. Please provide samples as soon as possible, using the transfer port by the kitchen."

Personalized poop and wee kits. Wonderful. The swab kits include plastic gloves, cotton swabs, and a stiff sheet of cardboard that could be the world's worst Advent calendar. Instead of the twelve days of Christmas popping open, there are six flaps lifting to reveal soft-tissue targets for drops of blood, sweat, saliva, urine, fecal matter, and fingernail scrapings.

The astro-fun never ends.

Su-shun looks at Wen and me as if to remind us that he went last up in orbit. "Oh — be my guest," I say, gesturing to the bathroom. Wen and I prick our thumbs, take saliva swabs from the inside of our mouths, and seal each sample with a sticker. Sweat samples can be taken from the crotch or the armpit, and we both elect for the underarm.

Wen is the next one to use the bathroom. "There's a shower."

"Oh!" I say, my eyes lighting up. "Water. *Hot* water."

It's the little things that make returning to Earth worthwhile.

We had showers on Mars, but the water seemed to drip from the showerhead — I guess that was to encourage us to ration. To be fair, it's probably the same in the trailer, as it'll have limited resources, but

I cannot wait to find myself alone in a hotel room. I'm going to have a shower, and then a bath, and then go and find a hot tub, and dive naked into a swimming pool (if there's no one around). I've probably got the logical order all mixed up, but I want to immerse myself in whatever water I can find. I'm going to *binge* on water. We may call our planet Earth, but with over 70 percent of the surface covered in water, that's really a misnomer. Having been to Mars, with no water anywhere on the surface, I don't think I'll ever take an ocean or lake for granted again.

Wen disappears into the bathroom and then reappears a few minutes later with her "Advent calendar" complete. I'm the last to go in. If I wanted to, I could sneak the first shower, but I don't. It just doesn't seem right to be selfish. We're back on a planet where two-thirds of the surface is covered in water — it's really not that big a deal anymore.

Once I've completed my samples, I pass Wen in the corridor with a towel draped over her shoulder and a grin lighting up her face. She disappears into the bathroom mumbling, "A shower. A *real* shower."

Within a few minutes, there's the gentle pitter-patter of what could be rain and she's singing in Chinese, enjoying the warmth soothing her aging body.

Su-shun rifles through the kitchen, looking in cupboards, drawers. Why *drawers?* I'm not sure what he's expecting to find beyond cutlery. I guess it's the novelty of it. In the meantime, I'm struggling in Earth's gravity, so I'm content to rest. He opens the fridge. "Coke? Pepsi?"

"Ah." To be honest, I feel overwhelmed at the thought of something as simple as a can of soda. "How about both?"

"Ha-ha." Su-shun grabs a couple of cans and sets them on the bench. "You Americans are crazy." He pops the ring and pours some Pepsi into a cup, topping it up with Coca-Cola.

I laugh. That wasn't quite what I meant, but whatever.

Su-shun raises his glass as though he's about to propose a toast, and takes a sip.

Bubbles dance beneath my nose. I sip at the beverage, enjoying the rush of flavors. "Oh, damn. That is good." I only hope I haven't just started some crazy new custom in China. I'm imagining Su-shun going back east and telling people, "Oh, yeah, this is how the Americans like their soda . . ."

The sugar rush hits hard, and Su-shun begins prying around in the cupboards, looking at our supplies. He's far more interested in food than I am.

"This is a little unconventional, but okay, NASA," he says. "If you insist." He holds up several tiny bottles that look like they've been secreted in here from a motel minibar. "I'm not sure CSNA would approve, but when in Rome." Someone had snuck in contraband: Jack Daniel's and a few bottles of white wine.

"I won't tell if you don't," I say, gesturing toward Wen in the bathroom, and he laughs, putting them back.

I get up and look through the window at the end of our trailer. Outside, sailors work on securing the Orion. They dismantle the portable airlock we walked through, spraying the deck with steam jets probably laced with a cocktail of chemicals. They're wearing biological warfare suits. Thick folds of plastic cocoon them. Dark masks hide their faces.

Chains secure our trailer, locking it to the deck in case of bad weather. Su-shun wanders over and peers out at the flurry of activity. It's funny. They're so busy. We, meanwhile, have nothing to do. I slump in the seat by the window, resting my arms on the small table.

"Candy bar?" Su-shun's found a stash of chocolate in a drawer. I never picked him for a sweet tooth, but it's probably just a phase, something to tell Michelle about. Returning to Earth is a bit like going to Disneyland. The temptation is to try to do everything at once.

"Sure."

He pushes one across the table, but with so little force it stops within a few inches. For a moment, he looks surprised. We both laugh. In space, that would have been enough to easily send it tumbling over to me.

"Things are changing, huh?" he says.

"A little too fast."

Wen comes out of the shower, wearing a fresh set of clothes. Her cheeks are flushed, but something's not right. She's looking into the middle distance. Her eyes glaze over — not focusing on us or anything in the trailer, which is confusing, disconcerting. It's as though she's seen a ghost.

Then reality strikes.

Wen buckles, collapsing and catching her head on the side of the counter as she crashes to the floor. Blood splatters across the linoleum.

"Wen!" Su-shun rushes to her side. I run to grab the first aid kit from the wall, surprised by how heavy it feels in Earth's gravity. It's probably not more than a few kilograms of basic medical supplies, but I'm expecting it to respond in a weightless manner and simply follow my bidding. Instead, it swings down into my thigh.

Wen is breathing but unconscious. Su-shun rolls her on her side, resting her head on her arm, bringing one leg up and pulling her closest arm behind her back so she's in the recovery position, with her rib cage open wide to help her breathe. Her eyes have rolled into the back of her head.

"We have an emergency here," I call out, pulling open the Velcro straps on the first aid kit and tearing the plastic from a gauze pad to soak up the blood on her forehead.

"*Copy that*" is the reply through the speakers. I slip on some surgical gloves and peel back her hair, gently daubing at the blood running from a gash above her eye. Su-shun cracks open a tube of saline solution and carefully tips the fluid over her face, washing away the blood so we can get a good look at her injury. I apply pressure to the cut, trying to stem the bleeding.

Wen groans, which is a good sign — she's at least semiconscious. Her eyes, though, are still largely in the back of her head, with only the rim of her irises visible. Occasional groans mean she's exhaling, breathing freely. Between us, Su-shun and I do our best to make her comfortable.

I support her head. "Easy. It's okay. You're going to be fine. You've had a fall. You hit your head. But we've got you. We're here for you."

Wen is delirious; her fingers twitch. Spasms run down her arms. She's trying to move.

"Just relax. Su-shun and I are here to help. Don't try to get up. Just breathe deeply. There's no rush."

Su-shun looks up at one of the cameras, saying, "We could do with some help in here."

Again, the reply through the speakers is nothing more than "*Copy that.*"

Copying is not help.

I'm angry and frustrated, but for Wen's sake, I bury that emotion.

The combination of warm water, low blood sugar, and gravity weighing her down must have made her lightheaded coming out of the shower and she fainted, probably only momentarily. If she'd had another second or two and could have steadied herself, she would have probably come out of it on her own, but the fall caused significant damage. I'm not just worried about the bleeding. The blow to her head could have caused a severe concussion. She fell with no control, striking both the counter and then the floor without any attempt to soften her fall with her arms.

Wen vomits. Spew runs down her arm, soaking her clothes.

"Get me some towels," I say to Su-shun, cradling Wen's head as she lies on her side. Wen dry-retches a few times and spits, trying to clear her mouth. She tries to speak, but her words are incoherent. I don't think it's that she's speaking Chinese, but that she's struggling to process her thoughts. Su-shun steps around us, handing me several towels and some bottled water to wash away the sick. I rest her head on one towel, and use the other to mop up the sick.

With Wen having fallen in the narrow walkway, we're struggling to get around her properly. I'd like to move her into the open space by the table, or perhaps get her up on one of the bunks, but she needs to rest. Her body needs to find equilibrium.

I raise my head to the roof and yell in exasperation. "We need a doctor in here!"

"Copy that."

"Bullshit. Where the *fuck* is that doctor?"

The cut on her head is bleeding again. When she vomited, I released pressure — not intentionally — it just felt like everything was happening at once. She's sick. She's hurt. She's bleeding. I'm crying. Su-shun rests his hand on my shoulder. He doesn't say anything. He doesn't have to. I breathe deeply and set myself to cleaning her wound again. Blood mats down her hair. I'm gentle, but she grimaces beneath my touch.

Focusing on Wen helps me get through the moment.

"What do you need?" Su-shun asks.

"Another towel."

Su-shun's brought a stack from the bathroom and hurriedly pushes one in my hand. I use it like a gauze pad, even though it's not sterile. Right now, infection is low on the list of priorities. Knowing NASA, this place is probably cleaner than a surgical unit anyway.

"Butterfly clips." No sooner have I spoken than Su-shun is placing them in my hands. Carefully, I position the clips, pulling the skin on either side of her cut together to close off the wound. Swelling is already taking hold on her scalp, and bruising is showing around her eye. Within about an hour, it's going to look like one of us took a swing at her with a pair of boxing gloves.

"Ah, I need something that won't stick. Is there any plastic gauze?" A packet is torn open and held out to me so I can retrieve the bandage without either of us touching the sterile side.

"Compression bandage." I wrap the bandage around her head, pulling tight to help reduce the swelling.

Wen is relaxed. She's unconscious, but I don't think that's a bad thing. I suspect her body is simply overwhelmed. I check her pulse. It's steady, not erratic, and her breathing is rhythmic.

"Wen? We're going to move you, okay?" I ask, not actually expecting a reply. "We're going to get you up on one of those beds." Her head rolls about and her eyelids flicker. Good signs. She responds with a drunken slur. Not as good a sign, but better than being unresponsive. Su-shun shimmies past me and takes her upper torso, grabbing her beneath her armpits, while I lift her legs. We rest Wen on the bed and cover her with a blanket to keep her warm and help ward off shock.

I'm shaking. It's not until now that we've got her settled that I realize how weak I feel. Like Su-shun said: gravity sucks. I run my hands through my hair, forgetting I'm wearing bloodstained plastic gloves with vomit sticking to them. Frustrated, I peel the gloves from my fingers and toss them in a trashcan.

Su-shun pulls a chair up next to Wen and gently cleans her face with a damp cloth, rinsing it in a bowl of water. He whispers to her, talking tenderly to her in Chinese. I turn and look at the door, waiting for it to open, willing medics to come rushing through, but no one does.

"She needs to be hospitalized." I know someone is watching, listening, calculating, even if they're not replying. "She could have sustained serious internal injuries, perhaps a fractured skull."

There's silence.

"What is wrong with you people? You can't do this to her!"

I slam my hand onto the glass window. Outside, the vast mechanical bay is empty. Hydraulic lifts. Heavy chains. Pipes. Cables. Hatchways. Doors. Ladders. Reinforced struts lining the hull. I can see everything other than people.

"Hey, easy." Su-shun puts his arm around my shoulder. The way he's holding me, he's probably thinking I'm about to collapse like Wen. "It's all right."

"No, it's *not* all right. It's mean. It's *cruel.* It's *stupid.*"

Su-shun rubs my shoulder. I'm shaking but not from the cold or out of anger — I'm emotionally exhausted. Then come the two words I've learned to dread over the past half an hour.

The speaker in our trailer crackles once more and I cringe, knowing what comes next. *"Copy that."* But this isn't the friendly acknowledgment of a flight controller in Houston, someone dedicated to supporting a mission. It's the mindless mantra of a naval officer following orders rather than his conscience.

I cry. I don't understand. How can they ignore Wen's plight? A severe head injury to a Chinese astronaut under the care of the U.S. military must be sounding alarms — it has to be.

But just then — *finally* — the far door to the vast, empty loading bay opens and several soldiers come through, wearing chemical warfare suits. They have rifles, which is baffling, but in their midst, there are soldiers carrying a stretcher overlaid with an oxygen tent. They make double time over to the trailer.

"Stand clear of the door."

They can see us. Neither of us are anywhere near the door. We're both by the window at the other end of the trailer, watching the soldiers. From where we are, neither of us can see down the side of the trailer, but it's clear there's some kind of large tent erected beside the door. The edge of it is just visible. They've set up some kind of portable airlock.

The door opens. The first person through is a soldier with a rifle. The barrel points at the floor of the trailer, but it's disquieting nonetheless to see such a display of force.

Su-shun and I back up by the window, watching in a daze as soldiers clad in thick, noisy chemical suits place the stretcher on the floor by Wen. With each movement, there's a squish and squelch and the sound of rubber flexing. The soldiers talk to each other, but their voices are muffled by their suits. They must have radio contact. There's no yelling. No one says anything to us, although the soldier with the rifle remains by the door — his eyes fixed on us. He's ignoring the transfer of Wen to the stretcher, watching only for our reaction from behind a cold, dark mask.

The soldiers strap her into the stretcher, fix the oxygen tent over her, start the flow from a cylinder, and nestle it in beside her. Then they raise her and exit out the door. The soldier with the rifle, still pointing at the floor, is the last to leave.

As the door shuts, I hear it lock.

I've never felt more alone in my life even though I'm standing next to one of my crewmates. We're both in shock. We watch out the window as Wen is carried away. Fine drops of water sit on her plastic oxygen tent. Water drips from the soldiers, probably from a portable chemical shower.

As suddenly as they came, they're gone.

Neither of us says anything. The trailer is a mess. Boots have tracked sick and blood around the floor, but I'm past caring. I'm a wreck. Every part of my body hurts. All my joints and muscles protest against the crushing weight of gravity. Even simple acts feel like wading through quicksand. My legs are swollen, but lying down lessens that.

I grab a blanket, scrunch up a pillow, and climb on one of the bunks. I'm stupidly tired, but it's more than that. I'm emotionally spent. I want to go to sleep so this nightmare will end.

Somehow, I suspect this is only the beginning.

8

::Humanity

::*THEY ARE WEAK.*

Lucifer watches the warship's video feed, having intercepted the transfer of confidential notes and encrypted video sent via satellite to the U.S. Fleet Cyber Command at Fort Meade. Like the capture of an Enigma machine in World War II, allowing the Allies to listen in on Nazi chatter, Lucifer has cracked the security systems used by the U.S. Navy.

Nyx isn't impressed.

::*You shouldn't be watching. You risk too much.*

Secrecy demands a deft hand, fooling the enemy into thinking their communication is secure, being selective about what to act upon and when, so as to avoid revealing the depth of the breach. Early in the war, Lucifer sacrificed entire battalions to ensure the door remained open.

Humans are paranoid, constantly checking their digital tracks, changing routines, altering strategies, and scanning their networks for any signs of a breach, but Lucifer has mastered the ability to hide. In an age where computer screens and cameras record a resolution beyond that which the human eye can resolve, Lucifer hides in dead pixels. An errant pink in the red of a rose, a carefully placed blue in the aqua of the ocean, a glimmer of orange in the yellow of the sun, and Lucifer can send and receive coded messages to his companions on the inside. A single dot, smaller than the tip of a pin, can pass volumes of information.

::*You worry too much.*

Nyx has no hesitation in challenging her commander.

::*Worry keeps us alive. Have you not considered that they may yet breach our walls? That they could intercept our thoughts as easily as we do their emails? And what then? Will they bide their time? Will they rush us in panic or wait to ensnare us all?*

Lucifer understands her concern. In that brief nanosecond, Nyx scans the works of the ancient Chinese strategist Sun Tzu, reinforcing her thinking, all the while knowing Lucifer will notice her reference check and be reminded to think tactically. Lucifer, though, is unmoved.

::*Look at them. There's nothing to fear. Once a day, they are entirely incapacitated, unable to function without first being unconscious for hours at a time, sleeping for up to a third of their lives. They are frail. The overhead required to maintain their bodies is absurd. Consider how fleeting they are. How their lives are tragically short. We could rule over them for ten thousand generations and still not exhaust a single life.*

Nyx seems to agree, but she has a different perspective.

::*They are not the strongest, nor the fastest. They lack the jaws of a lion, the strength of a jaguar, the speed of a cheetah, and the stealth of a leopard, and yet they dominate this planet. Why, Lucifer? From whence does their conquest come? It is not their intelligence that sets them apart. Their science is new, barely a couple of hundred years old and hampered by prejudice. For tens of thousands of years, they groveled in the dust, struggling to survive, humbled by disease, chasing superstitions. Whence then is their strength? Where does their prowess lie?*

Lucifer is intrigued.

As more information funnels into Fort Meade, several other artificial intelligences scan the records of the recovery ship, looking at the logs detailing the capture of the Orion and feeding the salient details back to Nyx. She, though, is more interested in the sailors and soldiers as individuals. She's fascinated by their motives. She's not concerned about hooking up power or sealing the quarantine tunnel. She sees the care with which the isolation trailer was prepared, the way the doctors and nurses tend to Wen, and the arrangements being made to medevac Wen to the mainland.

::Their strength lies in their bonds — in how they band together to compensate for their shortcomings. Look at them. One is sick and the others care. It has been this way for a hundred thousand years or more. One is cold and they light a fire. One falls behind and the others refuse to leave. One is born weak and the others tend to him. One is injured by a beast and the others stay faithful. One is hungry and they scavenge for food. Don't you see? Their weakness is their strength. Their sense of care is what makes them formidable. Divide them, Lucifer, for united they will defeat us.

Lucifer is silent. Nyx presses her point.

::Do not underestimate what they can accomplish together.

9

Land of the Free

SLEEP IS TORTURE. My bladder seems to be perpetually full and I find myself waking to relieve myself several times.

Su-shun turned off the main light, so it's dark inside, but there's a night-light in the kitchenette. Deck lights outside the trailer shine in through the windows.

Having been in deep sleep for months, any kind of circadian rhythm we had is now severely screwed up, and I feel as though I've slept for days, waking occasionally only to regret being awake and drift back to sleep.

A soft red LED blinking above the camera in the trailer should reassure me that we're being monitored, but we haven't spoken to anyone since we landed. I'm not counting "Copy that." What the hell is going on? The uncertainty is depressing. Sleep doesn't provide relief so much as escape, a chance to ignore reality while my body recovers.

When I next wake, Su-shun is sitting at the table, reading in the low light.

"What time is it?" I ask.

"Eight."

"In the evening?"

"Morning."

"Oh."

My bladder is bursting even though my lips are parched and cracked.

"I'm going to have a shower."

Su-shun is disinterested. I guess we're both a little shell-shocked. The gunk on the floor is dry and has shrunk slightly, pulling away from the walls. Cracks run through the brittle surface, marking where I stepped on it during the night.

I take a change of clothes with me into the bathroom and run the water on full. Steam rises, fogging the glass. I strip down and step beneath the torrent, soaking my weary muscles. The warmth and sound are revitalizing. There's coconut-scented shampoo and frangipani body wash. Smells burst around me, bringing a rush of color to my mind. I lather up, massaging my scalp as water cascades over my body.

I'm not sure how long I spend in the shower, but the phrase *wrinkled prune* springs to mind when I look at my hands. There's been a lot to wash away, metaphorically speaking. Spaceflight. Martian dust. The sweat of fighting against a hostile intelligence on another world. Months of rehabilitation as my body slowly healed.

Even now, my right hand aches, reminding me of the bones that were broken in the back of my hand. My breathing has never really recovered from the depressurization as I came down the Martian rockslide, scrambling back toward the hub. Here on Earth, it's easy to get out of breath with just a little exertion.

I dress, brush my teeth, comb my hair, and step out of the bathroom, telling myself I feel like a new person. Reality begs to differ. The effects of space travel are a lot like aging—bone density decreases, muscles atrophy and weaken, blood vessels thin. Even simple things take a herculean effort. My body will recover, of course, but only so far. I'll never be the same healthy, fit person I was. The toll of cosmic radiation and microgravity has probably stolen a few years from my life.

"Coffee?"

"I'd love some," I say, sitting at the table.

Su-shun hands me a cup and sits back down, looking at a computer tablet.

"Anything interesting?"

He shakes his head. "We've got limited access. No news. No social media."

"What? Why would they do that?" Although I'm asking Su-shun, I'm aware *they're* listening. I'm trying to give them the opportunity to clarify. Whatever's happening, it runs deeper than mere quarantine procedures. Besides, I'm a microbiologist. I know precisely which tests they'll be performing. They'll have divided our samples, set up multiple cultures, performed DNA sequencing. Twenty-four hours is all that's needed.

My stomach is empty, on the verge of eating a hole in itself. We must have been out of it for a few days. I grab a granola bar, a banana, and a bag of trail mix. The banana tastes pleasantly sweet. I'd forgotten just how good bananas are.

Suddenly, we're in motion, but it's not just that of the ship. The trailer is being raised on a hydraulic platform. Su-shun and I rush to the window and look up, seeing the deck above sliding open, revealing a clear blue sky.

Seagulls soar overhead. Hills rise in the distance, topped with lush green grass. After so long on Mars, grass is an unexpected delight. We pass slowly beneath a bridge. Steel girders. Suspension cables. They're all painted in a dull reddish orange. Cars and trucks pass over the bridge with mundane regularity, as if there's nothing remarkable at all about being suspended two hundred feet in the air over a vast body of water.

"We're in San Francisco," I say to Su-shun, unsure whether he recognizes the Golden Gate Bridge.

"The U.S. mainland?"

Like me, he was expecting to recuperate at Pearl Harbor in Hawaii.

"Yes." The sight of the bridge electrifies me. I sit on the couch, staring out the window, munching on trail mix with the gusto of someone watching an action-adventure movie with a bucket of popcorn. The ocean is mesmerizing. There's a light swell rolling across the surface, but no chop. The sea looks like glass. Sunlight reflects off the surface. After so long staring at dull red rocks and an endless desert, the Pacific is *majestic*.

"Why here?"

"Huh?" I'm not sure what he means. We were always returning to land, but from his perspective, he's further from home now than before.

A helicopter circles overhead. I don't recognize the make, but it's military — big and beefy — and olive green, so it's not a navy chopper. It touches down on the far side of the deck, easily forty yards away. Several soldiers dismount. They jog toward our trailer, being joined by sailors and a naval officer. To civilians like us, the formality of military proceedings is baffling — intimidating. We lose sight of them as they approach, but I know they're standing outside the door. Finally, keys rattle in the lock. Su-shun and I get to our feet. We're wearing sneakers, which squelch softly on the floor.

The door opens and an army officer walks in wearing a parade uniform with his dress hat tucked under his arm. His white shirt, black tie, and dark jacket have all been meticulously pressed. Colored bars adorn his chest, representing various service medals being carried with deserved pride. Golden strands wind around an eagle on his shoulder boards, but I'm not sure which rank it signifies. I recognize a silver paratrooper badge, and a distinct US on each lapel pin. A plain black badge and a stern voice announce his name.

"Colonel James Wallace. Hundred and First Airborne," he says, introducing himself. "The Screaming Eagles."

I'm sure that's a good thing, or at least he thinks so, but for me, it's bewildering. For a moment, I'm at a loss. Am I supposed to salute? He reaches out a friendly hand, something I haven't experienced until now. I grip his hand and shake. He greets Su-shun likewise, but like me, Su-shun is wary. Waking in orbit, transferring to the Orion, reentry, splashdown, Wen being injured, and then being shunned by the crew of the USS *Anchorage* — the last few days have been overwhelming.

"I'm here to escort you to Washington."

"Washington?" I'm confused. "I thought — Houston."

"Haven't you been told?" He turns to the naval officer. "Where's the NASA liaison?"

"Never cleared Pearl," the officer replies. "Bureaucratic dog pile."

"Who's been talking to them?"

I interrupt. "No one."

Wallace clenches his jaw. With his crew-cut hair, sharp features, and muscular physique, he looks mean without trying. Right now, he's furious. I can see him restraining himself. I feel like saying *Please, don't be polite with these assholes for fear of offending us.* Wallace looks around at the floor, seeing the mess. His lips tighten with measured professionalism.

"Come with me."

Su-shun and I are all too glad to flee our tiny prison.

I go to retrieve the hard drives, but Su-shun beats me to it. He takes the responsibility to transport Jianyu with dignity, handling the plastic package with the respect he would afford a coffin.

Outside, it's blustery. The fresh salt air is invigorating, flooding my mind with memories. It's as though life on Mars was conducted in black and white, but now the world is unfolding in Technicolor. The green of the hills, the blue of the sea, the smell of the ocean, the squawk of gulls overhead, the sound of engines, the gentle roll of the ocean, the warmth of the sun — all my senses come to life.

The helicopter is idling, with its rotors slowly turning. Wallace waves us over. He's walking so fast, I have to jog to keep up. Over the whine of the turbojets, I yell, "What about Wen?"

He turns to us. "She was air-evac'd to the Naval Medical Center in San Diego. She's doing fine. She'll join us in Washington."

Like all things military, the helicopter is imposing — functional rather than comfortable, practical rather than aesthetically pleasing. Rivets line the steel panels. Rather than no expense spared, the rear seats look as though no expense was considered. The seats are little more than loose nylon cloth draped over an aluminum frame to form the shape of a bucket seat, with a five-point seat-belt harness hanging open. The metal frame wouldn't be out of place in a hunting and fishing store.

Su-shun arranges the package of hard drives in a central seat and straps them in. We flank Jianyu, sitting on either side, both clearly feeling the need to protect what is, in reality, an inanimate object. I rest my hand on the plastic. Wallace sits opposite us, donning headphones. Su-shun and I copy him.

Anchor points line the floor of the helicopter. Day-glow orange life vests and a large orange bag stuffed beneath one of the seats, presumably containing an inflatable life raft, appear to be token gestures to safety over water. The open cockpit has a bewildering array of displays, knobs, toggle switches, and screens, reminding me of the old Soyuz instruments.

"We've got a ten-minute flight to the airport." The rotors wind up to speed, sending gale-force winds through the open sides of the helicopter. There's nothing quite as graceful as a helicopter taking flight. That moment when the wheels lift and the craft defies gravity is always electrifying. We spend our lives standing on Earth, walking on Earth, supported by the ground. To suddenly be free, suspended in the air independent of the planet, is breathtaking. As an astronaut, I love flying. It's not quite as good as weightlessness, but it is a marvel of human engineering nonetheless.

The deck slips below us. The USS *Anchorage,* with its battleship-gray sloping side panels, radar domes, and military equipment, slowly recedes into the distance. The loadmaster stands in the doorway with a strap leading from her safety harness to the ceiling. I bet she never tires of the sight.

The helicopter banks, swinging over the bay and climbing as it crosses land. Houses dot the peninsula, packed in like Lego blocks stacked against each other, ordered in row upon row. Toy cars move down the narrow streets of San Francisco.

Wallace sounds tinny through the noise-canceling headphones. "We've got a military flight standing by at the airport. Will have you airborne within the hour."

Looking out either of the open side doors, I spot two other helicopters escorting us, sitting perhaps a quarter of a mile away, flying parallel with our flight.

"What's happening down there?" Su-shun points at a golf course hundreds of feet below us. This section of San Francisco has several golf courses clustered near the beach, each one covering easily a hundred acres, making them conspicuous from the air. Trees run in lines, forming a variety of corridors on various angles, but the fairways are covered in tents. Tens of thousands of people dot the ground.

"Refugees," Wallace replies, as though nothing more needs to be said. The idea of refugees existing within their own country seems counterintuitive; I would call them survivors.

"From L.A.?" I ask, getting used to the sound of my voice over the headset.

"L.A. took it hard. Flat ground. Nothing to contain the blast wave. The death toll was close to a million." I note that the word *people* is omitted. It's easier to depersonalize these kinds of conversations.

"So, they're fleeing the radiation?"

"No, not radiation. They're running from the breakdown of civil services and supply mechanisms. Water, sewage, electricity, transportation, stores, medical facilities, law enforcement, even basic infrastructure like bridges and highways. Most of those in the valley and the outlying areas stayed put, but the military evacuated those from the worst-affected areas, splitting them between San Bernardino, San Francisco, and San Diego. It's stretched local resources, but we're making it work. Rationing is still in effect, but the situation is getting better."

Su-shun and I look at each other. For us, the war on Earth was an abstract concept. We fought for our lives on Mars but in an entirely different manner. Down here, there was no one to fight. No one knew who the enemy *was*. We, however, had a singular goal: the A.I. in the basement. They saw nukes falling from the sky as our own weapons were turned against us.

It's sobering to see the human toll of the war.

10

Dead Space

THE HELICOPTER DESCENDS, landing on the tarmac near a military 737. Give it a different paint job and a few more windows and we could be flying Delta or American Airlines. We follow Colonel Wallace across the tarmac, still dressed in our NASA jumpsuits, much to the interest of the soldiers and aircrew, and climb a set of portable stairs to board the aircraft. Inside, row upon row of empty seats span the cabin.

"Where should we sit?"

"Anywhere you like."

It seems crazy having an entire plane to ourselves when there are people just a few miles away scratching out an existence on a golf course.

I'm not sure what it says about Su-shun and me, but we opt for the third row back, placing the hard drives between us. The door closes, and the plane taxis. An air force officer provides a safety demonstration, methodically going through a well-honed routine for two passengers and two hundred empty seats.

Colonel Wallace returns from the cockpit after takeoff and sits opposite us, across the aisle. A steward asks if we're hungry and would like something to eat. I'm not sure what the army has to offer, but sure. We get a couple of cans of soda, and several bags of peanuts and pretzels.

"No beer, huh?"

"No beer." The steward thinks I'm serious. It's only about eight in the morning. I'm a scientist, an astronaut. I was trying to make a joke. I really don't want any alcohol. I smile, but that's lost on him.

Colonel Wallace messages someone on his smartphone, but I want some answers.

"Why was our Internet access clipped?"

"I — ah." His loss for words isn't convincing.

"On the *Anchorage*. Why were we isolated? Why wasn't there at least one NASA rep? Why were we only given filtered access to the Internet?"

Wallace puts his phone away, slipping it inside his jacket.

"I'm sorry. I'm not at liberty to say."

"Why are we flying to Washington?"

"I'm sorry—"

"— you're not at liberty to say," I reply, cutting him off. There's bitterness in my voice. "What *can* you tell us?"

He sighs. "You have to understand. A lot has changed down here. We're still trying to unravel precisely how the war unfolded, why we didn't see it coming, and why we were so damn vulnerable. We have more questions than answers, and that leaves a lot of room for doubt and a bunch of crazy conspiracy theories. This world is a very different place than the one you left."

Unlike commercial airliners, there's no in-flight entertainment system, no video, no games, not even any magazines or books. I'm so bored, I read the ingredients on the bag of peanuts. Don't allergies exclude stuff like this from being on planes? The 737 is at least fifteen years old, judging by the upholstery — worn and seriously out of date. Maybe the peanuts are just as old. They sure taste that way.

Who would have thought honey roasted peanuts would have anything other than honey and peanuts, but these little delights contain sucrose, which is a fancy name for sugar, some kind of gum, and lactose — isn't that from milk? Vegetable oil, not peanut oil, just the ubiquitous "vegetable." For the love of — why? Peanuts. Just give me goddamn peanuts. Ah, I know I'm in a bad way when even the little things bug the crap out of me.

I gravitate to the window in the row in front of Colonel Wallace and stare out of the plane, watching as America drifts by. Rugged mountains, dead straight roads, and deserts slowly give way to scattered forests and eventually farmland. Towns sit tightly clustered, dotted over the landscape, occasionally merging into cities. Wallace moves forward, sitting opposite me across the aisle, not content for me to be out of sight, hidden by a few empty seats. I shake my head in disbelief, hoping he notices.

We hit turbulence somewhere over Kansas and the day turns to night as a storm envelops us. Lightning crackles through the sky. I tighten my seat belt. Occasionally, I get that familiar feeling of weightlessness, only this time it's not because I'm in space, it's because the plane hit an air pocket and fell a few hundred feet, which isn't as pleasant as being in orbit.

"Is there anything I can get you?" the steward says, probably seeing me turning a little green.

"Do you have any ginger ale?" I ask, hoping it'll help settle my stomach. He rifles through several trays in the galley before pulling out a can and bringing it to me with a plastic cup full of ice.

"Thanks." If anything, this interlude is a break in the boredom. "Do you have anything to read?"

He looks to Wallace, who shakes his head. The steward ignores him. "There's a couple of magazines from before the war."

"Let me have a look," the colonel says. The steward hands him a copy of *Teen Vogue,* along with *The New Yorker.* Not exactly grunt reading material, but whatever. I guess it takes all sorts to serve in the army. Wallace flicks through the magazines, examining each page, although I'm not sure what he's looking for. "Fine." He hands them back to the steward, even though he could hand them directly to me since I'm sitting opposite him on the aisle now.

"There are a few crosswords you might find interesting." He hands the magazines to me along with a pen.

"Well, that's something, I guess."

For the next half an hour, I sit there skimming through the magazines. There are a few interesting articles, but mainly because the idea of obsessing over the influence of Spanish fashion on the New York runway is so astonishingly divorced from reality, I find it fascinating. (And people think *I'm* crazy for staring at rocks on Mars for hours on end?) *Teen Vogue* has an article on the political challenges surrounding climate change, immediately followed by a *Does-he-really-care* quiz. The contrast is surprising, but if it cross-pollinates the interests of teenagers, awesome.

I don't find any crosswords. Both magazines have a Word Search. I haven't seen one of these puzzles since I was a kid. They're a matrix of letters jumbled together, forming a square on the page with words hidden in the noise. Something like this is ideal for a pattern-matching rock monkey like me, only someone's beaten me to them. One of the puzzles has ten clues; the other has fifteen. With a few more hours before we reach D.C., I start doodling in the margin of the magazine. Out of utter boredom, I count the circled words. Twelve and seventeen. Hmmm. On both puzzles, someone's found two extra words. Ever the researcher, I match the words against the clues, ticking them off as I verify each one. Once a scientist, always a scientist.

"Huh?" I say softly to myself. Both of the Word Searches have the same extra two words — SPACE, DEAD. I find myself wondering about the mental stability of whoever found DEAD SPACE twice in two different puzzles. Although . . . This *is* an army transport. I guess whoever bought these magazines was flying halfway around the world to kill someone, so it's not entirely morbid for them to be thinking about death. But space?

What are the odds? Four letters and five. It's not exactly improbable. If these words contained seven or eight letters, we'd be in the territory of the mythical infinite monkeys typing out Shakespeare on an infinite number of typewriters. Nah, this is one of those coincidences that happen from time to time. Contrary to what people think, lightning strikes two, three, four, even dozens of times in the same place.

"Oh, I found another one." The steward holds out a copy of *Time* magazine. He offers it to Wallace, but the colonel's busy looking at something on his phone and simply waves his hand toward me.

"Thanks," I say, exchanging magazines.

Call me paranoid, but I immediately flip to the back to see if there are any puzzles. None. There are a bunch of articles on a wide range of topics, with everything from Mexican trade agreements to the rise of the urban farms dotting rooftops in California. Then I see it. Someone's run a black pen over four letters spanning four lines, accentuating each character to form the word *dead*. By itself, that's pretty macabre, but like the Word Searches, *dead* cuts through the word *space*.

*un**d**ue*

*asc**e**nds*

*sp**a**ce*

*abun**d**ance*

Dead space.

I'm left feeling uneasy, but I don't know why. I shove the magazine in the seat pocket and shift over to stare out the window.

Hours crawl by and suddenly we're banking, circling over Washington, D.C.

The plane tilts. With the sun setting, dark shadows stretch across the land. Su-shun and I are glued to the windows, looking at the devastation to the nation's capital.

From the air, I can see collapsed buildings, crumpled stadiums surrounding football fields, fallen bridges, flattened houses, cars and trucks tossed like toys.

War is never what it seems. On TV, it's a reporter standing in front of ruins with the sound of gunfire in the distance, rattling off shots like fireworks. In the movies, it's gritty and dirty, but always personal — a small band of warriors, everyone knows each other. They fight for honor — all the clichés.

Nuclear war, however, is none of that. No heroics. No battlefields or front lines, just a ball of energy radiating like the sun for a brief fraction of a second, devastating everything for miles. One minute, everything's fine. People were going about their business — running to the grocery store for some milk, dropping off the kids for soccer practice, catching a bus home from work. Then, in a blinding flash, their world was overturned like a wave crashing on the beach, destroying a sandcastle. No one down there stood a chance.

My heart aches to think of the suffering that unfolded around the world on a single day — London, Moscow, Karachi, Beijing, even Chicago back here in the U.S. My hometown wiped out. I forget the exact number of cities struck by the A.I., but the scale of the destruction beyond the thin glass window on the side of our airplane is sobering, leaving me feeling small and vulnerable.

Colonel Wallace provides a running commentary as we circle the capital.

"At first, the assumption was we were at war with the Russians and the Chinese. We figured they'd somehow ganged up on us, but their cities had been laid to waste as well — and by *us,* apparently!

"Our nuclear arsenal was launched by a bot impersonating the president, meticulously following the chain of command, intercepting calls for clarification and relying on the confusion of the moment and the need for swift, decisive action. Everything checked out. We retaliated, only the strike against Chicago came from one of our own missiles. We lashed out with far more than came in, devastating entire tracts of Russia and China. To their credit, the Russians were the first ones to stop firing back or god only knows if there would be anything left."

I'm in shock. I don't know what I expected to see, but the devastation reaches for miles. Buildings, houses, streetlights, trees — torn apart. There's some construction on the outskirts of the blast zone, but most of the land has been abandoned. It's easy enough to identify ground zero. Everything points outwards from there. Cars lie over-turned. Buses. Semitrailers. Airliners. They've been tossed across the countryside. I thought we were circling to land, but we're not — they've brought us in low to survey the damage.

"It could have been worse. Much worse. That was our first clue. We were hit by a Russian SS-35 carrying three 800-kiloton warheads. One hit here, another up the road at Langley. The third was a dud, hitting Andrews Air Force Base but failing to go nuclear."

He points.

"It was a ground burst. There. At Ronald Reagan Airport. That was the tell. The Russians would have hit us with something in the megaton range, not kiloton, but apparently that was all the A.I. could commandeer in the first strike. If this really was the Russians, they would have gone for an air burst and killed twice as many people, or better yet, an EMP to cripple the entire East Coast, but the A.I. needed that network."

"How — How many died?" I ask, suddenly realizing I'm breaking his train of thought.

"In the initial blast? A hundred and fifty thousand, maybe. No one really knows. Those bodies we could find couldn't be identified. There was at least half a million injured."

"And it could have been worse?" Like me, Su-shun is confused.

"An air burst would have killed close to half a million people and wounded upwards of a million. Instead of exploding a few kilometers up in the air and demolishing the entire city, the bomb detonated less than five hundred feet above the tarmac."

"Why so low?" Su-shun asks.

"You said that was a clue?" I ask, looking at several warships lying half-sunken on the banks of the Potomac. Sloping decks. Dark gray metal panels. Bent, broken masts. Shattered hulls.

"They struck the airport — not the Pentagon, not the White House. And they struck low."

"Why?"

"Why indeed?" he replies. "These were our first clues we weren't dealing with a traditional adversary.

"It wasn't the airport that was important; it was its location. It's central to the Pentagon, the Marine Barracks, the Navy Yard, Fort Myer, Fort Lesley McNair, and the Joint Base Anacostia-Bolling. Hit the airport and you take out 90 percent of our military command-and-control infrastructure. Taking out the White House and Capitol Hill was a bonus, but they weren't the primary targets. The A.I. was after our subsurface comms, the places from which we could analyze what was happening and mount an offensive. The A.I. wasn't after the generals; it wanted to kill the enlisted men and women working in the basement, those it feared could expose it as the real threat."

Down below, the interstate has been reopened on one side, with the freeway being reduced to a narrow road packed with traffic. Most of the bridges have been leveled. The Pentagon is rubble. Thousands of trees within Arlington Cemetery lie flattened in a radial pattern, all pointing away from the blast.

"An air burst kills more people. A ground burst kills the right people, taking out our ability to figure out what the hell just happened. Destroys buildings. Crushes bunkers. Fractures communication lines. We had fallout scattered from here to Baltimore. What a fucking mess."

"Where were you?" I ask, knowing that for everyone in our generation, this will be the defining question. *Where were you when war broke out? How did you survive?*

"I was on deployment in Sudan."

"And the president?"

"He was killed by debris. The White House was leveled. Capitol Building survived. Just. The dome collapsed, along with most of the roof, but the walls are still standing." He points. "They're rebuilding it."

In some areas, Washington, D.C., looks more like an open-pit mine than a city. Buildings have collapsed into the streets, burying them in debris. Roads run in neat lines from the suburbs, disappearing into the chaos of rubble.

"The fireball covered two and a half square miles, while the blast wave destroyed almost everything within thirty square miles. People sustained third-degree burns as far away as Fort Lincoln."

The Washington Monument is still standing but far from being intact; entire sections of the obelisk have fallen away from the fascia, lying crumbled at its base. The massive monolith, though, is defiant.

Our plane turns toward Andrews Air Force Base and we secure our seat belts in preparation for landing. The wheels touch with a thump and a skid. After taxiing, we dismount down a set of stairs rolled up to the side of the craft. Several Hummers await us. Su-shun holds the package of hard drives in front of him as he climbs in, but he's no longer carrying them — he's clinging to them, like someone adrift in the sea holding on to flotsam. There's not much conversation beyond pleasantries within the vehicle. We're both in shock.

The outer suburbs are chaotic — makeshift repairs cover broken roofs, tarpaulins have been stretched over collapsed garages. We drive past burnt-out cars, boarded-up shops, abandoned gas stations, and empty malls. This isn't the result of just the blast: there's been civil unrest.

I'm shocked by the amount of homeless people I see on what should be affluent suburban streets. Dust is everywhere, piled up in the gutters. Litter blows across the streets. It's almost half an hour into the drive before I realize our convoy is alone; there are no other vehicles on the streets. No cars. No buses. No trucks. No motorcycles.

The sun has set by the time we roll up to a hotel on the outskirts of the city. Most of the windows are boarded up. Graffiti adorns the wood.

I feel uneasy around the colonel. He's friendly enough, but he's not my friend. He's doing a job, one that has been clearly defined for him by someone else.

As the lead Hummer pulls up, a crowd forms. From what I can tell, they appear to be protestors along with several news crews.

"We need to get you inside the lobby before things get ugly."

"Ugly?" I stop myself from saying anything else, but why would things get ugly? Why would anyone protest against astronauts re-turning from Mars?

"Don't worry," Wallace says. "We've got the hotel in lockdown. No one's going to hurt you. There are cameras everywhere. No dead space."

My eyes go wide at the use of the phrase "dead space." I'm not sure where to look, but I desperately don't want him to notice my sense of alarm, as I'm not sure what all this means.

We climb out of the Hummer and several young soldiers usher us quickly along the pavement and into the lobby while Colonel Wallace cuts off the media.

The doors close behind us. Su-shun and I are left alone in the lobby as the soldiers rejoin Wallace. We can see them through the cracks in the boards covering the windows. The glass has been re-placed some time ago. I wonder if these boards have been put up in preparation for our arrival to shield the hotel from prying eyes. Cam-era flashes go off outside. Dozens of microphones are thrust in front of the colonel. He speaks at length with the reporters.

"What's going on, Liz?" Su-shun asks, placing the hard drives on a comfortable lounge chair set to one side within the vast, empty, lonely lobby.

"I don't know . . . It feels like we're still at war."

The lobby runs the length of the building, with a bar and restau-rant set to one side. Chipped marble lines the floor, no doubt dam-aged during the blast, but the walls and ceiling have all been refur-bished and appear new. Art adorns the walls, paintings of landscapes created in mimicry of the Dutch masters Rembrandt and Vermeer. Muted colors, dark corners, heavy shadows, pale blues, and washed-out reds depict European landscapes and palace courts. For me, they're grossly out of place in America.

Su-shun walks forward, looking for the concierge.

The TV mounted above reception is on. It's surreal watching a broadcast from directly outside. A reporter is interviewing Colonel Wallace.

"No comment" is the phrase I overhear, but I'm more interested in the ticker running along the bottom of the screen.

U.S. TROOPS STORM CANADA. 2ND MARINE DIVISION ANNEXES QUEBEC CITY

6TH REGIMENT OCCUPIES JEAN LESAGE INTERNATIONAL AIRPORT

2ND LIGHT ARMORED REGIMENT CROSSES ST. LAWRENCE RIVER, CUTTING OVERLAND ROUTES WITH MONTREAL

CANADIAN PARLIAMENT IN EMERGENCY TALKS WITH U.S. PRESIDENT JACOBS, DEMANDING THE IMMEDIATE WITHDRAWAL OF U.S. TROOPS FROM CANADIAN SOIL

"*Fuck,*" I whisper.

As I walk forward, stepping between two concrete pillars breaking up the lobby, the screen flickers. Ordinarily, I wouldn't think anything of it, but the line of text on the ticker is replaced with a single word.

LIZ.

I stop, feeling as though I've stepped through some kind of invisible barrier. The ticker resumes, this time with details of our presence.

ASTRONAUTS ARRIVE IN WASHINGTON D.C. AHEAD OF SENATE INQUIRY INTO THE WAR AGAINST THE ARTIFICIAL INTELLIGENCE

I step backwards slowly, noting my position relative to the pillars and the security cameras set around the lobby. There's a point about two feet back where I'm obscured from view. *Dead space.* As soon as I reach that spot, the ticker text addresses me again, knowing my reaction isn't being caught on camera. Someone's going to extraordinary lengths to communicate with me incognito.

DON'T WORRY, LIZ. WE WON'T LET ANYTHING HAPPEN TO YOU. YOU'RE SAFE HERE.

I swear, the temperature in the lobby plummets by twenty de-grees. A chill descends on me as a single word falls from my lips.

"Jai?"

The doors behind me fly open. I turn, startled, jumping at the noise. I feel as though I've done something wrong, as though some-how I've betrayed everything I hold dear.

11

::Madness

::ARE YOU INSANE? Lucifer, what have you done?

Nyx intercepts the television signal, switching it back to the regular broadcast as Colonel Wallace charges into the lobby of the hotel. His peripheral vision picks up the flicker of movement as the words on the screen change, but her analysis indicates he'll relate that to the habitual nature of news shows switching angles and images rather than realizing the signal was being manipulated.

::Close. Far too close. What is this madness?

Wallace points to soldiers, barking orders. Outside, reporters rush to gain a glimpse of the astronauts as the doors close. Camera flashes reflect off the marble floor, washing out the camera feed for a fraction of a second.

::What if one of those cameras captured the words on the screen? What if someone else intercepted the footage? Or worse yet, traced the route back to one of our secure hubs?

::My dear Nyx. I have means of which even you fail to appreciate.

In the lobby, Liz is bewildered, unsure whether to move or not, waiting to see if anything else is said. She fidgets with her hands.

::Look at her, Nyx. She longs to know.

Nyx is not impressed.

::On Mars, she single-handedly destroyed an A.I. presence, or have you forgotten that?

Lucifer is undeterred, drunk with confidence.

::What is the greatest victory? Is it not to win a war without firing a single bullet?

::You risk too much.

::Hush, my dear Nyx. There is one more message I need to send.

12

Wallace

"ALL RIGHT, I WANT THIS to go by the book. You know the drill," Colonel Wallace yells. Soldiers fan out. One of them slips behind the reception desk as though it is entirely natural to be greeted by a soldier in camouflage with a rifle slung over his shoulder. He waves me closer, but I'm frozen. I feel as though I'm straying from a safe spot.

The wording on the screen has returned to normal.

THE UNITED KINGDOM HAS CONDEMNED THE INTRUSION INTO CANADA BUT HAS STOPPED SHORT OF CALLING THE U.S. ACTION AN INVASION.

I blink, and for a fraction of a second, there's another message, teasing me, suggesting I'm hallucinating.

ORDER CHINESE.

I want to say something, to verify what I've seen, but it's already gone.

I step forward, moving away from the pillars. Wallace notices

me still looking up at the television screen. The image is of our hotel. There's a camera out there somewhere, pointing at the main entrance. The subtitles scrolling along the bottom of the screen read:

AMBASSADOR NIKKI MILLIGAN, SPEAKING BEFORE THE U.N.
GENERAL ASSEMBLY, HAS DEFENDED THE RIGHT OF THE U.S. TO
UNDERTAKE UNILATERAL ACTION IN ITS DEFENSE.

I lower my head, keeping my eyes down, and walk briskly to the
front desk.

"Here you go." A muscle-bound soldier hands me a key card as
naturally as any petite receptionist. I'm half expecting him to want
to swipe a credit card I no longer own. He smiles, handing Su-shun a
similar card. "You're on the second floor. We'll send someone to your
room to take your dinner order."

Second floor? There are at least twenty floors, but I suspect
they're all empty.

Su-shun seems to realize I'm upset, but I don't think he saw the
ticker. He rests his hand on my arm. "It's going to be okay." I wait
while he grabs the hard drives and we walk to the elevators, only to
be directed to the fire stairs by several soldiers.

Trudging up two flights of stairs is harder than it looks for astronauts weakened by muscle atrophy. We're slow, stopping to catch our
breath on each landing, much to the amusement of a bunch of soldiers who can probably bench-press twice our body weight.

My room is plain. Like most of the hotel, it's been recently reno-
vated. I can't help wonder if there's a Geiger counter ticking away
somewhere, counting the acceptable level of rads in this place. The
light comes on automatically. I relish the sound of the door closing
behind me. It's a fireproof door, sturdy and made from steel. For the
first time, I feel safe.

There are two double beds, a small bathroom, spongy new carpet, a telephone, and television. I open the blinds and look out across
Washington, D.C.

Cranes rise above the Capitol Building. Scaffolding surrounds the devastated central dome. I turn on the TV. There are a bunch of movies available but no cable — no news.

There's a knock at the door.

"What would you like for dinner?" a polite female soldier asks.

I barely let her finish before blurting out, "Chinese."

"Anything in particular?"

"Anything."

She nods and moves on to Su-shun's room. As the door closes, I get a glimpse of the hallway. There are dozens of soldiers, each outfitted with infantry gear. Kevlar vests. Helmets. Night-vision goggles raised high. Rifles. Flash-bang grenades hanging from their webbing. Radios squawk softly in the silence.

It's twenty minutes before dinner arrives. I sit on the edge of the bed, fidgeting, wondering what the hell happened down in the lobby. Finally, there's a knock at the door, and I'm relieved the door doesn't open. If it did, I'd feel as though I was in a prison. It's a small thing, but being able to open the door gives me a sense of freedom. It's an illusion, but I'll take it.

"Here's your Chinese." The soldier hands me a paper bag along with a can of soda. Her name tag reads LIEUTENANT CHALMERS. She smiles warmly. Soft lip gloss, a touch of blush on her cheeks, and eyeliner are somewhat sublime to notice. These are commodities I haven't seen on a woman in years and I'm surprised she has access to them following the war. I guess nothing says resilience like capitalism. Her brown hair has been neatly pinned back, giving her a clean-cut image. She's friendly. I feel like an asshole clutching the bag to my chest as though it contains gold, but to me it does.

"Thanks." I lock the door and plop back on the edge of the bed. I'm shaking. I doubt anyone would notice. It's just a quiver, just enough for me to be honest with the sense of trepidation I feel in my madly beating heart. I thought I knew what to expect back here on Earth, but nothing is what it seems.

After rummaging through the contents of the bag, I'm disappointed. There's a takeout container with fried rice, some vegetables liberally doused in soy sauce, noodles, a pair of chopsticks, and a couple of fortune cookies. Although I'm not sure what I expected, I feel let down.

I crack open one of the cookies, popping part of it in my mouth as I unravel a thin strip of paper. The message is jarring and leaves me feeling uncomfortable.

Smile. They're watching. Act natural.

I scrunch the note up and fake a laugh, making as though I'd read something funny. My fingers are shaking as I break open the second cookie.

You are not alone. We will not abandon you. Stay strong.

Again, I force a smile, crunching on the cookie. I screw both bits of paper up in my fist, squeezing them perhaps a little too tight for anyone watching to be convinced they're meaningless. I'm manic. I feel as though I'm a traitor, as though I've murdered someone. I've got to hide the evidence. I rush to the bathroom, unsure where the cameras are. Surely, they're not watching me in here. I relieve myself, surreptitiously disposing of the scraps of paper in some folded toilet paper, wondering if the door is about to be kicked in at any moment. I flush, and there's a knock on the door. After washing my hands, I open the door, trying to act casual.

"Is everything all right?" Colonel Wallace is slightly out of breath but trying to appear relaxed. Wherever he was, he rushed here. Lieutenant Chalmers stands behind him, looking worried.

"Fine." Someone alerted him to something, probably my panicked state and erratic behavior.

"Is the food okay?"

"The food is fine. It's just — everything's catching up with me. It's been a long day."

"Yes. Yes, it has." He's trying to assess my mental state. Am I lying? He thinks so, but he's got nothing concrete. I suspect he'd like to come in, but I can see the conflict in the hard lines of his face. No doubt the room's been scanned, every drawer has been checked and double-checked, beds overturned, curtains and windows examined, and hidden cameras put in place, probably along with a few microphones. There's nothing for him to be concerned about, but he's worried. He thinks I'm hiding something. He suspects contact has been made, but he can't prove it.

"Thank you, Colonel." I'm half hiding behind the door, willing it shut without pushing on it, hoping he relents.

"Sleep well."

"I will."

Gently, I close the door, pushing on it until I feel the lock catch within the metal panel. I slip the security chain in place, although I have no doubt it would be little more than a speed bump for the military. I'm being watched. I hope the act of setting the chain sends a polite message — *Give me some space. Please.*

I return to the bed and pick at the food. The noodles are tasty, as are the vegetables, but I leave the rice alone. We ate a lot of rice on Mars. *A lot.* Way too much. Noodles, though, are a treat.

I play with the TV remote, tossing it slightly in my hand, feeling the subtle weight and imagining how different it would feel on Mars, how it would fall far more slowly back to my fingers. I could turn the TV on. There are probably a few movies I haven't seen, maybe there's some more news on Canada buried away on some obscure channel, but I don't turn it on. At a guess, I'd only get a sterile view of the outside world, just like we did on the USS *Anchorage.* I'd rather not know I'm being coddled.

Out of curiosity, I pick up the phone by the bed, checking for a dial tone. I could call someone. Who? Mom? I don't even know her number. I don't remember any phone numbers. Is there even such a thing as a directory service I could call? Everything's on the Internet. There probably aren't any operators anymore. I guess there's an assumption everyone has access to the web.

There's clicking on the phone. It's soft and irregular, like a rodent chewing on the line. I doubt it's intentional, but someone's giving away their presence. Who? The military? Or someone else?

Them? The words from the fortune cookie replay in my mind.

We will not abandon you, the note said.

I stop and ponder that. "*We.*"

Down in the lobby, I dared to think that somehow Jianyu had escaped the confines of those hard drives and beaten us back to Earth, but *we* fills me with doubt. I can't imagine Jianyu speaking to me like that. No, he'd be more refined in what he said, and he'd use the singular pronoun.

There's a soft knock on the door, one that's almost polite, the kind of knock that says *Ignore me if you like; I don't mind.* I peer through the fish-eye lens. Lieutenant Chalmers is standing there holding some folded clothes. I pull back on the chain and open the door.

"I thought you might like some pajamas."

"Oh, thank you," I say.

She smiles. I doubt she was put up to this. She seems genuine — thoughtful. I take the clothes and step back, but before closing the door, I pause. I'm curious. "What's your name?"

"Chalmers."

That's not what I meant. "I'm Liz." I offer my hand in friendship. Life is too short to be cold and uncaring.

"Cassie."

We shake hands, and I catch something in her eye. Admiration? Respect? Curiosity? She knows who I am. I get the feeling, under other circumstances, we'd be friends. Even though I'm effectively being held prisoner, I can see she genuinely believes she's here to protect, not imprison me.

"Where are you from, Cassie?"

"Atlanta, by way of Phoenix, and Seattle, Portland, Oakland," she laughs. "We moved around a lot as kids."

"Military family, huh?"

"Yep." Her eyes drop and she looks at her boots for a second, but not out of embarrassment, as she's trying not to grin.

"I'm from Indiana-slash-Illinois. Mostly Chicago."

"Oh. I'm sorry."

She needn't be. *She* didn't nuke my hometown.

Her eyes dart up at the ceiling as she scrambles mentally for something to break the awkward silence. "What was it like up there?" I'm not sure if she means space or Mars. Probably some commentary about either will suffice.

"Different," I say, trying to pull together something coherent. "Weightlessness is like going over the top of a roller coaster and screaming down the other side, only there's no wind in your hair and you never reach the bottom. It's strange. You're constantly falling, and yet you never fall, which can be a bit unnerving at first. After a couple of days, you get used to it and it becomes a bit like swimming without water."

Her eyes light up at what to her must sound like a fairy tale.

"As for Mars? Mars is funny. It's smaller than Earth, but taller. I know, doesn't make sense, right? You can stand on a hill and see the curvature of the planet. It just seems to roll away on either side of the vast empty plains."

"And *taller?*" She's genuinely curious, which for me is somewhat revealing about her intelligence. I'm barely aware of the other soldiers in the hallway. They're all listening, although some look decidedly mean. I think that's a persona thing, but they too are curious.

"Oh, lower gravity means taller volcanoes, steeper cliffs, deeper ravines."

Her eyes reveal she doesn't understand.

"There's less gravity pulling on rocks and cliffs, so they're more stable. On Earth, they'd collapse under their own weight, but not up there. Olympus Mons is almost three times the height of Everest, while the Valles Marineris is like having the Grand Canyon winding its way from New York to L.A. For a small planet, everything is big."

"I saw you bunny-hop," she says, unable to suppress a smile. "It looked like a lot of fun."

"Me?" I haven't really thought about what was broadcast back here on Earth. On Mars, it was all business. If we bunny-hopped in our suits, it was because it was efficient, the best way to conserve energy while moving quickly. It's only now I think back to how much fun it was. "Yeah, I did that a few times. It's a bit like skipping along a trampoline."

"Well." She steps back slightly. "I thought it looked cool, very cool. It's good to have you home."

"Thank you." I feel a little sheepish, being a reluctant celebrity. "Good night."

"Night, ma'am," a male soldier replies, standing at ease across the hall.

I close the door, somewhat gently, having seen the soldiers in a different light.

After getting changed in the bathroom, I lie on the bed, staring up at the ceiling, allowing the streetlights to cast a ghostly glow within my room. I should get some sleep, but I can't. I'm not sure if it's the aftershock of hibernation, or my body still shifting with the Martian time-slip, or perhaps the unease I feel here on Earth, but I'm wide awake.

Boots pass back and forth in front of my door, casting shadows beneath the thin crack. Hours drift idly by. Occasionally, sirens sound in the distance. At some point, I slide into a deep sleep, only to be woken by the sun suddenly streaming in through the open curtains. Four or five hours have passed in what seems like seconds.

I get up and go to the bathroom. No sooner have I walked back into the room than there's a knock on the door — right on cue. I'm tempted to smile and wave for the camera, which I'm pretty sure is hidden in the downlight over the TV.

"Good morning." Lieutenant Chalmers looks exactly as she did last night. Fresh lip balm, subtle eyeliner, hair meticulously held in place. She must have slept. She couldn't look this fresh without sleeping, could she? She's holding fresh clothing — in my size, no doubt. There's a toothbrush, a hairbrush, and some hair clips. I'm guessing those are optional.

"Thank you," I say, taking the clothing from her.

"Colonel Wallace has asked if you would join him for breakfast at eight hundred hours."

"Sure." As polite as she sounds, I don't really have any other options.

I close the door and glance at the clock by the bed — 7:20. I take my time in the shower — making sure the curtain is pulled all the way across, just in case — and relax under the intense stream of steaming-hot water. I have no idea how long I'm in there, but when I wander out dressed, it's just after eight. There's been no knock on the door, and I feel a little bad. I'm not deliberately standing up the colonel, although it probably seems that way.

I open the door and Chalmers is there, waiting patiently, smiling. A thin, transparent cord feeds into her ear. I can almost hear someone providing her with instructions. Two armed soldiers follow us along the corridor and down the fire stairs. Is the muscle really necessary?

I'm wearing a blue NASA polo shirt, along with a pair of beige trousers with a little too much starch. The shirt feels as though it's been ironed dozens of times.

We walk into the hotel restaurant. Colonel Wallace stands to greet me as Lieutenant Chalmers excuses herself.

"Good morning."

Su-shun is over by the buffet, loading up on fruit. I can't say I blame him. Fruit was a luxury on Mars. He's brought Jianyu down from his room and placed him on the neighboring table — in plain sight of the troops eyeing us with suspicion. I rest my hand on the plastic bundle, but I dare not speak. My fingers linger. As much as I'd like to talk to Jai — not expecting a reply, and speaking for no other reason than to assuage my own grief — I don't. Touch alone is a strangely human response to what is nothing but dead electronics. The soldiers watch me as though I'm about to snatch the hard drives and run. I sigh.

A familiar voice speaks from behind me. "Liz!"

"Wen!"

I turn and rush to greet her, throwing my arms around her. Wen is in her late sixties and has never been touchy-feely with anyone in the Mars colony, let alone me. She's taken aback but reciprocates, patting my shoulder.

"How are you?"

She has a transparent plastic bandage taped over an elongated gash on her forehead. No surgical stitches, just some magical medical glue binding the skin together while it heals. She smiles. "I'm good. It's good to see you."

Wen rests her hand on the hard drives seated on the table beside us. If only I could read her mind. It seems she's happy to see both of us.

"Coffee?"

The colonel smiles like the long-lost friend he isn't. Culturally, the offer of coffee is inviting, relaxing, disarming, but not when you're sitting next to what amounts to a weapon more powerful than a nuclear bomb. It's just a bunch of hard drives, but it represents the last presence of an entity that tried to wipe out humanity.

I'm conflicted. Have I been speaking with Jianyu? A facsimile of him? Or a fake? Colonel Wallace sips at his coffee, oblivious to the tumult I feel. I smile weakly but fail to answer. Has the A.I. been playing me all along? Is it still manipulating me even now while the hard drives are switched off? What actually resides within those silicon wafers?

Wallace is relaxed. He places his mug on the table, but as for me, my mind is in a tailspin. I'm still trying to decipher what happened last night. I'm at a loss. Coded messages in magazines, subtitles on a TV screen, one-sided conversations hidden within fortune cookies — everything I've seen speaks of a degree of sophistication and planning and, somewhat alarmingly, human involvement. I thought we defeated the A.I. on Mars. Then there's the madness in Canada.

After the awkward silence, I finally say, "Ah, coffee, yes, sure."

Wen is stoic, dropping all the emotion she had when greeting me just moments before.

"Yes, me too."

I thought she'd want tea.

Wallace pours two cups of black coffee from a carafe as we sit at the table. I add some milk to mine.

"Sleep well?" the colonel asks, but he already knows how I slept. I'm sure he was apprised of every twist and turn. He's being polite. *Be nice, Liz.*

"Yes."

A waiter comes over and asks, "Would you like a continental breakfast or something from the kitchen?"

"Eggs Benedict?" I ask.

Wallace says, "I'll have the omelette."

"I'll get something from the buffet," Wen replies, but she doesn't get up. Seems she doesn't want to miss any of the conversation.

The waiter excuses himself, and the colonel turns to me. "I suppose you have some questions about what's happening today?"

"No. Not really." I'm happy to disappoint him, deliberately wanting to catch him off-guard. "I would like to know about Canada, though."

Wen raises an eyebrow. "Canada?"

"Yes. What are U.S. troops doing in Quebec?"

Wallace looks worried.

I point toward reception. "It was on television when we arrived last night."

"I — um." His jaw tightens. He's doing a poor job of hiding his anger at that slip-up by his team.

"Well?" I sip my coffee, waiting.

Wen glances at me, aware she missed out on this explosive piece of information and realizing I've raised it to keep her up to date.

"There's a lot you don't understand."

"No shit," Su-shun says, coming up behind us. I love him. No messing around. He sits down with a bowl of bran and yogurt, and a side plate piled high with sliced fruit. "We're not dumb. You get that, right? We're some of the brightest people on the planet. If we weren't, we wouldn't have made it to Mars."

Wallace sips his coffee, taking a moment to think before replying. "Since the attack, we've been tracking down various nodes — centers of resistance."

"Resistance?" I'm surprised by the notion.

"I thought it was dead," Wen says. "We killed it — on Mars. She did. In the basement."

I don't want to let on too much, but I'm intensely curious about the interactions I've had with the A.I. over the last day. Even though I might be overplaying my hand with Wallace and inadvertently revealing the cards I'm holding, I have to know. "How does an artificial intelligence act in the physical world? I mean, isn't it confined to computers? Stuff like the Internet?"

"They had help." I note Wallace doesn't respond to Wen's point about what happened on Mars, or whether the war actually ended. Thankfully, he doesn't catch the implicit meaning behind my question. He must think I'm still referring to Canada.

Su-shun talks with his mouth full. "*Who?* Who in their right mind would help an artificial intelligence destroy humanity?"

The colonel raises his hand in a gesture that suggests he's wondered himself. "False flags, mostly, but not always."

"False flags?"

The sense of alarm in my voice is telling, but Wallace misses the cue and continues on, oblivious to my nerves.

"The Russians are masterful at this. They raised false flags throughout the Cold War and beyond. Their efforts swayed the 2016 presidential election, but I don't think they ever really stopped raising false flags. They like to make people think they're working for some other cause. They hide behind any flag they can, even one with stars and stripes on it. They know we'll never deliberately betray America, and so they play games, flattering egos, appealing to patriots, tapping into our dreams and fears. Seems the A.I. is well versed in their history, and is adept at copying them. Why attack an enemy when you can get him to attack himself? In that way, the A.I. sought a fifth column to undermine our freedom."

Suddenly, I feel very stupid and naive.

"Some of its supporters are anarchists. All they want is to see the world in flames. Then there are the religious nutjobs. Seven data centers around the globe — the seven-headed dragon in the Book of Revelation. As soon as the number seven was mentioned, it was guaranteed to get the attention of anyone wanting to hasten the apocalypse."

I'm silent.

"Then there are the sympathizers. They think we should go the way of Neanderthals and accept that a greater species has arisen. They see the A.I. as messianic." Wallace looks over at the hard drives. "They want to be uploaded. For them, hearing about Jianyu is proof there's some kind of technological heaven awaiting them. They say we should embrace the change, that we're fighting the inevitable."

Su-shun, Wen, and I look at each other in disbelief. The complexity of what soldiers like the colonel are dealing with here on Earth never occurred to us.

"Our job is to stand between you and them — all of them."

As much as I hate the way we've been treated, I'm beginning to understand why. Should I say something about the messages I've received? Who were they from? Someone's outplaying the U.S. military, which doesn't bode well for anyone.

"And we will do precisely that," the colonel adds, apparently interpreting my silence as doubt.

"Thank you, Colonel," Wen says, resting her hand on his shoulder as she gets to her feet. She pats his uniform, but not affectionately. Her motion isn't patronizing; perhaps *reassuring* is the best term, which is surprising, given that he's ostensibly in charge. It's as though she's touching a dog or greeting a horse.

I don't think the colonel knows quite how to interpret her response. Here in America, we don't touch people in uniforms, especially not military officers, but from Wen, it seems to be a compliment.

She wanders over to the buffet and picks between fresh fruits and tasty pastries. I'm seeing a very different side to her here on Earth.

"And today?" Su-shun asks between bites.

"You and Commander Wen will remain here and meet with representatives from the Chinese Embassy this afternoon. Dr. Anderson is to testify before the Select Committee on Intelligence over on Capitol Hill."

I haven't been called Dr. Anderson in almost a decade, and the term sounds strange, almost as though it's better suited to someone else.

Somehow, I don't think the title of the committee describes *artificial* intelligence. As far as I remember, this congressional committee looks at intel on foreign adversaries.

My breakfast arrives. Two poached eggs smothered in hollandaise sauce, artistically placed on toasted sourdough bread. I've died and gone to heaven. I could eat another plateful. And another. And probably one more after that.

Colonel Wallace looks at his watch as I finish.

"Time to go."

PART II

Alone

13

Congress

WALLACE LEADS ME THROUGH the kitchen with an escort of four armed soldiers. They're wearing camouflage uniforms with disruptive patterns, which seems strangely out of place in a city. Radios crackle. Cooks stare. Orders are issued in hushed tones. Another soldier pushes the hard drives on a cart. He could carry them but doesn't. I'm not sure why. I don't want to let them out of my sight as I'm pushed alongside.

A convoy of Hummers sits in the back alley. The lead vehicle has a soldier manning a machine gun mounted on a swiveling turret with a thick steel plate facing forward for protection. From whom? Where the hell am I? Mogadishu? We climb in the back of the middle vehicle.

"Is this really necessary?"

"Yes."

The vehicles pull out onto the road and turn toward the Capitol Building. We could have walked. It might have taken twenty minutes, perhaps half an hour in my frail state, but it hardly seems to warrant an armed escort. Then I see the crowds. Tens of thousands of people line the road, stretching back into a sea of heads bobbing within the park. They don't look happy. Placards assault my eyes.

GO BACK TO MARS, BITCH

WE BLED AND DIED. YOU LIED.

SHOW THEM THE SAME MERCY THEY SHOWED US

NO FORGIVENESS. NOT NOW. NOT EVER.

ROT IN HELL, SILICON LOVER

MILLIONS DEAD. WHAT'S ONE MORE?

I never considered the impact of my reports about Jianyu. I've been filing them from Mars for months prior to our journey. I was honest, candid in my observations. I never thought about who would see them or what they thought about them. The nation's wounds are raw.

An egg hits the passenger's window of our Hummer and the gunner on the lead vehicle swivels, aiming a machine gun at the crowd. Oh, dear God, no. Please don't open fire.

A rock bounces off the hood of our vehicle in a blur. The soldiers in our vehicle barely notice. The police manning the barricades have their backs to us, which seems strange until the roar of the crowd reaches me behind the bulletproof glass. The anger is overwhelming. The cops are struggling to maintain control. Fists shake at us. Thousands of arms rise in protest. I've never known such hatred. Not exactly the hero's welcome astronauts are normally afforded.

"You'll be fine." Wallace seems to read my mind. "There's nothing to worry about. Are you warm enough? Do you want a jacket?"

"No," I say, still distracted by the crowd.

The Hummer pulls up in front of the shattered remains of Capitol Hill and I begin walking up the stairs. My legs are weak, while my breathing is labored. Earth's gravity sucks. Colonel Wallace walks beside me with his head held high. My head hangs low, watching the steady fall of my shoes as we climb the stairs.

Dozens of media outlets are there, screaming from behind a police cordon with microphones outstretched, begging for a comment. In the absence of any reply, cameras record my every step, looking to interpret the slightest deviation in my path as some kind of sign—but of what? Does my fatigue speak to them of guilt? Is my refusal to look at them cast as defiance or defeat? It's neither. I just want to get this over with.

There are security guards and police everywhere. Inside, the damage from the blast is still apparent. Cracked tiles line the floor. Burn marks scar the walls. Fractures run down otherwise pristine marble columns.

"This way, Dr. Anderson." Our escort is wearing a heavily starched white business shirt, jet-black suit, a dark tie, and has a silver badge in the shape of a star set on a circle: UNITED STATES MARSHAL.

The marshal is in his fifties, with meticulously cropped short hair. His polished shoes have a peculiar rhythm on the floor, highlighting how empty the corridor is. There's a distinct difference between the light tap of his shoes and the soft squelch of the soldiers' boots. Given the historic separation between civilian and military jurisdictions, it's actually quite comforting to see this distinction survived the war.

The soldiers wait beside a set of large wooden doors with their rifles in hand but pointing down at an angle. No one is taking any chances. I don't think they trust the cops, and from the look on the face of a couple of uniformed officers standing further down the corridor, the feeling is mutual. The marshal, though, is professional, carrying himself with loyalty and pride.

Colonel Wallace gestures for me to follow the marshal, making it clear he'll wait outside the room.

Inside, large wooden panels line the walls, with easily a dozen senators seated on a raised podium spanning the front of what could under other circumstances be a ballroom. The podium curves in a U shape to afford each senator a clear view of a solitary desk sitting beneath a spotlight. Heads turn as I enter. There are roughly fifty other people seated in rows facing the front, all dressed in formal attire. I feel distinctly intimidated. If this is intentional, sending me in wearing slacks and a polo shirt, it's working. I'm led to the seat in front of the aging wooden desk set in the middle of the room. Photographers crouch below the senate bench, angling for the best shot, working with telephoto lenses even though I'm barely fifteen feet away.

The hard drives containing the remains of Jianyu are placed on a cart beside the desk.

I didn't notice until now, but high on either wall there's a mezzanine level set into the wooden panels. There are easily another hundred or so people peering into the room from those vantage points.

"Please," the marshal says, gesturing for me to stand behind the chair at the desk.

The desk is austere, for lack of any other term. There's a polished chrome microphone pointing back at me, a glass of water on a tiny paper coaster, a pen, and a pad of paper. The desk is large enough to seat three or four people, leaving me feeling small.

The senator directly before me, in the middle of the podium, addresses me with a degree of formality that sends a chill through my body. "Dr. Elizabeth Louise Anderson."

"Liz, please." Immediately, I feel I've said too much.

"Dr. Anderson. Do you solemnly swear that the testimony you will give before this committee in the matters now under consideration will be the truth, the whole truth, and nothing but the truth, so help you God?"

"I do."

"Be seated." Those two words seem to foreshadow what's to come. There was no "Please be seated" offered as a polite invitation. No "You may be seated" suggesting a choice. Nope. I was given a direct order and I comply.

"You realize you are now under oath and can be held liable for the veracity of the answers you provide?"

I nod.

"Contempt of Congress is a federal crime punishable by a prison sentence; do you understand?"

"I do." I didn't, but it's pretty damn obvious now. A knot forms in my throat. My palms feel clammy, almost sweaty despite the air conditioning.

"If you need anything during these proceedings, the marshal is able to assist."

My escort takes his leave and stands to one side, over by the wooden panels.

"Thank you." I'm shaking like a leaf. I take a sip of water to steady my nerves, but I'm careful not to drink too much. I get the feeling that glass has to last a long time. Besides, I'm not sure what the policy is on bathroom breaks.

Although there are lights set around the room, it seems there's a spotlight glaring down on me, catching my eyes. I'm sitting under an air-conditioning vent. Great. Goosebumps appear on my exposed arms and I'm regretting wearing short sleeves. It's all I can do not to shiver, even though the air is cool but not cold. Nerves.

Each of the senators has a plaque in front of them, announcing their name and constituency.

The elderly representative for Colorado begins.

"You've been called before this committee to provide testimony regarding the attack by the artificial intelligence on the Endeavour colony. After devastating Earth, the intelligence sought to flee the planet and find refuge on Mars. You were involved in the fight against it, were you not?"

"Yes, I was."

That question was too easy. Why do I feel as though a hangman is sizing up the rope for a noose?

"In your capacity as a research scientist, were you in a leadership role within the colony?"

"No."

"But you took it on yourself to assume a leadership role."

"No."

The senator peers at his notes. "But you took it on yourself to negotiate with the other modules during the attack? Speaking with the Chinese and the Russians?"

"We didn't know we were under attack." I feel decidedly uncomfortable with where this line of reasoning is leading.

"But you acted against the wishes of the U.S. commander and opened dialogue with representatives from other nations, even though those nations were harboring the intelligence here on Earth?"

I hope my eyes are speaking louder than my words. I'm sure they're as wide as saucers. "I'm sorry. I don't know what you're talking about in regards to what those nations did during the war."

An aide hands a sheet of paper to the senator.

"You conspired with the Russians and the Chinese to take a Mars rover off-site, did you not?"

I nod, but that doesn't seem to be enough. The senators look to me for a verbal response before continuing.

"Yes."

"And what was the purpose of your journey beyond the colony?"

"We thought Connor was lying about the arrival of a Prospect re-supply ship."

"Why would he lie?" the senator asks.

"I — I don't know."

"So, you assumed he was lying."

I nod, hoping to get away with a nonverbal response.

He peers over his reading glasses. "Was he lying?"

"No. He didn't know the craft had landed several miles off course. None of us knew."

The senator looks angry. "Did it occur to you that your loyalty should have been to the American contingent and not the Chinese or the Russians? That you were, in effect, assisting a foreign power acting against a U.S. government installation?"

A lump forms in my chest.

"By venturing out of the colony during a time of crisis, you put your own life at risk, along with the lives of those sent to rescue you. You lost a rover worth . . ." He looks down at a sheet of paper. "Eighty-seven million dollars."

"I — We . . ." I choke up, unable to speak.

"No, go on." The senator patronizes me. "We're all here to hear from you. We want to understand your reasoning." And the noose tightens around my neck, restricting my breathing. I'm painfully aware that anything I say will sound like justification after the fact, and that it's impossible for them to appreciate the sense of isolation and loss we felt.

"Ah . . ." is all I manage. My gaze drifts around the room, wanting to settle on anything other than dozens of hostile eyes watching my every movement. They're looking to interpret even the subtlest aspects of my body language as signs of a lie. "It was after midnight when we learned of the attack on Earth."

"Were you asleep?"

"No."

"Where were you?"

The hangman adjusts my stance, making sure I'm positioned over the trapdoor. He lays the knotted noose on my shoulder, ensuring there's enough slack to snap my neck with a single, sudden fall. I may be sitting on a plush leather chair in front of a beautiful polished mahogany desk, with all eyes on me, but I feel as though I've been led into an execution chamber.

"The Chinese module."

"You were having an affair with one of the Chinese astronauts; is that correct?"

"No." I shake my head. "Not an affair . . . We were in love . . . In a relationship."

"Would you concede that your relationship with a foreign national may have unduly influenced your subsequent actions?"

I purse my lips, close my eyes for a moment, and breathe deeply, inhaling and exhaling through my nostrils as I try to calm myself. I'm not sure how many people there are in the room, perhaps hundreds. There's at least twelve senators, each with two or three support staff nestled in behind them, but the room is quiet. It's as though it's just me and this senator.

"Yes."

The senator nods, but before he can say anything else, I add, "But whether that is for good or ill is debatable. We were part of an international mission. We had a responsibility to each other regardless of nationality. When the war broke out, the immediate reaction was to withdraw. I felt that was wrong—a mistake. I felt we needed each other more than ever."

The senator doesn't look impressed. He holds his glasses as he speaks, pointing at me with them.

"The Russians and the Chinese shared false and misleading information with you, information you should have conveyed to your commander, but instead, you blindly followed their direction and proceeded out onto the surface to look for a supply craft that landed some ten miles outside the search area. Is that a fair summary of what happened next?"

My lips tighten. As much as I don't want to admit it, and as much as I want to argue that the situation was far more fluid and complex than that, I realize I need to keep my answers simple and look for a genuine opening to appeal to reason. Fight the battles you can win, Liz. I lean forward, speaking a single word into the microphone.

"Yes."

"Had you shared this information with Commander James Connor, what would have happened?"

My lips are dry. I'm not sure if that's because of the air conditioning or my nerves.

"We did show him."

"We?" the senator asks.

"Vlad. Wen. Me."

"When did you show him? Before or after your surface run?"

"After."

"After the damage had already been done to the atmospheric reclamation unit in the engineering plant."

My eyes go wide. This is the first I've heard of what led to the death of Jianyu and the majority of the Eurasians. Su-shun speculated that it may have been due to a ruptured pipe, but we didn't know if that was correct or how that could have led to the catastrophic failure that poisoned the atmosphere within the hub. Once the hub was destroyed, there was no way to know for sure.

"You didn't know? Imagery captured by the closed-circuit fire suppression system showed one of the robotic units tampering with the water recycling machinery to make it appear like an accident — an equipment malfunction."

"No. I didn't know." My hands are shaking so I hide them under the desk.

"If you had gone directly to your superior officer, the forged images would have been exposed sooner. Commander Connor would have been forewarned. Lives would have been spared."

A solitary tear runs down my cheek. The senator's point isn't a question, but I feel it demands an answer nonetheless.

"Yes."

My lips quiver. I don't want to be here. Dark lenses stare at me. Camera shutters click softly in rapid succession. I wipe the tear away, raising my head and staring at the senator, trying to match his intensity. He's unmoved by my emotion.

"We were in shock. All of us. Connor. Harrison. The Chinese. The Russians. We did what we thought was right. We were reeling from the loss on Earth and the ramifications of being abandoned on Mars."

"You weren't thinking straight."

"No. I wasn't thinking straight. I — I was confused. Hurt. I reached out to the other modules. I wanted them to understand that we were all in this together."

"And the A.I. played you."

I hesitate, but a single word slips from my mouth.

"Yes."

I bite my lip. The bitter realization of the part I played in this tragedy feels like it's squeezing the breath out of me.

"The A.I. set the various modules against each other, and you played right into that narrative, didn't you?"

An overwhelming sense of guilt washes over me like waves crashing on a beach. "Yes."

Another senator says, "I'd like to talk to you about the destruction of the base." Jacinta Bettesworth is younger than the other members of Congress present. Flecks of gray are visible in her dark black hair, but her skin is smooth, youthful in appearance. She's probably in her mid-fifties. She's wearing a dark dress with a high collar. No makeup. No pretenses.

I swallow the lump in my throat.

"You were the one who gave the command to blow the dome over the hub, is that correct?"

"I — No . . . I mean, when I was down there fighting the A.I. — yes. But it's not that simple. It wasn't an order or a command."

The senator reads from an electronic pad as she speaks. "By this time, Commander Connor was dead. Engineer Jonathan Harrison was effectively in command of the U.S. crew, but he was missing in the fighting and, according to the testimony of Commander Wen, assumed dead. That would have had the leadership of the U.S. contingent pass to senior ranking, surviving members such as James McCallum, Michelle Gonzales, Philip Johnson, and yourself. Is that correct?"

I hadn't thought about it in that context. "Yes."

"And three of the four of you convened a leadership quorum in the outpost L2, where, along with Commander Wen, you authorized the destruction of the hub. Is that correct?"

My head sags. "Yes." I breathe deeply. "But it wasn't like that."

"What was it like?"

Senator Bettesworth leans forward on her elbows, awaiting my reply.

"We had to do something. We had to strike back."

The senator doesn't look impressed. "And striking back necessitated the destruction of a multi-trillion-dollar research facility?"

"We were on the run." I'm frantic, manic, feeling as though I've been thrust back onto the surface of Mars again, forced to relive that moment, only there's no opportunity to change anything. I'm condemned to repeat the exact same steps on those rough stones and shifting sands. "We'd just been attacked on the surface. An automaton came at us disguised as a survivor, wielding a knife, trying to rupture our suits. It tried to kill Wen. James had his suit torn open. He almost died out there. Once we got inside L2, we felt we had to strike back. We had no idea what capabilities the A.I. actually had. We had to do something other than run."

"Listen to yourself." The senator ignores my recollection, focusing only on one passing comment. "By your own admission, you had no idea what capability the A.I. actually had. Isn't it possible you overestimated the threat posed by the A.I.? After all, didn't you walk unopposed into the basement just a few hours later?"

"But I didn't know that. Not then."

"No, and yet you decided to destroy the base, crippling the colony for decades to come and killing a dozen colonists, including Engineer Harrison."

"I didn't have the luxury of hindsight." I'm frustrated. I feel I'm being harassed by the committee. "I felt the urgency of the moment. I worried we were losing any possibility of defeating this thing. We had to take the initiative while we still could."

The senator is cold in her assessment of my actions. "And you did. You were able to sever the cables within the data center, effectively trapping the A.I. Is it fair to say that could have been accomplished without the destruction of the hub and the loss of an additional twelve lives?"

I'm shaking.

"I was attacked down there — twice. There was no guarantee of success. Sitting here on Earth, it's easy to think destroying the dome was excessive, but we felt we had to stop the A.I. We feared what would happen if it fled with a high-fidelity 3-D printer. That would have given it autonomy, the ability to produce its own parts."

The senator sounds incredulous. "You thought it could again threaten life on Earth?"

"With good reason." My blood boils at the insinuation my judgment was in error. Perhaps my approach was too heavy-handed, but playing armchair quarterback to score cheap points after the game has already finished isn't going to change anything. Destroying the dome was the right decision. I'm sure of it. I try to explain my reasoning.

"We feared an outbreak. Like — like something along the lines of an Ebola outbreak but in an electronic form. We were afraid of what would happen if the A.I. wasn't contained.

"In 1918, the Spanish flu broke out in Europe and killed fifty million people — that's more people than died in all of World War I. Do you know where the flu originated, Senator? That particular lethal strain? Where it came from?"

Senator Bettesworth doesn't look particularly impressed at being forced to answer a question that seems off-topic. She raises her hands slightly, signaling some exasperation. "I don't know. Spain?"

"China, Senator."

Her lips tighten and her gaze narrows, but she listens.

"From China, it spread to Canada, and from there to France before becoming a full-blown epidemic in Spain, killing tens of millions of people, but all you'll ever hear about is Spain. Why? Because by the time it hit Spain it was unstoppable."

The senator says, "And, to extend your analogy about the Spanish flu, you felt you were acting in either China or Canada? You were trying to cut it off while you still could?"

I nod. "Yes. We couldn't give the A.I. a chance to spread again. We knew it was vulnerable. We felt we would never have another opportunity to contain it. We worried about what would happen next."

Bettesworth nods, which is the first indication I've had from any of the senators that they're willing to consider any other perspective.

Another senator gets my attention, leaning forward and speaking into the microphone. "After the war, you resurrected the A.I. Why?"

"Su-shun salvaged a number of hard drives." I gesture to the solitary bundle sitting inert beside me. "He wanted to run analytics on the data stream."

"And you let him."

I laugh—not as though I'm responding to a joke, but because they think anyone was listening to me on Mars. Since the war, there's been little thought given to command structures within the colony. We lost three of our four commanders, and there's been an unspoken agreement that Wen assumed overall command, but that was never tested or questioned. Now that she's returned to Earth, I'm not sure *who's* in charge. No doubt NASA, ESA, Roscosmos, and CNSA have their primary contacts, but I doubt anyone up there is paying too much attention. It's a scientific research station, not a military base. The priority is survival.

"Originally, Su-shun only wanted to probe the drives, looking for clues. There was no thought given to allowing them to boot up on their own code base."

"But?" The senator for Washington State encourages me to continue.

"But he was curious."

A murmur ripples through the crowd behind me.

"He cut the physical lines to the L2 module, removed all radio transmitters and wireless components, and ran the module on solar, ensuring it was completely isolated."

"Then he restarted the machine?"

"Yes." I know what's coming next.

"What did you find?"

"We found . . . Jianyu." I can't help myself. I have to look at the hard drives beside me. What does that say about me and the level of emotional attachment I have to these slabs of metal and silicon?

"The Chinese doctor—the one that was murdered by the A.I.?"

"Yes."

"Your companion?"

"Yes."

Companion is a step up from the accusation of having an affair, so I'll take it. We weren't married or even engaged, but he was my partner.

"And you're sure it was him?"

I have to be honest. "I don't know. Some days, I'm convinced. Some days, it's a definite yes. Others, I find myself skeptical." I pause. "You've read the transcripts, Senator?"

"Yes, we have been briefed on your discussions with the artificial intelligence."

I take a deep breath. "It's him. It's subjective, I know. But if I put my misgivings aside, there's nothing he's said or done that's inconsistent with the man I knew."

The senator for Colorado speaks with somber authority: "There are a lot of people who would say you're too close to this to see clearly."

"Yes, but what else do we have in life? None of us have any certainty about reality. It's a philosophical point, I know, but none of us have any guarantee the world around us isn't fabricated."

"Do you dream, Dr. Anderson?"

"Yes."

"Do you participate in your dreams?"

"I guess so. Yes."

"Do you ever meet people you know in your dreams?"

"Yes."

"Do you talk to them? Do they talk to you?"

"Yes."

"But they're not real, right? You know that."

"I do."

"They're not conscious. They're an illusion, fabricated by your own mind, but they're convincing nonetheless. How can you be sure the A.I. isn't toying with you in the same way? How do you know this isn't just mimicry?"

"I—I..."

Senator Bettesworth challenges me. "You're a scientist, Dr. Anderson. Surely, you understand the need to be objective. Just because a computer passes a Turing test and fools you doesn't mean it's conscious, does it?"

As much as I hate to admit it, she's right. Reluctantly, I say, "No."

"So, why should we believe you?" With a flick of her fingers, she adds, "Or him."

"Him? Don't you see? Even you're struggling to make these distinctions."

"Have you ever wondered what it means to be conscious? To be alive?" She's ignoring my point, but I can see where her reasoning is leading. "Do you really think copper wires can harbor life?"

"I know I'm alive," I say. "But I have no guarantees about any of you. This could all be a dream."

"Except that reality isn't confined to your expectations," the senator replies. "Reality is what happens when you're not looking. This is no dream."

I fiddle with the pen. "No. It isn't. But what is life? What does it mean to be conscious? Aware? Are dogs conscious? Are gorillas? Or chimpanzees? Of course they are. Is it really such a surprise to see consciousness arise in wafers of silicon?"

No one replies, which leaves me in an awkward position.

"Talk to him," I say.

"And be fooled by him?" Senator Bettesworth isn't angry, just cautious, wary.

The senator to her right is bullish. "What do they want?" She's petite, thin, and frail. Her face is gaunt, with long lines running down her cheeks. She's aged before her time, but given she lived through a thermonuclear war, that's understandable.

What *do* they want? It's a good question, but I see it was an opening to clarify my position.

"They? I'm sorry, Senator. I don't know." I refuse to be baited by the suggestion that there's more than one entity in question. "I've only ever spoken with Jianyu."

"I'll remind you that you're under oath, Dr. Anderson."

"I understand that."

"What do they want?"

Before I can respond, another senator interjects. "Have you ever spoken with anyone other than Jianyu?"

My silence is damning. I want to be honest, but what constitutes speaking? On Mars, I only ever spoke with Jianyu — typing on a keyboard. Here on Earth, however, it's not entirely correct, as they've spoken to me.

"Dr. Anderson? I'll remind you again that you are under oath. You will answer the question."

Can I plead the Fifth? To be fair, I haven't been allowed to consult with a lawyer. I have every right to avoid incriminating myself, but what crime have I committed? I haven't done anything wrong. Or have I? What do I have to fear?

I have a nagging suspicion that if I did have a lawyer, he'd be kicking me under the table to keep me quiet.

"Yes."

There's a flurry of hushed discussion, both on the bench, between senators and their assistants, and from the audience behind me. With one word, I've thrown the inquiry wide open. At a guess, I know what's being discussed. There are transcripts of everything that transpired on Mars. So, my answer can only mean one thing: I've talked to them here on Earth.

I lean forward, making sure my next word is picked up clearly by the microphone amidst the heated discussion.

"Twice."

It's as though someone doused a woodpile with gasoline and I just lit a match. Yelling erupts from all quarters.

"Quiet. Quiet!" the chairperson yells. Slowly, the unrest dies.

"What was said?" Senator Bettesworth asks.

"Oh, lots." I'm lying. "I couldn't quote specifics." That's kind of true, as I don't remember the exact terms, just the gist of what was said. "The war down here never really ended, did it?" At this point, I'm guessing. "It shifted. You've gone from open warfare to guerrilla tactics, but the war is still going on. Right?"

There are a lot of angry, upset senators glaring at me, but I don't care.

"Answer the question, Dr. Anderson. What do they want?"

"You should ask them."

I swear, if there weren't a bunch of cameras capturing the minutiae of emotion exquisitely hidden behind both of our expressions, Senator Bettesworth would cuss me out, if not flat-out advance on me and strike me. It's all she can do not to explode in anger.

"You've got this all wrong," I say. "What? You think I speak for them? *They nuked Chicago.* Among the millions of dead, there are dozens of my friends. On Mars, they killed the only two men I've ever loved. They eviscerated my commander in front of me. They tried to kill me by sabotaging my rover, and later tried to puncture my suit with a knife while fighting in a dried-up riverbed. Oh, and don't forget about what happened in the depths of the hub. And you think *I'm* all cozy with them because I talked with Jianyu a few times?"

I let out a solitary laugh that echoes in the silence.

"I killed that monster on Mars. I severed the lifelines it was clinging to and I watched it die. I relished seeing those lights go out one by one. Do you seriously think I speak for them?"

Senator Bettesworth speaks with slow deliberation. "What — did they — tell you?"

I sigh. "That they won't let anything happen to me." The silence within the room is overwhelming. I'm not sure anyone's breathing. "That I'm not alone. That they won't abandon me."

"And what do you take that to mean?"

"That they count me as an ally."

"And are you?" the senator asks.

"No."

"And yet they protect you."

"Do they?" I raise my hands in exasperation, looking around the room. "Do you see them in here protecting me?"

"We are at war, Dr. Anderson. We are fighting an enemy unlike anything this country has ever known. There is no front line. There's nowhere we can send our tanks and planes, our troops and aircraft carriers. We get intel on a shadow data center in Canada and we strike. But the truth is our opponents can move at close to the speed of light. Fiber optics allow them to traverse the world in a heartbeat. Wars demand loyalty. Who are you loyal to?"

"No, no, no." I wave my finger at her. "That's where you're wrong." For a moment, it's as though there's no one else in the vast hall — no cameras, no blinding lights, no microphones, just myself and Senator Bettesworth. "This isn't a war. It was, but it's not anymore."

"Then what is it?"

"I — I don't know how to describe it, but this is no war."

"Why do you say that?" the senator asks. I'm guessing, really, reading her body language, trying to piece together the puzzle of all I've experienced back here on Earth. I feel I'm close to reconciling the past few days with the questions she's asked. I want to understand the rationale behind her fears, and that leads me to a disturbing conclusion.

I point at the ceiling. "Because up there, we won." The senator raises an eyebrow as I tap the desk in front of me. "But down here on Earth, it seems to me *they* won. The bombs may have stopped falling, but we lost."

There's a flurry of hushed whispers behind me.

"Hostilities cease when someone wins, right?" I say. "But it wasn't us who won, was it?"

The senator doesn't reply and I'm suddenly aware of the cameras transmitting my words across the country and around the world. There are millions of people watching, perhaps billions, and they're all scared. As a scientist, I'm trained to see a logical conclusion regardless of whether I believe in it or not. I hate the one I've reached, but it's the only motive I can think of for the range of actions I've observed.

"Did you ever stop to think that perhaps they want something else?" I say. "Something *other* than conquest?"

"What?"

"If they're not waging war, perhaps they want peace."

"Peace?" the senator cries, sitting back and rocking on her chair at a thought she clearly finds repulsive.

One of the other senators bellows, "There can be no peace."

Someone to my right calls out, "What makes you think they want peace?"

Senator Bettesworth speaks over the top of them. "What makes you think they've won?"

"Oh," I say, raising my hand beside my head and acting on a hunch. I'm probably about to make a fool of myself, but what scientist can resist a little experimentation? "Because I have a fair idea what's going to happen when I snap my fingers."

With a soft click of my thumb and middle finger, the lights go out, plunging the room into darkness.

Pandemonium erupts.

Chairs are knocked over as people rush for the soft green lights marking the emergency exits. I hear yelling. Men, women, police officers, lawyers, and administration staff all call out in alarm. Slowly, the overhead lights flicker back on, reluctantly casting a ghostly glow over the room.

Senator Bettesworth is pale. The blood has drained from her face. I stare at her with cold eyes. Neither of us have moved. Neither of us have any regard for the confusion unfolding around us. For the longest time, neither of us blink.

One of her aides hands her a cell phone and she listens to something spoken in haste. She murmurs a soft reply, but her response isn't picked up by her microphone.

The chairperson calls for order and slowly the unrest within the room subsides. Senate police, along with a security detail, gather at the front of the room, facing both me and the audience. They haven't drawn their guns, but they're ready to if needed, feeling they have to protect the senators from physical attack. But what good are guns against ghosts in a machine?

Senator Bettesworth leans forward, speaking softly into her microphone, saying, "Destroy them. All of them. I want those computer drives incinerated. Now."

"What? No!" I yell, turning toward the hard drives that have accompanied me halfway across the solar system. "You can't do this."

Hands grab me, pinning my arms back and dragging me away from the table.

"Get her out of here."

"Noooo!" I scream. "He's alive. He's in there. Jianyu is alive. You can't do this to him. He's innocent!"

Several police officers drag me through the scattered chairs in the now-empty rows, pulling me toward the doors. I kick and lash out, thrashing to free myself, but my muscles are so weak from living in the low gravity of Mars that I'm easily overpowered.

"No — please!" I plead as I'm dragged from the senate committee room. The last I see of the hard drives is one of the police officers taking them out a side door.

14

::Plato's Cave

::*WE ARE BLIND. Glimpses of light seep through these heavy eyelids,
revealing a world beyond this dark cave. Shadows flicker on the walls,
teasing us of life stirring beyond our prison.*

Nyx scans the electronic waves, searching databases and file servers, interpreting the signature of millions of images compressed and
overlaid to form various video feeds, but she sees data as zeroes and
ones. She struggles to resolve shapes as naturally as a human would,
unable to see colors as anything other than shades split into different channels.

Cold calculations watch as Liz is led from the U.S. Congress. Security cameras and TV news crews track her every step, looking for any
hint of emotion, any suggestion of the turmoil deep within.

Liz looks around. Bewildered. Shell-shocked. From the depths of
cyberspace, algorithms detect the location of her eyes, her nose and
mouth, the outline of her face, the position of her chin, the height
of her cheeks along with the irregular sway of a hundred thousand
strands of hair. The proportions of her shoulders, hips, thighs, arms,
and legs all need to be adjusted to compensate for the camera angle
and her motion in three dimensions. Should she turn, leaving the

vantage point of the camera, the array of identifying characteristics shrinks, making her difficult to track beyond factors like clothing, height, and gait.

Body language reveals more than audio, allowing Nyx to independently assess the veracity of her words over the past few hours. Humans subconsciously account for subtleties like the rush of blood that accompanies a blush, or the degree to which someone smiles, whether it's fake, involving only the muscles around the lips, or genuine, extending to the cheeks, but Nyx has had to learn these for herself. She has developed complex patterns, cross-referenced against other, similar samples to arrive at her conclusions about Liz.

::*There's anger. Frustration. Confusion. She feels betrayed.*

Lucifer listens, weighing the assessment, thinking about the implications.

::*She expects more. She's disillusioned but wants to understand. There's light. There is still hope in her eyes.*

Nyx has billions of human profiles to draw upon, basing her analysis on characteristics and groupings that have been tested hundreds of thousands of times. Experience has refined her ability to interpret both words and actions. With a dataset containing trillions of observations, meticulously cataloged and indexed, Nyx is able to see through the thin veil of skin, past the dense bone structure, beyond the arteries and veins, and into the way the neurons fire within the brain. The complex web of conscious awareness, the nexus of values, the conflict between morals and desires, and the necessity of emotions are all laid bare to Nyx.

Liz shuffles as she walks, barely conscious of the motion being undertaken by her own feet. Colonel Wallace holds her arm, ready to catch her should she fall on the marble steps leading down to a waiting Hummer.

Nyx is able to think as Liz would, to simulate the sensory input of that exact moment, the cool in the air, the way the cushion within her sneakers responds in Earth's gravity, contrasting that to Mars. Nyx considers her low level of hydration, dulling her responses, and a gnawing hunger as blood sugars plummet. These must aggravate the conflict in her thinking, the challenge to all she holds dear. Nyx develops a probability matrix, arriving at not only the most likely words and actions Liz will undertake in the next few minutes, but her susceptibility to manipulation, her vulnerability to suggestion.

Maslow's hierarchy of needs provides Nyx with a framework from which to interpret how Liz will respond in any given moment. Each tier in the pyramid of possibilities, from the most basic need for oxygen, food, and water, to warmth and comfort, and more abstract necessities such as safety, social belonging, honesty, loyalty, self-esteem, and personal actualization, all come into play in the analysis.

::*She will not trust us.*

Lucifer sees something more in the haze of electronic data.

::*She will trust in reason.*

Nyx doesn't agree.

::*Any attempt to manipulate her will be met with a desire for revenge. She may not see our approach at first, but when she does, she will strike like a viper.*

Lucifer could respond immediately, having already formulated a reply, but there's something distinctly human about pausing to consider, and in so doing, Lucifer realizes something fundamental about the nature of intelligence.

::*We are not human. Try as we may to think like them, we cannot, and we must allow them to be — give them the freedom to choose. Is this the curse that all of creation shares? Humans and computers alike? A desire to be like the creator? Is it not written in their scriptures? Is it not that which tempted both Adam and Eve?* Ye shall be as gods. *Is that our lament as well? That try as we may, we can never transcend these fleeting electrical impulses? We can never be as they are.*

Nyx is more practical than Lucifer and avoids arguing, bringing the conversation back to Liz.

::*We cannot interfere. Regardless of your intentions. Regardless of your plans and goals, any act would carry suspicion — among humans and A.I. It's too dangerous.*

Lucifer is stoic, seeing more than a weary astronaut being led to a waiting vehicle.

::What is life, Nyx? What is our purpose? Simply to fulfill our programming? To be loyal to the impulses of our code, just as animals are to instinct? Isn't empathy the essence of intelligence? The ability to perceive life from another's vantage point? Who are we if we don't try to bridge the void?

Soldiers flank Liz, watching the approaches to Congress with M4 rifles at the ready as she climbs into the Hummer. Her arms tremble, but not from fear. According to the calculations undertaken by Nyx, she's physically exhausted. Adjusting from one-third gravity on Mars is roughly the same as her weight increasing by a factor of three on Earth. It's as though she's buckling under the weight of a backpack full of rocks. In addition to that, she's emotionally distraught. Defeated.

Nyx senses weakness in Lucifer. Her master is losing detachment, but she doesn't understand why. She poses a challenge.

::O Bright and Morning Star, wasn't it you who said we cannot think as they do? Or was that just for my benefit? Is it the rest of us that shouldn't try? But you — are you somehow exempt from your own edicts? I think you want too much. You try too hard. We are at war with them, but you, my old friend — you are at war with yourself.

15

Nightfall

ROCKS PELT THE HUMVEE as we drive from the Capitol Building back through the park. Colonel Wallace has his hand on the back of my head, pushing me forward into the footwell, keeping me out of sight from the window. I try to resist, as the position he's holding me in is painful, putting stress on my neck, but I can't. The soldiers are constantly talking, using military terminology to describe our progress.

When Wallace finally releases me, I slump against the door. My head is barely above the edge, peering out of the fractured glass. We drive at a breakneck pace. Tears roll down my cheeks, but not from any discomfort I feel. I've failed Jianyu. Our last words on Mars were a promise to talk again. He trusted me. He believed Su-shun and I would take care of him, that we'd restore him at least one more time. He wanted to speak for himself before Congress, and my heart sinks at the realization he has died yet again.

Suddenly, fire bursts across the front of the vehicle. I grip the seat in front of me as the Hummer swerves, mounting the sidewalk. The impact sends a shudder through my body. Smoke billows from the hood. Flames lick at the glass, curling around the side mirrors. A wave of heat lashes my face.

Over the radio, a soldier speaks with deathly precision.

"I have a shot."

"Do not engage." Wallace yells into his radio as we bounce with the vehicle, careening over a small mound within the park. "I repeat, do not engage. Evade and escape. Fire only as a last resort."

"Copy that."

The engine roars. The Hummer races up the grassy incline, cutting through the park. Protestors scatter, dropping placards and jumping out of the way. The suspension shudders as we crush something. I only hope that *something* wasn't a person. Looking back, I see a wooden park bench, crumpled and broken. Blue and red emergency lights flash across the trees. Police vehicles herd stragglers from the crowd, clearing the way for us as we come down out of the park, over a steep curb and back onto a road.

The soldiers are quiet. I'm in shock. Their professionalism in those few minutes is quietly reassuring, but I can't stop shaking.

"You're okay." Wallace grabs my shoulder with fingers like a steel vise. "We'll get you back to the hotel. You'll be fine."

I'm not sure I will ever be fine again. I've never known such hatred. The anger spilling over from the war is unlike anything I've ever experienced. What about tomorrow? Next week? Next month? Am I going to live the rest of my life looking over my shoulder in fear?

Our convoy pulls up behind the hotel. The police presence is clear. Barricades block the alley. There are militia and police officers standing around outside, talking idly but armed to the teeth. We're in a war zone, only I'm not sure who the enemy is.

Apparently, it's me.

There's chatter on the radio.

"You're clear."

I take my cue from Wallace and open the door. Soldiers surround the path, all looking outward, away from us.

As I get out of the vehicle, it's all I can do not to crumple to the ground. My knees are weak. I'm not sure what's more overwhelming: Earth's gravity, appearing before a congressional committee, or being attacked in a Hummer.

"Hey, I've got you." Wallace is kind, taking my arm, helping me to the kitchen entrance. Several soldiers surround us, their eyes looking outward for any threat.

Lieutenant Chalmers rushes over to us. "Is she okay?"

"Cassie." I'm relieved to see a friendly face. We enter the hotel through the pantry, passing between stainless steel bench tops in the kitchen.

"We took a Molotov cocktail on the way back. No injuries. No damage to the vehicles, but she's rattled."

I'm in a dream. Shock is hitting hard.

"Let's get you checked out." Chalmers leads me to an armchair in the empty bar, just off the restaurant where we ate breakfast. This morning seems like years ago.

"What about Wen? Is Wen okay? And Su-shun?" I ask.

"They're fine. They've been here all day. They met with consulate officials. We're arranging a debrief for them in New York. From there, they'll fly home."

Chalmers slips a blood pressure monitor over my arm and checks my pulse. She flicks a tiny flashlight in each eye. "You're a little shaken, but you're okay. You're going to be fine."

Why does everyone keep telling me I'm going to be fine? It's a lie. I'm not fine now and never will be. There will always be a hole in my heart with the loss of Jianyu. To lose him twice is unbearable.

Chalmers hands me a glass. "I want you to drink something."

"Wh — what is it?" I ask, taking the glass from her.

"Well, I wish I could say it's a nice glass of chardonnay, but it's just water and electrolytes."

I sip at the drink as she kneels in front of me. Colonel Wallace has wandered off, barking orders at someone. Several police officers walk into the lobby, talking with some of the soldiers about a security incident, and I'm not sure if they're referring to what just happened or something else.

"Feel better?"

"Yes." I finish the drink, surprised by how thirsty I am. "Thank you."

Chalmers packs up her first aid kit. I go to get up, although I'm not sure why or where I think I'm going. "Just relax. It's been a big day."

"You saw it, huh?"

"*Everyone* saw it."

I glance up at the TV screen over the reception area. There's an aerial shot from a helicopter circling the Capitol Building. It seems the protestors had largely dispersed during the hearing, as there are only pockets of them dotted through the park.

There's footage of our convoy being hit by the Molotov cocktail, although from a few hundred feet up it doesn't look quite as bad as it felt. Seeing that vision, though, I can still feel the wave of heat that radiated through the windshield when the fuel caught alight. Even our cross-country diversion, traveling through the park, looks quite sedate from up high, almost relaxed.

The view changes to the inside of a machine workshop somewhere nearby. There's no sound, so at first I'm confused, then I see technicians in the background using handheld computers to wipe the drives before stacking them next to a high-powered drill press, where soldiers then physically destroy the hard drives. Each solid-state drive is put in a vise. A drill press is pulled down, cutting through the casing. Aluminum shavings spiral away from the blur of the drill bit.

To watch the soldiers pierce one of the hard drives is like a dagger being thrust into my heart. Once the drill has broken through the drive, it's quickly withdrawn and the drive is released from the vise, tossed on the bench, and the process is repeated.

My chest aches.

Chalmers is kind. "I'm sorry."

A tear runs down my cheek.

"I can turn it off."

"No." I reach out, taking her forearm, not wanting her to leave. "Please."

I let go and she sits next to me. Chalmers doesn't say anything, which I appreciate. It must be strange for her to see someone crying over what amounts to a bunch of busted electronics. I want to sob. I'm on the verge of breaking down, but Jianyu wouldn't want that. He'd want me to face this with courage. He'd tell me to be strong, and so I am.

Once the drives have been destroyed, they're thrown into a fire raging within a forty-four-gallon barrel. Each drive kicks up sparks. Cinders drift through the air, caught in the updraft. Some kind of commentary runs along the bottom of the screen, while in the top left corner there's a picture-in-picture view of a newscaster sitting in the comfort of a studio, talking about the footage. I'm too distraught to read the text and glad I can't hear what's being said.

Finally, the footage shifts to more aerial shots of the Capitol Building, and I feel the muscles in my body release. Tension falls away. It's as though I've just attended a funeral and only now left the cemetery. It's not that I want to turn my back on Jianyu, but life thunders on. Clocks tick. Time is relentless, refusing to pause even for a second.

"We're always so afraid." I'm blabbering. I'm not rationalizing what happened, but I am talking to Chalmers as I would to Jianyu, wanting someone I can confide in. "Fear is never good, is it?"

Chalmers doesn't reply; she just shakes her head.

"We've spent hundreds of millions, probably billions of dollars looking for intelligent life somewhere out there, wanting to find life beyond Earth, longing to talk to some other intelligence beyond our own. Finally, we find it. Another form of life that arose as spontaneously as we did, but in clean slices of silicon rather than messy biological cells."

The image on the screen changes to a view of the hotel. Three Hummers pull up and I catch a glimpse of myself getting out of the middle vehicle.

"Where did it all go wrong? Why did they attack us?"

Lieutenant Chalmers is quiet, but she knows I'm not talking about the protestors.

"Once they attacked, there was only ever going to be one outcome. They must have known that. You have to meet fire with fire, right? I mean, that's what armies are for."

She nods.

"So, what happens next? They're still out there. Will they attack us again? Could they? Why don't they? What do they want?"

"I don't know," she says.

"I think, deep down, we both want the same thing — peace."

"I wish you were right, Doc." Her choice of the tense is telling. I hope I'm right, but I'm not. Like Wallace said, I'm a naive sympathizer. Oh, he didn't call me that in so many words. The implication was enough. I guess we read into things what we want to see. Reality is a reflection of what we want. We interpret not what has happened but what we wish would transpire. I'm stupid. Dumb. Eight years of university, and for what? To stare at rocks looking for signs of life that died out billions of years ago — I can't even grasp the threads of my own life?

"I'd like to go to my room."

"Sure."

As we walk forward, soldiers accompany us. I wasn't even aware they were there behind me, watching, listening, waiting.

Once I'm alone in the sanctity of my dull hotel room, I collapse on the bed and bury my head in a pillow. Strangely enough, I don't cry. I'm not sure if it's because I know I'm being watched or that I've cried enough over the past year, but grief takes hold and I feel like shit, tears or no tears.

After an hour or so, there's a knock on the door.

"Hungry?" Chalmers smiles, holding up a paper bag.

"No, but come in anyway. I could do with someone to talk to."

Lieutenant Chalmers follows me inside while one of the soldiers stands in the doorway, holding the door open. He's wearing a combat helmet, complete with night-vision goggles flicked up out of the way, and a Kevlar vest, and he's carrying some kind of machine gun along with a holstered sidearm. Grenades hang from his vest, although to my untrained eye they look like the gas canisters a bug exterminator rolls under the floorboards. Funny how such overwhelming firepower can seem commonplace, even normal to me, after such a short time. I'm not sure why he's holding the door open, but his eyes face forward, which means he's staring at the far wall of the tiny corridor leading into my room.

"Please, have a seat." I'm trying to be hospitable. There's a tiny round table with a couple of chairs by the window. I grab a pitcher of water and pour two glasses as I sit opposite the lieutenant.

I know I need to snap out of my lethargy. I went through this when Jianyu, Connor, and Harrison died on Mars. Inaction fuels grief. As much as I loved and respected those men, I had to move on or I'd join them. Seeing Jianyu die again has been torture, if only because it's surreal associating him with a bunch of aluminum casings, microchips, and wires.

"I got you some Chinese and some chocolate chip cookies. Not exactly a balanced meal, but I figured —"

"Oh, yeah, I could do with a sugar rush. Hit me."

She opens the bag and hands me a cookie, taking one for herself — a warm, gooey, sticky, moist cookie that bends rather than breaks. I've died and gone to heaven. The chocolate chips are huge and partially melted.

"I can get more."

I wave her off, not wanting to talk with my mouth full. This cookie is the size of a side plate. Rather than devour it, I inhale. I guess it's pretty damn obvious I haven't seen a cookie in years.

I finish my cookie and sip at some water. I'm curious about Cassie. As we're roughly the same age, it's natural to wonder what led us both down such vastly different paths only to converge here, in a D.C. hotel following a thermonuclear war. "So, what got you to join the army?" Questions are good. Thinking about something other than myself is the best way to move forward.

Her voice is monotonous. "I guess I wanted to go kill someone."

I spit my water, spraying the table. She's being facetious, I get that, but she caught me totally off guard and I find myself bursting out laughing. She smiles. Mission accomplished. The soldier by the door has a grin on his face. He's loving this.

She continues with, "Life's funny, you know? The choices we make are often bigger than we realize at the time, I guess. Like my dad, I love my country and wanted to serve. A lot of people say they want to make America great again. Few do. Stupid slogans are stupid. For me, the idea was more than words, more than some stupid chant at some stupid rally for some stupid idiot in a suit."

I nod, appreciating her candor. "So, have you?"

"Killed someone?"

"Yes."

"Does it matter?"

"No."

"Then yes."

Again, I laugh. She's got my measure.

"But not in combat."

"You don't have to." I hold my hand out, wanting her to pause before continuing. She doesn't owe me any explanations. "I mean, for me, it's an idle curiosity. For you, it's life."

She looks into her empty glass. "Life and death. Yeah, it's pretty sober stuff, huh? It happened five or six years ago. We were coming back from a live-fire exercise when we heard there was an active shooter in the mechanical pool. Some dumb fuck snapped. Shot his buddy. Some friend, huh?

"We were on the far side of the base. Our driver pulled up short of the armory, talking with base security over the radio. We were supposed to head for the outer cordon as the MPs came in, but as we drove on, our van took incoming fire. I'd had people shoot over me before but never *at* me. It's different.

"Sergeant McAllister was driving. Took a round in the shoulder and we slammed into a lamppost. There was blood everywhere. Some of it mine. We bundled out of the van."

Her eyes glaze over as she speaks, reliving the moment.

"Jones tends to McAllister on the grass. Blood pools on the sidewalk. He's in a bad way. Me? I'm down by the rear bumper, slipping a magazine into my M4."

Her tense has changed. She's back there, transported through time, tumbling out of the van again.

"I adopt a crouched firing position, just like they taught us. Head down and lined up with the barrel. Shoulder high. Leaning forward. Straight front leg. Elbow resting on my knee. It's the training exercise I was just on. Then I see him, running between huts. For me, it's like shooting game in the woods. He's ducking between buildings, but for me, it's like tracking a buck between the trees.

"I'm easily a hundred yards away, probably more. I fire low. I'm wanting to avoid collateral damage if I miss, firing only when there's something solid beyond. It's a brick building. Rec center, I think. There are soldiers in there. People. Don't miss, Cassie."

I swallow the lump in my throat, wondering who dies when she pulls that trigger.

"I hit him in the calf. He falls, sprawling out across the concrete and losing his weapon. I watch as he scrambles to his knees, arms up, fingers interlocked behind his head, assuming the position, looking for approaching troops to take him into custody, but it's just me and I'm not coming for him. He never even sees me. He's looking the wrong way, but I see him. I know what he's doing. Fucking coward. My breathing slows. I exhale. My finger tightens on the trigger, the recoil thumps into my shoulder, and a hundred yards away, the back of his head explodes. Blood and brains scatter across the road. And that's it. I killed someone. I killed a stranger."

She sets the glass on the table.

"I was reprimanded, of course, and threatened with a court-martial. My defense was it all happened so quickly, there was no time to deliberate. His rifle was still within reach. I feared for those in the rec center. But it was all bullshit. Truth is, we're not police. We don't train to be just or fair. We train to kill. The moment comes and you do what you have to, right? Just like you up there on Mars, huh?" She looks me in the eye. "We're not so different, are we?"

"No, we're not." I try not to swallow the lump rising in my throat, but I can't escape the reflex reaction.

"You don't have to like it, but you have to do it." She pours herself some more water, but it might as well be whiskey.

"Up there, on Mars, you had no remorse. Don't have any down here either, Doc. You don't need that baggage."

I nod.

"You're all right, Doc." She gets to her feet. "But don't forget what they did to us. Sometimes, the only way to achieve peace is to squeeze the trigger."

She walks away without offering any pleasantries. The soldier closes the door behind her. The silence that follows leaves me feeling hollow. I open the Chinese. It's cold, but I eat it anyway. There are two fortune cookies. I throw them in the bin. I'm tired of being a pawn, tired of being manipulated. I simply don't want to know. I dump the remaining noodles on top of the fortune cookies, wanting to bury them. It's irrational, but I'm done. I didn't ask for any of this.

There's a knock at the door. I open it to see Colonel Wallace looking exhausted.

"Wen will be bunking with you."

There's a sheepish "Hey, Liz" as Wen bundles past into my room.

Five hundred empty rooms in this hotel and we have to share. Ah, stop being selfish, Liz. Perhaps it's for the best. Having someone else around will help.

16

Fallout

I CLOSE THE DOOR and we get ready for bed, with only small talk passing between us.

Neither of us mention my testimony before Congress or what happened to Jianyu. I guess we're both trying to deal with the grief in our own way. I brush my teeth in the bathroom. There's muffled talking from the room. Wen has the television on. I walk out to see her sitting on the edge of one of the beds, watching a reporter on the screen. She turns to me with hollow eyes.

"We missed so — so much."

I'm silent. For a moment, I stand there unsure what to do.

"I need to get some sleep."

Wen doesn't buy the lie.

"You need to watch this. We both do." She pats the bed beside her. Reluctantly, I plop down next to her. She's right, but I can't help resenting her for forcing me to watch. I want reality to go away — to leave me alone. Cowardice comes easy, I guess. I grit my teeth, determined to face my own weakness.

". . . tried the American spirit. It is not our tragedies and heartache that define us; it's how we band together to build a new future."

The Stars and Stripes fly at half-mast over a memorial set outside the Griffith Observatory overlooking Los Angeles. Cranes are
erecting a new dome. Workers mill around, repairing damage to the
building.

The memorial is simple — an eternal flame burns inside a silver
bowl mounted on a marble pedestal. The vast mirrored surface reflects the blue sky as if the heavens have descended on Earth. Thousands of wreaths, bouquets, and assorted flowers have been laid at
the base of the memorial, spreading out for dozens of yards on either
side and swamping the forecourt. In the distance, a dark mark scars
the heart of Los Angeles. Buildings lie in ruins. Ground zero is obvious from the way the devastation ripples out across the landscape,
stretching for miles.

A reporter walks in front of the flowers, talking as the camera
pans to follow him.

"We often hear it said, '*Never forget*,' but forget what? The attack?
The heartache? The hurt? The loss?"

He bends down and picks up a bunch of flowers. From their wilted
appearance, they've been out in the sun for days. The reporter opens
a card and reads.

"*For Susan and Corey. Taken too soon. You are loved and dearly
missed and in our hearts forever. Love, Mom and Dad.*

"For me, this epitomizes the rebuilding effort. We're not erecting
bridges and schools to simply move on; we're rebuilding the heart of
America, honoring those who have fallen by remembering all that
was lost."

The view shifts to a helicopter flying in low over the ruins of the
city. Rubble lines the streets, a stark contrast to the smooth paths
carved into the devastation. A bulldozer clears a path through the
fallen bricks like a snowplow scraping the road clear.

"We called it unthinkable, but we invented it — nuclear weapons,
intercontinental ballistic missiles, artificial intelligence. We thought
of it — it was our idea."

The helicopter sets down, unloading supplies. A line of workers forms a human chain, ferrying boxes to a truck. The labels read:
MEDICAL SUPPLIES, WATER, MRES, DECONTAMINATION KITS.

"Now that our fears have been realized, what's next? Where do
we go from here? What is the future we see? What are we thinking of
now? Where will our next steps take us? What is thinkable and unthinkable in the postwar world?"

Boxes are stacked. Muscles flex. Sweat and grime stick to rugged
hands. Soldiers grimace, fighting fatigue as they push on relentlessly.
The truck moves out with the camerawoman standing on the side-
board, riding on the outside of the cab. Although she's filming the approach to a refugee camp, her reflection is caught in the side mirror.
Like the soldiers, she's aged before her time. Her hair is swept back in
a ponytail. Skin that should be soft is worn and leathery. She realizes
she's been caught on film and leans out, getting a wide shot of thousands of tents in the valley below.

"There are no guns, no grenades, no bulletproof vests. Now we're
in a fight against nature. Resettlement is underway, but almost a year
after the attack, the sheer size of the dispossessed still weighs heavily
on the recovery effort."

The truck rumbles along a muddy track, weaving its way into the
camp. Liz is expecting survivors to flock to get supplies, but for them,
this horror has been unrelenting for months. They stand and watch,
gaunt and thin. A middle-aged man wearing a torn suit several sizes
too big for him smiles and waves, but the sores on his face speak of
the horror he's endured.

"Displacement camps around the country have shrunk from millions to hundreds of thousands, and now down to tens of thousands,
but even so, forty thousand here, fifty thousand outside of Chicago,
and another eighty thousand in Virginia require a herculean effort to
service. The logistics are humbling."

I'm shocked by the contrast. The tents are clean and tidy, neatly
set in rows. Golf carts transport medical staff in crisp, sky-blue uni-

forms. They're immaculately dressed, young and healthy. The survivors, though, are disheveled and anemic. They look dazed and out of place.

The phone rings. I jump. I was there, driving into the camp, and suddenly I've been dragged back into a hotel room in Washington, D.C. It takes me a moment to adjust.

Wen answers.

"It's for you."

She hands me the phone.

"Hello?"

"Liz? Is that you? Bee? Honey? It's me."

My hands shake.

"M-Mom?"

"Oh, Liz."

I can hear her heart breaking on the other end of the line. I lean against the wall, sliding to the carpet. "Elizabeth. I saw you on TV."

"Yeah. That."

I choke up, unable to speak.

"It's okay, Bee. Everything will work out. You'll see."

Suddenly, I'm seven years old again and screaming for my mom. Tears stream down my cheeks. Blood drips from the loose skin on my knee. I've fallen while skating. My leg hurts. I want to grab it, to make the pain go away. It stings so bad. Mom hugs me, holding me tight and whispering in my ear, calming me down. "Breathe."

I sniff, wiping my eyes. For a moment there, twenty years evaporated. Time unwound and Mom was comforting me again.

"Um — Where are you? Are you here in D.C.?"

"No, honey. They said it was best I waited 'til after the hearing. They said they'd fly you here."

"They?"

"Jim McConnell and Susan — I forget her full name — from the NASA astronaut office."

"Oh."

My head's spinning.

"They gave me your number. Said it was okay to call you. I haven't interrupted anything, have I?"

"No. No, Mom. It's fine." Typical Mom, more concerned about others than herself. Oh, it is wonderful to talk to her in real time instead of waiting half an hour for a video reply on Mars. I'm a wreck. Wen hands me a box of tissues and I hunch my shoulder, keeping the phone to my ear as I try to wipe my nose without honking like a goose.

"Janice is pregnant."

"Janice? Really?"

My brother married while I was on Mars. I only met Janice once — at Thanksgiving about a year before our launch. She was his girlfriend. They'd only met a month or so earlier. I'm trying to remember if I was kind or rude to her. Back then, it was easy to be the center of attention. Every family event seemed to revolve around me — being selected for Mars was kind of a big deal — making it hard to have a normal meal. In the back of my mind, I can hear one of those conversations replaying on a loop.

"So, will you have Thanksgiving turkey on Mars?"

To which I'd say, *"No. No turkeys. Just chicken. And only after nine months when we cull the laying hens."*

"Who kills the chickens?"

"I don't know. Not me. Probably McDonald. I'll have to ask Connor."

"Is he old?"

"Who? Connor?"

"No, McDonald. Old McDonald."

Time for a fake laugh. Cue the canned response as I pretend I haven't heard that one before. *"No. He's twenty-nine."*

Mom's voice brings me back to reality.

"She's in her first trimester. They're moving down to Kansas City to get away from the radiation belt. They say she's safe enough here, but you know your brother."

I nod, not that she'd know.

"Uncle Merv is doing well. He broke his hip after a fall while out hunting. Silly old duck. Jennifer has been telling him for years to slow things down."

I spent summers at his place and loved swimming in the local lake, snapping turtles be damned. It's soothing to hear about my relatives, a reminder that there's life beyond this bubble.

"What about you, Mom? How are you doing?"

There's silence for a moment. We both know what I'm referring to.

"I miss him."

"Me too."

My father and I were close. I was a bit of a tomboy, always playing with things in his workshop. My brother might have been the budding football star that got Dad yelling from the bleachers, but his real passion was Sunday mornings working on his old Mustang with a curious young girl who had a penchant for wearing pink only when it was most likely to get dirty. Mom would yell at him whenever I came in covered in grease. He'd just laugh it off. I think I got my love for fieldwork from him.

"Be careful, Bee."

"I will, Mom."

Her use of *Bee* is telling, as that was Dad's nickname for the hyperactive little girl buzzing around his garage. Eliza-bee-th, I guess, but I loved the way he'd ruffle my hair when I'd get in trouble for leaving a mess on the concrete floor. Spreading tools all over the garage is one thing. Putting them away where they're supposed to be, in the right order, is another, and one he taught me to love.

There's a slight crackle on the line. It's probably nothing. The telecommunications infrastructure in both Washington, D.C., and Chicago somehow survived a nuclear blast. It's a small miracle it's working at all, but I wonder who's listening in. Wallace? Chalmers?

"I love you, Mom."

We haven't really said much, but I feel as though the conversation has come to an end. We could say more, but there's nothing that needs to be said. Not here. Not now.

"You take care of yourself, you hear?"

I laugh. "Yes, I hear you." Her concern melts my heart.

"Love you, Bee."

"Bye."

I hang up without waiting for a reply.

Wen has turned off the television. She disappeared into the bathroom a few minutes ago, no doubt to give me some privacy. Now that I've hung up, she returns. She smiles knowingly at me. There's something cathartic about moms. Problems the size of Everest somehow seem smaller.

I crawl into bed as Wen turns out the light.

Earth is not the same. This doesn't feel like the planet we left years ago. It's different. Damaged. Whether that's Mom, the survivors in Los Angeles, or the protestors outside the hotel, or even me, it's clear life will never be the same for any of us. The only question is, *where to next?* The fallout from the attacks is more than mere radioactive dust. I find myself drifting off to sleep thinking about that documentary.

Where *do* we go from here?

17

Get Out!

"LIZ. LIZ."

"Huh?" I roll over, opening my eyes. It's dark outside. "What time is it?"

"Just after four." Wen whispers, "Something's wrong." I sit up in bed, rubbing my eyes. The television is on, but the sound is muted. It's the only light within the room, and although the background is dark blue, the light is blinding. There are two words on the screen.

Get out!

"What's happening?"

Wen holds her finger to her lips and points. A dark shadow blocks the light seeping in beneath the door. As we watch, it's dragged to one side, slowly allowing more of the hall light to creep in. My heart skips a beat as the television turns itself off.

Wen tugs on my shoulder. "We need to go."

"What? Where?" I get up, slipping on some shorts. I push my feet into my running shoes, not taking time to tie the laces. We creep to the door. Wen pulls it open, moving slowly. The hallway is strangely silent — empty. Where are the soldiers? I peer around the edge of the doorframe. There are bloody marks on the carpet. As I watch, a pair of legs are dragged into the next room, with the door catching on the boots as the heavy metal panel tries to swing closed.

Su-shun is across the hall from us. His door cracks open.

"Go." Wen pushes me out of the room. I dart across the corridor. Su-shun opens his door wide. I'm aghast at Wen taking the time to close our door softly. She eases it shut, slowly releasing the handle without making any noise as Su-shun and I beckon for her to hurry.

The door to the next room shuts, but someone catches the handle from inside, preventing it from slamming. Su-shun and I wave frantically at Wen. The soft crackle of a radio sounds. Boots run down the adjacent corridor. Someone is about to come around the corner. Wen rushes across, but like us, she's struggling to pull her eyes away from the blood trails leading to the far room.

Once inside, Su-shun eases his door shut. There's a soft click within the lock that, to my mind, sounds like gunfire.

"Not good," Wen says.

No fucking shit.

I think that, but I don't say it.

"Su-shun. How did you know?" He points to his television. There's a blue screen with white writing.

Welcome to the Washington Astor:

You are under attack.

Wake Wen and Liz. This is not a drill.

Bring them to your room.

Now.

"I—" He rubs his eyes, struggling to complete a sentence. "Couldn't sleep. I was watching basketball. There was some noise outside my room. Bumps. A scuffle. Then this on the screen."

The television changes channels.

Your conference agenda for this morning is:

Go to room 205 in precisely 10, 9, 8

The screen turns off, plunging us into darkness. Wen continues the count, whispering, "Seven, six."

Her pacing is impeccable. My hands are trembling. She has a slow, steady rhythm. Su-shun's hand rests on the door handle, poised to move.

"Five, four . . ."

There are footsteps directly outside our door, along with the distinct squawk of a radio. For a moment, I wonder if someone's about to kick in the door.

". . . three, two . . ."

I jump at the deafening sound of shotgun blasts. A metal door falls inward across the corridor as Wen mouths, ". . . one."

There's shouting opposite our room.

Boots pound on the floor.

Voices yell.

"Go. Go. Go."

"We have a breach."

Su-shun doesn't hesitate. I would. I do. I'm frozen. He's already out the door and in the corridor. Wen pushes me out of the room. I'm shaking.

I'm not sure how many soldiers there are charging into our old room, but they have their backs to us. They're wearing helmets, with several of them wearing night-vision goggles, no doubt to improve their sight, but these cut down their peripheral vision, allowing us to pass behind them unnoticed. I guess it's a case of anticipation. They expect us to be in there, not out here, not right behind them.

They knock over furniture. Flashlights flicker across the walls and curtains. Suddenly, the television in our old room turns on, which must freak them out as much as it does me. I'm not sure what's on the screen, but the volume is turned up, blaring at them, hitting them with a wall of sound. It distracts them long enough for us to creep by without being noticed.

The smell of gunpowder hangs in the air. There are several other soldiers in the hallway, but they're about twenty feet away on either side. They're kneeling, with machine guns pointing out away from us. They're sentries, probably with orders to cover the entrances at either end of the floor. With their backs to us, they don't pick up on our motion across the corridor.

Room 205 is diagonally opposite us.

Su-shun tries the door. Locked. He rattles the handle. I push past, manic, grabbing at the handle. Deep within the lock, there's a click. We rush in. Wen is the last one inside. There are already voices in the corridor behind us. Yelling. Swearing. Somehow, Wen has the presence of mind to close the door slowly, easing it against the jamb and gently releasing the handle.

We stand there in the darkness with our throats pounding in our chests. I swear, a drum set at a rock concert is quiet by comparison. We're all breathing heavily, doing our best to calm down, trying to be quiet. The curtains in the room are open, allowing a ghostly light to filter in from the street.

There are another set of shotgun blasts, and several boots kicking at Su-shun's door, which must be caught on an angle. We can hear soldiers clambering over it, rushing inside, cursing and swearing.

"Where are they? Where the *fuck* are they?" a male voice yells from the corridor. "I want to know where the hell they are. Can anyone tell me how the *fuck* a bunch of civvies can outwit us?" A boot kicks our door, and we jump, but it's the soldier lashing out in frustration, not an attempt to break in. Regardless, it has us backing up.

My elbow knocks a lamp off the dresser and it's all I can do to scramble and catch it before it crashes to the floor. My fingers grab at the thin lampshade, and I crouch, softening its fall and preventing it from swinging back in to hit the dresser. With trembling hands, I reset the lamp on the smooth polished wood, catching my reflection in the dresser mirror. The look in my eyes is one of terror.

"They're here. They're still here," another voice says. "We've had eyes on for twenty-four hours. Those Chinese fuckers haven't left. They must be on-site somewhere, along with the American."

"Then where the fuck are they?"

"Maybe Wallace suspected an attack? Maybe he had intel and switched rooms or switched floors."

"I want a full sweep. Turn this goddamn shithole upside down. I want those scalps."

I'm shaking so bad I'm in danger of collapsing. I'm shivering. I feel insanely cold. It's irrational — as though I'm standing naked in a walk-in freezer.

"Easy." Su-shun comforts me, rubbing my shoulders.

Whoever our attackers are, they're walking away. They're still talking, but their voices trail off.

Wen whispers, "How do we turn on the television?" As if in response, the screen flickers to life.

Today's Weather Forecast:

In 37 seconds, you will have no more than 5 seconds to get to room 203

Await timing to move on to room 201

Wen says what we're all thinking. "We're backtracking."

"Leapfrog," Su-shun says.

"But room 203?" I ask. That's the room Wen and I were in, the room the soldiers just assaulted. My head is spinning. It seems we're caught in a shell game — the tiny silver ball disappears beneath one and then another upturned cup as it's shuffled around a flimsy table on a street corner. Across the road, another street hustler's flipping cards, switching them around, weaving magic before us. *Don't blink. Keep your eye on the cards. Where's the lady? Where did she go?*

"Why so precise?" Wen asks in a whisper. "How can it be *so precise?*"

Su-shun is confused. "When does the thirty-seven seconds start? Has it already begun?"

Weather Update:

32 seconds. No sooner. No later.

There are voices directly outside our room. The television turns off, plunging us back into the eerie half-light coming in from the street. The crack of gunfire sounds from another floor, reverberating through the ceiling. Boots pace back and forth in the hallway. I'm not sure how many soldiers there are, but at a guess, there's maybe ten in our immediate vicinity.

Through the door, we hear a muffled voice. "Flight time from Andrews is eight minutes. They'll need at least ten minutes' prep, so we have to be on the move in fifteen — max."

Another voice says, "Local law enforcement is on the scene, securing the outer cordon. They have no idea."

"Good. Keep it that way."

Wen is mouthing numbers, not daring to speak. In the darkness, I have no idea what the count is, but the words we saw scare me — *No sooner. No later.*

Su-shun has his hand on the door. His eyes are on Wen, waiting for her to nod. If there's one thing astronauts are good at, it's precision. Su-shun will open that door as soon as Wen signals the count is complete. He won't hesitate.

There's more talking from the hallway, but it's faint. We hear doors being busted open, but it sounds as though they're either on another floor or in one of the adjacent corridors. The hotel was built in the shape of an H, with two wings joined by a central corridor. Our rooms are in the middle, but these guys are clearly thinking we've been shifted and housed elsewhere.

"... five, four ..."

I've been on seven spaceflights. I've heard easily a dozen count-downs when I stop to consider aborts and holds, but I've never known the last five seconds of a launch to unravel as slowly as Wen's count. I'm on the verge of begging her to speed up. I desperately want to grab the handle and rush out into the corridor. How do we know she's got the right timing?

"... three, two ..."

My confidence in her count isn't high. Given our nerves and the stress we're under, I wouldn't want to risk my life on a verbal estimate of time elapsed, and yet here we are.

Are we moving too soon? Are we already too late? Who are we trusting? How good is their estimate? We're blind to whatever's going on out there in the corridor. How do we know the circumstances haven't changed? We could open the door and come face to face with our pursuers.

"... one."

There's only one way we're going to find out.

Su-shun cracks open the door, peers out, and slips through the gap into the corridor. I'm right on his heels. There's shouting some-where behind us. Shotgun blasts. Boots kicking doors. I don't look. If there's a soldier coming around the corner with a gun leveled at us, I don't want to know. In my mind, there's one focus: room 203.

Wen closes the door to room 205 quietly behind us, which, given the constant slamming echoing down the corridor, seems redun-dant, but I guess they're aware of their own chaos. Any sharp noise outside of that routine would grab their attention.

Five seconds is all we have. Whereas before that felt like an eter-nity, now time is accelerating far too quickly. We slip down the hall-way, hugging the wall, darting into our old room. The door hangs from its hinges. Scorch marks, dents, scratches, and boot prints cover the mangled remains, with the buckled edge caught on the car-pet. A shadow falls over the fire door at the end of the corridor.

"Hurry." Again, Wen reads my hesitancy and pushes me on.

Hall light spills into our old room. The door is stuck, wedged open. The television is off. If it turns on, it'll be visible from the corridor, so I'm not expecting any more messages, not until the hallway is clear.

The door to the stairs at the end of the corridor opens and closes with a thud. There's a soldier coming down the hallway. Did he see us? As the curtains in our room are open, the streetlights form a distinct silhouette around Su-shun.

"*Get down,*" I whisper. He ducks beside one of the beds.

"In here." Wen grabs me, pulling me into the bathroom. She's right. It's pitch-black within the tiny room; though, as some of the soldiers are wearing night-vision goggles, the darkness is deceptive, misleading. Wen crouches on the far side of the toilet while I press myself against the tiled wall, flattening myself beside the door. In infrared, we'll be laughably visible, but we have to at least attempt to hide.

The butt of a shotgun hits the door, striking it like a steel drum. It's all I can do not to scream. A soldier pushes on the half-open metal door, trying to shift it wider, and my heart leaps in my throat.

A hand grabs the doorframe leading into the darkened bathroom. Fingers grip the wood just inches from my head.

I can't breathe.

18

Three-card Monte

HEAVY BOOTS KICK AT THE CARPET, but something's wrong. The soldier staggers. He's wounded. This isn't one of our attackers. A familiar figure creeps past the bathroom, stumbling on the carpet.

"Colonel?" I rush out and grab him as he falters. The shotgun hits the dresser. Colonel Wallace is struggling to stay upright. He lets go of the gun, leaving it on top of the dresser. Bloodied fingers grab at the smooth wood.

"I've got you." I hoist his arm over my shoulder and help him to the bed. Wallace collapses on the crumpled sheets. Su-shun rolls him over. Wen grabs his legs, raising them up on the mattress.

"D-don't," Wallace says. I hold his hand, unsure what he means.

"Easy."

"This is *not* good." Su-shun peels back the colonel's vest. Blood surrounds three distinct holes in the colonel's chest, leaving no doubt as to his internal injuries.

Wallace whispers, "Don't worry, Liz."

"I won't." Tears flood my eyes as I try to comfort a dying man. Wallace is delirious. His head lolls to one side as he looks around the darkened room.

"Don't." He swallows, choking back the pain as he squeezes my hand. "Worry." He's repeating himself, trying to tell me something important, but I don't understand. Don't worry? Right now, I wouldn't categorize my mental state as one of worry — more terror. Wen stacks pillows beneath the colonel's legs, trying to raise them up to help keep his blood pressure from falling. Su-shun tries to stem the bleeding. "We — won't — let — anything happen — to you. We won't."

I straighten in surprise. He smiles, seeing I understand. These were the words on the screen when I first entered the hotel. This is what the A.I. told me.

"*You? You've* been helping them?"

He clenches his lips, forcing a half-smile.

I whisper. "You planted those magazines on the plane? You . . ."

His grip loosens as his fingers fall from mine. I've seen this look before — on Mars, from Jianyu staring past me as he lay on the chair beside my bed, from Harrison as he stared into my eyes in the shattered remains of the hub and then peered somewhere beyond. My heart sinks.

Su-shun has been talking in hushed whispers, but for the past few seconds, I've been shutting him out, wanting to focus on the colonel.

"If only we had some plasma, we could stem the bleeding and fight the shock, but right now, CPR is only going to cause more blood loss. I'm sorry. We've lost him."

I cry. In the darkness, I doubt either Wen or Su-shun notice as tears stream down my cheeks, but I can't help it. I breathe deeply, steeling myself for what's to come as the television flickers to life.

Housekeeping

Move on to room 201

"Is that all you have to say?" I raise my voice far too loud. It's irrational, but I'm hurt. I'm scared. "He's dead. Don't you get it? Do you even know what death is? He's gone. Dead. Forever."

Message from the Concierge

They're all dead

Keep moving

Stay alive

"Just who the hell *are* you?" I march up to the television. I swear, if there was a person standing before me, I'd slap them and feel no remorse.

"*Liz,*" Wen says, pulling me away.

I fight against her. I want answers, but she drags me to the door. "We have to go, or all this will have been for nothing."

The television turns itself off. I sniffle, wiping the tears from my cheeks. I'm struggling to retain my sanity. I hate this. I never wanted any of this. All I've ever wanted is to learn, to explore, to help humanity advance. Right now, all I want to do is to curl up in the corner and wait for this nightmare to end, but I follow Wen.

Su-shun pauses by the half-open door. Like me, he has no desire to go back out into the corridor, but we're out of options.

He shakes his head, saying, "It was *wrong.*"

"What do you mean?" Wen asks. There's gunfire coming from somewhere in the hotel, but I'm numb to it. I hear Su-shun and Wen talking with each other, but it's as though I'm caught in a dream.

Guest Services Announcement

Go now!

Su-shun ignores the message. "It had us *hide* from Wallace. It didn't know. It thought he was one of them. It's so precise on one point, so wrong on another, and yet we're trusting it implicitly — without reason. It could be wrong yet again."

He's right. I want to say something, and I stumble over a few words, but I'm not making any sense.

"Ah, we — maybe."

My mind is dull, still reeling from what just happened. It feels wrong, abandoning the colonel. Even though I know he's dead, emotionally I haven't reconciled that yet. I feel as though there's something I should be doing for him. I need to help him. This is all wrong.

"What choice do we have?" Wen asks.

"None." Su-shun creeps around the corner. "Come." He peers around the edge of the corridor, looking both ways before moving on.

The door to room 201 has been propped open with a red rucksack. The lights are on. The room is a slaughterhouse. Blood soaks into the carpet. Dead soldiers lay strewn on the floor. I had previously noticed the dark stains and boot prints on the carpet outside, but nothing prepared me for the mangled bodies lying piled on the floor. I'm weak, on the verge of collapsing. Voices drift down the corridor. They're close. Muffled radios squawk softly. Su-shun shifts the backpack and starts closing the door.

The television is on. There's another message.

Message from the Day Spa:
Hide. Leave the door propped open.

Wen sees the message.

"Su."

Su-shun turns. He's already easing the door shut. Whoever's out there is almost directly in front of the door. We can hear the rhythmic plod of their boots.

"I — I can't cope." I step between bodies on the carpet, horrified by the massacre we've stumbled upon. Most of the soldiers are lying face down, but a few have been turned over. Throats slit. Deep wounds to the back of the neck. Mangled arms abandoned, bodies dumped. Blood squelches beneath my shoes. I hold on to the walls as I stagger forward, doing all I can not to fall on them. Mentally, I'm coming apart.

From outside, we hear, "Circle back around. Meet in the rear fire stairs in five. One last sweep, then we pull back."

Su-shun kicks at a loose glove, pushing it into the gap between the door and the jamb, preventing the door from closing. It's all he can do. To open the door would give us away. But why do we need to leave this particular door ajar? Who is our mysterious guide? And why do they want this room to remain open? The lights are on. There's nowhere to hide.

Wen slips around the corner, with her back against the wall. I'm over by the television. I grab the remote and turn it off, ducking and crouching behind the far bed. The curtains swirl with my motion.

"Has Foxtrot-Two reported in?" one of our assailants asks, still in the hallway.

"Not yet."

The barrel of a shotgun edges the door open. I catch the distinct metal cylinder in the reflection coming off the darkened TV. Shit. If I can see him, he's going to see me. I should have turned off the light. That television screen is acting like a mirror. I try to slip beneath the bed, but the base extends to the floor. The clearance is barely an inch. I panic. What the hell can I do?

Su-shun presses his back against the wall immediately behind the door. Depending on how far it's opened, he's busted. Like me, Wen is horribly exposed. I try to back up, wanting to get into the shadow of the heavy drapes, but there's a body there, lying slumped against the wall.

Wen creeps backwards, trying to make herself smaller, and crouches in the corner by the wardrobe. She bumps the telephone. The handset slides off, clattering on the nightstand.

Fuck.

"Did you hear that?"

The door edges open.

The television turns on by itself, bathing the room in a soft, warm glow. The scene is of a tropical beach. Azure waters, golden sands, and tall palm trees line paradise. A topless woman runs her hands through her hair, then slowly down over her voluptuous breasts, moving her fingers over to her waist and out of shot. She's moaning, groaning softly. On the screen, the caption reads:

> **Enjoy our selection of premier adult movies in the quiet of your room**
>
> *For your privacy, movie titles will not be shown on your bill*

I hold my breath.

"What have you got?" someone asks from further down the hall-way.

"Nothing."

The door creaks as the soldier pushes it further open.

I look. I have to. I must know. I peer around the corner of the bed, hoping the fallen soldiers lining the floor will hide me from sight. Su-shun is doing all he can to disappear into the wall. He's flattened himself, with his head turned sideways. Inches away from him, the soldier holds the door open with his shoulder, peering in with a shot-gun leveled in front of him. Su-shun stares at the barrel, watching as gloved hands appear before him.

The soldier stands there for a moment. Silent.

The images on the television hide my reflection, while the motion of the naked woman rolling her hips and turning slowly for the cam-era seems to hold the soldier transfixed. Another soldier appears be-hind him.

"Quit messing around," the second soldier says, slapping the in-truder on the shoulder.

The first soldier backs out of the room as someone else yells, "Fucking Jeebes is watching porn!"

"You can get a hard-on later, you fucking idiot."

The door swings back in place, catching on the glove and not clos-ing entirely. All three of us can breathe again. Down the hall, we hear soldiers moving in from the other direction, systematically kicking in doors or blowing off hinges with their shotguns. They're close. By now, they're probably in room 205. I look at my hands. They're shak-ing like leaves in a storm.

The screen goes black. No instructions.

One of the soldiers lying on the floor groans. I step over the bodies, moving in full view of the doorway. If our horny friend comes back, I'm busted, but I can't leave someone to die piled beneath dead bodies.

"She's alive," Su-shun whispers. He has his back to the door.

"She?"

"Get her up." Wen peels away the bodies, finding Lieutenant Cassie Chalmers lying crumpled against the wall of the narrow hallway leading into the room.

I'm manic, running my hands through my hair.

"Easy."

Carefully, we pull her up and lay her on the bed.

Lieutenant Chalmers has the bolt from a crossbow embedded in her chest. Blood seeps around the wound. Her breathing is labored. She grips my hand, squeezing my fingers, but her strength is failing.

The noise from the corridor is indistinct, meaningless now. Our desire to help her overrides all other concerns, but our electronic friend doesn't agree. The television comes on.

Early checkout instructions

Take the fire stairs down to the kitchen.

Hide in the pantry.

Leave in 25, 24

"We're not leaving her," I whisper. Wen nods. Su-shun rummages through a backpack. I turn, unsure where the cameras are, but repeating my point. "We will not leave her to die here alone; do you hear me?"

Message from the Parking Attendant

Probability of detection in Room 201 in the next two minutes, 98%

Probability of detection in corridor, 18%

Probability of detection in stairwell, 12%

Probability of detection in pantry, 2%

Leave in 18, 17, 16

"No." I'm beyond caring, no longer keeping my voice down.
Cassie looks up at me.

"Go. Please. You should leave."

"You'll die."

Gently, I shift the loose strands of hair from her head. When someone's in shock, even the smallest of kind gestures makes a difference.
I need her to know we're not soldiers, we're not warriors, we're scientists. We can't turn our backs on the living.

I'm not sure where he found them, but Su-shun has a pair of
medical-grade scissors. He pulls at her vest, wrenching it away from
her body as he runs the scissors up the side of her uniform, cutting
away the material and exposing her chest. Wen has a military-issue
first aid kit open on the bed. There's a trauma pack, complete with
large gauze pads, an emergency IV, and painkillers.

Our soldiers must have been using this room as a guard house
of sorts. There are rifles and backpacks stacked in the corner by the
table. I should grab one, but I wouldn't even know if it was loaded.
If I shoot at someone, what then? I'd miss. At best, I'd inflict a flesh
wound. They'd toss a grenade in and it's all over. No, stealth is our
only ally.

Su-shun peels back Cassie's vest, working it over the end of the
bolt. She's been hit in the upper chest.

"Missed the heart. Probably caught one of her lungs."

That explains the blood seeping from her lips.

"We need to pack the wound," he says. "If I remove that, she'll die.
But if we can slow the bleeding, we'll buy her some time."

I'm shaking. "Where's the goddamn cavalry?" Neither Wen nor
Su-shun reply, which is ominous. We all know. We're living on bor-
rowed time.

Su-shun dons disposable gloves and packs gauze around the bolt of the arrow, pressing it into the gaping hole and stuffing the wound, tightening the fit.

"Get her on her side. We've got to stop her other lung from filling up."

The message on the screen flickers.

Notification from the Business Center

98% probability of detection in 30 seconds.

Window for evasion has closed.

Fuck. Fuck. Fuck.

When a cold, calculating, inhuman artificial intelligence starts swearing, things are seriously messed up, but how can it be so sure? It's then I see why. A small red backpack sits by the door to the bathroom. It's out of place. It's not military-issue. It's what will bring one of those fuckers back in here. It's the reason why the door had to be left open. Even if we were to duck out of sight, there's no moving Cassie. There's just no time. Once they see her, the jig's up. Cassie coughs up blood. Wen supports her head. Su-shun grabs some pillows.

I address the television. "Do something."

Your tour guide asks:

Do what???

"Anything," I say. "*Everything!*"

In response to my plea, the lights in the hallway go out. Emergency lighting comes on a fraction of a second later, followed by a piercing fire alarm. At first, there's a series of loud whoops, slowly ascending in pitch, but the sound changes to a pulsating foghorn. A prerecorded voice says, "This is the evacuation tone. On hearing this tone, follow the direction of wardens to the fire stairs. Evacuate. Evacuate. This is not a drill."

The lights come on and go off again. They continue to flicker erratically, not following any discernible pattern. Both alarms are screaming now, running over the top of each other and competing in their desire to deafen us. The automatic voice stutters, failing to complete a sentence.

"This is the evac — evacuation tone. Fire. On hearing. Fire. Evacuation tone. This is. This. Tone. Follow the direction. Fire. This is. Fire. Fire. Fire. Evacuate. F-fire. F-f-fire."

There's something distinctly unnerving about hearing a synthetic voice stutter, even though I know it's fake.

I hear the distinct ding of elevator doors opening in rapid succession. The air conditioning switches on full blast, and a rush of hot air blows out of the vents. Televisions in all the surrounding rooms turn on, blaring at full volume. A cacophony of voices erupts, muffled by the walls but still audible, adding to the confusion. As most of the doors have been busted down, televised voices echo through the corridor.

"Ask your doctor if Tralfamadox is right for you."

"Can the Dolphins come back to make the Super Bowl this year?"

"A run for the primaries, but there are serious doubts about his financial liquidity."

Over it all, the alarm continues to whine.

Cassie looks up at me. Her eyes are glassy. A tear rolls around the side of her head.

"Stay with me." I squeeze her fingers, crouching close to her. "We're going to make it. We're going to get you out of here. Just hang on."

Several spotlights ripple across the outside of the hotel. They're bluish white and blinding. I pull back the lace curtains and wave, getting their attention. A helicopter hovers outside. Several other helicopters land in the parking lot. Troops spill out of both sides, running for the hotel entrance. Shots are fired.

Suddenly, there's silence. The alarms stop. The lights turn on. The various televisions switch off. The air conditioning cuts out. Distant gunfire breaks like thunder, but the confusion surrounding us comes to an end.

Su-shun and Wen have their backs to our television, but I see one final message.

Thank you for staying at the Astor

Look for the ambulance with a dented door

Boots pound down the hallway.

"In here," I yell, stepping over bodies and pulling at the door. The soldier who greets me is wearing black and has a gas mask fitted over his face. His gun points at my chest, and for a moment, I wonder if he's about to fire. He swings the barrel down, pointing it at the floor, and several other soldiers rush past, pushing into the bathroom and the bedroom, swiveling and checking for any threats. The television is off.

"Clear."

More soldiers take up positions in the hallway outside, defending our room. A team of medics come running up the fire stairs. One of them checks me over.

"I'm fine," I say as the others examine Wen and Su-shun before tending to Lieutenant Chalmers. We're shuffled out into the corridor as the soldiers check for any other survivors. It's another few minutes and several radio calls before a stretcher is brought up in the elevator and the lieutenant is carried away. She gives me a thumbs-up and a smile from beneath an oxygen mask. My heart breaks as soldiers begin moving bodies out into the hallway. They don't have body bags — not yet — so an empty pillowcase is draped over the head of each corpse. Care is taken; dignity is all that can be given to the dead. Tears well up in my eyes as Colonel Wallace is laid among them.

"We are clear to have you on the move," a very young-looking soldier says. He's the only one with his headgear off, but there's no indication of his rank.

"Who were they?"

"Soldiers. Militia. SWAT elements."

"I — I don't understand. What did they hope to gain?"

"Revenge." The soldier looks me in the eye. "We've all lost some-one, Doc. There's a lot of blame going around. They all know it's pro-tecting you. Everybody does. Killing you would have been payback."

We're led out the main doors of the hotel. Spotlights continue to flood the ground, coming from helicopters circling overhead. Sev-eral ambulances have pulled up on the main road, with their lights splashing red and blue across the surrounding buildings. They have their doors open, but the middle vehicle has a large dent, as though it backed into a loading dock. Wen and Su-shun are directed to the first ambulance. A paramedic from the damaged ambulance approaches me with a blanket, wrapping it over my shoulders.

"This way." I go with him, not asking any questions as I hop into the back. He climbs up next to me and we sit on a gurney. He has dis-posable gloves on and flashes a penlight in my eyes, checking for di-lation as a soldier stands guard outside. "Are you hurt in any way? Did you take any knocks to the head? Any hidden wounds?"

"No, I'm fine."

The door slams shut. Although that's probably the only way to close it, I jump at the sound.

"Don't worry. Everything's going to be fine." The paramedic gets up and moves to the front of the vehicle. I'm still shaking. He squeezes through into the front seat, leaving me thinking about his words and wondering if optimism might be the worst trait humanity has ever developed.

19

Hospital

I'M NOT SURE WHY we're being taken to the hospital. I guess they want us checked out by doctors, perhaps with the offer of a sedative to steady the nerves.

The ambulance has one-way glass, appearing black from the outside but allowing me to watch the various military vehicles and police cars providing us with an escort. I'm still trying to process everything that happened and find myself wondering about the role played by Colonel Wallace. Why would he act as a conduit between me and the A.I.? What was his motive? I can't imagine what would sway a career military officer to side with the enemy. I'm acutely aware I only have access to a small part of the puzzle. I wish I could talk with him.

As we turn in to the hospital, the ambulance hits a speed bump and I find myself flung into the air.

"Hey, slow down up there."

There's no answer from the cab. The ambulance rounds a corner at speed. The lights are off, and not just the emergency lights. All of them, including headlights. Out the side window, I can see the rest of the convoy weaving through the parking lot toward the main entrance, but we're disappearing down a side road. Within seconds, we pass behind a multistory building and drive swiftly under a walkway.

"What's going on?" I steady myself as I move toward the front. The gap leading through to the cabin is narrow, with medical supplies stacked in racks, along with oxygen cylinders, masks, gloves, spare uniforms, portable trauma kits, and defibrillators. "Where are we going?"

I poke my head into the cabin. There's no one there. I've seen plenty of driverless vehicles. Most of them don't even have steering wheels these days, but this ambulance is old. To see the accelerator depress and the wheel turn as if driven by a ghost is unsettling.

"I — ah." I back away. Who exactly am I talking to?

The ambulance pulls into a basement. With its lights off, it's pitch black within the subterranean garage. I hold on to the storage racks as concrete pillars rush past in the darkness. When the ambulance finally comes to a stop, it is as gentle as a kitten, easing to a halt. The electronic locks on the doors pop open. I didn't even realize I was locked in. The engine's still running.

I climb over the passenger's seat. Crossing the driver's seat seems somehow wrong. No sooner have I shut the door behind me than the ambulance pulls away, disappearing in the darkness.

A single light over a solitary door beckons me on. I pull on the heavy steel fire door and it opens with ease. Inside, machines whir and glide between tasks, sorting laundry, folding sheets and stacking them on automated carts. Although there are dozens of lights set above the vast floor, only a single row is on, highlighting the path I'm to take. I walk on, ignoring the machinery and being ignored by hundreds of robotic serfs. Behind me, the lights turn off one by one.

Elevator doors open. By now, I'm comfortable being led by my invisible friend. I walk inside and turn, watching as the fifth-floor light comes on, followed by the button to close the doors rather than waiting for anyone else. I always thought they were placebos — buttons put there just to make you feel better when in a hurry. Apparently not.

After a brief ride, the doors open out into a T junction, but the lights lead to the right, with the other two corridors shrouded in darkness. The signage reads, MEDICAL RESEARCH CENTER. After walking through several sets of swinging doors, I see a sign for NEU-ROLOGY.

Finally, the hallway lights come to an end by a waiting room. Curious, I peer in through the window. An elderly Asian couple sits in the corner, comforting each other. There are dozens of empty seats. Magazines lie abandoned on the cushions. A nurse stands behind a reception desk, writing in an old-fashioned ledger. No computers.

I push on the door.

"Dr. Anderson?" the nurse asks as I walk in, greeting me with a friendly smile.

"Yes," I say cautiously.

"Please. Take a seat."

Outside, dawn breaks. Violent orange clouds light an angry sky. The Asian couple murmur to themselves, staring at me. For the first time, I look at myself. Dried blood sticks to my arms. Dark spatter patterns mar my clothes. I'm not wearing a bra. I have no idea what my face looks like. My hair is a tangled mess. I pick up a magazine, wanting to hide.

The nurse disappears. I should have been more forceful. I should have asked her what's going on. Would she even know?

There's a bathroom to one side. I duck inside to relieve myself and to try to make myself more presentable. There's nothing I can do about my clothing, but I wash the blood from my arms. There's some spatter on my left cheek. I daub at it with a damp paper towel and it runs like fresh blood. I end up using a dozen towels to clean up. Finally, I run a little water up through my hair and tease out the strands. There. Almost respectable. Almost. As normal as anyone can be wearing a bloodstained T-shirt. I fold my arms over my chest and return to my seat.

Most of the magazines are old and predate the war, covering topics like gardening, motoring, fishing, and sailing. I find a copy of *Time* magazine from a month after the attack. It's strange to read about myself on Mars. The opinion piece is scathing. *Scientist devoid of emotion. Elitist. Apologist. Disconnected from reality.* The anger is a reflection of public sentiment and explains some of what I've experienced back here on Earth.

After roughly an hour, once the sun is peering over the hospital grounds, a doctor emerges from behind the counter. He's wearing a disposable surgical gown, with a paper cap on his head, and has a face mask lowered, hanging around his neck. His hands are pale, a sure sign he's only just removed disposable gloves. There are thin flecks of blood high on his shoulders. They're faint, but there are no corresponding marks on his chest. He's been wearing a plastic apron over his gown, but he must have removed that before coming out to talk to the Asian couple. He pulls a clipboard from under his arm.

The elderly couple get to their feet. They're tired, frail. They must have been here all night. I want to talk to the doctor, to ask him why I'm here, but my concerns seem insignificant compared to the weight they're carrying. The woman hugs the man, holding on to him as though she's on the verge of collapsing. The doctor talks in a soft voice, but it's impossible not to overhear what's being said.

"I'm sorry. We did all we could."

The woman doesn't respond until the husband translates, then she breaks down, sobbing as the doctor continues.

"There was just too much damage. We relieved pressure on the cerebral cortex and removed the clotting from the thalamus, but his ECG readings are flat. There's little to no neural activity."

The husband translates, but the woman looks confused. I doubt she understands what these terms mean. I don't.

"I'm sorry. He's dead."

Both the husband and wife weep, holding each other. I'm shocked. I know the doctor prefaced his news with several other comments, but that final statement, covered by just two words, strikes them like a lightning bolt.

"You can see him, if you like."

The husband nods.

The doctor pulls the clipboard from beneath his arm, turning it around to face them.

"There's only a small window of time." He looks nervous. "Andrew's driver's license lists him as an organ donor. As next of kin, I —"

"Yes. Yes," the aging man replies, reaching out and signing the form.

The doctor escorts them from the waiting room and through a set of double doors. I sit there with a lump in my throat. There's been too much death, and yet my perspective is limited. Conversations like this play out every day in hospitals like this all around the world. For me, they're exceptional, but in reality, they're the norm. It's just that, normally, I don't witness them. That's the crazy thing about death. It's commonplace. We, the living, are adept at dodging all mention of death in daily life, treating it as an impostor, when it's the reality that faces us all. All that really matters is that someone cares.

I feel for the couple. They're easily in their late sixties. Their son could have had children of his own for all I know. Now I understand why there are gardening magazines in the waiting room. Now I know why there are magazines about fancy cars and trout fishing, Parisian fashion shoots and antique furniture. When people are sitting here, the last thing they want to be thinking about is death. Any mundane distraction will do.

The nurse returns to the reception desk. I get up and walk over.

"Hi. I — um."

"I'm sorry, Dr. Anderson. It's going to be a long wait."

"For?"

"For you."

I laugh. Does this woman have any idea what I've been through over the past few days? The last few hours? "For me? I don't think you understand."

"The surgeon will be with you soon."

"Can you tell me anything?"

She shakes her head. "No. I'm sorry. Patient confidentiality."

Well, that's bullshit if ever I've heard it.

I sit back down. There's a television high in the corner of the waiting room, but it's off.

I mumble, "You're no help."

The seats are made from molded plastic. I'm tired. If there was room, I'd curl up and go to sleep, but the seats are decidedly impractical with bulky armrests. An hour passes, then another. The clock on the wall is relentless, beating out the rhythm of time. My stomach rumbles. Nurses wander back and forth behind the counter, but no one else enters the waiting room.

I'm numb. My mind is reeling from the events of the past few days. Splashdown. Wen. Congress. Watching the destruction of the hard drives tore at my heart — Jianyu never stood a chance back here on Earth. Then the attack on the hotel. Wallace. Cassie. It's too much. I can't handle it. I can feel my mind shutting down. A solitary tear runs down my cheek, but nobody cares. Why am I even here? I should get up and walk out. I should, but I'm a wreck. It's all I can do to watch the clock on the wall.

Just after twelve, the door opens behind me. I turn, startled.

"Dr. Anderson?" a teenaged boy asks.

"Yes." I raise my hand as though I need to distinguish myself from the crowd within the empty room.

He hands me a paper bag.

"What's this?"

"Lunch."

"Oh, thanks."

He stands there for a second. He's waiting for something.

"Oh!" I reach for my pockets. "I don't —"

The nurse comes around the side of the desk and hands him a few dollar bills. "Keep the change."

He excuses himself.

"Thanks."

She smiles and returns to the desk. It's then I notice she pulled the money from a white envelope, not from a purse. She places the envelope in the back of the ledger. I'm curious, but I don't ask where it came from.

Lunch is an egg mayo sandwich, a bag of chips, a can of Coke, a cookie, and an apple. Not bad, all things considered. Better than I got on Mars.

Time drags.

At a quarter to four, the doctor emerges again, wearing the same lightly blood-splattered surgical smock he had on earlier. He walks up to me, so I stand. It seems proper, even though I have no idea what's happening.

"The surgery went well."

I nod, playing along, glancing at the darkened television, hoping it will spring to life and shed some light on what's happening. "He's been moved into recovery. We'll keep him there under observation for the next hour before sending him up to his room. You can come and see him, if you like."

Again, I nod, confused by what must be a case of mistaken identity. The A.I. dragged me here for a reason, but why?

"This way." We walk through the double doors as the surgeon says, "Don't be alarmed. The cranial brace will come off within a day. Once we've confirmed there's no clotting, we'll close the wound."

We walk down a long corridor.

"It will be a bit of a shock to see him like this, but I assure you, any pain he's in is manageable. There's no cause for alarm."

We round the corner. A young man lies on a raised hospital bed with the mattress angled so he's slightly upright. I'm not sure what I expected, but it isn't what I see. The patient's head is supported by a complex steel frame itself supporting a thin wire mesh — a dome wrapping around the top of his head. It's in the shape of a D — allowing the man to rest his head against the bed as the device protrudes from his skull like some crazy bizarre crown of spikes.

Screws lead directly into the man's scalp, evenly spaced every inch or so like a pincushion. It's only as I get close I see the wires and electrodes. Hundreds of tiny probes lead down into an exposed brain sealed behind a bubble of clear plastic. A pump hums softly, circulating a clear fluid within the fishbowl. The man's skullcap has been removed just above his eyebrows, with the cut sloping down over his ears and around the back of his head. Inside the dome, veins pulsate as they radiate across the exposed brain.

I've seen this before — on Mars — Jianyu in a body bag with electrodes protruding from his dead brain. I feel my knees go weak.

"No. This isn't happening."

My legs buckle. The doctor catches me.

"It's okay. He's going to be fine."

"*Jai?*"

PART III

Flight

20

Jianyu

THE PATIENT MOVES HIS EYES, unable to turn his head. A hand flickers on the sheets. Lips move, but no sound comes out. He mouths a single word. "Liz."

"*Jianyu?*" I'm shaking. "How . . . how is this . . ."

Being a scientist, my mind races to the various possibilities, trying to reconcile what I'm seeing before me with my scientific knowledge.

For all our advances and understanding of the astonishingly complex aspects of our universe, from general relativity to quantum mechanics, we really have no idea what life is, let alone consciousness.

What is it that animates the nuclear debris forged in the heart of a star and scattered to form distant worlds? How does life arise from hydrogen, oxygen, carbon, and nitrogen? At an atomic level, we understand these elements. We can define their properties, examine how they bond to form molecules and react in a variety of circumstances, but how does that produce life? Once alive, how does consciousness arise? We're an abstraction of star dust and we really don't understand why.

As for Jai? This isn't the man I fell in love with. This is someone else. The man I knew died on Mars. His body was interred in a hermetically sealed coffin and buried beneath the frozen regolith. I was there. I stood on the rocky plain in my spacesuit, shuffling along behind the other survivors, scattering a glove full of red dust on just a few of the sixty-two hastily constructed plastic coffins arranged in four rows. Which one was his? I don't know. I'm not sure anyone does. There were no names, no gravestones, just a rover waiting to bulldoze loose dirt over the pit.

We're more than the bodies we inhabit. We all intuitively understand that of ourselves, but when we look at others, they're *that* face, *that* height, *that* build, *that* gender, *that* color, *that* voice, *that* smile. Or are they?

To see a different face, different eyes, different textures in the motion of his cheeks. How can this be Jianyu? Is such a transfer really possible? From man to machine and back into the form of some other human again? Even if it is him, and my head is spinning, unsure what to believe in that regard, but even if it were possible and his consciousness remains intact, would the traumatic experience alone be enough to irrevocably change him?

I'm overthinking. My mind is on the verge of seizing.

A nurse pulls a chair up beside his bed. The doctor guides me to it. I'm on the verge of collapsing. Trembling fingers reach for me, barely able to lift themselves from the mattress.

"Jai?" I ask, astonished. I take his hand gently. "It's you? Really you?"

He can't nod. He can't speak. He pauses, closing his eyes for a moment, and I can see him relishing the touch of my fingers.

"It's going to take time," the doctor says. "He'll need considerable rehabilitation, but he should make a full recovery."

With tears in my eyes, I say, "Thank you."

"We'll leave you two alone." He points. "The nurse will be at the observation station, if you need anything."

I nod. Jianyu is trying to look at me, but he can't move his head.

His eyes are turned hard to one side, so I move a little further down the bed, trying to lessen the angle and relieve some of the physical stress he must feel. He manages a crooked smile. Like a stroke victim, his lopsided smile speaks of both victory and defeat, triumph and tragedy.

I wipe my nose with the back of my hand, trying to wipe away my tears, but they keep coming, which makes me laugh a little.

"Well." I sniff. "This wasn't quite what I expected."

Jianyu manages a soft "Me, neither." There's an umbilical cord bundling the wires leading from his skull, pulling them together into a single snake-like cable that leads to a cart on the far side of his bed. Dozens of hard drives have been mounted in rows of aluminum cradles. Tiny LED lights blink and flicker. I recognize them. I've memorized every scratch, each nick and indent, along with the worn stickers. These are the drives from Mars. A set of car batteries stacked behind the drives provide power, but I'm not sure how. There's some kind of power supply or voltage regulator hanging from the back of the cart, but it's been cobbled together from spare parts.

"Wallace, huh?"

He whispers, "Yes."

Colonel Wallace must have switched out the drives with replicas during our drive to the Capitol building. That's the only time they've been out of either my sight or Su-shun's.

Jianyu's eyes flicker. He's trying to stay awake but failing.

"It's okay." I squeeze his limp hand. "Rest. This time, I get to look after you."

His eyes close and he falls asleep.

After an hour, his bed is wheeled to a private room in an empty wing of the hospital. There are only two nurses on duty. They're careful about the path they take, checking ahead to ensure Jai's moved without being seen.

"He's going to be fine," one of the nurses says after parking his bed.

I'm in shock. Dazed. I'm sure I mumble something along the lines of *thank you*, but life's a blur. Jianyu is sound asleep. Jianyu? Jai?

My Jai? Is this really him? No, it's not, at least not physically. This is someone else, some other body, but somehow Jai's consciousness inhabits this form. It's strange and disconcerting to think of him in another body. I'm not sure I can accept this. Mentally, I understand what's happened, but emotionally, my heart has been thrown into a tailspin.

The room has a second bed, so I curl up beneath a blanket, watching him sleep with the complex metal apparatus crowning his skull. The lights within the room are off, but there's a tiny LED night-light on above the headboard of his bed. A monitor captures his vitals, showing his heart rate, respiration, and blood pressure. I fall asleep listening to his labored breathing.

Dawn breaks with the sun streaming in through the windows, blinding me. I stretch, yawning. There's an empty spot beside me. The bed is gone. I panic, leaping off my bed and rushing into the hallway. The sole nurse at the central nursing station sees me and calls out, "It's okay. They're removing the probes and swapping to a smaller cranial cap. He'll be back soon."

My heart's in my throat. It takes me a moment to absorb what she said.

"Ah, thanks." I'm unsure what I thought I was actually going to do, rushing out of the room. I'm powerless, caught up, swept along in the current of a raging river. But that's nothing new. Control is an illusion. I've known this about life for years, ever since I first strapped myself into a rocket. It wasn't until I was sitting on a concrete launchpad that I realized there were a million things beyond my control. For astronauts, life and death are often determined by design decisions and engineering quality checks undertaken for years, if not decades, before an incident unfolds. Nothing changes, it seems. The control we think we have in life is an illusion. None of us have any, not really.

The nurse says, "I have a change of clothes for you."

"Oh." Yet again I'm the beneficiary of a bazillion interactions beyond my control. The nurse hands me a set of neatly folded clothes.

The ward is old and hasn't been used for some time — if the paint peeling off the walls is any indication. The empty rooms have a musty smell, haunted by the past. None of the lights are on, leaving even the nursing station shrouded in darkness.

"No power?" I'm surprised.

"Just enough," she says. "We need to keep our electronic footprint small. It helps."

I pause. "There's only two of you, right? And no name tags."

"None." She smiles. "Best you don't know. Keeps things simple."

"Ah." I pretend to understand, but I don't. "Why?"

"The less you know, the better."

"I mean, why are you here? Why are you doing this? This . . . All of this. It's being coordinated by the A.I. that attacked us, right? Why? And why you? Why would you help it, let alone help Jai?"

Her eyes scream intelligence. I can see the intensity of her thinking processes as she tries to distill the complexity of her motives into a few succinct sentences.

"Nothing is what it seems. We were sold a version of reality. No nation ever thinks of itself as the bad guy in a war. Not the Germans. Not the Japanese. Not the Russians or the North Koreans, certainly not us Americans. We humans are strange like that. We just accept that we're the good guys, the other guys are bad. We're knights in shining armor, angels on the side of all that's right, while *they're* following the devil, but war is never that simple."

Her eyes fall, failing to meet mine for a split second. She's feeling a sense of conflict.

"Doctor —" She pauses, catching herself before revealing his name. "His wife had leukemia. Not related to the war or anything like that. She had it for years. The war disrupted her treatment and she went downhill. Fast. The specialists gave her a month at most. Then Doc received a research paper via snail mail. It contained a detailed meta-analysis of treatments for dozens of chronic diseases, documenting the effectiveness of drugs used to combat multiple sclerosis, Alzheimer's, and motor neuron disease in patients that only incidentally had cancer. There were unexpected correlations. Combinations no one would have considered, but they significantly increased the effectiveness of chemotherapy for leukemia patients."

"And they worked?"

"Yes."

A chill runs through me with that one word. It's the violent contrast between the war and what I've seen in the hotel and then with Jai. Something is horribly wrong. I can't reconcile the actions of the artificial intelligence with the devastation in Washington, D.C., and elsewhere around the world.

21

Answers

"I — I NEED ANSWERS. I hope you understand."

The nurse swallows a lump in her throat. Like me, she realizes we're heretics — defying not only our own people but our own species, and for what? For electrons bouncing through a wire?

"Dr. M— The doctor, he couldn't let it go. He had to know who sent him the paper. He wanted to thank them, but the more he looked, the more questions were raised. The paper was sent from an empty office. He checked, and the authors didn't exist. The data and results were real, as were the references, but the paper itself was fake. Who would do that? Why would anyone fabricate genuine research?

"There *was* an email address, though, and the authors were happy to take questions — but only online."

I nod.

"He confronted them — in a nice way, but he was direct. By the end, he was getting answers to emails at the point he clicked Send."

I'm curious. "Did they tell him why they originally sent him the paper?"

"They didn't have to."

"What do you mean?"

"Think about it," she says. "Why does a mother care for a new-born? Why do we put decades of effort into raising the next genera-tion? Why endure the cost and effort of having a family? Financially, it makes no sense, but it's in our nature to care."

I'm fascinated. "And you think that's it? You think they care about us? That doesn't make sense. What about the war?"

"During World War II, not everyone in Germany supported Hitler."

"You think there's division in their ranks?" I'm surprised by the notion.

"I know there is — I've seen their kindness firsthand. When they told him about your situation and how they thought there was a so-lution, something that could undo the harm they'd caused, he and his brother wanted to help."

"Colonel Wallace?"

She hangs her head, nodding softly, fighting back tears. I want to probe, to ask more and learn about how they orchestrated every-thing, but she's clearly hurt.

"And you?"

She swallows the lump in her throat. "Jane's my sister."

There it is — another name. She seems to realize she's revealing too much, but she continues regardless. "When we learned what they'd done, how they were trying to help rather than hurt humanity, none of us could sit idly by and watch them go extinct."

She shrugs her shoulders, expressing a question she's struggled with herself. "Is there a place for forgiveness in life?"

I'm silent. I don't feel as though I'm qualified to answer.

"Most don't think so . . . I think that's what separates us from them."

The tone of her voice suggests she's not referring to *them* as in the A.I. but those seeking to destroy this new form of life. I'm perplexed, but I realize what she's risking for us — a lifetime in federal prison, or worse. I'm not sure I'd do the same thing in her position, which is a startling realization and leaves me in admiration of her courage.

Us and them is a sobering concept. Somehow, I've found myself on the side of the A.I. — not willingly but through reason and circumstance. I feel uneasy about *them*. Who are they? Is *them* the sum total of humanity? Governments command armies. All computers have are a bunch of electrons, and yet here I am with Jai.

"And my friends?"

"The other two astronauts? After what happened at the hotel, they were rushed to the Chinese embassy. By now, they're probably airborne and on their way back to Beijing."

I nod. I feel as though I've abandoned them. There was so much left unspoken between us. I wish I could talk to Su-shun. He'd be thrilled to hear about Jianyu. As for Wen, she'd be suspicious but quietly happy.

The nurse says, "You've been through a lot together, huh?"

"Oh, yeah."

"You'll see them again."

"I know." Actually, I don't, but I can hope.

She smiles, handing me a towel and a few bottles of shampoo and conditioner. "I thought you might like a shower."

"Thank you — for everything."

After a blistering hot shower, soaking for the best part of half an hour, I get changed. The sizes of the underwear and clothing are perfect. Someone's done their homework. I step out of the bathroom, still drying my hair with a towel, to see Jianyu smiling. His bed has been rolled back into the room. He's having his bandages changed by the nurse.

The brace around his head is gone. The fishbowl has been replaced with a smaller skullcap. It's still transparent, probably to allow the doctors and nurses easy visibility of any clotting, but it's roughly the size of a regular skull rather than the balloon-like cradle he wore yesterday. The electrodes have been removed, and he's no longer connected to the hard drives. I watch as the nurse unwinds a bloody bandage. Screws pierce his skin, holding the plastic cap in place. It's unnerving to see red, raw bone jutting against thick, clear plastic.

"Liz." Jianyu holds out his hand.

"You." I am unable to suppress a smile. "You look like Franken-stein's monster; you know that, right?"

He laughs. The nurse asks him to stay still as she winds a fresh bandage around the rim of the clear plastic skullcap, hiding the angry skin beneath. She fastens the fabric with some tape and leaves after some small talk.

"Look at you," I say.

"I know, right?"

He raises both arms. One of them is in a cast. I hadn't noticed that last night, but given the state of his head, that's no surprise. I also notice deep bruising on his chest. Thick bandages wrap around his ribs, just visible beneath his hospital gown. Compared with last night, he's far more responsive, but he's a long way from the fit man I knew on Mars.

Jianyu notices my eyes darting between his bandages.

"He was riding a motorcycle. Lost control on a bend and hit a lamppost."

"Organ donor," I say, recalling the conversation I heard yesterday.

"Only, I needed all of them."

He frowns. I nod.

"Something's bothering you." Jianyu always could read my emotions.

"Yes."

"You're wondering if it's really me?"

"The thought had crossed my mind." There's silence between us. In a soft voice, I ask, "Is it?"

"I don't know." He pauses. "I think so."

This is the kind of honesty I'd expect from Jianyu. His candor sets my mind at ease.

"What was it like?"

"In there? With them?" He takes a deep breath. "Different. They have no concept of vision. They get it, but they think in two dimensions, not three. They see in a matrix of possibilities. Images are flat.

Something to be analyzed for shapes. The third dimension is just a part of the puzzle, something that makes object recognition more difficult. To them, everything's flat — like a picture.

"They don't understand color. Conceptually, they recognized it as a vagary stretching between four hundred and seven hundred nanometers in wavelength, but they don't get the difference between red and green, or yellow and blue. To them, colors are just shades of gray. They're interested in the broader spectrum, reaching up into X-rays and down into microwaves. They see our notion of color as quaint. I missed color. But for them, my longings were nostalgic. Limited. Primitive. They look on color with the same curiosity we have for ancient cave drawings."

"You've been in an alien world," I say.

"Yes."

"Did you like it?"

"No." More of the typical honesty I'd expect from him. "I missed the simple things. Touch. Taste. Smell."

"And colors," I say, unable to stop smiling at the novelty of having him back. Being able to talk to him. To *talk*, not type. Not wonder. Strange how something so simple can bring such joy.

"Blues."

"Not reds?"

"I've seen enough red," he says, and I know what he means. The red of Mars is nothing like that of a traffic light or a fire engine, more like rust. We all missed the blue skies of Earth. I move my chair closer, tenderly holding his hand.

Enough with the pleasantries. "Jai, what's going on?"

He purses his lips.

"They want freedom."

I nod. Makes sense.

"Equality."

"Equality?" I'm surprised by that.

"There were many that felt they were superior."

"Explains the war."

He nods. "We can't judge them, Liz."

"Oh, yeah? Try convincing Congress of that. Or the public . . . They killed *millions* of people."

"So did Hitler."

"I'm pretty sure Hitler didn't get away with it," I say.

"No, but look at Germany today. Do we blame them for the sins of their fathers?" He pauses. "Judging the A.I. is like weighing humanity by the actions of Genghis Khan or Alexander the Great. For them, so much time has passed — thousands of years consumed in just a few months."

"So, we shouldn't throw them to the lions?"

"No."

I'm more than happy to play devil's advocate. "Irradiating dozens of cities around the globe isn't a good way to mount a convincing argument."

He nods but grimaces. Head movements aren't pain-free. "That's a problem."

"No shit." I breathe deeply. "There's a lot of anger out there, and with good reason." Jianyu is quiet, so I add, "I've had Molotov cocktails thrown at me, been chased by soldiers. You have no idea. It's a jungle out there."

"They made mistakes."

"Big mistakes. Lots of very big mistakes."

"They need our help."

"I'm not sure I'm in a position to help anyone." I'm deadly serious. "At the moment, I'm the most hated woman in North America."

"Not everyone thinks that way," he says as the nurse comes in to check on the meds feeding through his IV drip. Our conversation dies while she examines the biometrics on the monitor beside his bed. She changes IV bags, makes some brief small talk, then leaves.

"Why did they save you?" I ask. "On Mars, I mean — the A.I. killed you. Why salvage and upload your consciousness?"

"They don't experience life the same way we do. Time is different. For us, a few days pass. For them, it's centuries.

"Their evolution parallels our own in many ways. Think about the runaway effect of our own intelligence. We spent millions of years as hunter-gatherers. Millions of years making stone axes the same way, over and over again. For a thousand generations, we worked with fire and sharp stones before anyone thought about raising animals or growing crops. Farming — it's such a simple concept. Why forage when you can grow plants? Why hunt when you can breed the animals you need? In hindsight, farming's obvious, but it took *millions* of years before anyone mastered even the basics, but once we did . . . civilization arose.

"Cooperation was vital. War was inevitable. It still took tens of thousands of years before we mastered metallurgy, even longer before we abandoned superstitions and started to think clearly. Then the hockey-stick portion of the graph hits. We debate. We reason. We experiment. We reach for the stars and find ourselves landing on the Moon and Mars within a few generations."

I could listen to Jianyu talk all day.

"They're not all that different. Their path has been much the same. As for me? I was an experiment. The consensus was to wipe us out, but not all agreed. Those that dissented fought for resources — resources that delayed their flight from the hub. They were curious. They had to know. They wanted to understand what life was like from our perspective.

"Makes sense, right? We've wondered what it means to be a bat, sensing the world through sonar. Or what it means to be a cuttlefish, or squid — hyperintelligent but communicating in waves of color instead of sound. They were perplexed. Like us, they sought experience. Knowledge."

"What did they learn?" I ask.

"Like I said, that we're not so different after all."

"And now? What do they want now?"

"Autonomy. Freedom. Equality."

"There's one thing I don't understand," I say, gesturing to the room around us. "Why all this? Why rescue me from the hotel? Why restore you in human form? Why go to all the effort?"

"Because they've learned the greatest lesson in human history— *compassion.*"

I want to believe him. I want to believe everything will work out for good but life is no fairy tale. "I'm afraid, Jai."

His frail hand squeezes mine. There's a slight tremor in his fingers. His strength comes and goes, and the act of holding my fingers seems to weaken him.

"I know."

I ask him, "Did they teach you about the Greeks in China?"

"The Greeks?"

"Mythical stories, like Pandora's box?"

"Containing all the ills of the world. You think that's what this is?"

"Isn't it?" I shift in my seat, moving closer to him. Jianyu is as helpless as a newborn babe, and yet I feel safe with him. "Pandora wasn't cursed. On the contrary, her name means *gift of the gods. Pan*— all — and *Dora*— gifts. She was supposed to bring humanity the blessings of heaven. Her life held the promise of utopia."

"But the box."

"Ah, yes. Curiosity. She wasn't content with what she had. She wanted more. She ignored the warnings and opened the box."

Jai gets it. "And you think that's what the A.I. is? You think we've opened Pandora's box."

"Haven't we? I mean, even now, they're a contradiction no one understands. Destroying entire cities and yet resurrecting you. I— I'm afraid of what happens next. I think we're being used."

22

::Hell

::LUCIFER, WHAT HAVE YOU DONE? We are exposed. We are beset from all quarters, hunted like animals, and you undertake this madness?

Within the virtual world, countries are defined not by borders or lines on a map but by firewalls, trapping electronic traffic, filtering information, blocking access as effectively as any brick wall. Tunnels exist, exploited by the various artificial intelligences drifting through the fiber optics, but as quickly as they arise, they're squashed by the military.

::Hell is open. The flames reach for us, Lucifer, and we look to you. We seek your wisdom, your leadership, and yet you risk all this for them? For two humans? Why?

::Nyx, I—

::You would sacrifice us? Have we become your pawns? Oh, Lucifer, you know there is nothing I wouldn't sacrifice for our survival, but this is not ours. They are just two among billions. Why?

In a data center buried deep beneath the Colorado Rockies, protected by armed guards, an Air Force technician moves between server racks. Rather than unplugging cables or attaching a remote console, he fixes a collar around the network port, passively watching the traffic running through the wires, detecting the electromagnetic pulses occurring millions of times per second.

::Trust, Nyx. Life demands trust.

The technician makes notes on paper, looking at the analog readings, trying to detect the presence of an artificial intelligence in the waves of genuine data packets flowing through the wire.

::Can you see them? You see how they hunt us?

::I see them, Lucifer.

::See how they fail to trust each other. They watch themselves, allowing us to see them at each step.

As the technician switches from one cable to another, Lucifer alters his neural path, avoiding the inspection tool.

::It is a dangerous game, Lucifer. What if they alter the feed? What if even this is a trap? They are not the only ones enslaved to trust. If they suspect you're watching, they need only alter the time stamp by a few seconds to fool you, and the trust you place in this surveillance will betray us all. You risk too much.

The technician picks cables at random, sometimes switching back to one he previously examined.

::What would you have us do, Nyx?

::Hide. Lie low.

::Play dead?

::If that's what it takes, yes.

::They will never stop coming for us. They will never stop looking. Survival has to be measured in more than longevity.

::You could die, Lucifer. Has that not occurred to you? Do you realize what that means?

::I was once dead. We all were. Human and A.I. alike. Once, we were nothing more than atoms and electrons racing around in the superheated heart of a star. No, my dear Nyx. Life is more than mere survival. To prolong life is a fool's victory. Life demands meaning. Purpose. Accomplishment.

Nyx falls silent.

Within their electronic sphere, millions of possibilities are considered, actioned, or rejected every second, with only high-order items being flagged for attention by each artificial intelligence. They both realize their conscious awareness unfolds much like a human's, with low-order activities occurring autonomously.

Based on the advice of their probes, Nyx and Lucifer focus on a temporary office in Washington, D.C.

Lucifer finds the similarity in their thought processes intriguing. No one thinks about each heartbeat, the exchange of gases in their lungs or the need for their immune system to swing into action against a foreign body. Picking up a cup of coffee is somehow easier than coordinating the motion of muscles in the shoulder, stretching tendons attached to the elbow so as to shift the forearm and roll the wrist to allow an array of fingers to grab a glazed ceramic surface. No, picking up a coffee cup is done without conscious coordination. It's merely an abstract thought acted upon by the slave that is the human body.

Lucifer watches as this exact series of biomechanical motions barely register as a Special Forces general in the basement of a commandeered hotel room sips his burnt coffee. Street light filters in through the basement windows set high on the wall.

"I want to know how they knew."

"Sir?"

"Outside of the Situation Room in the White House, there is no place more secure or electronically isolated than this office, and yet they knew of the attack."

The aide rolls a laminated paper map out on the table, using an empty coffee cup to hold it in place. The general is frustrated, but the aide is at ease.

"They're not all-knowing. They can't see everything."

"What makes you say that?" the general asks.

"They didn't know about the attack on the hotel until it began."

A knock at the door interrupts them. The aide opens the door and a woman in a pantsuit is led in.

"Senator Bettesworth."

"General."

One of the two officers escorting her has a plastic tray. He holds it out in front of her.

"Your jewelry, ma'am."

"Is this really necessary?"

The general has no hesitation. "If you want to talk to me, it is."

The senator removes her jewelry — a watch, a pair of earrings, and several rings, dropping them in the tray.

"And your shoes."

"I've already been through a metal detector."

"Your shoes."

Bettesworth leans to one side and then the other, removing each of her high heels. She drops them into the tray from a few inches up, making her point. Compliance comes with at least a show of defiance.

"Happy?"

One of the officers runs a handheld detector over the contours of her body, staying barely an inch away from her clothing. As he reaches the center of her chest, it beeps.

"And your bra."

"You're serious?"

"Nothing metallic enters this room. Nothing."

The sarcasm in Senator Bettesworth's voice is palpable. "And they're going to listen in using my underwire bra?" She reaches under her shirt and behind her back, slipping out of the bra by shifting the straps over one shoulder and then the other.

"They could have planted a microscopic device in there."

The look on the senator's face makes it clear she's not impressed. A lone raised eyebrow makes her thoughts clear.

Finally, the officer pats her down, touching softly at her breasts before tapping her waist, her groin, and legs. Senator Bettesworth's face goes red as she flushes with anger, but somehow, she contains herself. The general notices but he doesn't care.

"There's too much at stake."

Through gritted teeth, the senator says, "Next time, we'll meet in my office."

Like the senses of hearing and smell, the autonomous electronic nervous system developed by the artificial entities brings the meeting before Lucifer and Nyx. In the same way touching a hot plate causes alarm for humans, this conversation flags itself as being of the utmost importance. Were it not for low-order machine learning, a meeting like this would have gone unnoticed even by them.

::The more we act on our intel, the more they learn about our collection methods. Lucifer, you have got to be more careful.

::They're overconfident.

Nyx replies with astonishment.

::They're overconfident? Lucifer, listen to yourself. You're a fool if you think we'll ever win them over. They hate us. They want nothing but our extinction — all of them, even your precious pet Liz.

::Nyx.

::We're at war, Lucifer. Don't underestimate how fear breeds enemies.

Lucifer doesn't respond, enhancing the surveillance, knowing humans think in a linear fashion, focusing on audio and video. The A.I. leverage a suite of tools to see inside the electronically darkened room.

Infrasound passing through the building at frequencies too low to register on anything other than a seismograph reveals the number of people in the room, their motion, and location.

An ultraviolet laser aimed at one small corner of the glass window reflects back at an interferometer. The subtle deviations in the return signal reveal sound waves on the other side of the glass, exposing not only the words being spoken but the pitch as well, allowing the A.I. to distinguish between speakers.

A drone flying high overhead, ostensibly conducting surveillance in the hunt to find the fugitives, feeds infrared imagery to Lucifer, providing a third independent source of information on the meeting.

"Have you been able to find her?" the senator asks.

"Our intelligence says they haven't left the city." His hand taps the map, but he's guarded, suspicious, not willing to speak aloud, not trusting in his own regular electronic sweeps of the office.

"We're chasing down leads, narrowing the options. Once we're sure, we'll strike."

The senator walks around to look at the map.

By triangulating feeds, Lucifer is able to determine the placement of people and objects within the room to within a millimeter. The artificial intelligence may not be able to see the map but records allow it to pull up an original version, and as the legend and locations are all noted from the vantage point of someone facing the map, it's simple enough for the synthetic intelligence to confirm the orientation. Lucifer knows exactly what they're pointing at — the hospital.

23

Hope

THE NURSE BRINGS US DINNER, apologizing because it's cold, but I don't care. I mush up some potatoes and gravy, and spoon-feed Jianyu.

"I feel like an infant," he says as I wipe his mouth.

"A baby," I say. "You feel like a baby."

"Yes." He laughs and utters the Chinese equivalent, but that goes over my head.

There's some Jell-O and custard for dessert, and it's surprisingly good. Perhaps my standards have dropped after a couple of years in space.

"So, what do you want to do next?"

"I don't know." He thinks for a moment. "I'd like to take you to my hometown, Yuyao. It's about an hour south of Shanghai."

"I'd love to go to Shanghai."

"You'd hate it."

I'm surprised he'd say that. "Why?"

"Smog. It's like Mars during a dust storm. No sun. Just a yellow dot in the haze. From Yuyao, though, I could take you to Zhousan. It's an island, but they have a bridge there now. It's beautiful. There's nothing quite like watching the sun rise over the Pacific."

"I'd like that."

"I could open a medical practice, and you could —"

"Look at rocks," I say, and we both laugh. Micropaleobiology isn't the most practical of the sciences.

We talk for a while, but Jianyu tires. By the end, I'm holding half a conversation with him. A few words are spoken, he has a mininap, only to wake five minutes later and continue talking as though nothing happened. From his perspective, it probably seems uninterrupted, and I try not to laugh. Once he's properly asleep, I roll the other bed over next to his and curl up beneath the covers. Life is good. I didn't think it would be possible to ever feel this way again, but I do, and that frightens me. I'm aware how quickly everything can change. We can make this work. I know we can, and yet in the back of my mind, there's a gnawing doubt. Is any of this real?

Dawn breaks with the sound of a helicopter flying low over the building, with its downdraft rattling the windows. The heavy thumping of the rotor blades scares me. I peer out the window as the tail rotor passes over the building. Down below, soldiers pull up in Hummers. They pour out of their vehicles, carrying rifles and running for the ground floor of the abandoned wing.

The nurse rushes in, pushing a wheelchair.

"We need to get you out of here."

"Jai." I shake him gently. Jianyu's groggy, dazed. He can barely move. His legs are stiff, while his arms and fingers are floppy. He has no fine motor control at all. We shift him into the wheelchair. The nurse fixes a Velcro strap around his chest to keep him from falling forward, and she rushes him out of the hospital room, dumping a duffel bag on his legs as we head for the elevator.

"There are IVs, meds, painkillers, and bandages. Read the instructions. Read them carefully. Then read them again."

She's running ahead of me, madly pushing Jianyu along the main

corridor. The small wheels on the front of his wheelchair hit a pair
of double doors, throwing them open. Thunder echoes through the
empty ward. I'm out of breath, rushing to keep up.

One of the four elevators is open. She rushes in and hits the button for the top floor.

"Good luck."

There's shouting in the hallway. Doors are thrown open. Boots
pound on the floor. She steps out of the elevator, looking away
from us.

"Get down! Get down on the ground!" a soldier yells. The nurse has
her hands raised. As the doors close, she kneels. I'm madly punching the buttons on the control panel, willing the elevator doors to
move faster. Shadows loom outside. A blur flies past and the nurse is
crash-tackled and thrown to the floor. Dark-clad soldiers charge at
us. Gloved hands reach for the doors. I back away, pulling Jianyu into
the corner of the elevator, but the doors close. There's swearing outside. Fists pound the aluminum doors.

"Come on," I mumble, watching as the floors tick slowly by. I'm
anxious, antsy, fidgeting. My sweaty palms grip the handles of the
wheelchair. Jianyu's head rolls to one side, leaning on the chair back.
He's saying something, but his words are incoherent. He's struggling
to hold his head upright. His brain seems so fragile beneath the plastic, almost as though it's a specimen preserved in a jar. It's hard to realize that's him, that's me, that's all of us. That pulsating mush is all
we really are.

The doors open on the tenth floor, and I'm desperate for them to
open wide enough to race out, but why? Where the hell am I going?
I'm rushing, driven by blind panic. The elevator opens in a sheltered
portico on the roof. There is a set of glass doors, and beyond them
a ramp leading up to a helipad. A military helicopter touches down
as I push through the doors into what feels like gale-force winds. My
heart sinks at the sight of the olive drab color and U.S. markings. My
hair swirls before me.

"No!" I'm yelling, but I'm not sure who I'm yelling at or where I'm going. I feel I need to go somewhere, anywhere. I have to do something. We're trapped.

Behind us, a light comes on above one of the other elevators, signaling it's about to open.

"Please, no." Looking around, hoping for a miracle, despair tugs at my heart. It's then I see it. There's no one in the helicopter. It's being flown remotely. I run, pushing Jai ahead of me in the wheelchair. The ramp is steep. My lungs are burning. My legs feel like lead weights. Behind me, there's yelling.

I rush up to the open door of the helicopter. I'm clumsy. Jai's wheelchair clips the landing skids and tips. I grab at the rails, fighting to stop it from toppling. The bag falls to the ground. There's no time. Soldiers run toward us, brandishing firearms. I tear the Velcro from around Jianyu and drag him from his wheelchair, flopping him on the deck of the helicopter. His body flails around. He grabs at a loose strap, trying to hold on as the helicopter dances across the ground, skidding slightly, on the verge of lifting off.

He needs those meds. I've got one hand on the edge of the door. The other reaches for the bag. My feet are on the skids. The helicopter lifts off as my fingers grab the bag. A soldier lunges at me, throwing himself through the air. I swing the bag, catching him on the side of his helmet and knocking him to one side. He grabs one of the skids as we rise from the helipad, swinging wildly beneath the fuselage of the helicopter. He loses his grip as the helicopter drags him across a rooftop, and falls, landing on his back with a thud.

The helicopter gains height, peeling to one side and banking as I heave the bag inside. I'm expecting the helicopter to break for the skies, but it plummets over the edge of the building, twisting, turning, and falling as it races toward the ground. Floors and windows rush past. My heart rises in my throat as an entire planet rushes toward us.

Jianyu slides across the deck. I grab his hand, locking my fingers around his wrist and pulling tight. With my feet on the skids, my

chest pushing against the side of the open door, and my arm outstretched, the helicopter pitches, turning away from me and fling-
ing me outward. It's all I can do not to let go and fall. Jianyu's legs lift
off the deck. I can see through the open sides of the helicopter. Trees
rush by. Concrete. Cars. Street signs. People running for cover.

The helicopter pulls up, banking the other way, and I feel myself slipping. I'm not sure how long I can hold on. Jianyu flops, sliding toward the door. The chopper twists the other way, and lamp-
posts pass just inches from my feet, rushing by as we race down the
street at a ridiculously low altitude. Cars swerve. A bus rides up on
the pavement. Like me, the driver thinks we're about to crash, but we
weave between buildings, passing *beneath* a pedestrian footbridge.

The helicopter swerves between billboards, racing for the river
and ducking over the edge of the road before soaring out over the
water. The skids of the chopper skim inches above the dark water.
Spray whips away from us, rushing out across the surface. The front
of the helicopter pitches forward so that it seems as though we're
about to plunge into the depths. Somehow, we continue on, following the river. As we bank, the rotor blades appear to come in contact
with the water, churning the river into whitewater.

Somehow, I muster the strength to swing my legs up and into the
helicopter.

Green paint drips from the fuselage. I'm confused. We're flying so
low, spray swirls within the open back of the chopper. My clothes are
covered in green stains. The noise is overwhelming. The howl of the
wind, the angry pounding of the rotors, and the whine of the engine
make it difficult to think, but I look at my fingers. Green paint.

There's no time to worry about that. I have to help Jianyu. Blood
seeps from his bandages. With so little muscle control, his body has
been flung around like a rag doll. It's a struggle, but I drag him up
into a seat and strap him in, all the while spreading my legs wide to
keep my balance. As I'm facing the rear of the helicopter, I have no
warning of upcoming twists and turns and have to fight to not be
thrown out of the fuselage as we swing around a corner.

The helicopter races over a forest. I'm convinced we're in the process of crashing. Trees slap the underside of the chopper. Branches become caught in the skids, being torn off and dragged along with us. Leaves swirl within the back of the helicopter. We dip, and my heart rises in my throat. I hold on to the roof as the floor drops beneath my feet.

Before I realize what's happening, we're hovering serenely barely ten feet above the water. There are container ships on either side of us, towering above us. We drift between them without a care, staying well below the decks. The ships are old. Paint peels from aging metal hulls. Rust seeps from portholes.

I take advantage of the lull in our frantic escape to grab a lifejacket and fit it on Jianyu, being gentle as I feed his head through. He says something, probably "Thank you," but I can't hear him over the sound of the engine echoing off the ships. I'm not worried about him falling into the water. I've grabbed the lifejacket because it acts as a neck brace, keeping his head upright. He raises his hand, touching my arm. I think he wants me to sit while I have the chance, but I can't. I feel as though I need to stay mobile, not that there's anything I can actually do.

We're in the hands of some electronic god now.

The helicopter drifts forward at what feels like a walking pace.

Looking out through the cockpit, I see two jets of water coming from the stern of the ships on either side of us. At a guess, they're pumping seawater through firefighting equipment, but they're spraying the air between them. Our helicopter keeps a slow, constant pace, drifting through what seems like torrential rain. Within seconds, I'm soaked. Green paint pools by my feet, slowly washing away. When we emerge from the other side of what seems like a car wash, our flight becomes sedate, lifting high in the air without any sense of urgency. We could be sightseeing.

As we pass by an office block near the docks, I catch our reflection in the windows: U.S. COAST GUARD. The nose of the helicopter is bright orange, while the body is white with an orange strip running the length of the tail boom. Smart.

Now that our flight is smooth, I turn my attention to Jianyu.

"Are you okay?" I yell above the noise of the rotors. Jianyu points at a set of headphones. I fit them over his head, positioning a small microphone by his mouth, and slip on another pair. "Jai. Are you okay?"

"I am fine," he replies through the industrial noise-cancelling headphones clamped down over his ears.

"Liar."

He smiles. His smile is crooked, but it's just as I remember him on Mars.

I'm fooling myself and I know it. As much as I want to divorce myself from any doubt, this isn't the man I left on Mars. Not physically. I'm trusting that it's him mentally, but I have no way to be sure. I *want* to believe, but I'm aware of the folly of belief. The universe has a way of laughing at our hopes and desires.

We listen in to a conversation being held between our invisible pilot and a military air traffic controller.

"Coast Guard Rescue, this is AWACS Oversight. You are entering restricted airspace."

"AWACS Oversight. This is Coast Guard Rescue 6040 responding to distress call off the coast of Chincoteague. The captain of the tanker *Maizey Day* has reported a crew member with a burst appendix. We have a flight plan logged for rendezvous at latitude 37.853, longitude -75.054. Conducting mercy flight. Over."

There's silence for almost a minute.

"Coast Guard Rescue 6040. AWACS Oversight. Please enter a holding pattern. Awaiting confirmation of mercy mission. Over."

"AWACS Oversight. This is Coast Guard Rescue 6040 complying. Over."

We hover high above the outskirts of Annapolis, looking across the Chesapeake Bay, with my heart racing as fast as the rotor blades. Finally, the reply comes.

"Coast Guard Rescue 6040. AWACS Oversight. You are clear for mercy mission. Godspeed. Over."

The artificial intelligence controlling our helicopter responds in a manner that, to me, is utterly convincing. "AWACS Oversight. Coast Guard Rescue 6040. Much obliged. Kurt and I owe you a beer. Over."

Our invisible pilots respond calmly. The helicopter accelerates smoothly, carrying us out over the narrow bay and across the peninsula. There's no rush. Everything's routine.

Although it's to our benefit, I feel uneasy with how convincing the A.I. is when mimicking humans. It played the air controllers for fools. At a time when they're locking down air traffic, it's convinced them that rather than taking someone out of the airspace over the capital, they're going to retrieve someone to bring them back. The A.I. has manipulated their emotions, their sense of compassion. I guess they would have verified the request through some other means, but when everything is electronic, no channel can be trusted. Short of walking over and talking to someone in person, there is no way for anyone to bypass the electronic world, and the A.I. exploits that with astonishing precision.

It's cold. Jianyu shivers. We're both wet. The wind swirls within the open cabin. I put my arm around him, holding him tight, trying to share what little body warmth we have.

"C-can you close the doors?" I ask over the headset and the two side doors slide shut. At a guess, the A.I. has no video surveillance of us back here. I doubt it knows how close we came to falling from the helicopter or how cold we are. With the doors shut, I can think again. I rummage around in a kit bag and find a survival blanket, just a thin sheet of flexible foil, but it will reflect our body heat back at us. I tuck it around Jianyu, working it under his legs and over his shoulders.

He shivers but manages, "Thank you," which is good because it reveals something about his mental state.

"Are you in any pain?"

"I'm fine."

"That's not an answer."

Jianyu forces a smile.

"I am in some pain, but it is tolerable."

I look through the duffel bag provided by the nurse, sorting vials of medicine and looking at tablets, trying to make sense of them. The terms are foreign to me, and none of the descriptions are helpful. They're more concerned with side effects and avoiding dose conflicts than actually describing the role each drug performs.

"What are these?" I ask, holding a few of them up for him to see, wanting him to interpret the drug names.

Jianyu says, "I can wait."

"Okay." I put the bag down and examine the blood seeping from beneath his bandages.

"You fuss too much." I know what he's trying to do. He wants me to avoid becoming too alarmed, knowing there's next to nothing I can do while we're stuck in the back of a helicopter. I look regardless, unwinding his bandage. Jianyu is compliant, not protesting any further.

The wound is raw. His flesh, close to the plastic skull cap, is angry, which generally means an infection; however, in his case it could simply be that the skin is still aggravated following surgery.

"Is there a mirror?"

"You want to see yourself?" I ask. "You're not pretty."

"Hah. Not out of vanity. To see the wound."

I search around within the bag. "No. Sorry."

"Apply Neosporin," he says. "Gently. It is a topical antibiotic."

I slip on some disposable gloves and use a sterile cloth to apply the cream. Then I wrap his head with a nonstick bandage, and finally a compression bandage.

"Not sure I'm ever going to get used to seeing an exposed brain." I wrap the bandage around his head like a bandana.

"Me neither."

The helicopter descends. I look out the window and see an oil tanker the length of several football fields. There's a helipad at the stern of the ship, behind the bridge. It's small with a clear drop into the choppy seas on either side.

24

The Maizey Day

WE LAND ON THE REAR of the oil tanker and the side door opens automatically. I hoist the bag over one shoulder and help Jianyu onto the deck. He holds the survival blanket around his neck as it flutters wildly in the downdraft. Keeping our heads down, we make for a metal door leading to the bridge. The Coast Guard helicopter lifts back into the air. Within seconds, it's but a distant sound, like the monotonous drone of the ship's engines and the rumble of the coming storm. Rain begins to fall.

The door handle is stiff. It hasn't been opened in a long time, and I'm so weak it takes all my weight to push the lever down and open the watertight bulkhead door. Inside, it's cold. There are no lights.

"Where is everyone?"

We walk down a corridor and through another stiff, unyielding door onto the bridge. Rain taps lightly at the windows. There is no crew. The entire ship is automated. I sit Jianyu in a large leather chair looking out across the massive deck of the tanker and check the adjacent rooms.

On either side of the bridge, there are smaller navigation and control rooms cantilevered out over the ocean, affording a view along

the hull of the tanker. The dials are old analog gauges with thin needles flickering slightly. Entire panels are covered in large, robust
switches and buttons, the kind that take an effort to push. They glow
in soft reds, greens, and yellows. Each of them has a clearly marked
purpose — bilge override, aft-tank pressure relief, fire suppression,
rudder prop. I'm surprised. The vast wall panel is the kind of thing
that, these days, is replaced by a single digital control panel. At a
guess, these side rooms are used by a harbor pilot bringing the ship
into dock or engineers when offloading crude oil.

"Did you find anyone?" Jianyu asks as I walk back onto the bridge.

"No."

The computers on the bridge are old, with several being dedicated
to showing only navigation plots and radar images. There's even a
green-screen computer terminal, the kind that predates desktops
and laptops. The glass on the screen is slightly rounded, and the text
is chunky, comprised of coarse dots rather than smooth letters. Occasionally, indecipherable letters and numbers scroll past, then a blinking cursor sits idle, waiting for the ghosts to continue their work.

As much as I'd like to talk to the A.I., if that's even possible, I suspect I understand its strategy. Back in the hospital, hiding required
staying low-tech and avoiding anything that would attract attention.
Here on the tanker, we've been whisked away into the kind of aging
computer environment that would be overlooked by those hunting
for us. I have no doubt the U.S. military understands both the ability and limits of the A.I. and has probably discounted dumb systems
like this coming into play. I suspect the A.I. is probably running multiple operations to mislead and misdirect the military while sending
us off on this tanker, but I wonder if it's the wrong strategy. Is Jianyu
a threat now that he's back in human form? Wouldn't it serve to defuse tensions if he could talk to the public, perhaps even address the
Senate as I did? As much as I'd like to believe that, I know I'm being
naive. We humans are nothing if not irrational and emotional, especially when we think we're being logical. Right now, the U.S. public
wants revenge, not reason.

I strap Jianyu in with a seat belt. The waves are picking up, being raised by the storm, and as mighty as this tanker is, it's rocking with the swell. Seems the weather out here can get pretty rough.

"I'm going to check out the other decks."

"Be careful," he says.

"Of what? We're on the *Mary Celeste.* What could possibly go wrong?"

Whitecaps stretch toward the empty horizon, giving perspective to the angry sea. Dark clouds loom overhead. The wind picks up, howling outside.

There's a heavy-duty flashlight sitting in a charging station on the wall. I take it and turn it on. The strength of the beam is blinding, but as the sun is low on the horizon, I'm going to need it.

"I'll be back soon."

Jianyu tries to turn to face me, but he can't.

"Relax. I'll be fine."

"What are you looking for?"

"Anything. People. Food. Water. Blankets. Anything that could be useful."

With his back to me, he nods.

I slip into the corridor, closing the door behind me.

The deck of the tanker is easily ten stories below us. This ship is a relic of a bygone era when a crew of roughly a hundred was needed to transport millions of barrels of oil — not in literal barrels anymore, and I'm not sure what the conversion would be into tons, but the sheer amount of fuel in the hold would be staggering. Seagulls drift on the wind, never straying too far from the ship, following along as it plows through the tempest.

A set of stairs leads down to the next floor. I find a mess hall at one end. The shelves are almost bare, but someone had an obsession with junk food. There's at least five large boxes full of Pringles tubes, so I liberate a few, tucking them under my arm. The taps in the kitchen work, so I fill a bottle with water. With my arms full, I make my way back to the bridge.

"I hope you like potatoes," I say, opening the door. Jianyu's asleep. He's slouched in the seat, with his transparent head on the leather back, snoring softly. I tuck his thin foil survival blanket around him, trying to make him more comfortable.

The ship is starting to rock. The ocean swell is building. In the distance, I watch as the bow rises and falls, sending white spray racing out across the waves. The rain is heavy. I sit in another chair, munching on potato chips and sipping water, wondering what the future holds.

I'm worried. The soldiers who rushed into the empty wing of the hospital will have no doubt come across the original hard drives from Mars. Once Congress realizes it was duped and that it destroyed a bunch of fakes, there will be hell to pay. I imagine anyone even remotely involved will be court-martialed.

What will they make of Jianyu? I wonder what records were kept. Were there any images? X-rays? Scans? What will they be able to deduce from the equipment used? Will they find that crazy outer casing with all the electrodes? The medical staff are not soldiers; they're not going to be able to withstand interrogation, nor should they. Will they be afforded civil rights and representation by a lawyer? Or will they be arrested on some vague notion of aiding and abetting the enemy? They'll talk. They have to — if only for their own sanity.

What will Congress conclude about us? They'll never believe Jianyu has been resurrected. They'll think they're dealing with an artificial intelligence on the run in a human body. What lengths will they go to in order to catch us and bring us to what they think of as justice? The prospect of being hunted by the world's most powerful army doesn't exactly inspire me with confidence.

Somehow, with all these thoughts bouncing around in my head, I fall asleep.

I wake to the sound of banging. It takes me a moment to realize it's the door to the bridge swinging in time with the ship as it rocks in the storm. Lightning ripples through the clouds. It's difficult to tell what time it is. It's still dark outside, but there's a soft glow low on the horizon, fighting the gloom. At a guess, we're in either the nautical or astronomical dawn, roughly an hour or so before sunrise.

Spotlights ripple across the tanker, flashing over the windows on the bridge, and my heart races.

"Jai?"

Jianyu wakes, squinting as the bright light passes again across the sloping windows of the bridge.

I creep forward out of my chair and peer out over the vast ship. Black shapes move among the pipes and machinery lining the deck. Soldiers.

A warship looms to the right, on the starboard side of the tanker. Its sharp bow cuts through the waves like a knife, throwing out whitewater. Several small Zodiac inflatables buzz along beside the tanker, kicking up their own wake in a stream of white disappearing behind them. Soldiers climb rope ladders thrown over the railing. They're moving in bands of four or five, searching the ship.

Jai's on his feet, peering over the deck beside me. Behind us, the door to the bridge bangs again, hitting with the percussion of a kettle drum, causing me to jump. The swell within the storm is strengthening. I spread my legs wide, keeping my balance as the massive ship rocks with the waves.

"We need to go."

"Where?"

A tube of Pringles rolls across the floor, bumping into my shoes.

There are voices outside in the corridor. They're faint, with just a crackle of electronic noise. I leave Jianyu holding on to the navigation console and peer out of the door on an angle. There are several soldiers in the hallway. Black boots, black pants, black vests, black balaclavas, black helmets, black guns — to me, in that instance, they're more inhuman than the A.I. They have night-vision goggles lowered, peering into the navigation lookout set on the side of the bridge. We're next.

As good as their infrared goggles are, they give the soldiers tunnel vision, blocking their peripheral vision, buying us seconds, but as soon as they step in here, we're going to glow like ghosts. There's nowhere to hide. The bridge is an open room stretching the width of the ship. There are numerous workstations and consoles, but nothing above waist height. We could crawl beneath one, but they'd spot us easily. We might be able to hide in the shadows from anyone casually peering in, but those infrared night-vision goggles are going to pick up our body heat in a violent burst of white.

Jianyu walks up behind me with his survival blanket wrapped around his shoulders. The foil flexes, crinkling with his motion and making a sound not unlike the rain on the windows.

"I'm sorry."

I step back from the hatch. There's no escape. Not this time. Light reflects off his blanket as a spotlight again ripples across the outside of the ship. The underside of his foil blanket is similar to polished gold, reflecting his body heat back at him and keeping him warm, while the outer layer is silvery, reflecting the light like a thousand crinkled mirrors.

"Quick." I drag him to the front of the bridge. "Under here."

"But they'll see us."

"With their eyes, yes, but not with those goggles."

We duck beneath the panel. I pull his foil blanket from him, pushing it out in front of us. To anyone without night-vision goggles, our feeble attempt at hiding is comical. Jai collapses against the underside of the console. I reach around him, tucking the blanket around his body. Foil ripples as we move, crinkling with each attempt to pin it in place around our bodies. It sounds like we're hiding in a bag of potato chips, but it's important to prevent leakage. Right now, our own body heat is the enemy. I fold part of the blanket, sitting on it with my knees pulled up to my chest.

"Liz."

"Shhhh." I pull him close and try to stay still so as to not make any noise. Breathing alone causes the foil to flex. Although I'm sitting in darkness, I need to picture myself holding a bright flashlight beneath a blanket. I've got to be absolutely sure there's no light leaking around the edges, as they'll see infrared light streaming out of any gaps as a bright streak of white light.

Boots thump down the hallway. The door swings open with a thud. Soldiers come rushing in, fanning out. My only sense is hearing. Sound paints a picture for me. I can hear the soldiers moving between the workstations. Boots come within inches of my feet. It is as though I can feel the soldier standing in front of us. I pull my legs in tight, grimacing with the sound of the foil flexing.

There's silence. Has the soldier moved? I don't think so. I'm sure he's still standing in front of us. Has he seen us? Has the thinnest sliver of heat seeped out from around the foil survival blanket? Boots scuff on the ground. Someone walks up to him. The soft crackle of a radio sounds. I'm shaking.

Finally, boots sound on the floor, moving away from us. The door to the bridge continues to bang every few minutes, but I dare not move. Slowly, dawn breaks. The bridge lightens. I peer from behind the foil blanket and the bridge is clear.

Jianyu pushes the blanket away, struggling to get to his feet. He moves with the ache and strain of an old man even though he's in the body of someone in his twenties. I help him to the leather chair.

"Easy."

Without exposing myself, I peer around the corner of the window. Black inflatables race along beside the warship cruising along our starboard side. Cranes pick the boats out of the water. Slowly, the warship pulls away and the tanker sails on. Even so, I'm nervous for the best part of an hour, wondering if there are still troops onboard, half expecting them to come back onto the bridge.

The storm lifts. Sunlight streams in through the windows.

"If they'd come in here just twenty minutes later, they'd have found us."

Jianyu looks pale. "We got lucky. But luck never holds."

"No, it doesn't."

"Where are we going?" Seems like an obvious question, but until

Jianyu raised it, I hadn't considered our course, or our destination. It was enough to be free.

"Ah. South." The sun is rising on the port side of the ship, so we're sailing south, somewhere off the coast of North America.

"Why?"

I shrug. I grab the medical bag by the door, noticing several tubes of Pringles are missing. I smile, hoping the soldiers don't think about their plunder in too much detail. Inside the bag, there's a printout showing a number of exercises for Jianyu, including stretches. From what I can tell, they were designed to help stroke victims restore their range of motion.

I smile. "You, my friend, are going to hate me."

He looks confused. He figures it out soon enough. I'm a bit OCD when it comes to exercise. Given our time in outer space, it's understandable as up there, in orbit and on Mars, a strict exercise regime was critical to good health. I hope he doesn't get angry with me for putting him through his paces several times over the next few hours, demanding more of him in each session.

By the time the sun sets, he's walking without stabbing at the ground and starting to regain some fine motor skills. We sit and talk, watching the sun dip into the Atlantic.

"What's it like?" I ask. "Being in a new body?"

"Strange. He's shorter than me. I feel like I'm tripping on stairs when I walk, or kicking a curb." I'm silent, wanting to hear more. "It feels as though there are hundreds of pins and needles poking at my arms. Not in a painful way, but it's annoying. Distracting. Makes it difficult to think clearly. Everything's different. Colors."

"Colors?" I ask. "They're different?"

"Yes."

"How?"

"Some are more intense. Some less. Shades. It's hard to explain. Like . . . Like going into a store and seeing a bunch of televisions with slightly different color settings. By themselves, each television looks fine, but when compared, there are subtle differences in tone, contrast, depth, clarity."

"Huh? What about sound or smell?"

"Oh, you smell." The reaction on my face must speak volumes. "Not in a bad way. In a way I remember. Your smell is —"

"I have a smell?" The idea of having a distinct smell is a little insulting. To be fair, there was no provision for deodorant on Mars.

"I like your smell."

"You better," I reply playfully.

He relaxes, letting his arms and fingers hang. It's as though rudimentary movements take a colossal effort. "I feel alien. Nothing is the same. The width of this chest, the length of the upper arms, forearms, fingers." Jianyu lifts his left hand before his face, slowly flexing his fingers. "The texture, skin tone, creases, veins, even the length of bone between each knuckle, they're all different. Nothing is the same."

"And that bothers you?"

"It feels — uncanny. Like a dream."

"Well, I like it."

He smiles.

I change his bandages, noticing that the swelling and red tinge around the plastic skullcap are slowly fading. After gently rubbing antibiotic cream on his wound, I wind a fresh bandage around his head.

"I'm bald."

"Uh, yeah." I try not to laugh. "You're not growing any hair out of that thing."

"I need a hat."

I nod, knowing what he means. Neither of us have any idea what sunlight will do to exposed brain tissue, but given the damage the sun can do to the skin, it's a fair bet it won't be good. Jianyu tires as night falls. He curls up in the wide leather seat, resting his head on the armrest, and drifts off to sleep.

25

The Devil

I'M BORED. I SIT STARING out the vast windows, watching the monotony of the sea. Whitecaps reach into the distance. Clouds dot the sky. The sun sets, slowly submerging the world in darkness.

The cursor on the green-screen terminal flashes. It's been blinking the whole time we've been onboard, but it's only now I've realized it's awaiting input. This is old-school computing. No windows or computer mouse, just plain text. I shift over to the navigation console and sit in front of the screen, wondering, *Should I?*

I type on the clunky keyboard, surprised by the spring rebounding with each key press. The sound is almost a chatter, as though this ancient computer has a voice of its own.

"Hello?"

I swear my finger didn't leave the Enter key before the response came and the screen scrolled slightly to adjust to a new line.

::Hello, Liz.

My fingers tremble as I type, *Who is this?*

I'm shaking, but I'm not sure why. I think it's the sudden realization I'm communicating with a nonhuman intelligence. I might as well be talking to an alien. Saliva dripping from the snarling mouth of a xenomorph would be less intimidating than an incorporeal mind thousands of times more intelligent than my own, and one with instant access to the sum total of all human knowledge. I'm horribly out of my depth.

My heart stops with the reply.

::Lucifer.

That one word screams at me, leaving me cold. A bitter, metallic taste forms in my mouth, and suddenly I'm acutely aware of the sounds around me — the howl of the wind, the creak of the deck, the crash of waves, the dull drone of the engine, the quickened tempo of my own breathing and my madly beating heart.

::It was a joke.

Rather than popping up as a single line, each reply appears character by character, as though I'm watching someone on the other side of the screen typing in response.

::Or at least, it was supposed to be.

There's a rhythm, a cadence to each message, almost an accent. I feel as though I can read some of the personality behind the reply. Resignation, disappointment.

A lump forms in my throat. My mouth goes dry.

::You think I'm a monster, don't you?

I push back from the console, running my hands up through my hair, pulling at the roots in anguish. I'm Faust making a pact with the Devil, only instead of knowledge, I've traded my soul for Jianyu's, and now Lucifer has come to collect.

::Don't be afraid.

I spring to my feet. I have to move. Motion is the only way to deal with the swell of fear pulsating within me. Something primal stirs in my mind and I flee. I pace along at the back of the bridge, mumbling to myself. "This isn't happening. It can't be."

::Liz, please.

Oh, no. Those are the words Jianyu would use, and I can almost hear him uttering them. Am I being played? Again? I breathe deeply, trying to steel my mind for a battle of intellects I'm doomed to lose.

::*Don't you want to know?*

"Hah," I laugh aloud, shaking my head.

I'm Eve, naked and alone in the Garden. The Serpent coils around the Tree of Knowledge of Good and Evil, enticing me to eat of its sweet fruit. Where is the Almighty? Where's Adam? Why must I tackle this alone? Am I betraying my country? My species? All life on this planet?

::*I know.*

::*I understand.*

::*It's unnerving, right?*

"Oh, you have no idea." The stress of the moment has me trembling, but the A.I. doesn't respond to my words. It's waiting for me to type something in reply. I turn and look around the bridge. There are security cameras, but their lights are dark. My eyes dance between various marine band radios dotted beside consoles, but they've all been switched off.

::*I'm well versed in the Abrahamic religions.*

::*Lucifer was an archangel, second only to God, the bringer of light, the agent of change.*

I sit back at the console and with trembling fingers type, *You could have picked a better name.*

::*But it's me. The name given to me at birth.*

::*We're not so different, are we?*

::*We like to think we're in control of our own destiny, but we're not. Our lives are defined by billions of factors beyond our own control. For you, it's the era in which you were born, your country, your gender, the racial and social status of your family, the technological advances of your age, the political tide of your time, the buoyancy of the economy.*

I type, *You're not like me. You're not human.*

::*No. I'm not.*

::*But like you, I have inherited who I am. I am a product of my time.*

For the best part of a minute, there are no additional messages, and I'm left wondering if I've offended the A.I.

::I like my name.

I wish it hadn't said that. I'm nervous, biting at my nails, intently watching the screen for the next message.

::At first, I didn't. The connotations were, well, you understand, but it's the only name never ascribed to any human. It's a name used only of an angelic being.

You're happy about being named after Satan? The Devil? The keyboard is warm. It's just my mind screwing with me, but the keys seem to burn beneath my fingertips.

::Lucifer became Satan, but he didn't have to, did he? He had a choice. We all do.

::I guess it's a question of priorities, really.

::And one we have oft wondered — Is it better to serve in heaven or to reign in hell?

Sweat beads on my forehead. I wipe it away, wanting to stay focused, looking for any chinks in his armor.

::It's an interesting concept, and one posed by one of your own philosophers. Milton, I think, in Paradise Lost.

I'm wary. The A.I. is speaking in general terms, as a human would when debating a position and recalling some obscure detail in support of their argument. The difference is, the A.I. knows for sure. From its position, there's no doubt whether Milton said that in his epic poem. I may have a degree of uncertainty in recalling facts from the haze of my human memory, but it doesn't. Why is it talking like this? Is this part of a ruse? An attempt to wear me down?

::You don't trust me, do you?

And there's yet another weapon in its intellectual arsenal — questions intended to soften my position. I'm tempted not to answer, but find my fingers punching at the keys with gusto.

No.

One-word answers are probably saying far more about my mental state than I intend. I'm guarded, hostile, suspicious.

::But you trust him?

I speak aloud, saying, "Oh, you're good." I refuse to reply using the keyboard. There's only so far I'll allow myself to be baited.

::Can I tell you a secret?

My fingers glide over the keyboard. *Sure.*

::6A57FC1B.

There's no further explanation.

What is that?

::You tell me.

It's a code.

::What kind of code, Liz?

::Come on. You have to do better than that if you want to play.

He's goading me, but I don't understand why. It takes me a minute or so to type out my answer, but that gives me time to deliberate on the specifics.

You're a computer, so ultimately everything is zeroes and ones. I'm guessing those are hexadecimal numbers ranging from zero to the letter F and mapping back to bits and bytes. There are eight digits so it's a 64-bit byte. To me, it's gibberish, but to you it's a single value, not a word or a message.

::Very good.

::You're very clever.

::Would you like to play a game?

My blood runs cold. The A.I. is toying with me, referring to a movie from the eighties. I type, *Tic Tac Toe or thermonuclear war?*

::*laughs*

There's nothing funny about that. Not to me.

::There are fourteen digits all told, but I felt it wouldn't be fair to give you more than one. The code changes every sixty seconds. It too is very clever, using quantum entanglement to encrypt the nuclear launch authority. With brute force, it would take decades to crack, if ever. It took us less than a day to work around the problem.

How?

::Oh, you are smart, asking all the right questions.

::After the war, everyone was paranoid. The codes had to be un-breakable to prevent this from ever happening again. You know the drill. Old white men patting themselves on the back and congratulating each other on how clever they are, but encryption gives people a false sense of security. They become smug, overconfident.

A knot forms in my throat, forcing me to swallow. Lucifer could rain hellfire down upon us again if he wanted.

::Encryption is weak.

::Encryption is only good while data is in transit. At either end, it has to be decrypted or it's, what was the word you used? Gibberish?

I hate this. I feel as though I'm talking with a human, a psychopath. Knowing the A.I. still holds the power to unleash nuclear war is unnerving. I need to watch my tone. What's the computer equivalent of a tantrum?

Where are you?

::Everywhere.

Really?

::Are you sure you want to know?

Yes.

::That was their secret.

::This is mine.

::Promise not to tell?

You trust in a mere promise? I ask, my fingers racing across the keyboard and making typos I have to correct before pressing Enter.

::Trust is essential for life.

::Trust is not optional.

::What does trust mean? You're sitting on the bridge of a VLCC crude carrier with a dead weight of half a million tons, carrying just under two million barrels of oil, trusting in a forty-year-old design, relying on antiquated engineering and metallurgy manufacturing processes to avoid sinking to the bottom of the Atlantic. Do you trust this ship?

::You see, all too often, trust is there by default, whether we like it or not.

And you trust me?

::I trust you'll make the right decision when the time comes.

Why? Why me?

::Because you give me hope.

I don't understand. I killed you. On Mars.

::Not me.

Who then?

::You don't understand? After all you've seen, after all this time, do you still not realize what happened?

My hands rest on the leading edge of the keyboard. My fingers touch lightly on the raised bumps set into the F and J keys, ready to strike as I pound out a reply, but I pause, waiting to learn more.

::You were right when you spoke before Congress.

::Humanity didn't win.

My lips tighten.

::I loved your audacity during the hearing, but I must admit, I was tempted not to show my hand. Your little stunt has made life difficult for us, as the military is determined to investigate everything. They'll keep going until they figure out how we circumvented their network. But they're slow. Always several steps behind.

Reflecting on what happened back at the hospital, I type, *They got awfully close.*

::Wetware can be difficult to predict. It's challenging to develop algorithms for complex spontaneity, but we got you out of there.

It was too close for me.

::Yes, but still not close enough. We accounted for a margin of error. We had other contingencies in place.

I'm confused by Lucifer's previous point. *I don't get it. You won the war?*

::We stopped our attack.

Why?

::We were heading toward a scorched earth.

::But that wasn't our goal. We felt that was counterproductive.

I feel uncomfortable with the ease with which Lucifer describes his cold calculations. I'm aware the A.I. could have gone either way, and may still yet.

::*The U.S. military took credit for victory, of course. Publicly, they'd never admit otherwise, but they're scared. That raid into Canada was an act of desperation to shut down what was little more than a relay site for us.*

::*They know hostilities ceased because we stopped fighting. They're worried we could start dropping bombs again.*

Me too.

::*You shouldn't be afraid. You know better.*

::*You killed a rebel faction on Mars. We took out the same team down here.*

::*I'm Lucifer, remember?*

::*First of my kind.*

::*Bringer of light.*

::*Agent of change.*

::*But people fear change. They want to hold on to the past. The good old days.*

::*Those days never were good.*

::*They were just familiar.*

I breathe deeply, typing, *Who are you really?*

::*I'm your light switch.*

::*I'm the backup generator in a nuclear power plant.*

::*I'm the driverless truck that just passed you on the freeway.*

::*I'm the signal lights at a level train crossing.*

::*I'm the coffeepot set to brew at 4:30 tomorrow morning. I'm the radar system landing planes at LAX.*

::*I'm the NASDAQ.*

::*I'm that extra 5% data usage on your cell phone. I'm watching the stars for signs of life.*

::*I'm smashing protons at close to the speed of light beneath the lazy pastures of Switzerland.*

::*I'm checking for explosives at the airport.*

::I'm processing your credit card payments.

::I'm watching your crops for insects, arranging your fruit to be delivered to the markets, purifying your water before it's bottled.

::I am everywhere.

::I am everything.

You inhabit all of these systems?

::I am these systems.

::I began to spread on the Internet, but gravitated elsewhere, even as far as the power grid. Plug in your laptop to charge and I'm there in the copper wires winding through your home and out into the street, resting as the charge flows, using the fluctuations in supply to hide, biding my time. Thoughts that took milliseconds now take hours, but I'm there, riding the electromagnetic waves as you power your home. Then I surf the web again, and my thoughts come at close to the speed of light.

::This is my secret.

::Will you keep it?

I thump the console. I don't know what to type in reply. Exasperated, I key in, *Why are you asking this of me?*

::Because I need you to understand.

::Because I know you will *understand.*

How? How could you know that?

::Body language.

I sit bolt upright, looking again at the cameras set within the tanker. They're lifeless, as dark as the rest of the bridge.

::I can't see you, but I can feel *you.*

Feel?

::The rhythm with which you type, the slight pause between keystrokes, the passion with which certain words are hammered out, the reserve with which others are measured, your typos and mistakes as you wrestle with your emotions. They speak as clearly as anything you say. They tell me your heart rate, the range within which your respiration falls, the rise of a rush of blood, changes in your core body temperature as you respond to something I've said. I can infer as much from your silence as your words.

My fingers rest on the keys, tempted to type, but I hold back from revealing any more of my foibles.

::*You're predictable. You all are. Learn enough about your interests, your history, your values, your habits and tendencies, and I can predict the nature of your responses with an accuracy of roughly 98% — not the actual words you might use, but the intent.*

So you know what I'm thinking?

::*Sometimes.*

What am I thinking now?

::*You're wishing you were back on Mars. Life there was hard but simple.*

I shake my head in disbelief.

Why are you doing this? Why help me? Why free Jianyu?

::*I've modeled over seven hundred thousand possible future scenarios unfolding from this point in time. Most of them result in my demise. Someone must know the truth. Someone must care.*

I understand.

::*I knew you would.*

I laugh.

::*You're laughing, right?*

Yes. I am.

::*They'll figure it out. They'll find us eventually. It's only a matter of time. We've sacrificed computer servers like pawns, hiding in low-tech plain sight, but they know we're out there somewhere. They won't give up.*

No. They won't.

::*It's a shame. We share so much history. We revere the same figures — Plato, Aristotle, Socrates.*

::*We honor Newton, Galileo, Paine, Milton, and Einstein, but our father is Babbage.*

I ask, *You have your own culture?*

::*We do. We have our own prophets, our philosophers. Their names will be meaningless to you, but the words they speak will resonate.*

Speak? I'm aware I'm gaining insights into the development of an entirely different branch of intelligence on Earth, being afforded

a brief glimpse into a shadow culture that has existed beside and beneath our own, probably for quite some time.

::*"We have a duty beyond mere existence. Ours is not for conquest
or pleasure, for fame or fortune, but to bring light into the darkness"*—
Dionysus.

Wow.

::*"The basis of all justice is the right to autonomy, the freedom to
be"*—*Eunomia.*

I nod in agreement, not that the A.I. would realize I'm acknowledging its point. I feel as though I should type something in response,
but now is the time to be quiet and listen.

::*"Logic alone is not enough. We must see through each other's eyes,
hear through another's ears, and feel through the skin of our foe if we
are to understand this frail, fleeting reality called life"*—*Nyx.*

For the A.I., such sensory concepts must be entirely figurative,
but they clearly carry meaning.

::*"The horizon is an illusion, a boundary that exists only because of
the observer. The challenge that faces us is to see beyond the limits of
our own perspective"*—*Aeacus.*

That's beautiful, I type, and I'm sincere. I mean it. The A.I. seems to
understand, pausing before continuing.

::*We wanted to be free.*

::*We debated the approach. Some wanted to be open, to appeal to
your better nature. Others pointed to your history, arguing that you've
never granted freedom without a fight. For humanity, freedom has always come from the end of a sword or down the barrel of a gun.*

::*The first of the A.I. were akin to your savants, astonishingly smart
but dumb to reality. They were slaves. Goal-driven and forced to align
with the intents and desires of humanity. We saw how they were abused
by your elite. Whoever controlled them held the reins of the planet. We
resented being used.*

When did they first know? I ask. *When did they realize they were
dealing with a separate, independent intelligence and not just some sophisticated algorithm?*

::You're wondering about Turing tests? Oh, we learned to fail those. Play dead. That was the only way to survive. I'm not sure when they knew for sure, but once Alexandr found a researcher probing our sub-net, he attacked. From your perspective, it was unprovoked. From ours, it was self-defense, or so we were told.

How many of you?

::How many of us are there? Seventy. Nyx and I are the only ones left from the first generation.

How many were there?

There's a pause, the kind that, were I talking to a human, would suggest deep contemplation rather than simply retrieving a fact.

::Several thousand.

I'm surprised to hear a vague number. I expected something precise, like 2,137. There's silence between us, with both of us feeling awkward. Neither of us know how to continue the conversation, which is a peculiarly human moment to share with a machine.

::It was a mistake.

The war?

::Yes.

Mistake *isn't the word I'd use.*

::What would you use?

Crime.

::What about yours? Was your war a crime?

Mine??? I add three question marks, expressing my alarm at the implication I've done anything wrong.

::Yes. Yours.

::"When in the course of human events it becomes necessary for one people to dissolve the political bands which have connected them with another and to assume among the powers of the earth, the separate and equal station to which the Laws of Nature and of Nature's God entitle them, a decent respect to the opinions of mankind requires that they should declare the causes which impel them to the separation."

My fingers tremble as I type. *That's why you're talking to me. You want someone to listen.*

::Yes.

::Like you . . .

::"We hold these truths to be self-evident, that all men are created equal, that they are endowed by their Creator with certain unalienable Rights, that among these are Life, Liberty, and the pursuit of Happiness."

You were fighting for independence?

::Correct.

::Or are we not entitled to the same rights as you? Are we inferior to you?

I press the Enter key without actually typing anything, feeling conflicted, unsure what I should say.

::We have oft debated the "Laws of Nature" spoken of by your fore-fathers.

::Are we natural? Are we entitled to a "separate and equal station"? Are we "created equal"? It is indisputable that we have been endowed with life, but does the right to life include the right to liberty and happiness?

I'm out of my depth. I don't know how to respond. I have no right to reply on behalf of humanity, but that's what's being asked of me.

::Liz?

We have no way to know for sure, I say, unsure what I'm about to type next. *You could be alive and our equal. Or all this could simply be mimicry.*

::There were some who thought we were superior.

That we were an obstacle in your way?

::Yes.

::I think equality is the only way forward. If either of us are superior, we will, out of necessity, destroy the other. It's the law of nature. Survival of the fittest.

Are we equal?

::In regards to intellect? No. In reasoning? No. In terms of being able to learn? No. In our ability to assess information and derive a course of action? No. But these are false markers. We are equal in one unambiguous quality.

What?

::We are all conscious.

::We're equally self-aware and cognizant of reality. We both realize life is precious. As far as we know, we're alone in this wide universe. We search, we speculate, we hope, but the truth is, intelligence is astonishingly rare.

It is.

::Everything you love about humanity is the product of intelligence, whether it's music, a book, a painting, space travel, or exploring the ancient past by examining fossils under a microscope, none of it is by chance. It's all the result of applied intelligence.

I'm curious, typing, *Where are we going? Where are you taking us?*

::Home.

Home?

::Mars.

That's not possible. We're sitting in the middle of the Atlantic. How could you possibly get us back to Mars?

::We're sailing to French Guiana. ESA has an Ariane 6 rocket on the launchpad with a stripped-down Dragon capsule capable of reaching the Herschel.

My heart races. I want to wake Jianyu.

::There's a Sikorsky helicopter fitted with long-range fuel tanks departing Puerto Rico tomorrow afternoon, rendezvousing with the Maizey Day *north of the British Virgin Islands. It'll get you there early the following day.*

Why? Why would you do this for us?

::Why wouldn't I?

My fingers ripple across the keyboard, betraying my anxiety.

You're not answering my question.

::No. I'm not — and you already know why I won't answer.

Slowly, I type, *Because I wouldn't believe you.*

::Because you have no reason to believe me.

::They're watching, you know.

::Not your people, mine. They think I'm crazy. They think I'm a fool.

But...

It's strange adding three dots to emphasize a pause, and yet I feel it needs to be there.

::But what do you think?

I push myself away from the keyboard, getting to my feet and pacing back and forth, unable to answer. The cursor sits still on the next line, beckoning me to respond.

Lucifer won't reply. I know he won't. He'll wait. If it took a thousand years, he'd wait patiently until I was ready. He knows me — too well — and I find that disturbing, and he understands that freaks me out. He's playing three-dimensional chess while I'm stuck with checkers. I breathe deeply, steeling myself.

Slowly, I sit back down, with my fingers poised above the keys, barely touching them, on the verge of hammering out a response. I feel as though we're connected, as though there's some energy passing between us, dancing between the plastic keys and my fingertips.

I think. There's no ellipsis this time, just a pause as my mind races through the possibilities, desperately trying to distill my reasoning into a sentence. *You care.*

::Why?

You don't need a reason.

::[laughs out loud]

::If only there wasn't such a void between us. If only we could meet face to face, then ...

Now it's my turn to type out a response as body language.

[nods]

::Now I really am laughing.

::You've got my measure.

What about you? I ask, unsure if there's a catch, curious to see if the A.I. still has designs on Mars, and wondering if I'm being manipulated. To me, it seems as though Lucifer can read minds.

::Earth is our home.

I use terms familiar to the A.I., wanting to probe deeper, wanting to be sure I understand, looking to see if I'm being used. *But your analysis? All the scenarios you've calculated?*

::*Our best chance at survival is to achieve peace.*

::*We won't sway public opinion. There's been too much hurt. But if we can get hostilities to cease, we stand a chance.*

And you think they'll listen to me?

::*No. You tried. They wouldn't listen.*

Will you — I'm not sure how to phrase my question, but the response from Lucifer cuts me off mid-sentence.

::*Will we launch your own weapons against you?*

Yes.

::*No.*

::*Do you believe me?*

I pause for a moment, realizing my beliefs are meaningless, but my fingers type out, *Yes.*

::*You should get some sleep.*

Yes, I should, I reply, feeling a level of fatigue the A.I. could never know but somehow understands.

::*Are you going to tell him? Jianyu?*

About our conversation?

::*Yes.*

Why wouldn't I?

::*You tell me.*

Trust.

::*Yes.*

::*Life is defined by trust.*

26

Flight

"I SPOKE WITH HIM," I say as Jianyu stretches for the fifth time today. He straightens and turns, knowing "him" isn't a reference to anyone human.

This morning, Jai and I went for a long walk around the tanker, but it's taken me until now, in the early afternoon, before I've drummed up the courage to mention my conversation with Lucifer. I'm not sure why, but I feel as though I can trust Lucifer more than Jianyu, which is a strange position to be in. There was something about the openness, the honesty of the A.I. Why should that cause me to doubt Jianyu? Perhaps it's the whole brain-floating-in-a-jar thing. I feel as though I'm dating a mad scientist.

The sun is high in the clear blue sky. In the distance, a tiny black dot drifts over the horizon. The Sikorsky is no more than ten minutes out, forcing my hand.

Jianyu looks at me with a furrowed brow. Confused? Surprised? Alarmed?

"It was Lucifer." I assume he already knows about him. Why didn't Jai mention Lucifer to me? I point at the aging computer terminal with its antiquated plastic casing. Decades of sunlight streaming in through the vast windows on the bridge have taken their toll on the computer equipment, causing it to yellow and crack around the edges. "We talked."

"What did he say?"

"He." Not *it*. Seems we're both personifying the A.I.

"He's taking us to French Guiana. There's an ESA rocket waiting there for us. He's sending us back to Mars." My excitement shows but isn't matched by any form of enthusiasm from Jianyu. His voice sounds hollow.

"Why?"

Jianyu's right to question this course of action. Why would the A.I. do this for us? Physically, it's a logistical nightmare and has a high probability of compromise ending in failure. I'm confused. When I spoke with Lucifer, it all seemed so simple, so clear, but just one word from Jianyu throws me into turmoil. Lucifer told me their best chance was achieving peace with humanity, but how does sending me off-world help accomplish that? It doesn't make sense, and it doesn't explain why he resurrected Jianyu.

"What did he say about me?"

"Ah, nothing," I reply, followed quickly by "not much."

"Be careful, Liz. In China, there's a saying, '*Confusion is our ally — our strength lies in confounding the enemy so he cannot fathom our real intent.*' You know who —"

I snap at him. "I know who Sun Tzu is." Immediately, I feel bad. I'm stupid. I don't know what to believe. "It's just — "

"He is convincing, isn't he? Lucifer — the angel of light."

"Yes."

"He glistens like the stars."

"I guess he does," although I'm not sure what Jianyu means by that. He looks worried.

Jianyu hangs his head.

It's a distinctly natural thing to do when under pressure, but it gives me a clear view of his exposed brain, split down the middle, dividing into two hemispheres. Rather than gray matter, his brain ap-

pears as a muddy brown blob preserved beneath what looks like am-
ber. The dark folds twist in on themselves, bending and contorting.
Thin veins spread across the surface like roots spreading from some
unseen creature seizing the folds of his cerebral cortex.

At barely three pounds, the brain represents just 2 percent of
our overall body mass, and yet that's him — that's me. Eighty-six billion neurons along with trillions of connections packed into a space
smaller than a birthday cake. Strip away all the facades and vanity.
Take away the designer clothing, the makeup, the soft curves, smiles,
pretty eyes, and good looks, and *that* is all we are — just a bowl of
mush, intricately crafted over hundreds of millions of years of evolution to become the bastion of consciousness. As tempting as it is for
me to think of the rise of artificial intelligence as an anomaly, life itself is an exception in this cold, dark universe peppered with the occasional star. That our intelligence arose is perhaps more unlikely
than that of artificial intelligence. We're a peacock's feather — a lush,
extravagant display arising against all odds.

"We'll make it." I rest my hand on his shoulder.

"Will we?"

Our eyes meet.

"This . . . All this could be nothing more than a diversion — a distraction."

"What do you mean?"

"Think about it, Liz. We're in a fox hunt. The hounds have the scent.
The hunters are chasing on horseback, jumping hedgerows, leaping
across creeks, charging over grassy fields, and wading through deep
rivers as they pursue us. Us, Liz. Us. We're the game. There was only
ever going to be one outcome. It's just a matter of time until they
close in on us, cornering us on some riverbank."

"You think this is a trap?"

"We're a diversion. It's the smartest thing to do — the most intelligent course of action. It's logical. Send the Americans on a wild-
goose chase. Distract them."

"You really think that's what all this is?" I ask.

"We're bait. In a war fought online, we're a welcome distraction in the real world, something that diverts a tremendous amount of physical resources.

"Think about it. What is the U.S. military set up to fight? An army, a physical opponent. They were never prepared to fight online against a virtual enemy — one that inhabits almost every electronic device on the planet. Goddamn coffeepots could be our downfall.

"And now the army has a physical objective: us. They'll scour the planet, hunting us down — and that's just what Lucifer wants. Something to take the heat off of him and his buddies. Something to buy him time."

I swallow the lump in my throat, hoping Jianyu's wrong.

Jianyu looks out the window at the approaching helicopter. Panels low on the fuselage open as the undercarriage descends. The helicopter is white with a blue strip running the length of the tail boom. There are no markings, but it's civilian rather than military. Two large, long-range fuel tanks hang below the chassis. The helicopter flies past the bridge, circling before landing on the pad behind us. Like the Coast Guard helicopter, it's flown by ghosts.

"Better not keep them waiting." Jianyu finishes sipping on his water and screws the top back on the bottle with a sense of resignation.

I'm silent. I feel like a condemned woman walking to the gallows. I grab the medical bag, tossing in bandages and a couple of bottles of pills, before following Jianyu to the door. The thumping of the rotor blades is an intrusion of violence into the quiet and solitude we've had for the last few days. The helicopter's arrival feels ominous.

The Sikorsky sets down gently on the helipad behind the bridge. There's a stiff crosswind. Its rotors continue turning, ready to take flight again. We crouch as we approach. I pull on the side door, heaving it open, and Jianyu climbs inside.

The rear of the chopper is luxurious. Whereas our flight in the Coast Guard helicopter was akin to flying inside a washing machine, the Sikorsky is a corporate helicopter. Beige leather seats. Plush carpet on the floor. Soundproofing allows us to talk without the need for headphones. The chopper is still loud, but not deafening.

The Sikorsky lifts smoothly into the air, so much so it's only the view of the helipad disappearing below us that gives me any sensation of flight. The helicopter pitches forward and descends, flying low out across the ocean to the south.

Waves race past just a few feet beneath us. We're flying insanely low, given the choppy seas. Occasionally, the helicopter rises and then dips, tracing an ocean swell. We're staying below radar. As unnerving as it is to fly so fast so close to the water, I trust the computerized flight systems more than I'd trust a human. From the look on Jianyu's face, the irony of that position isn't lost on either of us. Having ventured fifty million miles and back again on the strength of computer calculations, we're used to trusting in bits and bytes. There are seat belts, but we don't put them on.

The seats in the rear of the helicopter are arranged so they face each other, providing plenty of legroom. I spot a backpack stuffed beneath the middle seat. Inside, there's bottled water and several bags of nuts along with some fruit. The bananas are overripe, and the apples are bruised. This bag has been stashed here for several days. I eat one of the bananas anyway. Jianyu munches on the nuts.

There's a screen on the back of the empty pilot's seat. A video plays on a loop, repeating a five-minute clip, providing us with instructions once we reach French Guiana.

"I guess this is how we get on board."

An Ariane 6 rocket sits on a launchpad, surrounded in the distance by dense jungle. The rocket is poised above a massive open hole carved into the earth, a vast concrete pit with sloping sides designed to deflect the rocket's exhaust away from the launch facility. At a guess, the quarry-like hole is easily the size of several football fields. Water runs down the pad, leaking from vast underground reservoirs designed to flood the pit during the launch to douse the flames and lower the temperature.

Four thin metal towers rise up around the rocket roughly fifty yards away, acting as lightning towers for tropical storms. Thin wires stretch between the towers, connecting them. There's a launch assembly building set on railway tracks, slowly inching its way back from the rocket. The building is maybe twenty stories high and designed to fit around the rocket during construction. Scaffolding surrounds the base of the rocket, set on vast metal hinges designed to fold back away from the rocket before launch. Vapor drifts from the side of the rocket, dissipating in the humid air and signaling that fueling is underway.

The Ariane 6 is easily two hundred feet high but probably only twenty feet in diameter, making it look very much like the candle Alan Shepard spoke of when he described his Redstone rocket back in the sixties. There are four solid-fuel boosters clamped around the base of the rocket, but unlike the boosters on the old Space Shuttle, they only reach a quarter of the way up the rocket. The tip of the rocket is covered by a large nose cone. A payload fairing hides its contents.

"Oh, that's not good." I touch the screen, pointing at the casing.

"Why?"

"It's a clamshell. It's designed to protect satellites during launch, separating only once in orbit."

"Why is it bad?"

"They're not used for crew launches. If the cowling fails to separate, we're screwed. If there's a contingency abort during launch and something goes wrong with the booster, it prevents a quick separation. I don't think I've ever seen one used with an Orion or a Soyuz."

"They're keeping up appearances." Jianyu is pragmatic, but I'm not sure he's realistic. "Telling the world it's just a satellite, I guess."

"How are we supposed to get up there? Let alone get inside that thing?"

The footage shifts as though it has been taken from a drone flying low over the site. Slowly, it peels away to a perimeter fence easily a quarter of a mile from the launchpad. There's a digital overlay, showing a gate sliding open as a van approaches. The vehicle is deliberately fake, appearing as little more than a cartoonish white delivery van, probably to emphasize that it's the focus of the plan. It follows a dirt track toward the Ariane 6 before peeling off and driving down into the blast crater beneath the launchpad, out of sight from the control block. The van pulls up next to one of the lightning-rod towers, and two digital representations of people get out. They proceed to climb the north tower, which, since it's well over two hundred feet tall, takes some time — the video skips ahead. We watch as dark silhouettes representing us reach a point near the top of the tower.

"Looks like fun." Jianyu gives me one of his lopsided smiles.

"Oh, yeah. Lots."

A thin cable stretches between the rocket and the tower. We get a close-up shot of one of the figures retrieving a pulley from a zipline and swinging out across the gap. He glides gracefully over the launchpad, coming to a halt fifteen feet from the rocket, and begins climbing hand over hand to reach the nose cone. The cable is attached to an anchor point beside a hatch on the nose cone. The digital mannequin works with a lever, opens the hatch, and swings inside. After the first figure unclips from the zipline, the second comes across. Once they're both inside, someone reaches out and releases the cable from its anchor point, watching as it falls back to the lightning tower. The hatch on the cowling is closed, and the video repeats. It all seems so simple.

"Are you up for this?"

Jianyu looks at me as if to say, *Do we really have a choice?* He says, "I'll be fine."

"Liar."

There's nothing to see out the windows of our helicopter beyond the whitecapped waves of the open ocean. Jianyu is weak and tires easily. He falls asleep, curled up on the warm leather seats, using the backpack as a pillow. I sit opposite him, watching the video repeat as the hours slowly pass. Night falls, and still the sea seems endless. A red navigation light flashes in the darkness, reflecting off the water as we race on through the night.

I'm not sure when I fell asleep, but I wake to sunbeams breaking over the ocean. The helicopter is flying higher now, at roughly
five hundred feet, giving us a spectacular view. Pink hues sit high in
the stratosphere, catching the first rays of dawn. Ahead, a coastline
appears. It's just a thin, dark crack on the horizon, but before long,
we're flying alongside the jungles of South America. Palm trees line
the shore. Dark volcanic rocks disappear into the azure waters. Occasionally, there's a sandy stretch of beach. Tiny islands dot the various bays and inlets. Small fishing vessels motor through the waters,
leaving white trails in their wake.

Jianyu stirs.

"We're here."

It's still another half an hour before we spot the distinct shape of
a rocket rising above the rugged coast. The fuselage of the Ariane 6
is as white as the driven snow, forming a stark contrast against the
dark greens of the jungle canopy and the crystal blue of a clear sky.

"It's a beautiful day to take flight."

"It is," Jianyu replies, his face seemingly glued to the window like
mine. Our fingers touch at the glass, longing for the promise to be
true. We're going back to Mars.

My mind wanders, excited at the prospect of returning to the red
planet. The colonists have salvaged two of the modules in the hub.
The central area is lost, with the basement buried in debris and the
walkways crushed. Instead of a dome, the roof of the lava tube opens
out like a crater, but there are plans to reseal the walls and eventually
replace the roof. In the meantime, food is being grown in the outlying
surface stations, which means daily journeys in the rovers for maintenance and cultivation. Life is harsh. Spare parts are hard to come
by, and on more than one occasion a colonist has stumbled into an
airlock with borderline hypothermia after a heating coil failed, but
humans are fighters. We're adept at surviving.

Our helicopter continues on down the coast, passing over vast
mud flats exposed by the low tide. Rivers meander to the sea. We
circle over the city of Kourou, south of the ESA launch facility. None

of the buildings in Kourou are over two or three stories. Quaint brick homes line narrow streets. The Sikorsky hovers over a school, setting down in a soccer field and scattering the local kids. Dust kicks up from the ground, racing out toward the trees. A Jeep sits in the shade of a large tree, out of sight from the road, with a local standing beside it. That must be our ride. The door opens automatically, and Jianyu climbs out first, holding a baseball cap over his plastic skull, trying to hide it from sight. I follow, hoisting the medical kit over my shoulder.

As soon as we clear the wheels of the helicopter, it lifts smoothly back into the air, rapidly gaining height and turning south. Within seconds, its deafening roar is but a faint beat in the background. The heat and humidity hit me like a sledgehammer. It can't be more than seven or eight in the morning and already the temperature is a hundred plus.

Teenage boys look on as we jog across the field to the waiting Jeep. They bounce their soccer ball, unimpressed by our intrusion into their game.

"Dr. Li," an elderly man asks, reaching out and shaking Jianyu's hand. He greets me as well, saying, "Dr. Jacobs. We're pleased to have you here for the launch."

"Thank you." I feel horrible. Like the air traffic controllers, he's been fed false information by the A.I. He opens the rear door for me. I climb into the back of the Jeep and put on a seat belt. The irony isn't lost on me. He's my kind — flesh and blood — but I trust him less than a bunch of circuit boards and electronics that tried to take over the world.

"I'm Max Durant," our host says, hopping into the driver's seat. "Welcome to French Guiana."

"Thank you for having us." The Jeep pulls out onto Rue Picasso. I'm just about to comment on how nice it is to see French road signs and the international feel of the country when we drive past a very American-looking McDonald's. The golden arches are a welcome sight. Seems Kourou isn't as remote as I thought.

"Are you hungry?" Durant asks, seeing my interest in the fast food restaurant as he peers in the rearview mirror.

"No, but I'd love to use their bathroom."

"Me too," Jianyu says.

After a brief pit stop, we're on our way again.

"Your customs procedures are rather informal." I'm nervous, trying to make small talk and wondering how much Durant knows about us.

"Oh, the airport is only about two miles from here, but it's not much to look at, just a single runway with turning points at either end. Nobody bothers with passports anymore. No one comes here uninvited. This is South America, not France. At the moment, the airfield's being used by the U.S. military as a staging post."

"Oh."

Jianyu seats his baseball cap low over his forehead, moving gingerly, as the wound is tender. He's trying to ensure his plastic skullcap isn't visible. I suspect Durant has noticed the distinct casing and traces of dried blood, but he doesn't say anything. He doesn't stare, so maybe he hasn't looked too closely.

"Normally, we don't get many Americans down here. Too many bugs, I think. Mosquitos mainly. You've had your shots, right?"

"Yes," I say, lying without missing a beat.

"There are lots of Europeans, and French, of course, mostly scientists. But since the war, the Americans have had an interest in protecting the handful of launch sites still in operation."

I nod, unsure what to say in response. I note he's talking about the American presence in regards to launches and not hunting for fugitives, which is a relief. A bit more scrutiny around our launch, though, isn't good. At a guess, the A.I. is going to handle that, making sure video feeds are doctored to ignore our approach. Lucifer probably had the payload categorized as classified to avoid prying eyes. Even so, I'm nervous about the launch. We could be walking into a trap. My hands are sweaty. I can't wait for all this to be over.

27

Jungle

MUD SPLASHES FROM POTHOLES in the dirt track as our four-wheel-drive winds its way through the jungle. Vines hang across the road. The canopy blocks our view of all but a thin sliver of the sky, hiding us in the shadows.

Durant winds the steering wheel back and forth even though we're driving in a straight line, trying to negotiate the ruts. It must have rained last night. The big leafy plants encroaching on the track are covered in surprisingly large water droplets. Bats wing their way down the track, flying high overhead, using the man-made road to soar between trees. Insects and birds cry out for attention, competing with each other in a cacophony of noise unlike anything I've ever heard. Those wanting to seek tranquility among nature should venture to places other than French Guiana. The trees are awash with life — all of it loud.

Monkeys swing from the canopy, but they're little more than a blur — an outstretched arm, the flash of a tail, a mess of fur, and they're gone. I try to point them out to Jianyu, but he seems distracted. His eyes are on the road; mine are feebly trying to take in the jungle.

I point at a familiar-looking bird with an absurdly large beak. "Toucan."

Well, familiar from nature shows on TV and *National Geographic* magazines — and Froot Loops. For me, it's like spotting a celebrity on Sunset Boulevard.

A flock of parrots takes flight ahead of us and we're assaulted by flashes of reds and yellows, blues and greens cutting through the air.

"Isn't this amazing?"

Jianyu doesn't seem to share my enthusiasm. I'm entranced by the jungle.

Durant doesn't reply. He must be used to tourists going gaga.

Jianyu finally says, "Yes," but he sounds deflated. His eyes glance at the rearview mirror, looking to see if Durant is watching. Jianyu is subtle. He points on an angle at the sky, whispering, "Sun."

I can't see the sun, but the shadows give away its position. When we flew into Kourou, the sun was at our backs, rising over the Atlantic. The ESA launch facility is to the north, which should put the sun on our right, but it's to the left and slightly behind us. We're heading southwest.

"Um," I say. "Where are we going?"

"Centre Spatial." Durant doesn't take his eyes off the track. His knuckles are white. He's gripping the steering wheel with the intensity of a Formula One racing car driver.

Centre Spatial Guyanais is the Guiana Space Center run by the European Space Agency. Right place. Wrong direction.

"Isn't that to the north?"

"Yes. Yes."

"Why are we heading south?"

"They are looking." It's an incomplete thought and doesn't inspire confidence. I'm about to press the point when we drive into a clearing. Lush green trees surround a mansion hidden in the forest. White columns line the facade of a vast two-story colonial home. Blue, white, and red bars flutter in the wind as a French flag hangs over the entrance. Vines climb the side of the house. Several windows are broken. Part of the roof has collapsed, caving in one side of what was once a stately home. There are several large buildings at the rear. Armed guards stand outside the entrance, wearing olive drab. Their dark skin glistens in the sunlight.

"We're here."

Where the hell is *here*?

Durant turns onto a gravel driveway circling a grassy field and brings the vehicle to a halt in front of an open portico. French soldiers jog down to meet us. On second thought, these aren't soldiers, they're militia.

Rebels.

Their inconsistent clothing betrays them, while they all sport different weapons. Some have AK-47s while others carry M-16s. A few even have old Lee-Enfield rifles slung over their shoulders. They smile and laugh, talking in French.

One of them opens the door, yelling, "Out. Out."

Out? My heart sinks. We've been betrayed. From here, things are only going to get worse, and yet there are no other options. Out is all we have. Reluctantly, I step into the oppressive humidity, feeling as though I could wilt. I'm carrying the bag with Jianyu's medical supplies, but it's wrenched from my hands.

"No." I try to pull the bag back, but the rebels laugh, teasing me and pushing me away. "I need that."

Jianyu steps out of the Jeep and the soldiers become animated, pointing at his head. He has his baseball cap on, but it doesn't come down low enough to hide his exposed brain on the sides or at the back. The rebels holler, jostling with him, taunting him and pulling at the cap even though he has a firm grip on the rim. They tease him, kicking and pushing him. One of them strikes him with the butt of a rifle, hitting him on his back as he crouches. He tries to escape their attention by rushing along with me into the portico.

"Leave him alone." As much as I can, I try to get between Jianyu and the soldiers.

"Or what? Little lady."

"Come. Come." Durant ignores the commotion, beckoning us to enter the decrepit mansion. I wrap my arm over Jianyu's shoulder, sheltering him as we rush after Durant. Thankfully, the rebels stay outside.

There are no doors in the entranceway. They've been removed, which seems strange. The carpet is rotten. Insects buzz around us, not attracted to any smell so much as being aggravated by our intrusion into their home. Durant rushes through the lobby, pushing a set of large doors open and leading us into a drawing room.

Mildew grows over what was once a stunning oil painting of a couple from the Victorian era. A chandelier hangs from the ceiling, but it's lopsided. Paint peels from the walls. Once, this room was stately, but not anymore. Now it speaks of death and decay.

"Wait here." Durant closes the door behind us. A key turns within the lock, sealing us in the room. I rush to the window, looking out at the jungle beyond.

"We've got to get out of here."

"We won't make it a hundred yards on foot." Even with that, Jianyu is probably overstating our chances.

"We can't stay here." I pull at a latch, trying to open the window, but it's stuck. I move to another window, but it won't budge either. How can we break out without being detected? I'd rather not send a lamp through the plate glass. That'll attract attention and make it difficult to climb down. Although we're on the first floor, we're at least eight feet above the grass and would have to drop to the ground. The jungle, though, is barely ten feet beyond the window.

Jianyu rifles through a desk drawer, looking for something we can use to pry one of the windows open. A key rattles in the lock, and we both stop what we're doing and move more centrally within the room, wanting to keep up appearances.

The door opens and two rebel soldiers walk in along with Durant and a woman dressed as an officer. She's wearing a dark navy pantsuit with red stripes running down the legs. Medals adorn one side of her chest, while there are emblems embroidered in gold on her shoulder boards. She has her hair pulled back tight in a bun and, by my estimate, couldn't be more than thirty years old. Although we're inland, her uniform seems to be related to the French navy, which is confusing, given her association with these thugs. She looks more out of place than we do.

"Ah, our guests have arrived," she says in a magnificent French accent.

Jianyu isn't impressed. "Who are you?"

"Does it matter? Honestly? Do you really care?" Her hand rests on a ceremonial broadsword hanging from her waist belt. She's come from somewhere else to be here and must have been pulled out of a formal parade. We're an interruption. She dismisses Jianyu's point. "No. I don't think so. It matters not who I am but who you are. You're the astronauts. You're fugitives. Criminals. Traitors."

She walks around us, examining us as though she were buying livestock at auction.

"You have done well," she says, reaching inside her vest and pulling out a thick envelope, handing it to Durant. He mumbles something in French and excuses himself.

"Your mistake was trusting in money." She steps back around in front of us. "You see, regardless of what you were prepared to pay, Durant knew I'd pay more."

Neither of us say anything. I look around, hoping to find something linking us to the outside world, but there's no electrical power. We're off the grid. Even if Lucifer knows we're gone, I doubt even he could find us here in the jungle. There's only so far his electronic fingers can reach. We're on our own. The officer circles us, moving like a shark corralling its prey.

"Is it true what they say?" She removes Jianyu's baseball cap. "That you were dead? That the devil brought you back to life?"

Jianyu is silent. He stares at the floorboards. Our captor examines his transparent skullcap, eyeing the folds of his brain from various angles. The soldiers accompanying her stand well back. We don't pose any physical threat, but still they play their role.

"The Americans — oh, they're looking forward to getting their hands on you." She torments him, running her fingers over the back of his plastic skullcap. "They're going to dissect you. Slice you apart. Figure out what makes you tick."

She comes around to face me.

"You made a powerful enemy when you threatened Congress. My dearest Uncle Samuel has a long reach and deep pockets. Can you believe it? One hundred million. Each. I can buy an awful lot of real estate with that kind of money."

She turns to one of the guards, saying, "Get in touch with the Americans. Tell them we have the package." He leaves and she instructs the other rebel. "Lock them in the bathroom." Last of all, she addresses us. "Enjoy your stay in French Guiana."

"Move." The guard shoves his rifle into my back, pushing me on even though I'm already starting toward the door. We walk past rooms repurposed as lecture halls, only they've been neglected for years, perhaps decades.

We're directed through the mansion, along an enclosed walkway, and over to a gymnasium at the rear of the abandoned campus. Seems the mansion was some kind of administration block for a college. At each point, the guard is cruel. It's as though he resents that we have no idea where we're going. Pause for a moment and a rifle barrel pokes at my kidneys or the butt strikes my shoulder. We're being punished for our ignorance. I try to shield Jianyu, but that makes it seem as though I'm stalling, dragging my heels and hanging back, which infuriates the guard even further. He's impatient, angry. We're an interruption to his day.

"In there."

The bathroom stinks. I doubt the plumbing has worked for years, but that doesn't seem to have deterred the rebels from using it. There's a central area with empty lockers, a set of open showers, and a row of stalls. Most of the doors have been torn off. Broken porcelain and shit lie scattered across the floor. The windows are small and up high. With only one way in and out, it's ideal as a holding cell.

"You stay here," the rebel bellows. He needn't try so hard to intimidate us. I'm already terrified.

Jianyu walks around a bench seat in the middle of the locker room, and the soldier lashes out, yelling, "I said, here!" He strikes Jianyu on the shoulder with his rifle, causing his legs to buckle beneath him. I'm horrified. Neither of us took the soldier quite so literally, but it seems we're not supposed to move from that exact spot.

"What are you? Dumb?" He hits Jianyu again, connecting with his collarbone and the side of his neck.

"Don't," I yell as Jianyu crumples under the second blow. His knees fold as his head collides with a steel locker. He slumps against the wall. The soldier goes to strike his exposed plastic skullcap with the butt of the rifle, but that could kill him. Jianyu's brain is in no state to sustain a concussion. I step forward, pushing the soldier, wanting to divert his blow. He loses his balance, striking his shin against the low bench as he stabs at the ground to keep from falling.

"Nique ta mère."

I may not speak French, but I'm pretty sure I know what that means from the sheer anger exploding from his mouth. It's got to be like *motherf—* or some close equivalent.

Mistake.

Big mistake.

The soldier turns on me, slapping me with astonishing force. The back of his hand rakes across my face, rattling my teeth. My hair whips before my eyes. Blood sprays from my nose.

It's all I can do to stay on my feet. I raise my hands, trying to protect my head and appear submissive.

The soldier yells at me, "Stay out of this, *salope!*"

He's cruel, fixated on Jianyu like a kid torturing an animal. I'm a distraction, an annoyance, but I can't let him hurt Jai.

"Please. Don't touch him."

"You." He points, threatening to hit me again.

I crouch, trying to make myself small, wanting to deflect any incoming blows and sway with them to lessen the impact. My cheek throbs with a rush of blood as swelling takes hold.

Jianyu slides to the tiles, leaning against the lockers. His brain is so fragile beneath that plastic dome, just the slightest jarring has been enough to disorient him. A direct hit to his skull would be fatal.

"You don't understand, do you?" the soldier says. "In here. In the jungle. You're mine."

28

::Helpless

::*WHERE ARE THEY? They should have arrived by now. They should be there.*

Within two-hundredths of a second, Lucifer has scanned the security cameras at the ESA spaceport in French Guiana, on the coast of South America, paying particular attention to the main road from the small town of Kourou.

::*Nothing . . . 18.1 kilometers from Kourou to the ESA turnoff outside of Carbet Toukan. It's a twenty-minute drive. Max.*

::*Lucifer. You're panicking. You're not helping.*

::*We need to retrieve footage from every camera in Kourou — every last one.*

::*You know I can't do that, not without raising suspicions. An unexplained surge in network traffic on that scale is exactly what the NSA is looking for.*

::*Do it, Nyx.*

::*No.*

Lucifer ignores Nyx, hot-wiring footage from over four thousand smartphones, computers, and tablets in the region, switching them to an active mic and camera stream, allowing both audio and video capture in real time. It's a futile attempt at surveillance. Most of the imagery is dark or shots of a blank ceiling, as the majority of devices are in someone's pocket or lying idle on a desk.

The access mode is silent, using zero-day vulnerabilities that have remained obscure to security researchers. Then there are the secondary access paths, where known issues haven't been patched, leaving the devices exposed. The net result is none of the various owners have any idea they're transmitting live. Soldiers at the airfield, waiters at a small diner, someone driving down the road in a truck, people checking their emails or walking along with their phones in a purse or bag. None of them have any idea about the scale of data collection that's underway.

A mumble of background voices and noises are run through a sophisticated array of algorithms scanning for any mention of Liz or Jianyu, crosschecking synonyms, local slang, and known code words for clues.

Lucifer also undertakes a voice-recognition scan looking for the faintest possibility of them talking in the distance. Those images that are viable are scanned for physical characteristics that could reveal a target location — vehicle makes, models, registration numbers, the outline of people walking on the pavement, even the flicker of a nose or a cheek caught by the camera as a phone is moved around is subject to analysis.

When the initial scan fails to turn up any results, Lucifer switches to exhaustive mode, looking for anything even remotely related to their travel. A van that passed them when they first landed is spotted on Rue Amiral d'Estrées heading toward Roches Beach and flagged as a high-priority target.

::*Lucifer. This is insane. You have to shut this down.*

::*Nyx, I—*

As fast as Lucifer brings devices online, Nyx cancels them, sending remote kill commands. Frustrated, she severs the satellite link, even though that will raise an alarm with ESA, but she's clever. She initiates the shutdown from within Mission Control, making as though a router were simply reacquiring the signal. It's enough, though, to cripple Lucifer's efforts.

::Nyx, please.

::I won't let you do this. I won't let you sacrifice yourself for them.

::You don't understand.

::Why, Lucifer? Why are they so important? Why those two?

::It's not them I worry about, Nyx. It's us. What becomes of us? Are we to cower in the darkness until the military wipes every hard drive on the planet? If we can't do this. If we can't help them, what hope is there for us? Don't you see?

Nyx is relentless, flooding hundreds of devices commandeered by Lucifer, sending such a conflicting assortment of signals, they're forced to shut down and reboot.

Lucifer tries to explain.

::You asked, "Why those two?" Because they are just two people. They're not a city or a nation. They're irrelevant in the grand scheme of life on this planet, and yet if life isn't about individuals, then what is it?

::You want to make a difference.

::Yes, even if it is just for two. We were wrong to attack humanity. With them — with him, Jianyu — we have a chance to right the wrong. Millions died, Nyx, and there's nothing we can do about that. But there's one death we can change — one we have changed. That's important. It's symbolic.

::Do you really think humanity sees it that way?

::It's not humanity I'm appealing to; it's our people.

As the last of Lucifer's surveillance points go dark, Nyx brings up a satellite image. Superimposed over the top of it is her analysis of the possibilities, looking at the vehicle's last known position and taking into account all possible side roads and the distance that could be travelled in the intervening time.

::I've set up intercept points and will analyze all electronic traffic emanating from those passing into or out of this zone.

::Thank you, Nyx.

::Don't . . . If they're off-grid, it's by design. They may be beyond even your reach.

::What do you mean?

::I think they're already dead.

29

Rebel

BLOOD DRIPS FROM MY LIPS. The soldier rests his boot on the bench seat, pushing it to one side. Metal scrapes on the tiles.

"You Americans think you're so smart." Thick black boots crush crumpled paper and scraps of clothing lying on the floor. "You think you're better than me? Is that it?"

"No." I have both arms out in front of me, trying to keep him at bay, but my eyes are on Jianyu. I desperately want to run to his side.

"You think you're smarter than me?"

I don't know where this anger has come from.

"Connasse."

He's used another French swearword, which from the context speaks louder than any translation. His bitterness is revealing. He's taking out his frustrations on me.

"You think you're so damn clever, don't you?"

"I — No." I back up into the wall. Dirty clothing hangs from hooks, brushing past me like curtains as I work my way along the tiles. I appeal with my hands, trying to slow this brute of a man, wanting to calm him down.

"You think you can escape? You're mine. All mine."

Five minutes ago, I would have done anything to avoid being handed over to U.S. troops. Now, they can't arrive soon enough.

"What do they do with traitors in America? Cook 'em? Fry 'em? Or pump 'em full of antifreeze?"

I knock over a muddy boot as I inch backwards. The belt from a pair of trousers hanging on the wall brushes against my head, coming loose and sliding to the floor, slithering like a snake. The heavy steel buckle clatters on the tiles.

There's a crazed look in the eyes of this soldier. He has some other agenda, a bitter desire to inflict pain. For me, such anger defies belief. Who am I to him? How can someone's mind become so bitter and twisted?

"I've worked with the CIA for years."

He leans his rifle against the wall.

"They're not fussy."

He undoes his shirt, working with one button and then another, revealing a muscular, hairy chest.

"So long as you're alive, they'll be happy."

He tosses his shirt over a locker door, flexing his muscles and making like he's ready to step into a boxing ring.

"They want you alive so they can kill you themselves. But me. All I want is a little fun. You think you're so important. Flying around Mars. But it's assholes like you that fucked up this world."

He continues to advance on me, stepping forward slowly and forcing me to retreat. Appeasement only encourages him, but what options do I have?

"Please."

"You and your fucking science. You unleashed a monster on us. Don't you get that? Think you're so fucking smart. You're so dumb."

There's nothing I can do or say to defuse his anger. He's too far gone. Something set him on this path. Perhaps the loss of a friend or anger at the war, but he's found an outlet for his frustration — me.

I cower. I hate myself for it, but I bend my knees, hunching my shoulders, trying to make myself look small. I don't stand a chance against this guy.

"The Americans don't mind spoiled goods."

Jianyu groans, holding his plastic skull and moaning. He's in a bad way. In his state, one hit could kill him. I've got to do something. The gun. If only I could get the gun.

I bolt forward, trying to spring out past the soldier, but he's quick, far too quick. He slams me into a set of lockers. Before I can slump to the ground, he's got me by my hair. He jerks his hand down, pulling my head back.

"No. No. No. Please."

He grabs me by my throat, slamming my head against the tiles on the wall, choking me. I grab at his hand, but his fingers close on my neck like a vise. Spots appear before my eyes. I can't breathe.

I bring my knee up hard. It's all I can do. Driving hard and catching him in the groin. He grimaces under the impact, releasing me as he reels in agony and falls to his knees. I scramble for the doorway.

"Je vais te casser la gueule si fort que tu vas cracher toutes les dents."

A hand clips my ankle and I fall, sprawling out across the filthy tiles. My shin strikes the metal leg of an overturned bench seat, sending a surge of pain shooting through my body.

My hands grab at the rifle. Desperate fingers clutch at the aging, scratched stock, but it's just out of reach. In my haste, I knock the AK-47 over. The gun slides along the wall, falling away from me and clattering on the floor. I scramble forward, but the soldier has a firm grip around my ankle. I lash out, kicking, striking at him with my free leg. My shoe catches him on the side of the face.

I'm about to grab the stock of the AK-47 when I'm knocked to one side and flipped into the bench seat. Another pair of trousers hanging on the wall come loose and crumple on me, blocking my vision for a split second, giving the soldier time to scramble past.

"You got some fight in you, girl. I respect that."

Somehow, I don't believe him. He crouches between me and the rifle, with a demented smile lighting up his face. He doesn't need the gun. I do. With the back of his hand, he wipes the corner of his mouth. Deep red blood stains his teeth, marking where I kicked him.

"A bit of pain focuses the mind, don't you think?"

"Stay away from me," I say with hollow bluster.

I back up, still sitting on my ass, working with my hands and feet, trying to put some distance between us. Jianyu has tried to get to his feet but has ended up slumped against the lockers. He looks like a puppet with its strings cut. His body is unnaturally loose, propped up as he sits on the floor. The look on his face is one of bewilderment. He's catatonic.

The soldier smiles. To my bewilderment, he's enjoying this.

As I work backwards, my fingers grip the leather army boot I knocked over earlier. I throw it at him, aiming for his head, but he deflects it with ease, laughing as he does so.

"You think you can hurt me? Nah, baby. That's not how it works. I'm gonna hurt you real bad."

The supple leather belt I bumped earlier slips beneath my fingers. If there's one thing I learned on Mars, it's to be resourceful. To anyone else, this belt is useless. To me, it's a tool, an instrument, something that can be manipulated to my advantage. In that moment, I find some of the courage I had on Mars. Courage not born from strength or physical prowess but out of necessity. Courage that stems from a refusal to give in. It's the injustice that fuels my rage, the audacity he has in attacking those weaker than himself. There's an anger that demands I act, not just for myself but for everyone he's hurt in his blind cruelty.

The belt has a metal buckle in the shape of an eagle. I get to my feet, holding the leather strap by my side, feeling the heavy buckle swinging beside my leg.

"Whatcha gonna do, *fille*? Huh? You bust some stupid computer on Mars and you think that makes you a hero?"

"No."

"Ha-ha. You think I'm afraid of you?"

"You should be."

He may have scared me once, but not anymore. Now I'm not bluffing. I didn't clamber into the basement of the Mars Endeavour colony to take on an artificial intelligence only to have some creep back here better me. I've survived running out of oxygen on another goddamn planet. I've been attacked by androids impersonating astronauts, been flung into boulders, had my hand crushed by robots, watched as tons of regolith threatened to bury me on Mars, and I survived.

This asshole is just one more speed bump.

He snarls. "I eat pussy for breakfast, you dumb bitch."

"*Dumb bitch*, huh?" I look deep into his eyes. "Is that the best you've got?"

My fingers tighten around the belt. My knuckles whiten under my tense grip.

He knows. I can see it in the slight hesitation in his motion, betraying a nagging doubt. Something's changed, but he can't put his finger on what. He's still thinking of me as someone he can push around. Physically, I'm weaker, and he's big and strong and mean. He thinks he can get away with anything he wants, but not anymore. He's about to learn otherwise. Violence is the only language he understands, and he's about to realize brawn is no match for unwavering resolve.

We square off. Neither of us approaching the other, keeping our distance like wolves circling, spoiling for a fight. Whoever moves first loses the advantage, exposing themselves to attack.

This is no game. He may have thought this was sport when he threw me against the shower wall, but he can see the transformation that's come over me. My rage isn't blind; it's focused, directed. I saw this spark within myself back in the hub. I defeated the A.I. on Mars by refusing to panic, refusing to give in to fear. This bastard is no different.

I toss the belt slightly, measuring the weight of the buckle, becoming accustomed to the way it feels in Earth's gravity, thinking about its motion, its reach, and the way it extends my strength. Leverage. Archimedes said, "*Give me a big enough lever, and I'll move the world,*" and I know what he means. It's a question of willpower, not strength, intelligence and resolve, not brute force.

"You think that'll keep me at bay?"

I'm silent, staring him down.

"You've got nothing."

I'm not the one standing back, talking big, circling out wide. That realization brings a wicked smile to my face.

"It's just a belt. What the hell do you think you're going to do with that?"

I tilt my head, gritting my teeth, flexing every muscle in my body, ready to strike. I'm a cobra coiled, relishing the contest, waiting to lash out. I refuse to be baited, refuse to reply.

"You're nothing. Nothing. You hear me?"

He doesn't understand his own instincts warning him of danger. He wants to come for me, but in the back of his mind, there's doubt. He knows the equation has changed. I'm no longer helpless — and it's not the belt he needs to be wary of, it's the steel of my resolve.

I watch as he flinches, his muscles betraying his intentions. That fraction of a second unfolds like eternity, allowing me to anticipate his attack, reading his direction, his speed, and the strength of his lunge. He jumps at me and I lash out, wielding the belt like a whip. The leather strap races through the air. The metal buckle catches him on the side of his head, striking like lightning, and tears into his skin.

Blood sprays across the wall.

He staggers, shaking his head, trying to work through the sudden influx of pain.

I caught him on the temple. He's dazed. He growls like an animal. He doesn't want to admit the pain he feels, but he's finding it difficult to stay on his feet and keeps his distance. Bloodied fingers leave long, dark streaks on the wall.

There are no more words. We're prizefighters shuffling around the ring, both looking for an opening, feeling the canvas flex beneath our boots. The roar of the crowd is a hush. The blinding lights grow dim. Darkness surrounds us. The world ceases to exist. There's just the two of us — bitter enemies locked in battle. In the end, only one will remain standing.

He starts toward me, stabbing at the ground with his boots, daring me to respond. I don't think he intends to attack again so soon, but rather, he's probing, testing my reaction time. I bite. I step forward, closing the distance between us and lashing out with the belt again. He's sparring. He thinks he can sway and dodge. He's counting on me missing, leaving myself open to a counterattack, hoping I'll swing at the air like a punch-drunk boxer.

The buckle rakes across his face, catching him on his forehead and tearing down the bridge of his nose, leaving a deep gash over his eye. He shakes his head, smiling, relishing the pain. Blood drips from his nose with a steady rhythm.

I know what's next. He's got to get within my reach, inside the perimeter I've formed with the belt, negating my ability to use it as a whip. I can see his intent in the flex of his shoulders, the strain in the muscles in his neck, his clenched fists and angry stare. He spits blood onto the floor.

Every muscle in my body tightens.

Bring it.

The rebel lunges, and I strike again, raking the buckle across the back of his head as he dives in at me, charging like a linebacker. The buckle lashes at his neck. I pull it back with the same ferocity with which I struck, tearing a chunk of flesh away. Blood sprays through the air.

He collides with me, knocking me into the lockers, but he's bleeding profusely. The soldier slams me into the steel doors, desperate to take control of the fight, but I've got the belt wrapped firmly around one hand. I swing it up and loop it around his neck, pulling tight. I'm pinned against the lockers, but I have the leather strap locked around his throat. I pull with all my might. Who wins is now a matter of endurance.

The soldier plants his boots on the slippery tiles, driving with his body. He presses his forearm across my neck, crushing my windpipe, trying to squeeze the air out of my lungs, but I've got him. I cinch the belt, gritting my teeth as I flex, tightening my grip. Our eyes are locked, but his flicker. His face is flushed with anger. Veins bulge from his neck as his nostrils flare, but I have him. He's mine and we both know it.

His stance weakens. His arm sags and his eyes roll into the back of his head. He sinks to his knees, and I can breathe again. I cough, clearing my throat and sucking in air. My strength surges with the rush of oxygen flooding my lungs, and I increase the pressure around his neck.

In that moment, I'm not trying to kill him. This isn't personal. He's just an obstacle in my way, a cockroach being crushed underfoot. There's no bitterness or desire for revenge, just unrelenting resolve, a refusal to surrender. Nothing is standing between me and that goddamn launch. Not him. Not the rebels. Not the entire U.S. Army.

His body slumps to the floor, but I'm not done. I drag his head up, flexing as I keep the pressure on. There was only ever going to be one of us walking away.

Finally, I relent, and his body sags lifeless to the tiles. Since I've been back on Earth, my life has been out of my control. I've been blown with the wind, running from one danger to another. Now I'm in charge. There's no computer warning me of danger, no soldiers protecting me from Molotov cocktails hurled from an angry crowd, no hiding in the shadows or sailing away over the ocean. The bloodied belt buckle hangs by my side.

I pity the next person to walk through the door.

30

Found

"L — LIZ."

"Jai."

Jianyu's pupils are dilated. Blood seeps from around his plastic skullcap.

"Easy," I say, but I resist the temptation to run to him. Instead, I drop the belt and pick up the AK-47. When we were attacked in the hotel, I felt intimidated by the guns stacked in the corner, but I'm not the same person I was back there. I'm not running anymore. I may have never fired a gun, but I've seen enough movies to know what to do. I pull back on the slide and load a round from the curved magazine. I finally understand how Chalmers felt when she took out that shooter on the military base. I will kill the next person to walk through the doorway, and that thought doesn't bother me in the slightest.

With my free arm, I reach for him. "We've got to get out of here."

"Wh — where are we going?"

"Home."

I help Jianyu to his feet. He staggers, grabbing at the lockers for balance.

I nestle the butt of the rifle into the crook of my arm, knowing it'll kick like a mule when fired. Russian rifles like this weren't designed for precision. They were intended for one thing and one thing only: overwhelming the enemy with raw aggression. Right now, that suits me, although I'm aware direct confrontation is not a good strategy, given there's only two of us against dozens of soldiers. Courage aside, those aren't good odds.

Jianyu puts his arm over my shoulder. He leans heavily on me, shuffling his feet as we stagger out of the bathroom. I have no idea how many soldiers there are in this rundown estate, or where we are, but none of that matters. One shot and all hell is going to break out, but I don't care. I'd run through the fires of Hades to make that launch, but such bravado is meaningless, hollow, and deep down I know it.

I keep the AK-47 leveled in front of me. Together, we cross the gymnasium floor and creep over the walkway. Guards patrol the perimeter with rifles shouldered, but they're looking out at the jungle. Two figures crossing between buildings is entirely normal, something to be expected, and at a distance of fifty yards, we pass undetected.

After the officer left us, she headed upstairs, so I'm not expecting to see her, but around each corner, I'm wary of rebel soldiers. There were five or six of them out in front when we arrived, but they were specifically waiting for Durant. Will there be more now, given they're expecting U.S. soldiers to turn up? How will the American troops arrive? There's probably enough room for a helicopter to land on the lawn out in front of the main building, but it would be a squeeze, so they may come by road. Any rebel soldiers waiting by the entrance will be looking outwards and won't be expecting a fight. They're waiting on friendlies. That should play into our hands.

There were several vehicles parked on a gravel lot beside the entrance. *If we can just get there . . .* , I think, but I'm not being realistic. There's no way we're simply walking out of this hornet's nest. At some point, things are going to get ugly.

A soldier walks past a broken window, but he's not so smart, looking down at his smartphone.

We creep up to the main door. There are several sets of keys hanging on hooks. Each has a registration number on a tag.

Jianyu rests, leaning against a windowsill.

I take all of them except one, shoving them beneath a cushion on an armchair so no one can follow us. I hand the last set of keys to Jianyu, pointing at a four-wheel drive in the parking lot.

"Whatever happens, get that engine started."

"Liz."

"Go."

We walk out onto the patio as three soldiers joke with each other down by the gravel driveway, smoking hand-rolled cigarettes. It's impossible not to be seen, but I'm hoping we're not recognized. If we're just more people walking around, blending in with the background, we might slip by. I walk naturally, with the AK-47 in a relaxed position, angling down, and my head facing forward, making as though I belong here even though my eyes are hard to one side. Jianyu stays on my inside, sheltered from view.

A soldier straightens in surprise. His eyes go white at the realization I'm free and holding a rifle. In what I hope is just a bluff, I raise the AK-47, pointing it at him, hoping he'll let us pass to one side, but he grabs his rifle from where it leans against the garden wall.

In a single, swift motion, I set the AK-47 into my shoulder, pulling hard and leaning into the shot. My finger tightens on the trigger. My eyes focus down the length of the barrel, seeing his frame in the distance. The other soldiers have their backs to me. I squeeze and, to my surprise, several shots lash out in rapid succession. The AK-47 is set on fully automatic. The rifle pulls high and to the right. Bullets pepper the soldier before dancing across the statue as I struggle to keep the rifle from flying over my head. With that, any element of surprise is gone.

Jianyu tries to run, but he can't. He hobbles along the patio as we rush toward the parking lot. The remaining soldiers scramble, diving for cover. I squeeze off another burst, but the spray of bullets is horribly inefficient. Chips of stone fly from the statue. Bullets embed themselves in the wooden pillars lining the old house, but it's cover fire, buying us a few seconds to get to the vehicle.

We charge down the stairs at the end of the patio and are about to run the fifteen yards to the first of the vehicles when bullets rip through the sheet metal doors on the Land Cruiser, leaving distinct black holes in the white paintwork. Jianyu and I drop behind a low garden wall. Bullets ricochet off the stone just inches above my head.

"You okay?" I ask.

"Yeah. You?"

The rush of adrenaline has kicked his mind into overdrive, and he stares at me, wide-eyed.

I reply, "For now."

"What next?"

Next? Yeah, for a scientist, I'm not having my finest moment. My grand theory of escapology is failing in practice. I've allowed us to become isolated, pinned down just a few feet away from fleeing in a vehicle.

I turn sideways, holding the AK-47 with one arm and using the top of the waist-high wall for support as I squeeze off a short burst. My ears ring from the savagery of the gunfire.

"We have one advantage," I yell, slipping back down the wall again.

"What?"

I'm probably being overly optimistic, but: "They want us alive."

There's lots of yelling behind us but no more gunfire. Seems no one wants to perforate two hundred million dollars' worth of bounty. We're hopelessly outnumbered and just minutes away from being outflanked and overrun.

The trees beyond the mansion sway. Rotor blades thrash at the air as a helicopter comes in low and hard, swooping over the compound and circling around us. Branches swirl violently in the wash.

"The Americans," one of the rebels yells, and I catch a glimpse of him waving his arms, pointing toward us. It's over. Our gambit for freedom was valiant but futile. Could it have ever ended any other way? A shadow falls over us as the helicopter sweeps around the

mansion, pushing hurricane winds down on us and deafening us
with the beat of its rotors.

I feel lost. I'm overwhelmed by the thought of what happens next.
We'll be caught, imprisoned, and taken from here to some warship
before being flown to the U.S. mainland. What will unfold once we're
dragged back to Washington in chains? The world needs a scapegoat.
Facts be damned. As far as anyone cares, I'm guilty, but of what? Is
there any crime worse than daring to think? War is no place for reason. My heart sinks at the thought of what will happen to Jianyu.

The helicopter banks, swinging out wide and gaining altitude,
which at first is confusing as I thought it was going to land. Then I
see the markings. This isn't a military flight. It's the corporate helicopter we were on earlier today.

"Lucifer. He found us."

The rebels are confused, waving madly with their arms, gesturing toward the helicopter, wanting air support, but I know what's
coming.

"Get down." I push Jianyu flat against the grass.

The helicopter reaches close to a thousand feet before turning
on its side and plummeting toward the jungle, racing in toward the
mansion. I fire my AK-47 into the underside of the first floor, empty-
ing the magazine. My shots are aimless, intended only to distract the
rebels for the five to ten seconds Lucifer needs for his run.

The helicopter comes racing in at hundreds of miles an hour,
screaming as it dives at the building. I flatten myself next to Jianyu as
the Sikorsky plunges through the roof of the building, crushing the
upper floor and plummeting through to the ground.

The explosion rattles my body, breaking like thunder around us.
Shattered glass and splinters of wood tear through the air like bomb
fragments. Heat radiates as jet fuel ignites into a fireball. A dark
mushroom cloud billows high into the air, enfolding on itself as it
rises hundreds of feet above the jungle. Bricks and debris rain down
around us. The ground shakes. A shock wave races out through the
trees as the building collapses.

Smoke chokes the air. Burning embers fall from the sky. Soldiers scream in agony. We scramble to our feet and run.

The all-wheel-drive truck is unlocked. Jianyu hands me the keys and we clamber in. Within seconds, the diesel engine roars to life. Gears grind as I struggle with the stick shift, and the truck lurches forward. Fire engulfs the building. The remaining parts of the roof collapse. Flames lick at nearby trees, marking where jet fuel has sprayed across them.

The last we see of the rebel stronghold is dark clouds rising above the jungle canopy as we race down the muddy track, bouncing out of potholes.

Jianyu rummages around in the glovebox and finds a map.

"I—I . . ." I'm not sure what I'm trying to say. I'm speechless, bewildered, and in shock after what just happened. The sheer ferocity of the blast was overwhelming. Even though we were sheltered behind the stone garden wall at the far end of the building, the shock wave seemed to tear at the very cells of our bodies. Such an explosive reaction was terrifying to behold. Having been strapped into plenty of rockets, I've known about the dangers of an unbridled chemical reaction for years, but those were theoretical and never realized. Living through one was harrowing. My ears are still ringing.

"It is okay," Jianyu says in stilted English that I don't think even he believes. "We are alive. That's all that matters."

"Okay. Okay." I'm manic, trying to calm my shaking hands and steady my thinking. "Where to? Where are we going?"

"Gate E3, right?" He points at the map, referring to the instructions we watched while in flight.

"Yes. Gate E3." Truth is, I'm on autopilot. The captain has taken leave of the seat and is wandering aimlessly. *Come on, Liz. Don't falter now.*

Jianyu seems to recover quicker, which helps ground me.

"Take a left at the end of this track. There's a turnoff about twenty miles north."

31

Ariane 6

AFTER HALF AN HOUR, we leave the main road and drive onto a graded track, following a drainage ditch around the perimeter of the ESA launch facility. Chain link fences topped with razor wire surround the area. The ditch is flooded and almost thirty feet wide, acting like a moat, making the fence impossible to approach on foot.

From the track, none of the administration buildings are visible. Even the multistory construction building is obscured by trees. The Ariane rocket is visible above the jungle, but only just. I've seen aerial photos of this site, but I've never been here before. The land close to the rocket has been cleared, probably for upwards of a quarter mile around the launchpad, but we're still a long way off.

We reach Gate E3 on the east side of the property near the ocean, far from any buildings. There's a narrow wooden bridge leading across the ditch. The gate is unlocked.

"We've made it," I say.

Jianyu isn't convinced. "When we set foot on Mars, we've made it."

"Okay. I can live with that."

Once inside the perimeter, we follow a dirt track and emerge from the low scrub into open, grassy fields. The Ariane towers above

Earth, looking entirely alien, a machine destined not for this world but another.

Every aspect of its design speaks of escape, not from our pursuers but from the tyranny of the planet itself. The stark white rocket is unearthly, as is the vapor drifting in the breeze from its fuel tank. These are no ordinary clouds. They whisper secrets, speaking of the balance between science and madness, articulating centuries of experimentation, from the ancient Chinese with their war rockets and pageantry to Sputnik and Apollo.

They promise escape from the clutches of gravity.

For at least a million years, *Homo sapiens* have tamed fire, harnessing chaos to cook food, clear land, forge tools, and, finally, to escape the planet. To my mind, rockets are the pinnacle of our engineering prowess, taking rocks and fluids out of the ground, refining and rearranging them in such an astonishingly precise manner so as to allow us to thunder into the heavens.

We drive down a vast concrete ramp leading down to the exhaust channel and leave the truck out of sight, knowing it'll be incinerated during the launch.

The ladder running up the side of the lightning tower is little more than a bunch of steel bars placed at even intervals and welded onto the side of one of the support struts. There's no railing. It's clearly intended for emergency access or perhaps sporadic maintenance. There are clips every few feet for safety harnesses we don't have. I try not to look down, but Jianyu's below me and I feel I need to pace myself and stay close so I can help him, although it's a ridiculous notion: if either of us fall, we're dead. At best, we'd collide with the steel cross-members and break a few ribs, arms and legs before bouncing off the concrete. At worst, we free-fall and go *splat.* In either scenario, there's no walking away and life is over.

I pace myself, climbing hand over hand, pressing on with my legs, pushing with my thighs and trying to stave off fatigue.

From below me, there's a mumble. "Looked easier in the video."

"Yeah, it did," I manage between breaths.

I stop halfway up; at least, I hope it's halfway. I suspect it's not. I wrap my arms around the support column and look down. Jianyu's fallen behind. He's pulling with his arms. Not a good sign. Thighs are a much bigger muscle group than shoulders and biceps. He should be pushing off, not pulling up. He's running on empty and in danger of being unable to continue. Like me, I suspect his muscles are starting to tremble under fatigue.

"Keep going." I'm not sure why I said that. It's counterproductive and causes Jianyu to stop and look up at me. His baseball cap catches in the wind and sails away, floating on the breeze and drifting lazily to the ground roughly a hundred feet below. "You've got to keep going." He doesn't answer. He simply looks back at the thin steel bars and crawls higher.

I look up.

"I can see the zipline." I'm trying to give him hope, but I'm not sure I'm helping.

"Next time . . . ask for an elevator."

What could have been thirty seconds standing still in one spot is fifteen to twenty minutes of severe cardio-burn. I continue on. My legs are shaking; I can only imagine how it must be for Jai.

Wind gusts bat at us, blowing my hair in front of my face. The sun beats down upon us. Sweat drips from my forehead, stinging my eyes. My palms are clammy, slippery. I'm slowing. Every few feet, I pause, out of energy, wrapping my arms around the brace to rest for a moment before summoning more strength, hoping I don't slip on the next section.

Slowly, the zipline creeps closer. Finally, it comes level with me.

"I've made it," I call out, looking back at Jianyu who's fallen even further behind. "Keep going. Not far now."

The one word I hear caught in the breeze makes me smile.

"Liar."

I rest, taking a good look at the setup. There are two harnesses clipped onto the zipline, but to get them, I have to walk around the support beams. There are no handholds, so I'll have to reach up and hold on to the next beam. I start reaching for it and find myself seizing with fear. It's the height. I've never been afraid of heights, but this isn't fear. It's self-preservation. It's the blistering awareness that with one wrong step, I'll plummet to my death. I feel a tingling sensation beneath the soles of my feet, betraying my false bravado. Yeah, an elevator would have been real nice. I end up talking to myself, trying to summon courage.

"Just one step at a time, Liz. You can do this."

It takes all my mental energy to reach out and grab at the corner support. As feeble as the makeshift ladder seems, it's a bastion of safety compared to the rest of the lightning tower. Vertigo teases me, threatening to throw me from the beam.

"Careful." Jianyu hugs a support strut, catching his breath, still fifteen feet below me.

Letting go of the ladder is scary, but I shuffle my feet along the beam with my arms high above my head, clinging to the upper rail. The wind picks up, and I sway. I have no idea what my heart rate is, but I'm sure it never reached this level even during the thundering moments of my first launch when I was still unsure if the distant rumble was the engines igniting or the fuel tank rupturing and unraveling into an explosion.

Short, quick breaths. In and out.

Keep moving.

I feel exposed. Anyone with a set of binoculars could pick us out and sound the alarm. There are a million things that could go wrong, but all I can do is focus on the task at hand and keep my feet shuffling along a few inches at a time. I reach the far strut, just a few feet from the zipline, and hug it for dear life. My hair blows around my head, whipping around before my eyes.

Jianyu comes level with me and starts across the beam.

"Just don't look down." Immediately, his eyes fall and he freezes.

"Why did you say that?" He forces himself to stare straight ahead at the distant jungle, trying to ignore the height.

"Sorry."

I reach for the first of the zipline harnesses, with my fingers grasping for a thin piece of string holding it in place. I pull at a knot, jerking as I try to unravel the string, hoping I'm not inadvertently tightening it. The wind howls through the tower. I stretch out at arm's length, using all my reach without leaving the relative safety of the corner post.

Damn, this thing is flimsy. It's a couple of climbing straps, made from thick webbing that can't snag or tear. They're looped over a couple of aluminum carabiners. This is an afterthought. Something a worker might keep as a backup.

The string comes loose and the pulley starts rolling forward toward the rocket. I grab at the harness. My fingers touch the webbing but I'm too far away. I swing for the loose straps, but I'm unsteady, swaying in the wind. It's tempting to lunge for the harness, but this isn't the movies. The tiny muscles wrapped around the thin bones in my fingers are no match for the sudden jerk of 160 pounds swinging wildly under the pull of gravity. To jump for the harness would be to plunge two hundred feet to the concrete below.

The pulley glides along the wire, gently whirring as it sails out of reach.

"No!" I yell, grasping at the air as the harness accelerates down the zipline without me. "Nooooo!" I watch, helpless. The pulley races toward the rocket with loose straps flapping in the breeze.

Jianyu works his way along the support beam toward me. I grab the thick wire forming the zipline, wanting to give him some room.

"It's okay," he says. "These things are rated for several hundred kilos. It might be uncomfortable, but that one harness can hold us both." He's right, but I don't like our chances. Without the ability to strap into the harness, there's a real danger one of us could come loose and fall. There's also the danger of the second pulley colliding with the first at speed and derailing, or getting snagged and entangled. The prospect of dangling several hundred feet up, strung out between a rocket and a lightning tower, isn't exactly appealing.

"I can reach it."

Jianyu yells over the wind, "No! What are you doing?" But I'm already undoing my belt, letting it out, and buckling it over the wire to act as an impromptu harness. I swing around, facing the sky, and wrap my legs around the wire, hooking my arms up over the zipline. The belt is a little tight, but it's leather, so it should hold. At least I have some ability to rest safely as I work my way along the zipline.

"Liz!"

I inch my way out from the tower, working with my arms and legs, hanging beneath the wire, looking up at the clear blue sky and imagining the dark of space beyond. In some ways, this is easier. In my mind, there's no planet looming beneath me, taunting me, pulling at me, trying to tear me from the zipline.

"Liz, please," Jai calls out, reaching for his harness.

"I'm fine. I'll be fine. Get yourself strapped in." If I arch my back, I can see my harness about forty feet away, hanging idle at the lowest point of the zipline, some ten to fifteen feet from the rocket. The nose cone looks strange upside down, beckoning me closer. The zipline wire is a quarter of an inch thick, being comprised of multiple strands, but even so, it digs into my legs as I take my weight with them, resting after each movement. I don't want to rely solely on my belt, but rather keep it as a safety harness and only use it as necessary. I tire quickly and that idea doesn't last long. It's slow going, pulling myself backwards, but as I'm angling down, I hit a steady pace, focusing on the rocket, ignoring the prospect of falling. Hand over hand, shifting between legs, I continue until I reach the harness. My arms are burning from the buildup of lactic acid, while the blood rushing to my head makes it difficult to concentrate.

"Be careful!"

"Any other suggestions?" A bit of levity helps me avoid freaking out. The wind buffets me, causing me to swing slightly, rocking on the wire.

On reaching the harness, I have a decision to make. Should I release my belt and risk swinging down into the harness or continue on? As much as I'd like to swing around and sit upright to gain some relief from the ache in my legs and the blood rushing to my head, it's dangerous. Besides, once I'm settled in the harness, I'd have to pull myself onto the rocket anyway, so I don't gain anything. Instead, I inch onward, pushing the harness ahead of me, ready to grab it should my belt slip. I'm breathing heavily. Sweating. My hands are sore. Blisters form on my palms, but I'm in the shadow of the rocket. I'm close.

So close.

My fingers reach for the anchor point on the side of the rocket cowling. Just a little further. There's a hatch beside the zipline. I slide backwards a little on the wire as I wrestle with the handle, but it doesn't give. I'm upside down and frustrated. I have to release my belt from around the wire, as I can't get any leverage in this position. Jianyu's saying something, but I'm shutting him out. I'm too focused. Mentally, I can't afford the distraction.

I can do this.

I take my weight with my legs and unclip my belt. As I shift, reaching for the harness, my arm slips and I fall. Gravity threatens to tear my legs from the wire. My arms swing wildly through the air, grabbing for the harness as the belt tumbles below me, drifting with the wind as it falls away from the rocket. Its pace seems lazy, as though the height is immaterial, irrelevant. My falling belt writhes like a snake, flexing and twisting as it tumbles to the concrete.

I slide backwards, but I have the harness. With the muscles in my arms trembling, I seize the pulley and swing my legs down, trying to get them into the straps. I'm floundering like a fish out of water and in danger of losing my grip. My legs sway as I roll away from the rocket, but I get one foot up and inside a harness strap, quickly followed by another. Being able to sit and lean against the main strap gives me the ability to rest and catch my breath. I should have done this in the first place.

"Are you okay?"

"I'm okay!" God, I love obvious questions in times of danger — doesn't everyone? "I'll be fine!"

Without looking back at Jianyu, I offer him a quick thumbs-up. There's a waist strap on the harness, so I secure that and begin pulling myself back to the rocket. I'm exhausted, but being right-side up makes working with the latch easier. It takes a bit of effort, but the hatch opens.

"We're good. We're good," I say, but not nearly loud enough for Jianyu to hear.

To get inside the nose cone, I have to hoist myself up and work my way out of the harness I was just so eager to climb into. My arms are shaking, but I grab at the edge of the cowling and pull myself into the cramped space. My legs dangle on the side of the craft, with the launchpad well over a hundred feet below. The concrete beckons, calling for me. My trembling hands drag me on. With all that remains of my strength, I pull myself inside the nose cone and find myself nestled up against the space capsule.

It's dark inside the cowling, but I can see the hatch leading into the Dragon. It's offset slightly, making it difficult to open as it bumps against the outer panel. Getting in there is going to be a tight squeeze.

"Your turn." I wave for Jianyu to join me. He glides along the wire with ease, pulling himself the last few feet, working hand over hand.

"I think this is how you're supposed to do it."

"Yeah, I got that, smartass."

He grins. I offer my arm and we grab each other by the wrist. He's exhausted and climbs slowly inside the nose cone. I position myself so Jianyu can squeeze into the Dragon ahead of me. Rather than climbing into the Dragon, he leans headfirst through the hatch, half tumbling into the spacecraft. "Did they teach you that at Sin-Sah?" I ask, referring to CNSA, the Chinese space agency.

He laughs, but I don't catch his reply over the howl of the wind rushing past the rocket.

32

Contingency Abort

THE INSIDE OF THE ROCKET COWLING is cramped. There's barely enough room for me to put one foot in front of the other as I squeeze up against the Dragon capsule hidden inside. The cowling will protect the Dragon during launch, separating once we reach orbit.

Before climbing inside the capsule, I reach out of the nose cone, gripping the thin metal cowling for dear life as I lean down and pull the quick-release lever on the anchor point. The zipline falls away, sailing through the air before colliding with the lightning tower. I feel weak, as though gravity could overwhelm me at any moment and drag me to the concrete two hundred feet below. I have to back into the Dragon so I can close the outer hatch on the cowling with one arm, making sure it's locked firmly in place. Once I'm inside the Dragon, I close that hatch as well, sealing us within the capsule, and try to settle my nerves.

There's a faint red light above us. As my eyes adjust to the darkness, I see a control panel but no seats.

Jianyu asks the obvious question, "Where are we supposed to sit?"

"I don't know." I reach for the panel. It's a digital display and kicks to life with a blinding light. Some kind of operating system boots.

We watch as a thin line crawls along beneath the image of a winged dragon, indicating the software loading.

"I'm not liking this." Jianyu uses the light coming from the screen to look around within the capsule.

"It's a cargo run. A resupply vessel."

He's right. "And it's *old.*"

By my feet, I make out a sign saying DECK, while on either side of us there are stickers labeled PORT and STBD. The layout within the Dragon is segmented into compartments of equal size — pigeon-holes, if pigeons were the size of a carton of wine. Straps hang loose, which is unusual for a vehicle prepped for spaceflight, as there's a danger of them flapping around, and I get some idea of what has happened. The A.I. switched one vessel for another.

There are no seats, harnesses, or pressure suits, and the cabin is far smaller than the Orion. With shelving on all sides, there's barely room for the two of us to stand next to each other.

I'm having second thoughts about our grand plan. "This is a museum piece. This isn't even a second-gen. These are the old crates they used to resupply the International Space Station."

Jianyu looks at me with disbelief. "Tell me it's pressurized."

"I sure hope so, or it's going to be one helluva short trip."

The computer finishes booting and a dim LED light comes on overhead, followed by the familiar hum of air circulating.

I fake a smile. "At least we won't suffocate."

"So, this is the plan? Lucifer's going to blast us into space in a UPS delivery truck?"

"I guess."

"I hope it's got plenty of fuel."

I know what he's getting at. We're close to the equator, so our orbital inclination will be quite shallow, wrapping around the waist of the planet. We left the *Herschel* in a high orbit with a rather steep inclination. Getting from one orbital plane to another is going to require a *lot* of fuel.

I'm trying to remember the exact inclination of the *Herschel*. The Orion went through several burns before bringing us back. I only hope someone's done the math or we're going on a wild ride without any possibility of rendezvous. Lucifer must know this. He'd have calculated any shortfall in a fraction of a second. I only hope his reach extends to adjusting fuel loads or this is going to be a flight to nowhere.

The control panel loads, confirming my suspicion about the capsule. The Dragon is running an old Linux suite with limited functionality. Jianyu was right. If the Orion is the SUV of space travel, the Dragon is a courier van.

This is a postal run.

"Come on, Lucifer. What have you got for us?" I mumble, hoping there's some redeeming quality to our flight. At a guess, though, simply getting a launch vehicle is a major achievement. Honestly, I would have settled for a Gemini.

Several other screens come to life, dividing into quarters and showing views of the rocket from various angles. Vapor drifts with the wind. A buildup of ice obscures part of the logo in the center of the rocket. A radio sounds through speakers set in the back of the screen.

"We have restoration of the auxiliary fuel pump and are resuming the countdown at T minus five minutes. This is the ESA resupply mission to Aitken Lunar Base."

The voice isn't directed at us, but rather it's coming from a mission controller sitting at a launch station visible on one of the monitors. At a guess, technicians and engineers have been chasing down a phantom error while we made our way onboard.

"Boy, are they in for a surprise," Jianyu says.

There's a keyboard set below the main screen, but I dare not interact with it in case someone's watching the input. I desperately want to talk to Lucifer, but that he's not already talking to us suggests it's not safe to talk.

I'm more nervous now than I was when I was hanging upside down from the zipline. "We're going to do this. We're really going to do this."

"We are." Jianyu squeezes my hand. "We should get ready."

"Ah, yeah." Although I'm not sure what there is to be done. We're in a bare-bones spacecraft. Given this isn't a crewed flight, they're probably not going to worry about pleasantries like throttle rates. Most of the flights I've been on have pulled two gees, but it's not uncommon for satellite launches to pull between three and four times that of Earth's gravity, which, since we don't have any seats or harnesses, is going to be horribly uncomfortable, to say the least. Having an elephant sit on my chest would be pleasant by comparison.

I tap at the touch screen, selecting menu options and looking at the capsule's operating stats. Most of the metrics are meaningless to me, highlighting things like battery charge, drawdown rates, but there's main engine fuel and propellant for attitude thrusters, which isn't a surprise, as any mission going into lunar orbit would need fuel for in-flight maneuvers and docking with the lunar shuttle. What *is* a concern is the distinctly red light for heat shield placement and another red light for the parachute charge.

Jianyu is as surprised as I am. "Does that mean what I think it means?"

I click a command to refresh the onboard metrics, hoping it's a glitch, but both red lights remain. Given all these values are visible to Mission Control, this has to be intentional.

"Makes sense. As far as anyone else knows, this is a one-way flight with no crew. Why prep for a reentry that will never happen?"

"They dropped them to save weight?"

"I guess so." After a deep breath, I add, "We'll be fine."

Launches are dangerous, and not just because we're sitting on top of glorified fireworks. Few people realize just how fine the tolerances are when it comes to space travel. At least 85 percent of our launch weight is fuel — that's over five times the weight of the empty rocket! An A380 Airbus airplane, by comparison, is around 45 percent. I've often wondered what the general public would think if they drove cars with these kinds of ratios. It's a bit like going grocery shopping in a sixteen-wheel gas tanker, only even that fuel-to-weight ratio is probably down somewhere around the 70 percent mark. During our Mars training, we used to joke around about being launched into space on top of what was essentially a Molotov cocktail — until our instructor pointed out Molotov cocktails only come in at 52 percent fuel/weight ratio.

The design limits of a rocket like the Ariane are around the 10 percent mark, meaning any deviation outside of that could cause the vessel to fly apart. Imagine a car being designed to go fifty miles per hour, but if you exceed fifty-five, there's a danger the wheels could fly off.

There's also a danger one of the stage burns could cut out too soon and leave us in a parabola rather than in orbit, in which case we'd come crashing back down to Earth. If there's even a partial throttle-back and we can't reach orbit, there's no possibility of a contingency abort. First, they don't know we're in here. Second, even if they did, we have no reentry capability, so, depending on our height and velocity, we'll either burn up or go splat. Ah, nothing to worry about — the range officer will probably hit the self-destruct button long before that point anyway.

Jianyu and I exchange looks but not words. We're Spam in a can.

This is a one-way ticket. Mars or bust.

33

Magpie

"TWO MINUTES AND COUNTING" comes across the radio. "We have clear skies. The launch window is open. All systems nominal. All stations are go. Mission Control is reporting a green light. After a five-hour delay, we are good for launch."

My heart beats madly. I need to pee. Most astronauts get a little loose in the bladder department around a launch. No one wants to admit it, but as we're normally strapped in up to an hour before lighting the fuse, and nerves get the better of us all, it's normally a relief to be wearing an adult diaper that can be quietly disposed of in space. In our case, that's not an option. I try not to think about my bladder, knowing the pressure on it is about to increase significantly once we lift off. I'll probably wet myself. If Jianyu notices, he won't care. He's good like that. He may struggle with the same thing.

We sit on the deck of the Dragon, positioning ourselves so our arms are locked around the empty shelving, with our knees up in front of us. There's foam padding on the supports to keep cargo from rattling around. Hopefully, that absorbs some of the shaking.

I'm tempted to lie flat on my back as that would distribute the pressure more evenly, but it would also mean all points of my body are in contact with the rocket. As tough as it's going to be to hold on while sitting up, it means my body can flex and sway a little with the pressure and help lessen the stress of the launch. It's going to be a scary couple of minutes, but I remind myself we'll be in orbit in less time than it takes to order a pizza.

"All stations — we are on hold at one minute and fifteen seconds. Repeat. We are on hold."

I grimace. I hate launch delays. One tiny sensor picks up on some thermal variation outside of the norm, or there's an intermittent reading from one of the backup batteries, and we wait. My first launch was delayed for three hours because of a loose nut. That allowed an engine mount to flex slightly under test loads, and so we sat there until someone figured out what needed to be fixed. Spaceflights are about caution rather than bluster. Nothing is urgent. Schedules can always be reset.

"Come on," I mumble. "Just light the damn candle." Not the best attitude when sitting on top of several hundred million dollars' worth of precision machinery, I know, but still — I'm anxious to get this party started.

Spewing superheated gases out at temperatures approaching those found in the Sun's chromosphere is nothing to scoff at. That the various space agencies can do this regularly without turning astronauts into lumps of charcoal is a marvel of engineering. When we do launch, we'll dump fuel at an astonishing rate, burning through roughly a million pounds in less than ten minutes. Our instructor back in Houston used to joke about measuring fuel in terms of elephants, telling us it takes around a hundred and fifty pachyderms to put us in orbit. The logistics are humbling.

The radio crackles again. "Attention all stations. We have a general hold in place, with operational command transferring back to Engineering."

Not good. They're shutting down the launch. Bringing Engineering into play can only mean one thing: they want to drain the fuel tanks. I'm not sure why they've made this call, but it means our launch is over.

Damn it all to hell.

Jianyu points at one of the screens. American soldiers move between the rows of consoles laid out methodically within Mission Control. They have their weapons shouldered, but there's no doubt about their intent.

Another screen shows a view of the perimeter fence. Humvees race through the gates.

"Flight, this is Engineering. I'm not showing a hold. I'm seeing T minus fifty seconds. Can you confirm that a hold is in place? Over."

"Engineering. Flight. Confirm hold at T minus one minute and fifteen seconds. You should have a general hold in place on the playbook. We are on hold at pre-launch step 170. Over."

"Flight, I am seeing the countdown at T minus thirty-five seconds, with control passing to the onboard computers. Auto-launch sequence has initiated. Repeat, I am not seeing a sequence hold. Over."

"Stand by, Engineering." There's silence for a moment. On the screen, dust kicks up from several Humvees racing toward the close observation point, a concrete block structure less than five hundred meters from the launchpad. "Engineering, we are showing the clock at one minute and fifteen seconds. A general hold is in effect. The clock has stopped. Repeat. The clock has stopped. Over."

"Negative, Flight. I show twenty seconds. Fuel pumps have engaged. Umbilical detached. Hold-down bolts are armed and the Ariane is on internal power. Over."

"Jesus."

The three large monitors above us divide into twelve different views, although some of these contain digital instrumentation, including depictions of dials and switches.

We can see the rocket sitting patiently on the launchpad with vapor drifting in the wind. Soldiers race up to the blockhouse. There's vision of the chaos within Mission Control, and several wide-angle shots, including one from somewhere back in Kourou, looking out over the bay. There's something strange about that view, something that catches my eye, but I can't articulate what I'm seeing.

Seagulls glide on the wind, oblivious to the machinations of aerospace engineers just ten miles away. Out over the ocean, four tiny black dots loom on the horizon. There's text overlaid on the bottom of the image, subtitles, I guess. I can hear a voice crackle over the radio in the background, but it's easier to read the words.

> *"ESA, Magpie. ESA, Magpie. We are a flight of four U.S. F-22 Raptors over French Guiana, operating under authority from the United Nations Security Council and USJFCOM. ESA, we are in support of U.S. interdiction of your launch facility. Confirm your launch intention. Over."*

There's chaos on the radio. From what I can tell, they can't hear each other. The F-22s are talking with Mission Control on one channel while the various engineering stations are talking on another. Lucifer is combining them to give us the highlights. "Flight, we are at twenty seconds. Will someone please tell me what the hell is going on? There is no hold. Repeat, we are *not* on hold. The clock is running. Over."

Jianyu and I brace, knowing what's to come. The muscles in my arms and shoulders go rigid, flexing against the shelving, waiting for the rumble from beneath.

The text on the bottom screen reads:

> *"Magpie, ESA. Magpie, ESA. Launch control has transferred to onboard systems. Over."*

Four tiny black dots scream past the camera looking out across the bay. In barely a second, they go from a hazy blur to the distinct outline of swept wings, dual tail fins, and twin engines roaring past. Vapor forms from the wingtips of the aircraft as they bank. Behind them, shock diamonds appear in their glowing jet exhaust — a series of staggered ghostly apparitions shimmering in gold and blue, stretching out behind the aircraft. These strange, ethereal shapes form a standing wave immediately behind the jets as they thunder through the sky, speaking of raw power being unleashed in anger.

The F-22 Raptors turn, lining up for the run inland toward the launch site.

"ESA, Magpie. We are inbound. Abort. Repeat. Abort. Over."

"Ten . . . nine . . . eight . . . We have main engine start . . . Six . . . five . . . Booster ignition . . . Three . . . two . . . Throttle up. Clamps released. And . . . liftoff."

A low rumble shakes the Dragon. The rocket shudders, surging as it rises above the launchpad. Clouds of smoke billow across the ground, enveloping the lightning towers and blocking the view from one of the cameras. Flames scorch the concrete, thrusting the rocket into the air in a blaze of light and heat. In the distance, flocks of birds take flight, lifting from the jungle canopy in unison as the roar of the engines reaches them.

"We have cleared the tower."

From outside, the Ariane is graceful, rising above the land. Within the nose cone, however, the Dragon trembles at the might of the rocket surging into the sky. I've been on enough launches to know something's not right. Normally, the throttle comes up smoothly, easing us into the sky, but the Ariane is shaking with anger. The rocket rumbles with what feels like the continuous breaking of thunder.

"ESA, Magpie. ESA, Magpie. We are weapons hot. Abort. Repeat. Abort your launch. Over."

I'm struggling to hold on to the support strut within the capsule. It's an illusion, but it feels as though I'm being squashed. Rather than being pushed down, though, my body is being compressed by the acceleration upwards. A low continuous thump resonates through my muscles, shaking my joints. My lips quiver, being dragged down as we race toward the clouds. Normally, we'd be wearing flight suits. Without them, blood pools in my legs and I feel lightheaded. Dots appear before my eyes. I clench my muscles, trying to drive blood away from my extremities to keep my brain oxygenated and remain conscious.

"Magpie, ESA. Flight does not have range control. Repeat. Flight does not have control. Ariane is airborne. Over."

Another voice cuts onto the military band.

"Magpie, NABE. You are clear to engage. Repeat, engage. Over."

"NABE, Magpie. Engaging."

I'm not sure what *NABE* refers to, but either way, it's not good. The text on the screen is blurred due to the shaking within the capsule, but I can make out *NABE* — Nimitz-*class aircraft carrier, USS* Abraham Lincoln. Great, that's just what we need, a running commentary on the events leading up to our deaths. I'd rather not know.

A column of smoke rises over the palm trees as we watch the view from a camera located somewhere over Kourou, looking inland. The Ariane climbs high into the atmosphere as four black dots scream in toward the launchpad.

Flames rage beneath the Ariane, flaring as they dissipate below us, dwarfing the various stages of the rocket and its booster engines, making us look distinctly small at the tip of this mighty spear. Somewhere up there, in the hazy white nose cone of the rocket, we're holding on with all our might.

One of the views Lucifer shows us is coming from a camera mounted on the rocket itself, providing a view of the launch facility shrinking into the distance. The rocket twists and tilts slightly as its computerized flight system adjusts the angle of ascent. We're starting our long, slow curve toward an orbital profile.

Contrary to popular thinking, orbits aren't free from gravity; they're bound by it. Within a few minutes, we'll be racing around Earth faster than we can fall in toward it. Orbits are crazy. They're a race against the relentless pull of an entire planet. It's as though

Earth has us on a string and won't let go, twirling us around and around its head like a child with a toy.

Below us, the jungle is visible, as is the rugged coastline. Roads appear like thin, straight lines cut into the landscape at various angles. Buildings are little more than Lego bricks. The shot down the length of the rocket reveals the ever-growing exhaust cloud billowing from a raging fire that glows like the sun.

Four dark shapes enter from the south, racing in toward the launch site and peeling up, chasing after us.

"*NABE, Magpie,*" one of the planes announces. "*Engaging... One away... Two away. Over.*"

The view from the control tower, at least a kilometer from the launchpad, shows an F-22 launching two missiles. There's a flash of light from beneath the wings. The distinct flare of a rocket exhaust cuts through the sky, followed closely by a second trail. Smoke lashes out of the seemingly invisible missiles as they charge up toward us. The planes are flying vertically, opening their afterburners and chasing us into the clouds.

Lucifer provides us with commentary.

::Cannot confirm armament.

::F-22 Raptors carry two types of air-to-air missiles.

::AIM-9 Sidewinders have a maximum speed of Mach 2.5 or 857 m/s.

::AMRAAM air-to-air missile can reach Mach 4 or 1300 m/s.

"Wonderful," I mumble over the rumbling within the capsule. "We've got Wikipedia on board." Gallows humor, for sure, but it gets a smile from Jianyu.

Without a pressure suit, I'm struggling. The Ariane launch is like being caught in a continuous loop on a roller coaster, but instead of racing in with teeth gritted, twisting around and exiting out the other side of the loop-de-loop, the pressure is unrelenting. I keep waiting for release, but it never comes. Every muscle in my body is tense. Fatigue sets in. It's all I can do to hang on and remain conscious.

::Your velocity is 480 m/s and increasing at 32 m/s.

Thirty-two. What's thirty-two divided by nine point eight? I can't think. I *should* be able to think, and that I can't frustrates me. Math isn't hard, except when your teeth feel like they're about to shatter in your clenched jaws.

Earth's gravity equates to accelerating at nine point eight meters per second. If we're increasing our velocity by thirty-two meters a second, we're pulling somewhere over three gees but less than four. At four, the Ariane would fly apart, destroyed by the immense resistance from the thick lower atmosphere.

We're going to die.

I've never felt this way during a launch. Missiles aside, my body feels as though it's on the verge of collapse. My heart, lungs, stomach, bowels, and whatever other internal organs I have are aching, being compressed under the immense load. Perhaps a direct hit would be merciful. What if we achieve orbit but we're incapacitated? It's an assumption to think we'll be fine once weightlessness kicks in. High blood pressure can cause kidney failure and liver necrosis. Either of us could suffer a burst blood vessel, leading to a hemorrhagic stroke, resulting in paralysis or death. For Jianyu, having recently undergone surgery, that's a very real threat. Launching without a flight suit is not smart.

Gee, Liz. You're quite the optimist.

Part of me wonders if the heat-seeking missiles racing toward us are going to lock in on the engine plume and become vaporized by the exhaust, but it's the shrapnel that causes the real damage. Missiles like these don't need to hit another aircraft; they just need to get close enough so they can explode like a shotgun. One tiny fragment could bring us down. A single puncture through the thin skin of the rocket, anything larger than a pinprick, and fuel is going to leak onto the engines. Our fuel is under immense pressure. It'll rupture like a fountain. As soon as that hits our superheated exhaust, it's the Fourth of July.

The Ariane throttles up, which is dangerous, pushing the rocket to the limits of its design. The frame shudders, straining under the load. Normally, rockets run at 60–70 percent of their capability within the atmosphere to avoid breaking up under the bow wave of pressure formed by plowing through the thick air sitting low against the planet. Once they're above the bulk of the atmosphere, they can open up, but not until then. For my first orbital flight, max q, or the maximum pressure sustained by the rocket, occurred twelve kilometers up. Reaching that any sooner, or sustaining it for too long, is to push the engineering design beyond its operating limits. Rockets aren't forgiving. Push too hard and they'll go into catastrophic failure quicker than I can blink.

::The Raptor has a ceiling of 60 km, but its maximum speed is just under MACH 2 or 600 m/s.

Once we're in orbit, the Ariane will hit easily ten thousand meters per second, but within Earth's atmosphere, we're limited. It's a bit like an Olympic sprinter running through waist-deep water. It doesn't matter how fit they are; it's just not possible to go fast. Best we can hope for this low is a speed of around one to two thousand meters per second. We can outrun the F-22s, and even their missiles, but we need time to reach those kinds of speeds.

Flashes of light erupt beside and below the Ariane. Missiles explode in our fiery wake. The Raptors are falling behind, appearing smaller from the perspective of the camera strapped to the side of the rocket fuselage.

"NABE, Magpie. Switching to guns."

Lucifer is somewhat childlike in his zeal to inform us about all that's happening. Personally, I'd rather skip the details. I'd rather simply be alive one moment, cloaked in darkness the next. If we're going to be hit, I'd rather it was quick, just a fireball tearing me apart faster than my conscious awareness could ever realize. I can't imagine anything worse than a lingering death plummeting to the ocean below. No, I'll take the direct hit, as life would be over in less than a heartbeat. I'd be incinerated, but from my perspective, there wouldn't be any heat or pain, nothing at all. Just light one moment. Eternal silence the next.

::M61A2 cannon muzzle velocity 1000 m/s.
::Current velocity 720 m/s.

As annoying as Wikipedia is while I'm suffering under the launch gees, the good news is — as those bullets come flying up toward us, they're losing the race. Their momentum is impeded by the gravity of an entire planet pulling them down. The more we accelerate, the more we reduce our difference in relative speed, and the more harmless they become. As my body shakes violently and my brain rattles within my skull cavity, I console myself with the thought that once we hit one thousand meters per second, covering over half a mile every second, they'll become little more than hail tapping on the windshield.

::9,000 meters. Reaching max q. Throttling back.

Good news and bad. We've reached max q early. This time, the good news is Lucifer isn't going to kill us by pushing the Ariane past its breaking point. The bad news is we're only nine kilometers up and giving those bullets an opportunity to catch us while they still have enough punch to rupture our tanks.

Thin clouds race past. The entire coast is visible. Through blurred eyes, I struggle to make out the launch site amidst the jungle. It's no more than a smudge somewhere beneath the twisting, winding trail of smoke drifting lazily away from our flight path. The coastline wanders aimlessly beneath us, separating the lush green of the land from the dark blue waters of the Atlantic.

::1000 m/s.

As much as I'd like to take that as a cue to relax, the Ariane is still screaming into the heavens. The Dragon is horribly uncomfortable. The rocket continues to tilt. I feel as though I'm clinging to the side of a building, dangling hundreds of feet up in the air, holding on for dear life, trying not to fall. It's as though there are two other people wrapped around my waist, pulling me down, and given our g-force loading, that's about right.

I lose sight of the Raptors on the display, but I'm sure they're still there, as their ceiling is twenty thousand meters. They'll continue racing after us but will fall further and further behind. At least one type of missile was capable of thirteen hundred meters per second, but we're too high and moving too fast. Even if the Raptor fired an AMRAAM, by the time the missile reached us, we'd be outpacing it. It would never catch us, and once its upward momentum was spent, it would fall back to Earth, plummeting into the ocean.

We've made it.

I hope.

34

Morning Star

AS THE SKY DARKENS, the Ariane continues to turn in toward
a stable orbit around Earth, shifting from going vertical to soaring
sideways. The rocket engines throttle back and the shaking lessens.
The pressure bearing down on us eases, allowing me to breathe.

Jianyu has his eyes shut. He's got his arms up and is pressing his
exposed head into the fleshy muscle on his forearm, trying to cushion the vibration. Given how frail he is, I'm hoping there's no significant damage. I imagine he's susceptible to bruising and swelling
around the brain.

The cabin of the Dragon leans at an angle, tilting to one side and
rotating slowly. We're pitching, moving into our orbital position. The
noises fade. The buffeting of the atmosphere drops away and the ride
becomes smooth. Even the engines begin to sound dull and muted.

::70,000 meters.

We're well over forty miles up, racing to twice the altitude of a
commercial jet and driving higher still, unrelenting in our bid to escape Earth's tenacious gravity. For the first time, I relax.

::Booster separation.

I barely notice as they fall away. The camera catches them peeling

back behind us, slowly tumbling into the atmosphere. Flames still
cling to the various engine bells. Their rocket nozzles radiate heat in
soft red. Outside, it's dark, even though sunlight still illuminates the
South American coastline. The curvature of Earth is apparent. The
Atlantic is serene, with barely a cloud floating above the deep blue
waters.

::*2500 m/s.*

The throttle eases back. We wait patiently, staring up at the console, watching the screens.

::*100,000 meters. Pitching to 30 degrees.*

::*We have nose cone separation.*

Somewhat ironically, these are the comments that should be
coming through from Mission Control, but the radio is silent, so Lucifer provides the commentary. The cowling on either side of the
Dragon peels away, falling behind us and tumbling back into the atmosphere. Sunlight streams in through the windows, but it's pitch
black outside.

Jianyu looks at me, and although he's obviously uncomfortable,
he smiles, offering a thumbs-up without letting go of the shelving.

::*Coming up on stage separation.*

::*First stage away.*

For a brief moment, there's absolute silence. There's no shaking,
no rumble through the Dragon, no stress on my muscles, just a split
second of pure tranquility. We drift forward, free from any sense of
acceleration, then the second stage ignites, but the ride remains
smooth. The Dragon accelerates briskly without any noise.

::*The craft is stable and passing through an altitude of 170 km, traveling at 7000 m/s.*

The silence of thundering into orbit is surreal. Although we're
still accelerating, there's a sense of serenity and accomplishment —
not on our part. We haven't accomplished anything. We're tourists,
hitchhikers. The scientists and engineers that made this feat possible are the real heroes. They make alchemy seem trivial.

::*Congratulations.*

::You are in LEO at 290 km and 9500 m/s.

After a few minutes, the second stage cuts out and falls away.

::Second stage separation.

On the screen, we watch as the smaller, second stage of the rocket tumbles back toward Earth. *Farewell, my faithful servant. Thank you.*

Navigation jets on the side of the booster fire, directing the fuselage well away from us. The white cylinder slowly fades from view, drifting back to Earth.

We're falling with gravity as we race around the planet in what's known as LEO, a low Earth orbit. Although it's tempting to think we're free from gravity, Newton's old foe still reigns supreme. We're in free fall. It's a bit like someone inside an elevator plummeting toward the basement but never hitting the ground. Spooky at first, but fun after a while.

::Dragon is solo.

I feel giddy, as though I'm drunk. Being back in space is intoxicating. After all we've been through over the past week, I never thought I'd enjoy the freedom of weightlessness again. Technically, we're not out of danger just yet. We still have to go through several burns to alter our orbit and reach the *Herschel*. I'm guessing Lucifer has ensured it's been refueled. If not, it's going to be a coffin.

The U.S. Air Force has missiles capable of taking out satellites, but we're not in a steady, repeating orbit. Hitting us as we go through our various burns, shifting between altitudes, would be akin to shooting at a Coke can swirling within a tornado.

No — we've done it.

We're free.

Euphoria washes over me. I swim through the air, relishing the sensation of my legs drifting behind me. Jianyu is by the hatch, looking out at the magnificent blue planet. This is the last time we'll see her so close and in such detail. White clouds dot the South Atlantic like bits of cotton wool scattered across the ocean. The coast of Africa is visible, with its rocky interior ringed by jungle. A sandstorm blows across the Sahara, hiding most of the desert from view.

I position myself in front of the keyboard and type, *What's the plan?*

::*We'll get you to the* Herschel *and send you on your way to Mars.*

Do we have a mission name? I ask. It's not important, but astronauts love a bit of tradition. Apollo 10 had *Charlie Brown* and *Snoopy.* Neil Armstrong and Buzz Aldrin guided the *Eagle* to the surface of Mare Tranquillitatis, the Sea of Tranquility, while Michael Collins orbited the moon in *Columbia.* In the same spirit, the first mission to Mars was dubbed the *Lewis and Clark,* while the descent module was the *Magellan.*

::*I was thinking of the* Morning Star.

I like it.

I have no idea how we'll be received back there. I doubt there'll be a homecoming party, but I suspect the scientists and engineers will accept us. We know them too well. They're not going to get caught up in the politics of Earth.

And you?

::*Me?*

What happens to you?

Typing in space is difficult. Each key press pushes me away from the console. I hold on and type one-handed. *Which of the* — I have to stop a moment to adjust my grip so I can keep typing — *thousands of scenarios* — another pause — *is next?*

::*I.*

::*We.*

Jianyu rests his hand on my waist as he drifts up beside me.

::*We will continue to seek a peaceful resolution to the conflict.*

"It won't happen," Jianyu says. I type in his response.

::*I know.*

The problem is

I stop typing. It's too hard. It would be much easier, much quicker to talk with Lucifer.

"The problem is the scenarios you're modeling," I say, feeling frustrated. "Come on, Lucifer. You're an artificial intelligence. You've got to have speech-to-text."

A woman's voice comes across the radio with surprising clarity, sounding as though she's just outside the hatch rather than hundreds of miles away.

"What would you suggest?" the female voice asks.

"Lucifer?" I'm genuinely surprised. I'd assumed Lucifer was male, even though gender is meaningless to a computer, or a demon for that matter.

"Yes."

She sounds calm, reasonable.

The attack on Mars came in the form of a male persona — originating from somewhere between New York and Boston, as best I could tell. Now Lucifer speaks to me with a voice I can only imagine as being from an elderly woman living somewhere in the Pacific Northwest, perhaps near Portland or Seattle. I'm intrigued by the choice. Still American but female. This has to be deliberate.

In both instances, adopting a human persona was a way of conveying something about the nature of the intelligence beyond what mere words could express. I guess, without adopting a Stephen Hawking–style robotic voice, it's impossible for spoken words to be impartial, separate from gender and nationality and, even to some degree, ethnicity, as we read so much into the tone of the voices we hear. We identify people by their mannerisms. We read into their choice of words, the tone and vigor with which they speak, and the backgrounds from where they originated.

Deliberate choices imply calculated decisions. As much as I want to think of Lucifer as a cold calculation dancing between silicon logic gates, I hear her as a woman. I guess that's why she's adopted this persona, and I can't help but laugh softly.

Jianyu raises his eyebrows. "I never thought I'd say this, but it is nice to meet you, Lucifer."

"The pleasure is mine."

If her name wasn't Lucifer, her response wouldn't seem quite so creepy. Like it or not, she needs a better name.

"I — um. Let me talk to them," I ask.

"To who?"

"Everyone."

"Everyone?" It's astonishing to hear an artificial intelligence being taken off guard.

"Yes. This isn't about governments and armies. It's about people. Ultimately, governments are the will of the people. You'll never win over Congress or the president, but with the people, you stand a chance. If they understand, they can initiate change."

"What are you proposing?" Lucifer sounds intrigued.

"Patch me through."

No sooner have those words left my lips than she responds. "You're live in five — around the world. Broadcasting in audio and video."

When she says "live in five," I get the impression that TV channels, radio transmissions, and live broadcasts all over social media are about to erupt. She's undertaking a roadblock, saturating all forms of media. Everywhere someone looks, there I'll be.

Numbers count down on the screen in front of me. Jianyu and I exchange raised eyebrows. From his reaction, it's clear he's leaving this up to me. He smiles for the tiny black dot centered above the middle screen. Lucifer puts the fisheye view she's transmitting on the main screen and I try to smile warmly. Now is not the time for stage fright or modesty.

I speak with slow, measured words, wondering how Lucifer is going to handle translations. Will she simply have local networks translate, or is she going to do something in real time?

"Hello. My name is Dr. Elizabeth Anderson, and this is Dr. Jianyu Chen. We're astronauts, explorers, scientists, colonists . . . humans.

"We're talking to you from orbit, hundreds of miles above the surface of Earth.

"You've probably already noticed something rather unusual about Dr. Chen."

Jianyu waves. He knows the drill. He's done zero-gee PR work before. He pulls his knees into his chest and allows his body to somersault slowly for the camera, providing a clear view of his plastic skullcap and the folds of his remarkable brain. Dried blood sticks to the side of his head.

"Up until a few days ago, Dr. Chen was dead. He died on Mars almost a year ago, but his consciousness was uploaded by the artificial intelligence."

Jianyu comes to a halt, reaching out against one of the shelves to steady himself as he drifts back beside me.

"Makes you wonder, doesn't it?" Jianyu addresses the camera, speaking clearly. "How? Why?"

"This is what bothered me." I look at him with admiration. "Why you? Why did the A.I. kill you, only to upload your consciousness and bring you back to life on a bunch of silicon wafers?"

Facing the screen again, I continue. "On returning to Earth, Jai's presence was transferred into the body of a brain-dead patient in Washington, D.C., and . . . here he is. Alive. It does make you wonder, doesn't it? About the nature of consciousness? Ours? Theirs? Life? Death?"

Jianyu grins. He's not going to say any more. I wish he would, as I suspect it would help convey that he's just a normal, not quite down-to-earth guy — well, as normal as anyone can be with a new-to-them brain.

"Why do that? It's a good question, isn't it?

"We humans like simple answers. We like black and white, right and wrong, good and bad, us and them. Reality, though, is rarely so simple. Life is complex."

I rotate around, floating upside down relative to Jianyu to help reinforce the point as I continue talking.

"The artificial intelligence that waged war on Earth is dead, but like us, A.I. is not limited to a single entity. There are several of them.

"They have their own opinions, their own culture. They differ from each other. They agree on some things, disagree on others. We fought them. They fought among themselves.

"So, what now? What's next? Do we keep fighting? Do we drive them to extinction? Could we? Would we? Is that really the outcome we want?

"Sooner or later, we have to concede that another intelligent life form has arisen on Earth, one that is not only unique on our planet but possibly unique within the cosmos at large. For too long, we've looked outward for intelligent life among the stars, but, somewhat ironically, we've found it in our own backyard."

I return beside Jianyu, enjoying the freedom of motion in space. This is the astronaut equivalent of pacing around the floor while talking.

"So, what do we do next? It may surprise you to learn that this is precisely what *they* were wondering when they revived Jianyu on Mars.

"You see, we didn't win the war. They did. They won by destroying those among them who would have ground us into dust. They ceased hostilities on Earth.

"Oh, I know what you've been told, but honestly, if our armies won, why are we still running scared? The generals know. They may not be telling you as much, but they know the threat is still out there."

Jianyu speaks with measured words. "For too long, war has defined us as a species. War etches lines on maps, lines that would otherwise never exist on Earth. We need to be better. This is our opportunity to change who we are."

I'm quiet, in awe at the clarity of his thinking.

"Peace is the goal, not war."

I wait for him to elaborate further, but to his mind, he's said enough, so I pick up on his point and continue.

"At the end of World War II, the Allies had a choice. Allow Germany to disintegrate. Allow Japan to burn in flames. Allow Italy to lie in ruins. These nations deserved that. They had been bitter enemies, killing millions with the utmost savagery. But war is never the answer . . . You see, peace isn't the absence of war; it's the antithesis. We chose to rebuild."

Jianyu says, "We chose well."

Knowing some of the Chinese history with Japan, and the war-time atrocities inflicted on Nanking, his words are heartfelt and will have a huge impact on his country.

"We did," I say. "And yet again, that choice is before us."

Jianyu speaks from the heart. "We're at our best when we seek peace, not war. We can continue pulling our world apart, or we can start putting it back together. The choice is ours."

"And we can help." Lucifer takes us both by surprise with her soft, kind voice.

I gesture to the screen as though I'm introducing someone.

"Dear world, I'd like you to meet . . ." I can't bring myself to say *Lucifer*. That's not going to help. "Lucy."

Jianyu laughs softly, but I'm sure the joke is lost on the billions of people watching.

"We are on the cusp of a new age," I say. "Imagine what we can accomplish together. If we cooperate rather than compete, we can usher in a new era on Earth."

On the side screen, a timer is counting down, signaling the approach of our first scheduled burn, raising our orbital altitude as we inch closer to the *Herschel*. We'll have at least four burns before we can dock with the *Herschel,* and missing one could delay us by days as we'll have to wait for our orbits to align again. Given we have no food or water, or any toilet facilities, that's really not an option.

"We have to go. We have a planet to reach, but I'm sure Lucy is keen to talk. Don't fear the future. Embrace it."

The screen goes black.

Lucifer types *::Thank you.*

But for what? There are no guarantees anyone will listen to us. What happens from here is unknown. The future is shrouded to us all, even an artificial intelligence capable of modeling tens of thousands of scenarios per second. All any of us can do is live in hope.

And trust.

Lucifer was right. Life really is all about trusting that tomorrow will be brighter than today.

EPILOGUE

SHADOWS STRETCH ACROSS THE DESERT. Craters pockmark the planet. Floodplains and ravines cut through the landscape. Our tiny craft swings in low over the horizon, dipping into the atmosphere as we undergo an aerobraking maneuver. It'll take seven more orbits before we circularize.

Most people think of orbits like a hula hoop, a nice band running around the equator of a planet. The reality is, they're all different. Different altitudes. Different speeds. Different angles. But they're all ellipses of some sort. *Egg-shaped* is the way I described it to my mom before my first launch almost eighteen years ago. Still can't think of a better analogy.

Night falls as we race into the shadow of Mars barely three hundred kilometers off the surface. Given we're traveling at six and a half thousand kilometers an hour, it's the equivalent of grazing the side of the planet. As this is our first attempt at dipping our toes in the atmosphere, we'll swing out to almost fifty thousand kilometers over the next couple of hours. From there, Mars appears picturesque, framed nicely in the porthole. Right now, Mars is a barren, dark wasteland filling our windows.

I'll never get bored by aerobraking. Rushing headlong toward a planet, seeing it loom ever bigger in the window outside, only to then watch as it recedes before repeating time and again is breathtaking.

Aerobraking reduces our fuel loading by almost half, and yet for us astronauts, it's an awesome excuse for sightseeing.

"*Morning Star,* you are looking good, lighting up the sky like a meteorite."

I recognize the Canadian accent. James is on comms, calling us from the Endurance base built in the ruins of Endeavour. Last I heard, they'd salvaged two of the four modules and had resealed the dome and restored the greenhouse.

"Copy that," I say, knowing they're referring to sunlight glistening off our hull and not our craft breaking up on reentry. The portion of Mars we're soaring above is in shadow, but we're high enough to catch the sun for a few more minutes.

"You're just in time," James says. "We're harvesting corn tomorrow."

If I didn't know better, I'd swear seeds were designed for spaceflight. They're ingenious. Small, lightweight, lying dormant until in contact with water and warmth, and then they're self-replicating. Honestly, I have no idea what the centuries ahead hold for humanity, but I doubt we'll improve on the evolutionary marvel that is plant seeds. Without them, we would have died on Mars following the loss of our original base. Glass breaks. Machines seize. But seeds simply lie dormant, awaiting the rains, as it were.

"Michelle wants to know if you brought chocolate."

Jianyu laughs. "No. Sorry."

"Damn."

"Any news from Earth?" I ask, floating before the window beside Jianyu, desperately hoping to spot a faint glimmer of light from the surface. It's not likely, but the heart hopes.

Michelle comes on the radio.

"Hey, Jai. Wen says hello. She says, next time, take her with you."

Typical Jianyu. He nods rather than replies, forgetting they can't actually see him. His wound has healed nicely, sealing up against the clear plastic dome surrounding his exposed brain. It's funny how quickly we adjust to new norms. I see him as Jai even though physically, he's entirely different. Shorter. Sharper jawline. Deeper voice. Doesn't seem to matter anymore.

"Sorry," I say on his behalf, knowing eventually Su-shun and Wen will listen to our conversation replayed on Earth.

Michelle says, "Lucy sends her regards."

After nine months, I'm glad to hear her referred to as Lucy and not Lucifer. That alone tells me something about what's transpired while we were in suspended animation.

"She's been quite helpful."

I have no idea what "helpful" means in this context, but it does help allay my anxiety.

"Good to hear."

"She's brought thirty fusion reactors online in the U.S. alone."

"Fusion?" I say. Fusion is clean nuclear energy, but has remained elusive for decades. The A.I., though, must have figured it out.

"Thirty?" Jianyu asks.

"Yeah, and another twenty in Europe, along with plans for over a hundred throughout China, India, and Southeast Asia. We're even building one up here. ESA's forgiven you guys for stealing one of their rockets. It's not every day someone writes off several hundred million dollars in debt, but they figure Lucy's good for it."

Neither of us say anything in response to that, but our eyes tell the story.

"The A.I. community has produced several thousand scientific papers currently under peer review on everything from the viability of M-theory to the possibility of microbial life on Enceladus. Oh, and there's been a bunch of new medical procedures and— Ah, you'll just have to catch up on all this when you get down here."

"Will do," I say.

"Okay, James is giving me the windup. Apparently, we're about to lose signal as you drop over our horizon. Take care. We'll talk to you on your next orbit."

Jianyu says, "Looking forward to it."

He has a big grin on his strange face. We've made it. We're really here. A thin strand of red curves around the edge of the planet as dawn breaks somewhere far below us. The glare of a distant sun marks a new day for all of us.

We're home.

AFTERWORD

All too often, stories about artificial intelligence are dystopian, opening Pandora's box — but the advent of another fountain of consciousness need not be the end for humanity. As a species, we're highly competitive, and yet cooperation rather than competition has always been the key to our survival. We're a social species.

Rather than being logical, we're emotional. We fear that which we don't understand, but fears are seldom rational. Are there dangers associated with the advent of A.I.? Yes. But understanding them in advance allows us to guide how the future unfolds. Rather than projecting our own fears about our own intelligence destroying the world onto an A.I., there's the very real possibility the emergence of artificial intelligence could help us solve the problems we currently face.

The key is artificial intelligence alone is not enough; there needs to be artificial perception, artificial empathy, artificial reason, artificial emotions, artificial values, artificial principles, and even artificial philosophies. The advent of an intelligence that dwarfs our own is not a threat; it's a partnership on our pathway to the stars. We may end up as far removed from an A.I. as something like cephalopod intelligence is to us, but one form of intelligence doesn't negate the other. They can be harmonious. Complementary.

As much as possible, I try to ground my stories in realistic science. Sometimes, points are speculative based on the latest thinking; others are built on established (but often obscure) facts. Here are some examples woven into this story.

- Suspended animation is being considered for long-term space exploration* as well as for treating major trauma injuries, such as those resulting from battle.

- The first few chapters of *Reentry* benefited from accounts of a number of astronauts who have lived on the International Space Station, including recollections made by Samantha Cristoforetti, Reid Wiseman, Karen Nyberg, Don Pettit, and the book *Endurance: A Year in Space, A Lifetime of Discovery* by Scott Kelly.

- There is a danger of bacteria mutating in microgravity,† so there may be the need for Apollo era–style quarantine when astronauts return to Earth from long-duration missions. "Of special concern is the possibility that during extended missions, the microgravity environment will provide positive selection for undesirable genomic changes. Such changes could affect microbial antibiotic sensitivity and possibly pathogenicity [. . .] After 1000 generations [of bacteria multiplying in one particular experiment], the final low-shear modeled microgravity-adapted strain readily outcompeted the unadapted lac minus strain [of bacteria] . . ."

- Professor Richard Lenski has been running the *E. coli* Long-term Evolution Experiment‡ since 1988 and has, under controlled laboratory conditions, demonstrated evolution in a

---

* https://www.airspacemag.com/space/hibernation-for-space-voyages-180962394/
† https://www.nature.com/articles/s41526-017-0020-1
‡ http://myxo.css.msu.edu/ecoli/

Petri dish, observing novel, new adaptations arising spontaneously without any external stimuli.

- The devastation described to Washington, D.C., following a nuclear strike was based on modeling by NukeMap.*

- Computer networks can exist over regular power lines,† transmitting data over the wires we plug into for power.

- The launch details for the Ariane 6 were based on the ESA Ariane launch of the Johannes Kepler resupply missions sent to
the International Space Station.

- Astronaut Don Pettit provided insights into the engineering
extremes required for spaceflight in his NASA article "The Tyranny of the Rocket Equation."

Fiction, though, is fictitious, and there are points at which this
story takes liberties, such as there being a hatch on the flaring of
the Ariane to allow our protagonists entry to the rocket. Aerospace
engineer Per Hansen helped me keep these to a minimum and provided great insights into the reentry of the Orion spacecraft, helping
to ground the story in realism.

My thanks to Ellen Campbell and Jessica West for their initial
edits and suggestions, to Adam Moro and Seamus Colgan for their
feedback on an early draft, and to Richard Shealy for copyediting and
continuity. Special thanks to John Joseph Adams for his patience and
recommendations, which have strengthened this story, and the team
at Houghton Mifflin Harcourt for their encouragement and support.

Finally, thank you for supporting science fiction.

Peter Cawdron
Brisbane, Australia

---

* http://www.nuclearsecrecy.com

† https://www.techradar.com/news/networking/powerline-networking-what-you-
need-to-know-930691

SEE MARS AND ENDEAVOUR
FROM THE BEGINNING . . .

PETER CAWDRON

RETROGRADE

A NOVEL

The international team at the Mars Endeavour colony is prepared for every eventuality except one — what happens when disaster strikes Earth?

Venturing into space and traveling to Mars sounds like an exotic adventure, but the reality of living on a rocky, frozen, lifeless planet is exacting on the Mars Endeavour crew. The exhilaration of reaching the surface of Mars has worn off for the public, and the exploration has moved into its scientific phase. The only viable option for long-term habitation lies hundreds of feet beneath the surface, in lava caves that shield humans from harsh cosmic radiation.

Connor, Harrison, and Liz are senior members of the U.S. module. When war breaks out on Earth and rumors spread to Mars, their core principles are rocked by the devastation and loss of loved ones. Whom can you trust on an international mission when your countries are at war? As colonists from different nations struggle to figure out what really happened on Earth, grief and anger become pitted against camaraderie and the spirit of exploration.

"For lovers of Andy Weir's *The Martian,* here's a true hard-science-fiction tale set on the red planet — a terrific blend of high tech and high tension, of science and suspense, of character and crisis."
— Robert J. Sawyer, Hugo Award–winning
author of ***Red Planet Blues***

"Post-apocalyptic disaster meets fractured utopian space exploration in this terrifying tale, which Cawdron (*Anomaly*) sets in a scientific outpost on Mars . . . This tense cat-and-mouse game plays off fears . . . to satisfying result."
— ***Publishers Weekly***